T0129872

Thank you to my daughter Megan, for encouraging me to write and suggesting I had a story in the first place, and for supporting me with editing and advice. And thank you to my friends: Shelley, for being my biggest cheerleader and instilling confidence in me, and to Helen for encouraging me to have faith in myself to pursue my dreams.

Thank you to all of my daughters for putting up with me all those hours I was caught in my own world… writing! To Rosalyn for encouraging me to believe in myself and that wonderful things are always about to happen, to Alison for reminding me to embrace my life, the truth, who I am, and that I can stand on my own two feet and do it by myself. And to Gwen for being a constant reminder of generosity and strength, giving and brave, gentle and kind at the same time, facing the world, following her passions, never giving up.

A File of a Life

Christina McKinney

authorHOUSE®

AuthorHouse™
1663 Liberty Drive
Bloomington, IN 47403
www.authorhouse.com
Phone: 1 (800) 839-8640

Published by AuthorHouse 11/09/2018

ISBN: 978-1-5462-6609-9 (sc)
ISBN: 978-1-5462-6610-5 (hc)
ISBN: 978-1-5462-6608-2 (e)

Library of Congress Control Number: 2018912983

Print information available on the last page.

This book is printed on acid-free paper.

Contents

Chapter 1

The Meaning of Roses
(1972–1975)

The voice inside pushes a way to reality, whatever that is. Recognition, awareness, sensing, feeling, just drifting on emotion bare and clean—that's my course now. No steady, sure, and planned purpose. Just living and trying to learn to love or be loved.

I can't watch the time; time simply has no place for me, and no place has time for me. Just drifting. No port, no one, just me.

Soft sleep sometimes brings sweetness and peace. But it sometimes reveals hard and painful torture to my unsteady mind, wavering, tossing, clashing, and clanging.

But with it all comes movement. I'm being swept away each day into a new and changing world. It's my world. It's changing within the changing world. Will it ever fit into the little slot so that their revolutions may spin congruently?

But I can sense and feel and know it. If only I could turn myself inside out a bit so that I may share with and show to others. Silly me is so selfish in this quarter; however, it happens too frequently that the fineness is

> misused and misinterpreted so that I myself am feigned into believing the contrary and I look ugly in the mirror of so many faces.
>
> Tipsy, topsy, turned, and twirled, but going. Tip it this way, then that; it's crystal clear. It turns just slightly, and again the hazy confusion …
>
> Bobbie, 1965

Louie chauffeured her to school like he did every morning in his shiny, black MG. He was so proud of his little black car. He polished it nearly every day. The inside was bright red and in meticulous condition. It smelled like new vinyl. The backseat armrest was positioned in the center of the bench and served as a sort of chair. Jill sat up high on her armrest-throne so she could see out of the window like a princess observing her subjects. Her grandfather adoringly reveled in the pleasure of serving her.

The day had begun like any other. The temperature was moderate as usual. The sun pierced through the morning chill as Jill stepped out the back door. She immediately felt its warmth fading in and out as it tried to force its entrance onto the day. It comforted her. Jill breathed in the cool air.

Her slightly bulging belly was sufficiently stuffed with oatmeal and strawberries. Looking down at her black leather shoes fastened with a buckle that stretched across the tops of her feet, she nodded approvingly and gripped her lunchbox. Inside were a peanut butter and jelly sandwich, a box of raisins, and a thermos filled with water. It was the only lunch she would eat.

Jill stood on the back porch watching her grandfather lovingly as he pulled the black car out of the garage to prepare it for its morning drive. It was like the MG was about to enter a parade when it was pulled out of that garage. Louie made certain it was in show-worthy condition each and every time. Hardly a week went by that he wasn't approached with an offer. His eyes sparkled with pride, and the hint of a modest grin hung on his face when someone asked. He always shook his head as if it were the most absurd idea in the world.

He would never part with his little black MG.

Jill observed her grandfather polishing the shiny black paint with a white cloth as she stepped off the porch and into the light, her nearly white-blonde and smoothly brushed hair reflecting the sun. She smoothed the skirt of her dress with one hand and glanced down at the rippling folds that fanned out into a perfect circle encasing her long, skinny legs. She watched her grandfather with admiration, and he looked up and smiled when he saw her.

"Is my little girl ready for school?" He grinned at her.

A small smile formed out of the corner of her mouth, and she nodded.

He said, "Well, come on then. Let's go."

Jill walked toward the car while her grandfather held the door open for her to climb in. The glistening red vinyl was sticky as she crawled across it to the armrest that formed her throne. She disapproved of the stickiness and abhorred the way her knees stuck to it. She moved in such a way as to limit the number of times her hands had to touch it.

Her grandfather closed the door and walked to the other side. He was neatly dressed in trousers as usual and wore his beret-like cap that reminded Jill of a chauffeur in an old movie. He was bald with a thin band of short, gray hair that wrapped around the back of his head from one ear to the other. He had a modest short mustache that was almost taller vertically than it was horizontally, like a little German mustache. He always seemed to be chewing on something: a piece of grass, a toothpick.

The windows were rolled down, and Jill could smell the strong scent of the tomato vines growing next to the garage. Making their way down the driveway from the backyard to the front, she noticed the gentle perfume coming from the roses that lined the front yard. Jill glanced at the pansies in the flowerbed by the front porch. She wished she could get out and look at them. She never tired of searching for their little faces, which Louie assured her were there. Jill searched and searched for the faces every day, and she never saw them, but she told her grandfather she did because she wanted so badly to believe they were there. It was part of the reason she looked so hard; she was determined to find them one day.

It was quiet as they drove down their neighborhood street. The city was just waking up. "Grandpa, is that where the fish place is?" Jill asked.

The question somehow seemed important in order to place the information in its proper location in her mind.

"No, not really. Well, yes, sort of. Over that way and down a few streets."

The answer satisfied her for the moment.

Neighbors made their way to their cars with cups of coffee, steam coming off the tops. Most of them carried the morning paper under one arm with the look Jill thought all adults seemed to have, one of silent resignation.

She took in the sights and breathed in its aliveness as they made their way to the private Baptist school where she attended kindergarten. Jill relished the sights and the pleasant sensations that absorbed into every pore of her body. There was something pleasingly satisfying about the city.

The MG pulled into the long driveway, around to the back of the building, and then into the large schoolyard where children were spread across the playground. To Jill, it was like she was pulling up in a horse and carriage every time. She always wore a dress, and it was always spread neatly over her knees and the armrest. This morning was no exception. No other cars were ever there. Theirs seemed to be the only one. It was one small detail that bothered her and initiated the separateness she felt—and that would intensify shortly after her departure from the car.

As soon as Jill stepped out of the princess carriage she suddenly felt small. Her grandfather left, imagining all was as it should be. But to Jill, it was like she had stepped from the comforting carriage into a big ocean that separated her from everyone else. She felt so out of place, like she didn't belong there at all.

She stood on the blacktop that stretched forever across the schoolyard and met with the grassy fields. She watched the kids playing, laughing, and having fun. For her, she may as well have been on the moon. She wanted to join the other children but could not. So she observed from a distance as if through a glass that she could see through but they could not. In that moment, she realized there was no possible way to break through the glass. The distance was too wide. She would forever be trapped on the other side. She felt like a ghost walking on the wrong side of everything.

She never quite felt like she belonged to that old life anymore after everything had changed. Her mom linked her to that old life. Without her, she no longer belonged here either. She was a quiet observer now, disjointed, frozen, her feelings and her thoughts disconnected. It must have happened then when her mother left, and perhaps not that very instant, but slowly, over time.

Jill wasn't sad exactly, just separated.

The school bell rang, and she walked at an even pace toward the classroom. She didn't drag her feet as if in dread, but she didn't run either.

Once there, the activities of kindergarten occupied her mind, cutting and pasting letters endlessly. It seemed like that was all they ever did. But Jill didn't mind. Cutting was her favorite thing; she could do it for hours.

"What do you have there, Jill?" the teacher asked.

"A mother helping her child," Jill replied.

The teacher smiled and nodded as if it were some big discovery.

Jill wondered at the teacher's endless surprise at illustrations with mothers and fathers doing nearly the same things in all of them. The atmosphere was friendly nonetheless. The children happily cut and chattered quietly as the teacher made her way around to all of the tables. The smell of construction paper and Elmer's glue gave her a pleasant satisfaction. The room seemed like a wonderland full of color and fun things to do.

The teacher was kind, and sometimes, when her grandmother was there after the school day had finished, the two would talk over her. She never listened to what they were saying, but she could feel it was about her. The attention felt like warm sunshine hitting her back. They would talk about how Jill was beginning to talk to other children but how she continued to play quietly by herself while the others played together. The year before she had tried to begin kindergarten but she cried so much her grandparents returned home and didn't force her to go. Several months had gone by when she wouldn't speak to anyone. In preschool she would sit in the same corner playing with the same bucket of toys by her self. One day she got up and asked another quiet little girl to go outside. They went on the swings, carrying their dolls together, and after that, they played on the swings everyday. The teacher had told Harriott it was Jill who broke the silence and initiated contact. The teachers and Harriott were overjoyed and made far too big a fuss over it Jill thought. Going to kindergarten was like starting all over again, only in a far bigger pool. It was like jumping from a swimming pool into the ocean, and Jill still hadn't mastered how to swim. The parts to her stroke weren't integrated, and yet that wasn't it either. She could not advance even if she had wanted to. She could not reconcile let alone coordinate the pieces. Nothing made sense.

In between class time in kindergarten that day, a beautiful woman that seemed like an angel to Jill, wandered throughout the school. She seemed to be someone significant and roamed the hallways and the play yard endlessly. She was forever stooping down and listening intently to every word every small person had to say as if the fate of the world hung on those words. Later Jill would discover this woman was the principal's wife. She was radiant and vibrant. Today, she meandered from child to child during lunchtime. Long low-lying benches made for small children attached to school lunch tables lined the narrow room that was the cafeteria and opened up onto the outdoor hallways. Jill sat at one of the outdoor tables and opened her lunchbox, neatly removing each item and placing them carefully onto the napkin her grandmother had provided. She didn't talk. She mostly listened to the low humming chatter around her. It was a happy sound, like busy hummingbirds. Jill opened the container that held her peanut butter and jelly sandwich and delighted at the feel of the soft bread between her fingers. The smells around her were the same every day, a mix between play dough, spaghetti and paint.

It was then that the beautiful woman bent down to Jill, entering Jill's own child-world. Jill looked up into the angel's face in awe. That day she told the woman with the beautiful wavy blond hair and blue eyes that she looked just like her mother. Jill couldn't stop looking at her. The woman nodded and smiled. After school, she saw the woman and Harriott talking. This time Jill tried hard to listen. She knew they were talking about her and she wanted to know what the beautiful woman was saying, but she couldn't understand. Harriott's face cringed into a worried expression. The woman turned to Jill and they both stared at her intently. Jill observed the anguish on her grandmother's face and worried she had said something wrong to the beautiful lady. But the angel turned her shining eyes towards Jill and her attention fell onto her like a warm ray of light. It felt to Jill like she was being enveloped by the sun and she relished the moment.

Some days later, Jill found herself at the angel's home. Her backyard was enormous and it was littered with dozens of children and outdoor toys. The sound of children's laughter, clinking sand pails, and squeaky swing sets filled her ears. Jill ran and played with the toys. She didn't play with the children. The glass was still there, but at least she was close to them and the small house felt safer and comfortable enough to get a little nearer. She felt almost like she belonged. She was at someone's home and not in a vast schoolyard. That made a difference. But most of all, she was at the angel's home. After that, the beautiful woman invited Jill over regularly. She had two children of her own; one about Jill's age, a boy named George, and a younger little girl named Tammy. Sometimes the woman called her Tamantha. Jill loved that name. When the larger group of children fizzled out of the house and went home, Jill found her self at each progressive visit remaining behind longer and longer alone with them. In time she even had her portrait taken with the family. Everyone commented how Jill looked just like one of their own.

She spent the night with them, went to the store, did art projects. One day, when Jill walked into their home, a distinct and overwhelming smell of burnt baking and paint took over the house. Jill was quickly ushered to a table where dough, paint, brushes and small blocks of wood were lined up ready for assembly. She marveled at the endless excitement of something new once again. She never knew what to expect when she walked into their home. The beautiful woman hurriedly explained what Jill needed to do as if it was urgent. It was not a nervous sort of urgency. It was the kind of urgency that can't be contained due to unleashed excitement. Jill took up her place at the table and picked up a roll of clay. She kneaded it and rolled it, glancing around the table to see what everyone else had come up with and tried to decide what her creation would be. Finally she decided on mushrooms. Those were easy enough. She rolled out a stem and placed it on the wooden block towards the bottom. Then she rolled out a thicker piece for the top and flattened it out, shaping it into a plume. She rolled tiny bits of clay into little balls and placed them on the plume. Her mushrooms would be polka dotted. She handed them to the mother. "Nice job, Jill!" Carefully she removed them from the wooden block. Observing Jill's concern for their removal, she reassured her that they would be placed back as soon as they were finished baking. Jill's brow smoothed out and she answered, "Ok," with a sigh of relief. The placement of her mushrooms was critical.

The oven was hot and it made the kitchen warm. "Sit down over there, Jill. They will be ready in no time." She wore large hand mitts as she turned the other clay figures over on the pan. She worked quickly to accommodate all of the children. Jill observed with interest and could have sat like that for hours. When Jill's were done baking, they were placed on a drying rack to cool and before she knew it, she was back at the table, painting her mushrooms. She decided the plumes should be red. With the brush she carefully stroked paint around the mushrooms pausing every now and then to inspect everyone else's work. When she eyed the beautiful woman's she was astonished. She stopped to get a good look and her mouth dropped open. "It's a garden with a little girl!" Jill said. "Yes," the woman looked briefly in her direction. Jill's eyes were big with admiration. "It's beautiful." The woman smiled. She couldn't take her eyes off of the extraordinary collection of colors in the garden.

The most delightful activity was sitting down with all of the little girls while the principal's wife combed Jill's long hair and put it up in all kinds of styles. Choosing which rubber bands and clips to use was the most difficult task and involved great deliberation and discussion. Deciding what the style would be for the day was the highlight.

When it was time to go home, Jill lamented the departure. Harriott and Louie's house felt warm and safe, but the principal's wife and her family's home were beyond comparison. It was a real family.

After the long day at school was finished Jill stepped into her carriage back to her princess-world and went home. Everyday the routine was the same. She stepped out of the little black MG and walked across the long wooden front porch and in through the front door. She kicked off her black leather shoes and walked towards the brightly lit kitchen to see what was happening there. Harriott was wearing her pink and black apron covered in large flowers. It looked more like a smock than a cooking apron. She stood at the counter cutting beans. It seemed like she was always cutting beans. She walked across the hardwood floors covered with drab yet clean old-fashioned large round rugs, and through the arched doorway. The house felt warm and reassuring. There was a musty worn out smell like an old wooden farmhouse intermingled with the aromas of home cooking that constantly wafted into every room. It was a small house, but it felt plenty big to Jill. It was quiet but for the tedious routine tasks of running a home carried out in a labor of love and the soft drone of the large black and white television set the size of a large piece of furniture that took up a significant portion of the living room. It usually played the news which felt to Jill as intense as if the events were happening right there in the living room. Otherwise, the only show Jill watched was the clay-mation, *Gumby and Pokey.*

The patio out back was a simple slab of cement covered with green turf. It was meant to look like grass. The fake grass disturbed her. It just wasn't right and a far cry from the real thing. Jill balanced on the sliding glass door tracks peering out at a hammock that swung from the rafters. It was Louie's favorite sitting place. He was in the hammock sure enough, reading the newspaper. He would do that for hours in the warm sun. "Hi Pokey," she said. He looked up, "Well, hi there," he answered, removing the spectacles from his face. She called him Pokey after her favorite show. Jill continued her walk examining the long row of tomato plants in large pots on a ledge that ran the length of the backyard garage. He suggested she sing to the tomato plants so they would grow better. Jill doubted this worked, but after Louie's third request, she obliged him. It was a silly song and it was a silly thing to do she thought. She couldn't wait to be done with it.

Beyond the cement slab patio and next to the tomato vines there was a simple swimming pool surrounded by a fence covered with thick green ivy. The pool seemed huge to Jill. At the shallow end Harriott often had her practice swimming for the reward of a strawberry after each lap. The pool had a very deep section on the other end that always held a certain enigma for her. Jill made her way slowly around the pool's perimeter examining the width of the cement walkway around it before deciding to pull out her red tricycle. She had decided it was just wide enough to make laps around with the bike. She gingerly climbed on, barely reaching the pedals and carefully made her way around the swimming pool. She loved the brightness and the gleam of the sun reflecting off the red paint. She observed it with satisfaction and inspected the perfect handlebars. The second time around the pool she went a little faster. Her third loop around she went so fast she clipped a corner and went right in the pool, tricycle and all!

Louie dove in to the water as Jill lamented her sinking red tricycle. She thought her grandfather was going in to save it when to her surprise he swam to her instead. He grabbed her. She was confused and said, "Grandpa, what are you doing? Save my tricycle!" He replied tensely and out of breath with a distraught look on his face, "I'm saving you! Are you okay?" "Of course, why wouldn't I be? I can swim." She had had hours of excruciating swimming lessons, wearing her embarrassing rubber and floppy flower covered cap Harriott insisted that she wear in an outdoor pool ten times more massive and cold than this one. "Please! Go get my tricycle!" she cried. Her grandfather seemed immensely slow, wasting precious time heaving Jill out of the pool and then climbing out himself when she could have easily gotten out on her own without his help. Both of them were dripping, their clothes soaked through and they both smelled like chlorine. The old man heaved some more and gasped for air. Jill was surprised how out of breath he was for such a little swim. She was so impatient and distraught over her lovely red tricycle. Louie examined her much too slowly and she found this terribly tiresome and unnecessary. He was wasting precious time and she imagined the deep water had swallowed her tricycle up for good.

"Grandpa?" she asked, trying very hard not to be impatient for she knew she'd better watch her manners by the look on his face. "Are you going to get my tricycle, or is it gone forever?" Her little brow was furrowed in worry and she was afraid far too much time had elapsed for a rescue. He continued heaving, still out of breath and a little annoyed. He finally answered, "I'll get your tricycle. But you are much more important than that bike. That's why I got you first." Then she understood even if in her mind it was the tricycle that was important. She replied simply, "But Grandpa, I know how to swim." He nodded his head disbelievingly. She was perplexed, but when her grandfather finally dove in a second time and returned to the surface with the little red trike, Jill thought her grandfather was a hero. She jumped up and down and clapped her hands, then proceeded to inspect her red tricycle thoroughly. She looked up at him adoringly with a huge smile and announced, "It's ok Grandpa, it's ok!" "Yes," he answered and he couldn't help but smile.

Harriott walked out with a platter of raw hamburger patties. "Are you ready to fire her up Gramps?" "Yeh, yeh," he replied like usual. "Put em there and I'll stoke up the grill as soon as I change out of these wet clothes." Harriott took one look at the water dripping off of the tricycle and Jill and clicked her tongue disapprovingly. "That's why we stay away from the edge dear, isn't it? Well, I've told you." She cast a disapproving look Louie's way before walking back to the kitchen.

The familiar charcoal smell of meat wafted into the house and as Jill came out of her room with dry clothes, she walked back and forth from the kitchen to the grill several times, waiting impatiently. Soon everyone was sitting around the heavy round wooden table for dinner. A finger trail had made its way through the butter. "Jill, did you do that?" "No Grandma, I didn't," she answered innocently, but Harriott gave her a stern sideways look and said, "Jill, you can't do that." "Yes Grandma," she said. Jill loved butter and she couldn't help it. Harriott brought out the string beans and the noodles. Louie set the patties on the table. They ate them as usual without buns. It was a simple dinner and was repeated most nights. Sometimes a salad was added. And if they were lucky there would be fresh strawberries from the garden in the front yard where the vines grew beneath the roses. Harriott added a bit of sugar to the cut berries, causing the juices to flow out, and sometimes even a dollop of cream on top. Jill always stood on the stool and watched in awe at the transformation of the fresh raw berries into this delectable dessert. The tricycle incident was the talk of the dinner table that night.

After dinner Louie let Jill crawl up on his lap to read. She begged to have her favorite stories read over and over again. "'The Lion and the Mouse,' Grandpa!" Jill chanted. To her, the warmth of her grandfather's lap as well as the excitement of an adventure to read about and imagine in her mind were almost more pleasure than she could bear. His lap was warm and comforting, and she felt safe. Jill could sit with her grandpa for hours like that but eventually he shoved her off his lap. She unwillingly cooperated.

Jill loved her grandfather dearly. When he rose from the chair, Jill's eyes followed him as he disappeared down the hall. She never let him out of her sight. Every time he opened the front door to go somewhere, Jill came running. It became imperative that he never go anywhere without her. For one, it was a welcome break from Harriott, who was constantly telling her what to do. But secondly, her grandpa seemed to do all kinds of interesting things, and she had to see what he was up to. Louie did all the errands and he took care of all the problems. Jill was always curious.

The most exciting event by far was the nightly walk with their dog, Muffer. The outings seemed so adventurous and the darkness of the night, mysterious and exciting. That night, Louie stood at the door ready to turn the handle when Jill caught him. "Grandpa, where are you going? Are you going on a walk?" "Yes Jill," he said. It was dark by then and very near to bedtime. Jill begged to go, her grandfather holding Muffer's leash in his hand. Louie had almost slipped out without her. She would have been devastated if he had escaped. Her grandmother sighed while he patiently waited for a verdict. "Ok," Harriott said. "Let me put some shoes on her." Once she put her shoes and a sweater on, they departed. She was a bit frightened of the dark and yet felt completely safe with her grandfather, who could protect her from anything. Jill held Louie's large hand, feeling his warmth and smiled up at him. It was cold outside, forcing them to walk briskly. As children often do, Jill only felt it momentarily and then forgot about it entirely. The outings and mystical walks included any number of new adventures and she couldn't wait to see what they would be tonight. Mostly they were stories conjured up in her own mind. She strained her eyes to see into the darkness as they passed each house. The thing that marked the apex of every walk and held the greatest enchantment for her were the cathedrals and life-sized saints lit by glowing yellow light they passed under. Her skin prickled with excitement as she approached them towards the end of the walk. She always stopped and gazed at them. This she would never tire of seeing. For this reason she could never miss a walk with Louie.

On Jill's first birthday without her mother, Harriott threw her a party. Jill was turning five, but rather than invite a few friends her age, Harriott invited her own. Jill went to greet them when they arrived and everyone greeted her back cheerfully. That lasted a couple of minutes and then the adults got to talking and Jill was left standing in the middle of them. She glanced around and saw there was no one interesting to talk to or play with so she left the room. She went to the hallway where she could play alone. She could do this for hours with the small toys she pulled from the living room closet where they were kept. She played happily until she remembered the party going on outside and began to get up to join them before anyone noticed she had disappeared.

But then she began thinking, "Here I am alone and it's my party. There should be kids here." In the back of her mind she thought she ought to feel that a party without kids is not fun. However in reality, she liked to play by herself, and honestly she didn't mind. She forced herself to think how she ought to feel, maybe like other kids would have felt in this circumstance. Her mind continued down this path and more thoughts followed. The slightest tinge of pity took form, an emotion she hadn't experimented with before. The odd part is she saw herself as a quiet observer slowly forming these thoughts and timidly allowing a feeling to emerge. She saw herself controlling the process quite clearly. She thought the thought of pity matter-of-factly, and then she tried the feeling on for size. She backed up and pulled the feeling away and thought about it some more. The thought seemed trivial and not much to regard but the feeling on the other hand … did she like it? She tried again, letting the feeling of pity flow into her small body like a stream filling up with rain and spreading out like a fan. It filled her veins and it felt almost tingly and satisfying. Right then and there she made up her mind, "Yes, I'll hang onto this."

Harriott walked in to the hallway and stopped when she spotted Jill. "Why there you are! Whatever are you doing sitting here in the hallway by yourself! It's your birthday of all things, for peats sake. Come and join us!" As Harriott said this, Jill allowed a small frown to form; the new pity-feeling was pushing her to do this. Even though the decision had been made, Jill continued to be aware of the newly formed idea and now she was experimenting with it on others. Jill put her head down as if she were sad. It was easy. She knew she was doing it and she succumbed to its power. It was a brief almost imperceptible exchange between the two of them. Harriott was alert to it immediately. "Why honey, what is the matter? Ohhhh … oh dear, you have no little friends to play with, oh my goodness …" Now the process was complete. It had come full circle. Not only did the feeling flood her body with a most pleasant sensation, but it commanded power too. Until then, Jill had never questioned the idea of playing by herself in her make-believe world. In fact, she liked it. She was very used to adults and had no problem with them. Her grandmother persuaded her, "Ok Jill, come now, we mustn't make the guests wait. That is rude. We can have a good time anyway, ok?" But Jill knew she had succeeded in making her grandmother feel guilty and she almost felt badly about that. The newly formed habit, however, was there to stay. Jill never did reverse the decision and the longer it stayed the less aware of it she became.

Jill remembered vividly the day she had arrived at Harriott and Louie's house to live for good. At the time, she had no idea what lay in store for her. The night began at Effie's home, where Jill had been living for nearly two years with her mother. They had long since packed up and left their life in Washington with her father. Since her father had always been away so much of the time for as long as she could remember, nothing really felt amiss. In fact, it was quite the opposite. Living with Effie, Jill was surrounded by all kinds of family and a constant stream of friends. The backyard was a playground full of fantasies. It backed up over an empty canyon and swept down over three long hills. Jill would run through the sage weeds that enveloped her with their sharp scent and permeated her nostrils and instantly triggered memories whenever she smelled sage thereafter. Giant berry bushes became the food and magic spells for all kinds of adventures. She would never forget the feeling of rolling the tiny hard red balls between her fingers. They were tangible proof that her stories were true. One time she put one in her mouth even though she knew better. She had always wanted to know what it would feel like to roll it over her tongue. But she quickly took it out fearing the reason she knew she shouldn't have done it. What if it was poisonous? She worried the rest of the day, but nothing happened before nightfall. She was safe.

The enormous Weeping Willow that swung down over the lowest hill provided a perfect fort. The yard felt magical to Jill for other reasons too. Purple grapevines hung over the fences and when the tiny green grapes emerged, Jill was ecstatic over the miracle of real grapes she could eat. Although, when she tasted them she could not seem to remember a time when they didn't taste incredibly bitter. She never lost hope however that one day she would pick one that had finally ripened into the sweet fruit it was meant to be. Rhododendrons covered in hundreds of pink and white flowers surrounded the patio. The patio was made of giant cement squares and that too seemed magical for some reason. When Jill wasn't sneaking around the house early in the morning climbing onto the counter and secretly eating salt she shook from the saltshaker, she was in the yard for hours on end in her make believe world.

The afternoon before Jill departed the familiar life of Effie's magical house, a large group of people poured into the living room. Effie sat alone in a dark corner huddled in a blue upholstered armchair, her legs curled up underneath her. Her head was down and she spoke to no one. Jill dared not intrude into her cold silent cocoon. Dozens of longhaired blond men with handle bar mustaches that hung down to their chins littered the small living room, talking and talking. They were up so high, and she was down so low, the gap separated her and them into two different worlds. She tugged on her uncle's shirttails and followed him around the living room until he had to come down. She asked "Where's my Mom?" "She's not here," he answered. Jill persisted, "Well where is she then?" He tried to ignore her and walked away but he couldn't shake her loose. She followed him everywhere. She tugged at his shirt and he came down once more and she asked again, "Where is she?" Impatiently he answered, "I don't know." Two more times this went on, Jill insisting, "I know you know where she is," but it was the same reply. Finally, and impatiently he came down for the final time and said, "I don't know. She's at a restaurant." Now she was getting somewhere and she wasn't about to let go until she got more answers. She followed him around the living room more closely than ever. "Which restaurant?" she asked. "I don't know which restaurant. A restaurant, ok?" Jill knew she wasn't going to get cooperation, but she tried anyway. "Who is she with then?" "I don't know!" James was exasperated. "Yes you do!" she insisted. "She went alone, OK?!! Now will you leave me alone?" Jill continued to follow him and questioned him further, "Why did she go to a restaurant by herself? She would never go to a restaurant alone. Why would she do that?" Jill pictured her mother sitting alone at some restaurant but she couldn't imagine it. One last time James swung around and practically shouted, "Well this time she did!!" and he stormed off. Jill knew the conversation was over.

Before long it was dark and her father appeared at the door. Jill was surprised. She could hardly believe it! He did not enter the house. He remained in the doorway while he and Effie mumbled above Jill's head. Jill stood directly beneath them trying very hard to figure out what they were saying. It was something intense, she could tell that much. She finally gave up trying to make sense of their heated disagreement; their voices were like a faraway gurgle of unintelligible words. Suddenly her Father took her hand and said, "Come on." They walked down the cement path that led from the front door to the driveway empty handed. The air was chilly and the sky was so clear it was possible to see nearly all the stars and the Milky Way too. It was a typical dessert night. Jill asked, "Where are we going?" Her father answered, "To grandma and grandpa's." "Really?!" Jill replied.

This meant fun! As they approached the driveway in the dark Jill made out a small orange and silver truck. "Wow! What's that for?" Her father did not answer. She asked, "What's in it?" "Nothing," he replied. Apparently the truck was empty. Jill climbed up high into the great big cabin and sat on the huge empty seat. Her father had to lift her in. The seat was cold, but she didn't care. She sat up high and proud. The truck made a loud grumbling sound as it choked into motion. In the dark, her father pulled out of the driveway. Suddenly Jill remembered, "Wait! Where's mommy? We can't leave without her!!" Paul answered, "Well, this time she's not coming." "We're going to grandma and grandpa's without mommy? But why? We never go to grandma and grandpa's without mommy." Paul was silent. She asked again. More silence. She asked several more times. She couldn't leave without her. She just couldn't. Finally, in his deep voice her father said, "Be quiet." Jill continued to badger him but he said "Silence" with such finality that she knew she couldn't continue. Jill sat silently the rest of the way. She did not know why they were traveling late into the night alone without her mother.

They arrived at her grandparents' a couple of hours later. They had been waiting for them and greeted them at the door. Harriott ushered her weary son and granddaughter into the house and led them into a very large empty room with one enormous bed and a nightstand. Harriott pulled the covers down and helped Jill in. "Is this where I'm sleeping?" she asked. "Yes," everyone answered. The bed was large and it swallowed her up she was so small. Jill observed her father, grandmother and grandfather lined up by the side of the bed like it was a procession. Jill stated firmly, "I can't sleep here." The big bed was the only problem on her mind. "Why not?" Harriott asked. She didn't budge from her place at the side of the bed. Jill knew right away there would be no negotiation. "This is where you have to sleep tonight dear. It's the only bed we have." "But it's too big," Jill protested. "There's much too much room." The bed must have been the size of a living room. "Who's going to sleep with me?" she asked. "No one," Harriott answered. "I don't want to sleep alone," Jill replied. She hadn't slept alone for as long as she could remember. At Effie's house, her mother and she had always slept together. "I can't sleep alone," she began to cry. "Yes you can," Harriott said tenderly. "Look, you have your teddy bear." Jill glanced lovingly at her bear. His ears had been sewn back on so many times he was ragged. But he was perfect. Every time she looked down at him, the ears reminded her of how magical her mother was. She remembered the first time it happened. Mala, her dog, had ripped his ear off when Jill had teased her with the raggedy bear, taunting the adolescent puppy as she tore off at rip roaring speed in giant circles around the yard tearing up the damp green grass. There they sat in the kitchen afterwards, her mother on the stepladder stool that sufficed as the head chair of the eat-in breakfast nook where they ate every meal. Her mother quietly sewed the ear back on as Jill sat at the table watching the transformation. Jill thought she was magic being able to do that. When she'd finished, she handed the bear back. Jill was astounded. "His ear is back on!" "Yes," her mother had replied. Jill hopped down from the table running through the house, "His ear is fixed! His ear is fixed!"

When Jill finally settled down, reluctantly accepting there was no other option but to sleep alone in the giant bed, everyone knelt to the ground and said the Lord's Prayer. This was strange. They never did this as far as she could remember, and they were so serious, Jill thought. When everyone left the room, and she was alone in the enormous bed, she huddled into one small section at the upper left corner. She was afraid to stretch out. The bed was like a giant vast void she might fall into. She felt the coolness of the sheet touching her skin when she moved. The open space between the bottom and the top sheet that formed where her body spread them apart and slipped off into oblivion was too much to fathom. She pulled her self into a tight ball. A terror crept over her and she tossed from side to side trying to hide under the covers. She squeezed her eyes tightly shut so if anything terrible happened, she wouldn't have to look. Then she glanced down and remembered the bear. She breathed a sigh of relief and hugged him tight. She thought to herself he was the only thing she had in the world in that moment. It was the only thing she had departed Effie's house with. At least if it was going to be one thing, it was the most important one she thought to herself. She tried to fall asleep. It took a long time.

She heard the adults discussing the dilemma of no clothes the following morning. Harriot turned to Jill and said, "Well, honey, let's go shopping." She got to pick out three dresses that day. One was pink and white plaid with a dropped waist and a wide ribbon to go around. Another was white with small flowers. The last was navy blue. She got a pair of shiny black leather shoes that buckled on top that day too. The white dress with the little flowers became her favorite. Jill insisted on wearing it every day. Harriott didn't argue. Every night thereafter Harriott made her put the flowered dress under her pillow. She didn't want to part with it even in her sleep; it took some negotiation to finally arrive at an arrangement. After she fell asleep, Harriott snuck in, took the dress and washed it, folded it neatly and put it back under the pillow. Jill wore it again the following day. Did anyone wonder at her wearing the same dress day after day Jill later wondered?

As the days wore on, Jill received no straight answer as to the whereabouts of her mother. She asked and asked over and over again at first. After a while, she stopped asking. Her questions were never answered. The explanation that was given time and again was this and it was always Harriott who did the answering. "Grandma, where is my mom?" First Harriott turned slowly around in a most painful way, her forehead furrowed into a look of Jill wasn't sure what. "Your mom was like a rose," the story began. "But where's my mom?" She tried hard to keep Harriott focused, hoping to get a straight answer this time. "Honey, she was like a rose." "You said that already," she interrupted. "But where is she?" "She was like a rose." Harriott repeated this line over and over as if this explained everything. Jill stood there waiting and hoping. Harriott stared imploringly into Jill's eyes. "You know," she would say. She made a gesture with her hands like she was rolling something out. Jill just looked at her imagining if she looked hard enough, she would understand. Then Harriott finished the rose story: "Your mother was like a beautiful rose. And you know what happens to roses?" She would wait for Jill to fill in the rest. Jill thought to herself, "yeah, you pick 'em and they're pretty." She tried hard to search her mind for the answer to the rose story but her mind was blank. With an immensely painful look on her face Harriott continued. "Well, you know how a rose opens and the petals fold out one by one?" "Yes," she answered, wondering when or if Harriott would ever get back to her question. She was beginning to lose patience. "Well, you know," and Harriott would pause dramatically, making the roll out hand gesture again. "No," Jill would say after an intolerably long pause. "The petals start to fall one by one until …" and again the imploring look of agony. "And then what?" she asked. She was beyond impatient. "The flower is gone," Harriott would say tearfully. Jill thought, "Ok finally the rose story is over." "So where is my mom?" And the story of the rose would begin all over again. Jill sighed in exasperation and walked away. As time went by, although Jill persistently kept asking, she would only wait long enough to hear "The rose," before she sighed and walked away. Eventually she stopped asking altogether.

Whenever she asked the question, and no one would answer or gave some lie, it widened the gap more and more between her mind that could make no sense of it, and her heart because her feelings were betrayed. Jill retreated into her make believe world of fabricated explanations. It seemed perfectly natural to fill in the blanks. Jill regularly pulled one of the heavy dining room chairs up to the tall window that overlooked the long wooden front porch. Jill would stare out over the front lawn and wait for hours. She was looking through a glass then too, a glass that separated her from reality and the stories in her mind. She would imagine her mother walking up at any moment. She tried to imagine what might have taken her away. A long vacation? Traveling around the world? Maybe she was really sick and she would come back once she was better. The stories always included a compelling reason for her absence. Jill would reenact the coming home scenario over and over again, imagining what it would be like, how she would feel, how she would react, and how happy her mom would be to see her again finally after all this time. She was never sad or angry or upset. The sessions made her feel better, mostly because they seemed so real and likely to happen one day. She was sure of it.

Harriott came to the window one day while Jill sat there so patiently and for so long looking out over the porch. The tall windows framed by the old white painted wood were cold. The long wooden roofed front porch cast a shadow across the hall. Harriott had been polishing the heavy old dining room table and casually asked why she sat like that at the window so often. Jill replied like it was the most obvious thing in the world. "I'm waiting for my mom to come home and I want to be here when she does." Harriott gasped and appeared visibly shaken, Jill observed. "Why are you so upset Grandma? What's wrong?" Harriott got down on her knees and took Jill's hand while her other covered her mouth and all she said was "Oh Jill, oh Jill." Jill stared at her and waited for her to stop. She always thought Harriott was far too emotional.

Now and then Paul visited from New York. The visits seemed few and far between, perhaps once a year. Time seems to last much longer for a child. Perhaps it was more frequent than that. Jill wasn't sure. A couple of times her father took her to New York. She stayed with friends of his and their son. The father was a fellow pilot for the same airline her father worked and his name was King. To match his royal name he carried a silver clip fastened around several hundred-dollar bills. Jill knew this because she asked him one time if he always carried them around. He said indeed yes, always and in that denomination. Jill thought he loved showing off those hundred-dollar bills. She was amused to watch him whenever an opportunity came to flip out his clip fastened around those bills. He would dramatically pull them out of his pocket and flamboyantly roll one crisp bill out and hand it over to whoever the lucky recipient was.

During her time in New York, Jill saw her own father briefly in-between his work trips before and after the stays with the dramatic King and his son. Jill's father returned one time and took her to the Empire State building. She only remembered the top, but it always stuck in her mind as something significant. It wasn't only because the view was breathtaking; it was because her father was there, and it was one of the rare times she felt warm and close to him.

Another time or two Paul took her to San Francisco to visit his brother. Jill relished the rides on the back of Paul's motorcycle, hanging onto him intimately, her hair whipping in the wind, cruising up and down the steep hills of the beautiful city, passing the charming trolley cars along the way. At her uncle's apartment, Jill was both enamored and bothered by the live stuffed penguin sitting by her uncle's front door. It disturbed her. She hesitated whenever she passed it, deeply overwrought and yet fascinated at the same time.

Most of her father's visits, however, consisted of plane rides. On one occasion Paul arrived and they drove to one of the small airports nearby to rent a plane. She walked out on the tarmac holding Paul's hand on one such visit. They walked between the planes. There were many different kinds. Jill took the privilege for granted getting to see so many planes close-up and to ride in them. She got to choose the color. They wove in and out of the planes searching for the right one. This was of the highest importance as far as she was concerned. "I like the red one!" she told her dad. "No, not that one, it's not the right kind." She sighed and continued searching until she found another red plane. "This one!" "Ok!" he grinned. He was just as excited she thought to herself.

Paul busied himself getting the plane ready. Jill watched him and walked around it, feeling it's smooth surface, touching the blade of the propeller, holding the long rod that held the wing above their heads. He inspected every part of the plane. "Why does it take so long? Do you have to do all that?" Jill whined. She wanted to get going. Paul told her sternly and in a most somber way, "It is absolutely imperative. This isn't a car driving down the road. An accident you might survive. One failed mechanical part in the air and the entire plane could drop out of the sky. Plane crashes usually end in death." Jill looked at him wide-eyed and nodded, swallowing hard. Her father mumbled to himself as he walked away, "Damn lawyers and weekend pleasure pilots, think they're pilots, taking frivolous rides. Don't know a damn thing what they're doing. Don't take flying seriously. Not a lick of 'em do their inspections thoroughly. Takes time, but dying is pretty damn inconvenient too. Most small plane accidents can be avoided." "I'm almost done," he called over his shoulder. "Tell you what, you can take the chalks out from the wheels." "Okay!" That meant it was nearly time to go.

Paul entered the plane first. Ducking his head under the wing that reached out from the roof of the plane, he entered through the small opening. He had to crouch to get in. Jill climbed in after him so she could sit in the co-pilot's seat. There was a steering wheel in front of each of them. Jill was fidgety with excitement. Paul grinned and told her "Sit still! And put your seatbelt on." "Oh yeah," she said. She picked up the heavy metal buckle and shoved one end into the other. It made a loud clinking sound as it clicked into place.

He started the engine and the propeller sputtered into motion. In seconds, it was impossible to distinguish the separate blades. There was only one propeller on the small aircraft at the nose of the plane. The sound was deafening. Now they had to shout to hear each other. Paul taxied towards the entrance to the runway and stopped. A plane landed in front of them and headed their direction, maneuvering around them before it turned into the aircraft parking area. Paul took out the radio receiver and spoke into it. Jill felt so proud and important when her father spoke in his deep-throated commanding voice, but she could never make out the words on the other end. She wondered how her father could understand what they were saying. "Clear for take-off" he would say. "Ok. Roger that," he replied after the mixed up garble on the other end. Her father turned the plane in a 360-degree circle jerkily applying the brakes while he peered out from beneath the highest point of the windshield. Jill asked him one time why he did that. He told her he was checking for other planes over the runway. "Why?" she'd asked. "We don't want to take off if there are other planes in the sky above us do we?" Jill shook her head "no."

Paul moved the plane out onto the runway. Once he made it to one end, he revved the engine and the plane began to move forward. The plane picked up speed and the engine roared louder and louder. Soon they were moving so fast, Jill knew the best part was about to happen. She loved the take-off and she never tired of the sensation of lifting into the air. The entire weight of her body pressed into the seat with force as they rose up. Her stomach and chest brimmed over with a tingling sensation she could barely endure. She was beyond excited. Jill looked out the window. She watched the houses and cars get smaller and smaller. She was lulled into a mesmerizing state of contentment at the beauty of the horizon, the mountains, the clouds. Everything was so intense in the small plane. She could feel every movement and she could see everything for the entire flight. They never rose above the clouds.

Next came her second favorite part, controlling the steering wheel. "Can I?" she looked at him. "Yeah. Go ahead." She pulled the u-shaped wheel towards herself as far as it would go and felt the plane pull her with the force of a house into her seat. This was better than take-off and Jill relished it. Out of the corner of her eye she kept track of her father's response and waited for him to say "Ok, enough." He always said it with a chuckle. Secretly, Jill thought he enjoyed the thrill just as much as she did. Jill pushed the steering wheel back in towards the control panel and the plane leveled out. After testing the extremes, Jill pushed and pulled the steering wheel in and out repeatedly, delighting in the roller coaster rise and fall of the plane. Jill's stomach dropped and she felt there was no thrill that could compare. Jill could continue this game for hours, but eventually Paul said the inevitable, "Ok, that's enough." Jill could tell he was amused even though his face was serious. Landing was the worst part, mostly because it was over, but also because the sensation wasn't nearly as thrilling.

They drove back to her grandparents' home quietly after parking the plane. The ride was over and she knew Paul would leave again as soon as they arrived. Perhaps he would stay for dinner. Jill hoped.

Poor Effie; all the while Jill lived with her grandparents, she was forbidden to go to Effie's house, even though it was the home Jill had lived for the two years leading to her mother's disappearance. She would never forget that house or Granny's big yard full of sage and the gigantic willow tree, or the intriguing berry bushes that filled her imagination with fantasies. It destroyed Effie. She was heartbroken over losing Jill she later admitted. She lost not only her daughter, but Jill too, all in one day. Jill also missed Effie and wondered why she had been taken from one grandmother only to be with another. Effie was so alone.

The differences between Harriott and Effie were like night and day and maybe that explained the odds they were constantly at with one another. Harriott was girlishly immature and prone to jealousy. She envied Effie immensely. Effie was beautiful and she was a lady. She dressed in designer clothing, and looked like a graceful model. Harriott, in contrast, was simple. Her hair was unadorned and never fussy. Perfectly smooth waves rippled through her naturally grey curls. It was short and pressed to her head, giving her the appearance of a flapper girl from the 1920's. It must have fit well with the times back then and her affinity for dancing when she was young; she could still do the Charleston. She prided herself that she never once went to the beauty parlor or fussed with girly vanity. She didn't need to. She could rise out of bed in the morning, run a comb through her hair, and be perfect even if not glamorous. It was a natural down to earth look. It suited her.

Harriott was thick and stout in stature. Her fingers were wide and her hands large. She hated that. But she had grown up a farm girl. She knew hard work. Tragedy took its toll. During the depression, her parents lost their farm and the eight children were parceled out to alleviate the expense they could no longer afford taking care of them. Harriott was given to a family at the age of twelve to work as a servant in a family's home until she grew up. She ironed sheets, washed dishes, helped cook and care for the children. In time, the family came to love her, and when she departed

South Dakota for good, they gave her a parting gift, a cut glass bowl that she carried on her lap while she traveled on an old fashioned bus all the way to the budding city of Los Angeles when it was not much more than a dusty little town. She was merely eighteen years old, but ready to begin a new life.

Despite Effie and Harriott's differences and three long years later, Effie was for some unexplained reason granted permission to take Jill home with her one day. It was an exciting day because it was the first time Jill stepped foot in Effie's house since her mother had gone. Jill was happy beyond words. Effie pulled up to the driveway of Harriott and Louie's home to get Jill. The two of them got into Effie's car and pulled away without a backwards glance. It was a long drive but the weather was beautiful and the sun was out. Jill could feel the heat piercing through the rolled up car window even with the air conditioning on. The anticipation filled her with longing and excitement. When they pulled into the long forgotten yet familiar driveway, she shouted with joy. Jill secretly hoped she would find her mother there waiting. Everything looked just the same and Jill jumped out of the car after they had rounded the corner to the backyard garage. She ran into the house up and down all of the hallways, searching every room. Effie stood in the kitchen, watching her enthusiasm. "Where is she?" Jill demanded. "Where is who?" Effie asked. "My mom!" Effie's forehead wrinkled and she looked sternly at Jill. "Well she isn't here." "Oh," Jill sighed disappointedly.

Then she remembered the backyard. The first thing she did was run to the precipice that overlooked the sloping long hills that eventually turned into the large canyon. Jill stood there and the memories flooded back, all of the fantasies and the magic of that backyard. And there at the bottom of the third hill stood her beloved willow tree. She eyed it adoringly and with a carefree abandon tore down the first hill letting her hands fly out to her sides, brushing the sage plants and tall grasses to either side of her. When she reached the second hill she didn't stop. She kept running until she reached the willow tree. She turned towards the first fence that partitioned off the backyard from the remaining slopes beyond it. She touched the dainty leaves of the dangling wispy branches that hung nearly to the ground. It was much bigger and overgrown now. Then she raced back up the hills feeling and smelling the intense wonderful smell of sage that she remembered so well and that triggered the memories of so many long forgotten stories played out in her imagination so long ago. She took in the sites of the red berry bushes and the purple grapevines crawling up the sides of the fences, inspecting everything was still there. As she ran up the hill she shouted as the wind blew through her long blond hair, "I remember! I remember! I remember!" When she reached the top where Effie stood, she turned and ran down the sloping hills again all the while shouting, "I remember! I remember!" Effie stood at the top watching her and smiled a painful yet happy smile at Jill's contagious joy.

Though Jill was ecstatic over her visit to her long remembered home of the past, there was something hollow about the place that never went away for years to come. The house seemed to be aware of the emptiness too and it felt like ghosts roamed the hallways, casting an endless shadow on the ones left behind. It was only the two of them now.

Jill didn't realize at the time what it was that precipitated the breaking of the unspoken rule to go to the forbidden home of Jill's previous life. Things were changing, and something big was about to happen. Jill was sure of it. Her father showed up one day after she returned to her grandparents' home after the visit to Effie's. He took Jill outside to the passageway that formed a sort of corridor running the length of the side of the house and the two of them faced each other. In the middle of the long driveway, Paul leaned back against the black MG that was parked there, and he began to speak. He barely got half a sentence out before Jill shouted, "Yes! I'll go with you! I choose you!" Paul laughed and tried to be serious, "Well wait now, you didn't hear me through, we need to be sure, you need to think about this. Let me finish."

The question her father had posed was this. "Jill, the woman you met is going to be my wife and we are giving you the choice to live …" That was where Jill had cut him off. She had dreamed of living with her father for as long as she could remember and she already knew the answer long before he'd voiced the question. "Ok," he continued with a smile that spread from ear to ear, betraying his seriousness and belying his equal joy, "to live with me or to …" Again she cut him off, "With you! With you!" she chanted hopping up and down. He couldn't contain his contagious grin and a chuckle that tickled him down to his toes. Obviously he was just as giddy and excited as she was, but at the same time, he attempted to enforce a methodical process for arriving at such an important decision. The grave circumstances commanded it.

"Let me finish now," he said. "You don't need to, I already know what you're going to say," Jill said impatiently. He knew as well as she, the decision was a foregone conclusion, but he was determined to follow through the motions in order to give it fair consideration. "Jill, this is a very big decision, you could stay here with grandma and grandpa." "No! No!" she interrupted him again. "Well now, we need to give this serious thought." "I don't need to, I already have my answer," she said. "Well, nonetheless we aren't going to make a hasty decision until you've had more time." "But I don't need time!" Jill said. "We shouldn't make important decisions in a rush." "But my answer will be the same now as it will be later," Jill explained impatiently. "All the same," he informed her, "We will wait." Jill replied, "Ok. But my answer is that I will go with you." She wanted to make absolutely certain that he departed with her final answer.

Only days later, Jill was taken to her mother's grave on the very day she boarded the plane to live with her new family, her father and his new wife. Jill stood looking at the tombstone with her mother's name on it for a long time, cold, gray indelible words written in stone. She was solidly behind that rock. It's where she had been all this time, resting in the sun. The sun shone down nice and hot now too. She felt the heat of it on her back, her neck, and her head. She cleared the grass away so she could read her name better. She felt nothing but a wave of understanding that fell down on her and all around like the sky and the warm air enveloping her with the comfort of knowing. It was a relief. Finally she understood. Finally she had the answer. The separation was complete. Her mind finally understood, but she would never get the chance to feel what she may have felt when it happened. Maybe she would always feel that feeling of chasing the something she should have felt. Perhaps it was some place deep inside now, a slow invisible feeling that would never go away, hidden from her consciousness. She would walk through life with a constant gap between her self and the world outside, between her mind and her body, her thoughts and feelings forever disconnected.

In this way, Jill moved in with yet another family to begin a new life. Her grandparents joined her. For whatever reason, Harriott caused a great deal of havoc for nearly everyone, so much so it became a family joke. She and Louie moved in with Jill's father & his new young wife for three long months when they came to drop her off on the other side of the country. They couldn't let go of her, nor she them. She wanted so much to be with her father, and a young family where she thought she belonged. But living with Harriott and Louie had become her stronghold during those three long years after her mother had died. Without them she thought many years later, she could not have made it through. They gave her comfort and constancy at a time when she needed it most. No one else could possibly have done that. It was the stability of those few years that would carry her through the rest of growing up that she couldn't have endured had she not had them in her life. She couldn't let go, and nor could they. They stayed far too long.

When Paul remarried, their dog came too. The dog was Jill's dog. After all, they had nearly the same birthday. Mala followed Jill everywhere. She protected her fiercely even after they'd been separated for the duration of her time with Harriott and Louie. That was one thing about Paul. He was loyal to a fault. He would never abandon anyone, and that included their beloved dog. Mala waited outside the houses of Jill's friends for hours while she was inside just to be there when she came out and to escort her back home. Jill discovered many years later that her mother had bred her beloved Mala. She'd never known that. She found the picture with all the pups, her mother, Bobbie, holding one close to her chest. She found the letter describing how they'd almost died. She had saved every one of them. Whenever Jill and her father looked at "their" dog, there was a quiet understanding of her importance. She was the last thread connecting them to the memory of what once was. It was a small detail they both held onto.

The presence of in-laws was not a good start to a marriage. It paved the way to a rocky road and the treacherous winds of resentment and anger constantly blowing Jill's way. She had clung to Harriott and Louie and was afraid to let them go. She wanted all of them with her, her grandparents, her father, this strange new woman who everyone wanted her to call mother. They had even promised to pay her a dime each time she would. She never did, not even once. Jill knew no one could ever replace her mother and there was no one else in the world she would call that name.

She was only seven, but Harriott and Louie were wrapped around her fingers. They heeded her every whim. They were blind to the destruction they left in their path, and so was Jill. Their only mistake was in loving her too much. Slowly Jill broke the ties and they left, leaving her to adjust to yet another new life. She discovered a newfound freedom, sitting on top of gigantic dirt piles, getting as dirty as she pleased, running around like a street rat, and barefoot too. The process began before Harriott and Louie had departed for good. It was wonderful. Harriott would come out in a dither, scolding to get inside and take a bath. But Jill was so stubborn and determined to hang on to this new freedom that after the bath she would go right back out and sit in the dirt pile just to show she could do what she wanted now. Poor Harriott. It must have been hard for her. She was losing control and with it the attachment she so tightly held to her. Jill loved her dearly. She was a blessing at such a crucial age and during such a difficult time, tenderly caring for her like no one else could. But Jill embraced her new life. She was with young people, finally, like Jill thought she ought to be. That had been her wish the whole of the time she had lived with her beloved Harriott and Louie. As quickly as she had latched on to her grandparents, she latched on to this new life just as tightly.

Chapter 2

Dr. Zikler

(1970 – 1972)

There isn't anyone that I can tell how I feel … because they all have their problems and their little spheres of living and my state is inconsequential. The people who would be more likely to listen and care I can't tell either, because I care for them and I don't want to confuse or distress them.

So, what do I do? Just plod along hopeless, plod lonely on. But it's so hard and so painful and my load seems heavier and heavier; my knees are buckling and my head is bending low.

I am very willing, anxious even, to help other people with their load, but no one can help me. In this very particular sense, I am the most alone person of my experience. I know well that this sounds very much like over-indulgence in self-pity and a very strong tendency towards egocentricity. But where do you draw the line? Since I can't tell anyone how I feel I think would indicate the opposite. Right now, I am confiding to myself, just an outward expression of what troubles me … but no one knows, no one at all knows how I am being crushed and torn and twisted; how hard and unrelentlessly my heart aches.

And it will get worse before it ever gets better because I'll go on hurting; and I'll go on keeping it to myself; and people will go on never understanding me. So, I'll always be alone. Always, ever since I was a child and now and from now on ... always.

Please God, help me, please give me strength.

Bobbie, February 24, 1964

Bobbie lay in bed with the covers pulled over her head. It was noon already and she had yet to face the day. Jill toddled around embarking on one endeavor after the next. She was a happy child and the discoveries were endless. Jill could entertain herself for hours. A knock came at the door and Bobbie struggled out of bed, still in her pink nightgown, hanging past her knees. Her hair was tangled and day-old mascara exaggerated the dark circles under her eyes. It was Louie and Harriott, Bobbie's in-laws. It was common for them to spring surprise visits exemplifying the intimate relationship that existed between them. But their visits also masked another goal: to check up on things. They were concerned. They knew there were struggles in the household of their son and their beloved daughter-in-law. Harriott and Bobbie had a close relationship, and Bobbie had divulged much to her. Harriott mostly listened. She had worried and lamented from the onset her opinion that her son was not ready for marriage. To the contrary, Bobbie's Mother, Effie, saw in her son-in-law the savior of her daughter and the remedy for her affliction – as well as the prodigal male figure that would fill the void that her husband had made when he left their lives so many years ago. He was the answer to their half-empty family. What's more, just as Effie's husband had been, he was a pilot by profession, a most notable and prestigious addition to the family. He was a perfect replacement.

Bobbie opened the door and forced a smile. "Mom! How wonderful to see you. Dad, what a terrific surprise." Her voice was dull and flat. Louie and Harriott were never judgmental or angry over her condition. They only worried about her, and all of them. They stepped into the house, noting the house in disarray, toys scattered everywhere. "How are you Bobbie? Are you okay?" Harriott asked already knowing the answer, but attempting to get Bobbie to engage in conversation and to draw her away from the gloomy thoughts she knew were circling in her head. "Oh I'm fine," she replied mechanically as if she were reading a script to a play. "Do you mind if I make you a cup of tea Bobbie? I think it would do you good," Harriott offered. Bobbie forced a reply. "I don't really feel like one, but if you insist go ahead." Louie searched for Jill and found her in one of the bedrooms emptying the contents of the lowest drawer of a small nightstand. She was still in her red pajama one-sie all zipped up the front with padded feet. Her favorite wooly boot slippers lay in the hallway. They had long since been removed. The double layer was far too hot and made her feet sweaty. Louie bent down and called her, "Look who's here! It's Grandpa!" Jill turned and squealed with delight and ran into his arms. He picked her up and felt her damp cloth diaper that had leaked through the red pajama fabric to his arms. "I have an idea Jill. Let's go get changed, ok?!" He tried to sound excited. Jill complied and happily held Louie's hand as they walked down the hallway to the bathroom.

Harriott entered the kitchen with Bobbie following reluctantly behind. She halted at the doorway and gasped but then quickly covered her disbelief. The kitchen was a disaster. "Jill's been busy alright," Harriott tried to make light of the situation. She didn't want to upset Bobbie in her state of depression. "Every pot and pan seems to have been emptied out of every cupboard, including every item in every drawer she could get her hands on." She got down on her hands and knees and began to pick it all up. Bobbie blandly added a hand; bending over appeared to take all the effort of the world. Harriott ran into a big pile of sugar in one corner of the kitchen as well as a smattering of smaller piles nearby. Harriott quietly commented half to herself, "Well, I can see what Jill had for breakfast this morning." Harriott quickly had the floor cleared so they could at least walk around the kitchen. Next she put the kettle on to boil and examined the next stage of order at hand. The countertops were littered with dirty dishes and half opened boxes of dried foods of one sort or another. Cans lay on the counter with a can opener that looked like an afterthought to an attempt at dinner. Harriott quickly tidied up best she could and told Bobbie to sit down while the water boiled. Next she opened the cupboards and looked for some oatmeal to cook for Jill.

The water came to a boil and Harriott poured it into a teapot with loose tea secured in a tea ball strainer and put the lid on. She placed a little teacup in front of Bobbie and informed her the tea would be steeped in three minutes exactly. While the tea steeped Harriott swept through the kitchen once more, collecting last bits of debris and emptying it into the small kitchen trash pail. It was overflowing, so she announced she would be right back, all the while keeping a close eye on the time. Tea was serious business for Harriott; it had to be done just right. She left the kitchen via the back door and carried the trash pail to the side of the house where the large metal garbage bin was sitting and opened the lid. She gasped when she noted the abundant number of empty aluminum beer cans. The smell of old beer wafted up to her nostrils like the stench of spilled Budweiser and Coors the morning after a college party. Harriott came through the back kitchen door with the empty pail and put it away under the sink. She did not bring up the beer cans. She knew it was a problem and Bobbie wanted to hide it. She could see Bobbie had neatly tried to conceal the evidence as soon as Paul had disappeared on his latest trip to who-knew-where. He would be gone for days at a time. Harriott knew Bobbie didn't want her to know, so she pretended not to. The last thing she wanted was to humiliate or upset Bobbie while she was in this state.

The tea was ready so Harriott carefully lifted the tea ball out of the pot and set it onto a small plate with a clink as the metal hit the glass. She brought the little teapot to the table where Bobbie sat forcing herself to appear congenial. Harriott poured some tea into the little cup, set the teapot on a hot pad and covered it with a tea cozy, and then she got a cup for herself. Louie entered the kitchen with Jill smiling in her new dry clothes. Harriott remembered the oatmeal sitting on the stove still simmering and grabbed a dirty bowl. She cleaned the little bowl with hot soapy water and dried it with a towel before ladling some oatmeal into it. She went for the brown sugar then halted, bringing it down slowly from the shelf. She commented, "We'll just put a dab of sugar since we know a certain little one has had plenty of sugar already for one morning." Harriott eyed her little granddaughter with a sideways glance and a scolding tone in her voice. Jill looked up with her big blue eyes innocently as if she were an angel who could do nothing wrong. In Jill's mind, she hadn't. Louie pulled a chair up to the table and sat down with Jill still in his lap. Harriott placed the bowl of oatmeal in front of her. Louie began lifting mouthfuls into the toddler's mouth.

Harriott stood in the middle of the kitchen with a spoon in one hand. "And how are we doing over here? What can I fix you to eat my dear?" Bobbie's head hung down, cradled in her hands like she had the biggest hangover in the world. "Oh I'm not hungry," she answered as if the words were an immense struggle to get out. "Oh come now," Harriott insisted, "You must let me make you something. I'm not going to let you starve before we leave." "You can if you must, mom, but I can't guarantee I will be able to eat it." Bobbie called her mother-in-law 'mom' in the old-fashioned way; it suited their relationship. "Have you had anything at all to eat yet today?" Bobbie looked up as if the question were an abstract formal inquiry that had nothing to do with her. It took a great deal of effort to search her mind for the answer. Finally she replied with a small, "No." "Well then," Harriott concluded, "Let's see what I can whip up."

Before long, Harriott cooked up some noodles with a nice sauce and some cubed beef. There were no vegetables in the house, so a nice green salad or string beans would have to be foregone. She placed a small plateful in front of Bobbie. She stared at it like she didn't really see it. Harriott encouraged her, "Alright now, none of that. Better take a bite or you will most definitely offend me." Bobbie lifted her fork and stabbed a very small piece of meat covered with sauce. She put it to her mouth in a way that looked like she might be contaminated by it if it touched the insides of her cheeks. She chewed with labor and forced it down. "There's a good girl," Harriott nodded in satisfaction. They watched her, making sure she had at least a meal-sized portion before she left the table. "You'll feel much better I assure you with some food in your belly." "Now you have some leftovers so you will have something to eat for dinner, ok my dear?" "Ok, thank you mom. It's very kind of you," Bobbie acknowledged her mother-in-law's efforts.

Harriott and Louie remained there for the rest of the day but had to leave by evening. Harriott worried over the state of affairs. However, they lived two states away and couldn't come every week to check up on her. It was fortunate their son was a pilot now, so they could fly anywhere they wished for free.

Two days later, Paul came home from his trip exhausted but happy to be back. Bobbie had pulled herself together and was feeling better. The medication seemed to help. She tried to act excited that he was home and even stood in the kitchen preparing his favorite dinner: her special secret marinade soaked over a nice rib-eye steak that he loved so much and baked potatoes. Two artichokes boiled in a large pot. Artichokes were a tradition in Bobbie's family. All new guests were introduced to them if they had never had one before and even if they had. It was a special occasion when the artichokes were brought out. Paul was easily indoctrinated to the tradition. He now loved them too. He sauntered into the kitchen and breathed in the good smells. He set his pilot's hat on the counter and breathed a sigh of relief to be home. A big grin spread across his face. He delighted in the fanfare welcoming him home. Bobbie smiled warmly and he came over to her. He hugged her from behind and kissed her on the cheek. Jill sat on the floor playing with her toys as her mom cooked and made small sounds to make sure Paul knew she was there. When her father turned to her, her face lit up and a smile from ear to ear greeted him. Paul opened his arms wide as he knelt on the floor and he giggled at his small daughter reveling in delight at the sight of him. She played her part and came running. Paul commented to Bobbie not taking his eyes off Jill, "Wow, she's grown even since I was gone! Look at her Bobbie! She looks more and more like you every day." Bobbie turned briefly from her cooking and smiled.

Paul disappeared to take his uniform off in the bedroom and headed for the garage. Bobbie glanced up and reminded him dinner would be ready any minute. "Um. Ok." He muttered appearing to be only half listening. Bobbie was already beginning to feel frustrated and he'd only just returned. He would disappear into that garage for hours.

Bobbie set the dishes on the table beginning to feel her exasperation rising within her. She knew she would have to go get him even though he had just seen the food was nearly ready. She opened the door to the garage. He was leaning against the workbench in his tattered jeans and a white short-sleeved t-shirt guzzling a beer. This irritated Bobbie even more. She thought to herself, "Here we go again, he's already at it and he's only been home five minutes." With an edge of irritation Bobbie announced, "Dinner's ready. Right now." She knew he wouldn't come for another ten minutes and make them all wait. So she added, "the meat will get tough if you don't hurry." He glanced up like he'd only just heard her and set down his beer. "Oh! Ok, yep I'm comin.' Oh boy! Steak!!" Bobbie finished putting all the food on the table and pulled Jill up to the high chair. Bobbie had ground a small portion of everything in a grinder for Jill's dinner. Jill loved that. Bobbie always commented on it. Paul strode in as if the world waited on him and took his place at the head of the table. It was as if his entrance wouldn't be grand enough if he didn't arrive at least five minutes late. Tonight's dinner was special. That's why it was only five unlike most nights when he would saunter in halfway through the meal or sometimes after everyone had finished. In the beginning they waited for him, but Bobbie got tired of it and eventually gave up.

Paul was appreciative. He wasn't trying to be disrespectful. To the contrary, he was truly oblivious to the effect his interactions had on nearly everyone that was close to him. He lived in his own world most of the time and for Bobbie it was disappointing that this was the marriage she would have to endure for the rest of her life. She had serious doubts. She was sad that the happy life and future family she had envisioned might not be so happy after all.

During dinner it was plain to see how much he enjoyed the meal. There was an audible "Mmmm" at every bite and in between mouthfuls he commented things like "This is my favorite, oh isn't this steak great? I don't know how you do it. It's the best steak I've ever had. How do you manage to get it perfect every time?" And when he got to the artichoke and began dipping each leaf into the melted butter with a small dash of lemon the "Mmmm's" started all over again. It was the kind of compliment that would flatter any chef. To Bobbie, however, the gestures felt empty. It was simply that the elevation of status that her food obtained seemed to matter more than acknowledgment of her, and this is what shadowed any compliments, dwindling them down to almost nothing. It was what darkened her mood.

Paul could never seem to grasp an understanding of this. When dinner was finished he rose from the table and rubbed his belly, grinning with his charming and endearing smile, declaring "Well! That was a fabulous dinner!" He headed immediately for the garage where there was another refrigerator. In it contained rack after rack of cases of Coors beer. Paul opened the door and reached for one and proceeded to peel back the tab with a loud snap as it broke off, exposing the small hole from which he poured one huge gulp down his throat. For him, it was the most satisfying dessert to any meal, and especially this one. He turned to his workbench and scanned the multitude of projects that lay scattered from one end to the other. Harriott always said from the age of two, Paul was in the garage constantly looking for what to do and what he could possibly make. Whenever she asked him what he was doing, the answer was "making-doing mom."

Paul had studied electrical and aeronautical engineering and his passion had always been flying. In fact, from the time he was a small child he would stand outside the fences of small landing strips and watch the planes landing and taking off one after the other. When he was sixteen, he took a job as a paperboy and saved every penny to take flying lessons. Hour by hour he accumulated enough time to get a license and in college he worked as a car mechanic where he saved all of his money for flying too. His dream was to become an airline pilot and to this his father, Louie, told him time and again, "Give that up Paul, it just isn't possible. We don't have the money for such a lofty dream. And in addition to that there is no way you could fly a commercial airplane. That is out of our reach son. Set your sites on something sensible. Working for the post office for instance like me. It's a stable income and a very decent job. Be realistic son." But Paul never lost site of his dream or wavered once at its possibility. By this time he had met Bobbie and she worked as a teacher's aid after having dropped out of college one semester short of graduating. Her view was that "a piece of paper" didn't matter. She worked other odd jobs and contributed to helping him achieve his dreams. Louie, however, continued to express his doubt. In fact, he declared on one occasion, "Why if you become an airline pilot son, I'll buy you a plane." This was equivalent to declaring its impossibility because that was indeed impossible.

Louie had worked three jobs in order to support his three adopted children. He wanted to give them a good life, and they certainly were comfortable, meaning they never went hungry, although they did eat nearly the same simple food of mostly green beans, meat patties, and egg noodles every night. They lived extremely frugally. Their home was solid. Paul and his two siblings had grown up in the simple but quaint little home with red tiled shingles, wood floors and arched walkways and a little swimming pool and a garage out back that stood apart from the house on Malcolm Avenue. Louie and Harriott had chosen well; they bought their home at a time when they were able to afford to pay in full after two short years the sum total of two thousand dollars. Having this obligation completed prior to beginning their family was a good start. Louie and Harriott were simple and came from a hard life of farming in the mid-west where they grew up during the depression. Louie lived with an uncle from the time he was thirteen after both parents had died. As Harriott had done, Louie migrated to Los Angeles around the same time.

The two of them worked small jobs to get by in the then small dusty but quickly growing town of L.A. One day, Louie accompanied a friend who was meant to escort Harriott to a dance. At the last moment the friend backed out and Louie decided he'd better go anyway so as not to stand Harriott up. They went dancing that night and Louie was not too keen on that, but he did it anyway. After that, they danced every Sunday night for six long years. Harriott was twenty-six by then and her mother told her "Dump him. You're not getting any younger. No one will want to marry you if you wait much longer." Harriott patiently said to her, "Well, we'll see."

One day Louie asked Harriott to accompany him to a house he wanted to look at. After looking at the home the sellers asked, "Well? What do you think? Do you want it?" Louie turned to Harriott and asked, "What do you think?" Harriott replied quietly, "Well, it's very nice." The sellers answered, "That's super! You'll take it then?" "Why yes, I think we will," Louie said. "And you are of course married?" they inquired already assuming the answer was yes. Louie shifted his weight uncomfortably and he looked awkwardly at the ground and back up at them. "Well, no we're not." The sellers became serious and said to him, "We cannot sell a home to an unmarried couple. It's not decent and it's most certainly not possible." Louie turned to Harriott and said, "Well, I guess we'd better get married." Harriott answered as if they were having a conversation over what can of beans to buy at the grocery store. "Well, that would be fine." And that was how Louie proposed to Harriott and how they came to own the home on Malcolm Avenue.

Two years later, on the date of their final payment of the home, they invited the sellers over for dinner to present them with the money. The couple was impressed by their diligence and responsibility, so much so that they got up from the table after dinner to announce and present

Harriott and Louie with two tickets for a cruise to Hawaii so they could celebrate a proper honeymoon. And that was how Harriott and Louie came to experience a most unfathomable voyage and to a most unexpected destination.

Their family expanded in a most unusual way. Since they were not able to have children of their own, they adopted three from other families. Each child had their own story and each came by word of mouth and on account of perilous circumstances. One of them was even offered via a friend via a friend from a mother who'd had an affair while her sailor husband was out to sea. When he came home he was livid and gave an ultimatum: it was either the child or he. Harriott called Louie on the phone and asked calmly and in their typical choose-a-can-of-beans-way, "Honey, would you like a baby girl?" Louie answered, "Why sure honey, if that's what you want." "Well," Harriott began, "The pickle is, we would have to take her today." Louie replied just as calmly and matter-of-factly, "Well that's fine with me dear, if that's what you want." Harriott came home with a baby girl that night.

Paul came from different circumstances. He was the result of a teenage pregnancy, the young mother of whom happened to be the daughter of the Superintendent of the Los Angeles School District. Since he held such a prominent position in the community and it was a shameful predicament, the girl was whisked away to another town, hidden from view and from scandal. Harriott and Louie were informed of the need for a home for the child. They delightfully agreed to take him. This would be their first addition and beginning to their new family. Louie would come to spoil him no end.

Paul grew up in the Malcolm home in this way, with loving parents who provided him with a traditional upbringing. A rather unusual child, smart but peculiar, he came to be remarked on by everyone with comments such as "That's Paul. It's just the way he is." It was the best anyone could do to explain let alone try to understand his behavior.

Embarking on a marriage and creating a family of his own, therefore, was a most unseemly endeavor. What was perfectly fine to Paul was not to everyone else. He lived somewhere forever lost in his mind far away from everyone and it was hard to guess where he was. He could be absolutely charming and downright friendly with outsiders, warm and generous and kind with his family and genuinely so. He was handsome, tall and dark with sparkling green eyes that lit up when he was amused and an engaging grin and dimples that drew one in like waves hugging a beach. The thing was, the water retracted back out to sea just as quickly as is the nature of a wave. His quirkiness got in the way. When he disappeared, no one knew where he went. He could be talking to someone and his voice would trail off. He would look somewhere else, as if he were engaged in a dialogue with the universe, imagining something, figuring something out, coming up with a million and one more ideas.

It was all of this Bobbie came to know too late. The process of falling in love must have been enough to engage his attention for a while, but in time, his true nature became apparent. Bobbie was heartbroken. The marriage her mother had thought would mend the holes in Bobbie's mind only made them worse. It was a burden beyond measure and a difficult load to bear, especially for someone with an already fragile mind that teetered back and forth between depression and the ability to function in regular everyday life. Bobbie was constantly on the verge of mental illness. The question was, with her condition, was she strong enough to withstand it? Bobbie clung to the ideal of a perfect marriage and a perfect family with a house full of little ones running around her feet; she loved children. In fact, at their wedding she had invited her entire classroom of children, the little girls in matching dresses running around as flower girls. In accord, Paul was perfectly willing to oblige this charming picture of togetherness. It could happen all around him and it was just fine. He didn't assume exactly that he could watch it all unfold without his involvement. To the contrary, he didn't even realize it was what he was doing.

Regardless of everything, Bobbie loved her little girl. Jill held a special place in her heart, being the first to grace their newly formed family. When Bobbie was in a good constitution, she was the most gracious of mothers. She adored Jill and doted on her. She dressed her in pea coats, boots and the latest fashion of baby dresses. Though money was tight, Effie ensured that these most important necessities were procured. One must always look her best in public, and Effie was not about to have her first granddaughter looking like a peasant girl. Little did Effie know at the time, this would be her only grandchild.

The following morning, Paul woke up and Bobbie was in the kitchen feeding Jill breakfast. Bobbie finished giving her the last bite and pulled Jill out of her high chair and wiped her face. Placing Jill on the floor near them where her toys were spread out on the ground, Jill occupied herself immediately. Bobbie asked Paul what he would like. Paul was quiet and a tad grumpy. His jerky swift movements clearly communicated this. Bobbie got the coffee grounds to make coffee. Paul curtly informed her, "I'll do that." He didn't like anyone doing things for him when he was like that. In those moments, he needed to have control. Bobbie dropped the grounds on the counter as if they were going to burn her hands and backed up, letting him have the space where she stood. She did this dramatically, emphasizing – mirroring back to him rather, the abruptness of his behavior. She got out of his way and went to the fridge, looking for something she could make for breakfast. She got orange juice and set it on the table, then pulled out some eggs. She knew he liked eggs, especially over easy, yokes still runny. She grabbed the bacon too. He loved bacon. Gingerly she crept well around Paul as he continued with the process of making his coffee. A spiky shield enshrouded him. She pulled out two frying pans and set each on a burner. Next she peeled the bacon strips apart and placed them side-by-side in one of the pans. She washed the filmy grease off her hands. After the bacon was going she picked up an egg. She cracked it over the edge of the other pan and dropped it in. She cracked the next one. Carefully she waited for the exact moment to flip them. This was a tricky task keeping the egg yolks runny without breaking them. Gingerly she attempted to scrape away at the edges of one egg. It wasn't ready yet. While juggling the task of perfectly flipped eggs she checked the bacon to make sure it didn't burn. It was already sizzling steadily. She turned the heat down a notch and went back to the eggs. Now it was ready. She was sure. Timing it to be just fast enough but careful too, she slid the spatula squarely under one egg and went for it. Made it! The yoke remained in tact. It wobbled a bit as it hit the pan so she knew it was still runny. She went to the next and attempted to repeat the process. One, two, three, flip! But oops, it hit down too hard and out of an ever so slight tear the yoke came running out and quickly hardened into a solid yellow mass. "Darn it!" She pulled the first one up off the pan and set it on Paul's plate. "Thanks," he forced out with a voice that had an edge to it. She removed the other egg that was still in the pan and put it on a plate to the side and cracked two more in the pan. She took the bacon off of the stove and put each piece one by one onto a plate covered with a paper towel. She placed the plate of bacon in front of Paul. He eyed the bacon and allowed a barely audible grunt escape his mouth. Bobbie turned to the stove and attempted once again to do the tricky flip. She was successful! She immediately brought the egg to Paul once it had finished cooking; she slid it onto his plate carefully so as not to break it in such a silly way. The next yoke broke. She took both of the broken egg yokes and sat down to join her husband. They ate in silence until Bobbie interrupted it. Paul was almost finished and she knew as soon as he was, he would abruptly bolt for the garage.

Breaking the silence and skirting around what she really felt, she attempted to engage him in a conversation. "The bills came in while you were away." Another grunt. She brought up the car repair and he glanced up, "Oh yeah?" He was thinking how he could've done it himself to save money, but Bobbie had been stranded and he wasn't there. The conversation did not advance. In fact, he seemed even more irritated than ever. Bobbie attempted again, this time more casual talk and Paul became itchy to leave. He nearly walked out on her mid-sentence before she said, "You going to run off like usual?" "I have no idea what you're talking about," he answered. "How do you not know when it's what you do every single time we try to talk?" He put his head down in exasperation. He really didn't want to deal with this now. Bobbie changed the subject to lighten the mood. "The neighbors asked about getting together." Bobbie knew Paul liked Dave. They had a lot in common. He looked up vaguely interested, "Oh yeah?" She wasn't going to change his mood, and she knew the conversation was going nowhere. "Well, invite them over," he suggested. He turned towards the door.

She couldn't stand it anymore. She confronted him, "Why don't you ever notice me?" He glared. "I notice you." His mood was turning dark and he hated more than anything wasting time on nonsense. "Did you see I've dropped fifteen pounds in the past three weeks?" "No," he said, in a barely audible voice that seemed to be coming from somewhere far away. He was half listening to what seemed to him an irrelevant fact he could not relate to. Bobbie had been desperately trying for months to impress him. She thought if she were skinnier, he would notice her. Instead, she only looked gaunt. "You're fine the way you are," he said. He really couldn't understand where this was going, and it certainly was cutting into his more pressing goal of getting back to his project. He pictured it on his workbench. Bobbie raised her voice, "Fine! Run to your garage! You don't do anything with this family anyway!!" Paul glanced up, daggers in his eyes, mostly because he was annoyed at being bothered but also because he could not see a connection between Bobbie's erratic statements in response to unrelated events that weren't even happening. Hadn't he eaten breakfast together with them? "Don't you see what's happening?" "No, I don't," he answered flatly.

Jill began to cry. The toddler felt the thickness in the air building as she sat on the floor. She had stopped playing some minutes before. The tension built inside of her until she couldn't hold it in any longer. Her barely audible cry grew until she became aware her parents were looking at her. Bobbie's face melted and she ran to Jill. "Oh we're so sorry, we're upsetting you!" Paul softened too. "It's ok Jill, we're just talking." Jill relaxed when she noticed their faces were less angry.

The day continued and went back to normal, whatever that was. For Bobbie normal was an endless and mundane torture. Some time after the breakfast incident, she went to the cupboard and reached for one of her medications. She had been seeing doctors for some time. She went to more than one doctor, five to be precise, and each of them gave her various medications. She stockpiled them for future use. When things became intolerable, she would empty one of the bottles down her throat. She was slowly sinking into a slump and it was getting worse. She went through the motions of the day, caring for Jill, picking up the mess around the house. Paul stayed outside nearly the entire time. Even hunger was not important enough to tear him away from whatever he was doing. He wouldn't feel hunger even if he had it. He came in once, maybe twice for a few brief moments only to use the toilet, saying not a word, in deep thought, and headed straight back to the garage.

By evening, Bobbie decided she'd had enough. She was tired of everything. She was tired of life. She rolled one of the bottles around in her hand, feeling the hard cold plastic, fingering the lid and listening to the rattle of the tablets rolling around inside. It was a full bottle. She emptied all of it into her mouth, swallowed and waited. Some stuck in her throat so she chased them down with a tall glass of water. She stood at the counter in the kitchen and leaned against it staring at the clock, watching the second hand swing around five full circles and listening to the rhythmic ticking. It seemed to take forever. The waiting was unbearable. She walked out of the kitchen and stumbled down the hallway to the bedroom and sat on the bed. Paul was still in the garage.

She could feel her head begin to spin and she knew it was time. In her hazy fog she picked up the phone and dialed 9-1-1. She mumbled over the receiver that she had overdosed on her prescription medication. Several minutes later, the ambulance arrived. Paul leapt from his workbench and to the door when he heard the sirens, his heart sinking and muttering, "Oh God, not again." He grabbed the metal doorknob to the garage-kitchen door and swung it open so hard it banged against the wall, and ran across the house, letting the door slam behind him. He answered the front door and the paramedics stood on the doorstep asking what the emergency was. Paul knew enough to know it probably *was* an emergency.

He opened the door wide and invited them in. He said in a low voice it was probably his wife and he didn't know she had called. He led them to the bedroom. The paramedics exchanged looks as they walked down the hallway wondering how the husband didn't know there was an emergency. Paul quickened his step. Even though this scenario repeated itself fairly regularly, it put a tightness in his heart every time. He entered the room and everyone crowded in the doorway. Bobbie lay passed out on the bed with the empty bottle in her hand. She wore an orange t-shirt that was scrunched up around her waist. Her three quarter length blue pants protruded from underneath. One of the paramedics sat on the bed next to her making the bed sink and Bobbie rolled towards him slightly. He lifted her arm and gently felt for a pulse. Another paramedic kneeled onto the mattress on the other side of the bed causing Bobbie to roll back. He bent over her, supporting his weight with his opposite hand over Bobbie, and turned his head sideways placing his ear over her mouth and nose. He listened for breathing. A light trace of warm air blew into his ear and he looked up at his partner and nodded, confirming her breath. Paul picked up the bottle of medication and read the label, nodding "yep." He handed it to the paramedics who were still reading her vitals.

They shook her, but there was no response. She remained limp and unconscious. One of them radioed the doctor on call at the hospital and read the label on the bottle. The other paramedic put an oxygen mask over Bobbie's face while explaining to Paul that she still had a pulse and was breathing. They were only adding the oxygen for extra precaution. He said they were looking for signs of shock. He informed Paul, "At this time she appears to be stable, but there's no guarantee that could change at any moment."

The paramedic put down his radio and gave instructions where to put the stretcher that had been carried into the room. They put Bobbie on it and strapped her down. One of the emergency crew stood behind with Paul and explained what was going to happen next, and to get any background information he could. Paul stood idly by, helpless and with watery eyes. He confided this wasn't the first time. He didn't include the fact that this was one of dozens of attempts at ending her life. She had been doing this since long before he'd met her. She had told him she was thirteen, in fact, the first time it happened.

After everyone had packed and left, Paul went to the neighbors and asked if someone could stay with Jill while he went to the hospital. She had long since been put to bed by Bobbie earlier in the evening. He told them there had been an emergency, leaving out the details of what had really happened. Again.

Paul grabbed his jacket after downing a couple of beers and aggressively sucking the smoke from a cigarette into his lungs and climbed into his car. He headed for the hospital in the dark. It was cold and rainy, a typical Washington night and it was difficult to see. The lights glared against the drops of water on the windshield. When Paul reached the hospital, he parked and walked through the emergency room doors. He knew the drill. He was surprised the staff wasn't beginning to recognize him. He and his family were almost regulars. Paul informed the front desk he was there and he was taken back to his wife, still unconscious. He was made to wait in a chair in the hallway until a doctor came to explain what was going on.

Half an hour went by before a doctor approached Paul. Paul had stepped out two times by then to smoke a cigarette. "Bobbie has overdosed on Darvon. The bottle given to me by the paramedics indicates this was a prescribed medication." He waited for Paul to fill in the blanks. "Yes, my wife sees a psychiatrist." He left out the fact that she saw more than one. The bottle's label would no doubt indicate what doctor would be informed this time. "I see," the doctor said. "Well, we have her stable now. She's going to be ok. But she'll have a really bad hangover in the morning. We have given her some medications to take the edge off as well as to keep her blood pressure normal. We want to keep her stable. We're going to keep her here for the night for observation until her body is able to clear itself of the toxins. And I would suggest she see her psychiatrist as soon as possible as this appears to be a suicide attempt." Paul nodded. The emergency room doctor concluded by saying, "I will be needing to inform Dr. Hagen, her psychiatrist about the situation." Paul looked at the doctor intently and nodded his head. He already knew this. "I understand," he said. "That'll be all unless you have any questions." "No. I don't think so," Paul answered. "Ok then. Go home and get some sleep. You look terrible," the doctor told him. "Actually, can I see my wife first?" "Of course. Follow me." They didn't need to walk far. She was inside a big room around the corner. There was a curtain that divided the room into two sections. Another patient was on the other side. Paul looked at his wife, pale and ashen, knocked out cold with tubes running in and out of her, one in her arm for the IV, and another in her nose for oxygen. Sticky round patches covered her chest. He lifted her hand and held it between both of his. He looked at her and shook his head. "Why do you keep doing this? I don't understand." He said it as if she could hear him. He bent down and kissed her forehead. "I'll be back in the morning."

Paul pulled the car into the driveway of their house, walked in and thanked the neighbors. "She'll be ok," he told them. "She just fainted," he lied. "They're keeping her for observation." It sounded like a good enough explanation. The neighbors showed their concern and said they were happy to help and to let them know if Paul needed anything at all. He said he thought he would be fine. Jill was asleep the entire time. Bobbie timed her episodes conveniently with Jill's bedtime. Paul walked to the garage and opened the fridge, grabbed a beer and lit another cigarette. He shed no tears this time, but he leaned against the workbench with intense concentration staring at the garage door. He smoked the cigarette and drank the beer and that turned into three more beers and several more cigarettes. The cool carbonated liquid draining down his throat and the puffs of smoke escaping his lips, blowing into the air washed away some of his anxiety. He was up late into the night, eventually engrossed in his work. His projects served multiple purposes.

The next morning he drove to the hospital with Jill. He arrived to find Bobbie awake and sitting up in bed trying to eat applesauce. Paul walked through the door to her assigned room carrying Jill in his arms. She was smiling and excited at all the commotion of the hospital. When she saw her mother she squealed. Paul set her on Bobbie's lap, in part to remind her what she could have left behind. Bobbie put her arms around Jill and hugged her tightly. Jill hugged her back. Paul stood idly at her side and didn't know what to say. Their eyes met, and Paul's teared up. "I thought I'd lost you," he said to her. His affection was like honey to Bobbie. She soaked it up all she could. At least he was paying attention to her.

An hour or so later, they went home together. Although they drove in silence most of the way, Paul seemed somehow alive and present to Bobbie. He was kind, and it was like it used to be, when they'd first married. They talked easily, in a carefree way absent of the tension and heaviness of lost dreams and disappointed lives. It was a happy moment and they were connected. Even Jill felt the happiness and joined with her toddler jibber-jabber.

When they arrived home, Paul made sure Bobbie was comfortable and rummaged through the kitchen for something to make for dinner. He made boxed macaroni and cheese and brought it in on a tray for Bobbie to eat in bed. He stayed with her while she ate and they talked. Bobbie enjoyed the attention but eventually got up to get Jill ready for bed. After that, there was not much to do and Paul went back to the garage. Bobbie was ok with that. Their family was like a family again even if for one night.

Bobbie woke the following morning feeling contemplative. The cycle had completed itself and she was at the cusp of another revolution. She removed her brushes and paints from the closet where she kept her art supplies and arranged the brushes in a cup. She placed the cup and the handful of paint tubes she'd grabbed next to an empty canvas propped on an easel from the spare bedroom and began painting. In one hand she held the palate and with the other she dipped the brush into the colors she squeezed from the small tubes, mixing them together into small splotches of varying colors, creating the shades she wanted. The smell of the oils reminded her of college and the endless hours spent on art projects. She touched the tip of her brush into a soft shade of green and stroked it onto the blank whiteness that stretched before her. The sight of the grassy green color she had chosen pleased her and the feeling of smooth paint gliding over the canvas gave her a familiar satisfaction. She often painted when she felt not only compelled, but as a way to push through her emotions. It was an expression of something within that needed to let its self out. She did this with writing too.

Bobbie had studied art in college and had painted and sketched since as long as she could remember. Bobbie's work was scattered throughout her mother's house. There was a large portrait of her favorite pet dog, a German Shepard named "Shep." There were self-portraits of Bobbie, and paintings of Jill that were half realistic and half not. There was one portrait of Jill with unrealistically large blue eyes holding a single red balloon in one hand and Bobbie hovering in the sky above, peering over a cloud larger than life, watching her, like an eerie premonition of the future.

As the brush swept across the canvas shapes took form allowing her subconscious mind to pour onto it what she was holding inside. She was very peaceful and it was difficult to tell if it was the painting that brought her peace or the peace she was feeling that enabled her to paint. As figures emerged, so did feelings and thoughts she normally kept repressed. For the moment, she felt safe to let them out. Painting provided a release for her feelings because she gave them to the painting. It was an escape. Her soul had been redeemed temporarily though it came at a cost. Steadily the cup would empty itself again until there was nothing left and nothing to do but desperately cling to whatever measures would fill it back up again.

Two days later it was time for another trip and Paul stormed through the hallways trying to get ready. Even Jill knew to stay out of his way. She braced herself against the hallway wall to make room for him as he flew by. He did not speak. The intensity in the air could be cut with a knife. No one dared step in his path. Jill was barely two but she could already sense these unspoken rules.

Paul was absent for two days this time during which Bobbie slipped in and out of depression. She drifted through normal everyday life. She was barely hanging on. Through her multiple doctor visits Bobbie accumulated more psychiatric drugs. Every day she reached into her personal drug inventory and took what she needed, depending on the tide of her moods. Many times she took uppers and downers simultaneously along with others to combat the multitude of emotions she was feeling that day.

Paul returned from his trip to a house in disarray. It was quiet and dark with the exception of a small noise in one of the bedrooms. Paul walked across the living room before noticing small green balls placed meticulously around the living room floor. They made a trail from one corner of the room to another, down the hallway and throughout the house. Paul bent down to pick one up and mumbled to him self, "Well I'll be damned." It was a frozen pea, only the peas had defrosted by then. Paul gingerly dodged his way across the floor to put his flight bag down and take off his shoes. He hopped across the house to see what was going on. First he found Jill, happily planting peas one by one ever so carefully, creating a perfect trail across the guest bedroom. The precision with which she spaced them nearly perfect equidistance apart thoroughly impressed him. Paul was in awe. The laying of the peas in the guestroom completed the house. He was so amused he smiled and nodded his head in recognition of such an accomplishment. Jill looked up and smiled back a knowing reflection of her proud masterpiece. Paul couldn't help but let out a hearty chuckle. Then he remembered his worry over Bobbie and left Jill to continue with her work so he could check on her.

When he entered the master bedroom he found her lying in the dark still in bed with the covers pulled over her head. The blinds were drawn. He checked his watch. It was mid-day. He wrinkled his forehead and went to the bed, tugging at Bobbie's shoulder. She groaned and pulled away. "Bobbie, wake up. Why are you still asleep? What are you doing?" Paul asked. She struggled to open her eyes as he flipped on the light. It hurt her eyes and she squinted. "Oh hi, it's you," she said. "Yeah, it's me." He was happy to see her but concerned to come home to the house in its current condition. "Do you realize what time it is?" Paul asked her. "No. What time is it?" she answered half interested. "It's nearly noon. Jill is busy planting peas all over the house and you're still asleep," he told her. "What?" She sat up and looked around. "Come," he said, "Follow me. But watch your step or you'll smash peas into the carpet." The defrosted peas were just waiting to be mashed into artistic splotches of green on beige carpet-canvas. Bobbie climbed out of bed and slipped on her slippers. Paul shook his head, "Eh eh, better keep those off. You won't have enough precision to step around the peas." Bobbie squinted to see, a quizzical look on her face. When she saw what had happened she put her hands to her face, "Oh my God." All she saw was an endless mess and it was overwhelming. She went back to bed and put her face in a pillow. Paul looked back and realized she was good for nothing. He went to Jill and gently took the bag of peas from her. She was perplexed and a little startled someone had interrupted her nearly completed work of art. "That's enough," Paul said patiently and he picked her up. Jumping over and across one line of peas to the next, he made his way to the kitchen. However, the peas were there too. And the freezer door stood wide open with all of its contents nearly defrosted. A chair sat at the front of the fridge. Paul shut the door to the freezer and tiptoed between peas before putting Jill in her high chair. "Here," he said, "Have some peas." Jill smiled and put some in her mouth. Paul was on his hands and knees for hours picking up peas trying hard not to smudge them into the carpet.

Bobbie got out of bed and the usual cycle-post-airline-trip repeated itself. This time there were no explosions. Nothing notable happened. There was no fancy meal waiting for Paul that day. Minimal daily functioning was all Bobbie could manage. A couple of days later, however, Bobbie carelessly left a cupboard open containing her pills. Jill had long figured out by then how to pull a chair to formerly inaccessible places and get whatever she wanted. By the time Bobbie discovered Jill steadily stuffing the colored pills into her mouth, it was too late. Two bottles lay empty on the floor with a few tablets scattered next to them. There was no telling how many she had eaten or how long it had been. Alarmed, Bobbie yelled for Paul and he came running. He saw what had happened. It wasn't the first time. "Grab your jacket," he said. She grabbed one for Jill too and they ran to the car, Paul holding fast to Jill, keeping his eye on her. Once in the car, Paul handed Jill to Bobbie. Bobbie held her on her lap. Paul sped down the road to the familiar hospital it seemed they had only visited days before. And they had. The road was wet and covered with a layer of old yellow and brown leaves. A few dry leaves fluttered across the road as the car drove over them.

They rushed into the emergency room explaining what had happened. Even though there was a waiting line, a nurse took Jill in her arms and went back with the small child and told Paul and Bobbie to follow. In moments, despite other emergencies around them, doctors appeared. A small child who had overdosed on pills took precedence over broken arms and hips, elderly high blood pressure and the regular smattering of crazy people. If the hospital staff only knew … in truth, this small family more accurately fell into the latter description. They put tubes down Jill's throat and told Paul and Bobbie to stand back. They allowed them to stay in the room provided they would stay out of the way. They needn't have worried; they had seen this before. It had happened too many times to count.

Jill was still conscious but they had to work quickly. A body so small would not tolerate high doses of potent psychiatric medication. They pumped her stomach and retrieved dozens of little pills. The doctors marveled at their retrieval. "One more time," the doctor said. They pumped some more to be sure, but nothing came up. Jill had to be held down and she was not happy. They pulled the tubes from her throat carefully and Jill screamed and cried once they were out. She coughed uncontrollably. Bobbie came to the bed to hold her. "By the look of the tablets it doesn't look like they had enough time to dissolve much. We'll keep her overnight just to be sure there are no adverse reactions," the doctor informed them. Eventually Jill was wheeled to a room with two other children. She was tucked in bed and Bobbie pulled a chair up next to her. Jill fell asleep in seconds. It was an exhausting ordeal. Bobbie slept next to her.

Paul went home and straight to the garage for a beer and a cigarette. He smoked one cigarette after the next. He went to the fridge countless times that night to retrieve a beer. He was awake late into the night. Well after midnight, an idea came to him. He decided to scour the house for any sign of pills. He knew all of the hiding places. They were everywhere. Paul gathered all of them and sat at the kitchen table. He painstakingly opened each and every capsule. A large bag of sugar sat on the edge of the table and once a significant number of capsules had been emptied, he began filling them with the sugar. The capsules felt hard and rubbery as he rolled them between his fingers and that made them easier to grip while he patiently spooned small bits of sugar into them one by one until they were full. Sugar covered the table from the excess that had spilled out as he poured. Carefully, he put them back together. Once done with one batch he filled one pill bottle after the next. It took hours. In the morning, he put the bottles with the sugar-filled tablets back in their hiding places. One had to marvel at the painstaking amount of patience to empty and refill each and every one of those capsules. But Paul thought to him self, visiting an emergency room required painstaking patience too.

He went to the hospital to pick up the girls and to his relief once again, they were lucky. Everyone was fine. They drove home this time not quite as happily as the last. Paul was frustrated. The only thing that put a bit of happiness into his mood was the knowledge of his sugar secret.

Several days later when Bobbie lay on the bed with a couple of empty bottles in her hand, she called for Paul to come quickly and told him what she'd done and that they'd better call for help. He told her, "It's ok, lay back down and go to sleep. You just ate a bunch of sugar." It was dark, so he couldn't see the expression on her face but he wished he could have.

Two weeks went by since the sugar overdose and Bobbie had gone to the doctor to replenish her supply. She set her newly accumulated stash on a small table stand in one of the bedrooms. It took seconds for their lightening fast toddler to grab them and put them in her mouth. Paul came flying into the room after Bobbie had yelled in alarm, desperately trying to remove them. She pried Jill's lips open with one hand and Jill stubbornly clamped her jaw down onto her mother's fingers. Bobbie forced her mouth open and used her pinky finger to sweep from one side of Jill's mouth to the other pulling more of them out. Several dropped onto the floor. She lifted Jill from behind pulling her legs into the air, letting her head fall towards the floor, using gravity to shake the remaining tablets loose. Paul got down on the ground, holding her jaw open and searched for more. He worked quickly to remove the last couple, glancing up occasionally at Bobbie with a menacing glare. Bobbie cringed desperately, pleading for Jill to be ok. She knew she had messed up again. "I think we got them all, but I don't know if she swallowed any," he told Bobbie. His voice had an edge to it. His movements were abrupt and jerky, clearly communicating to Bobbie his dissatisfaction. He curtly informed her "This is the last time I'm taking Jill to the hospital. If you can't keep your medication out of Jill's reach, then you take her to the emergency room from now on." Bobbie did not reply. She picked the toddler up in her arms and cradled her soft blonde head in her hands, pulling her to her chest.

Things continued in this vein for some time. The moodiness of both of them was the most difficult part. Bobbie became more despondent. Her mind was in constant turmoil and she chewed over the state of things again and again. By this time, Effie, Bobbie's Mother, was well aware there were problems and she had some knowledge of the part Bobbie's condition played in the duo's troubled life. But it was easier to pin the blame on someone else. Paul had let them down.

It was about this time Bobbie began making a list that led to the formation of the decision she ultimately arrived at. The list included no compelling reason to remain in her current situation.

Tuesday, January 5, 1970: stays out late in garage – goes to Burle's and then devours six drinks beer. No common interests other than boating, camping. Over controlled personality, won't talk out probs. Drinks beer excess. Stays out late in garage, sex, no common interests. *Questions*: Can I move out in 2 weeks? How much alimony & child support, duration of divorce, see other men, new car, what if he harasses me (he doesn't know I'm going this far – and he says he still loves me although he knows something is wrong – he may fight it – will not be forced to keep up his alimony?

Progressively her handwriting became crooked and sloppy, jerky even, not at all like the familiar neat round handwriting of her regular journal entries, reflecting her despair and uncertainty. Her decision had been made and she wrote another list that included items for a departure:

January 28, 1970 – ball, bicycle, blouses, iron, diaper pail, … make-up, eye shadow, pancake make-up, white top, car key chain, fill out application for Aero Space, and county jobs.

It was around this time Bobbie made the final move. Paul was away on a trip and she made her rounds of the house, selecting items to take with them. It was difficult on two counts, one because she would be flying, and she could only take a limited number of items, and two, she wanted to be fair to Paul and constantly found herself deliberating over every item and whether he would need it or not. She did not need a great deal of household supplies. After all, she was going back to live with her mother. Effie already had everything to run a household, so there was no need for duplicates.

Bobbie decided to bring her wedding dishes. These she would hold onto. Her mother had gone to a great deal of effort picking them out. Plus, they were worth a considerable amount of money. Effie never chose anything less than the highest of quality. She did not buy to excess, and much did not matter to her. However when it came to clothes and dinner entertainment that was another matter entirely.

Bobbie did not have a great deal of clothes and neither did Jill. A portion of the few they had, however, Effie had bought for them. The clothes easily fit into one of the two allotted suitcases permitted each of them on the flight home. Bobbie put her make-up and beauty items in a hard-shelled oval case and closed it tightly. Other than that, Bobbie carefully selected only the most meaningful items and those were mostly small gifts given to her by her dearest friends. The baby book would need to come, including the baby diary marking important milestones. It was mostly empty. The first few baby accomplishments were neatly penned in, but the entries trailed off around the time Jill began to walk and the marathon game of touch and tag got faster and faster trying to keep up with a toddler.

By the time Bobbie was finished, the bags would barely close. She had to sit on them in order to get the large metal and leather belts to buckle. Paul would be home the following day and the airline tickets had been purchased by Effie. They arrived as planned, while Paul was gone.

Bobbie vacillated between feelings of relief and feelings of doubt. She continued to belabor the question; was she doing the right thing? Her convictions about marriage were steadfast and conservative and yet, the unfolding of her own was a mess. Neither she nor Paul knew what they were doing. Both of them had insurmountable problems they could not handle. And they certainly could not help each other. This was not the happy marriage Bobbie had envisioned. Her heart was wrenched and every bone in her body ached terribly. It was not an easy road to take, and even more difficult to carry out. Part of her still loved Paul, but she knew she could not change him. The only thing left to do was to wait. It was the confrontation she dreaded most.

The following morning, Paul arrived home, exhausted and jet-lagged. He walked in the door to find four suitcases lined up in the entryway. A few haphazard carry-on's and the box of wedding dishes lay next to them. Paul noticed the bags and briefly puzzled over them. Bobbie was in the kitchen sipping coffee. She had already taken a cocktail of several pills. This helped her composure, and yet her hand was shaking.

Paul put his flight back down next to the other suitcases and went to the kitchen, still in his uniform, hat in hand. "Where are you going? I didn't know you were planning to go somewhere. Is it to your mother's? That is where you're going, isn't it?" He waited for Bobbie to answer. Her hand began to shake a little more and she set the coffee mug down. She put her head down for a moment trying to compose the tears that were beginning to well up around the edges of her eyes and then she looked up.

Her eyes were glistening. Paul noticed her hand trembling and assumed it was the medication. "Bobbie we don't have the money for a trip right now." He was worried about finances. She tried to speak but the words wouldn't form. Paul glanced behind Bobbie and noticed Jill, sitting on the floor, dressed in her nicest dress, a bonnet and matching coat, including tights and matching shoes. She was ready for the trip too.

Bobbie got up from her chair and faced Paul. "I'm leaving." "I can see that." He could sense this was something more than just a trip but he wasn't sure what. The words that came out of her mouth next were ones that would destroy and shatter him. "I'm leaving for good Paul. I think you've known this hasn't been working for a long time. Neither of us is happy." Paul's head started to fog up. "What do you mean?" "I can't do it anymore," she said. "Jill and I are leaving." His eyes began to glass over even though what was happening had barely begun to sink in. "Don't go." He knew there were problems, sure, but in his world, loyalty trumped all else. This held a double-edged sword, however. Loyalty ensures safety – and freedom to do as you please in the surety that your partner will have to endure whatever comes their way. Bobbie had shattered this with a few simple words. She had violated the laws of his universe. He was crushed.

Paul fingered the edges of his pilot's hat and he looked down trying to think of the magic words that would end the situation unfolding before him. "I'm going Paul. We're leaving now. Our flight is at 2:00. Do you care to escort us to the airport or shall I call a cab?" Paul looked at her, his body rigid. His shell was beginning to form. "I'll take you," he replied in a deep voice tinged with anger and erupting feelings he couldn't embrace but was trying desperately to control. Bobbie got up from the table and said, "Come on Jill. We're going on a plane now. We're going to see Granny." Jill had a vague understanding. She sensed the heaviness. Bobbie smiled to reassure her.

Paul hadn't moved from the edge of the counter since the start of the conversation. He leaned against it in the same position, his head down, his hands and fingers wrapped around the back of his neck like he was willing it not to happen. "Bobbie, please don't go. I love you. Please don't leave me. I love you both. We're a family." Bobbie drummed up all the courage she could muster. She had to be strong and she was determined to stick to her convictions. "Paul, I can't do this anymore. You're always in that garage. You pay absolutely no attention to me. We don't have a relationship. We do nothing together. We have nothing in common with the exception of camping and boating, and that isn't enough." "But we do have a lot of fun doing that, you can't deny it can you?" He pleaded with her. A slight smile formed at the corner of her mouth. "Yeah we do," she said. Paul thought he'd made a break, but she forced a frown and mustered every ounce of courage and strength within her. She felt terrible for Paul, but she was not about to budge. She knew what she had to do. "It's not enough Paul. It's over." Bobbie turned away from him and pretended to straighten Jill's coat so he wouldn't see the pain and the tears forming in her eyes. This was the hardest thing she'd ever done. And it wasn't over yet.

"Come on, we have to go now or we'll miss our flight," Bobbie said. She couldn't withstand another second. Paul slowly moved through the kitchen, the keys to the car on the counter. He reluctantly reached for them. "This can't be happening," he said to himself. He moved towards the door and picked up two of the bags, one in each hand and walked towards the car. Bobbie let out one deep breath and got up, lifting Jill off the floor with her. She mindlessly picked up the toy Jill had been playing with and placed it in her hand. "Here, you can play with this on the plane." Jill blandly took it even though she'd nearly worn out her interest in it.

Bobbie put Jill in the car and went back to the house to pick up the smaller items while Paul retrieved the other two bags. They loaded the car in silence. Bobbie got into the car, breathing in the damp Washington air for the last time. Jill sat on the seat between them without a seat belt. Paul climbed in to the driver's seat and shut the door. He turned the key in the ignition and started the car. He backed down the driveway. Half way to the airport one tear ran down Paul's face. "I can't believe you're doing this." He tried desperately to control his voice. Bobbie remained quiet and tried not to look at him. "Please don't go." He pleaded one last time, but the event was already in progress. He tried to imagine in his mind this wouldn't be permanent. "What if we take a break and then you come back?" Bobbie shook her head and spoke after a long silence. "No Paul. I'm done." Paul gripped the steering wheel and stared ahead, slightly angry that he had no control over the situation.

They drove in silence the rest of the way. Paul was in shock and he was heartbroken; after this rejection, Paul would close his heart for a very long time. They arrived at the airport in front of departures. Paul pulled the bags out of the trunk and placed them on a trolley for the baggage man to take to check-in. Bobbie held Jill in her arms and faced Paul. He was already facing her with his arms loosely dangling at his sides like a puppet unaware its arms are attached to its body. A brief moment of connection spanned the space between them and Bobbie said "Goodbye" for the last time. Instinctively they moved towards each other. Every journey begins with a hug by the one left behind. They hugged each other and Paul choked down a sob. Bobbie felt the bubble rise and escape with a small gulp from his chest, and she choked down her tears and pulled away. "Goodbye Paul," she repeated. Paul pierced his lips together tightly and nodded farewell. Bobbie had already turned and walked away, but Paul stood glued to the spot where she had hugged him for the last time and stared after them until they disappeared through the doors. Hardly aware of the movement of his own body, he got into his car and drove away.

Bobbie arrived at her mother's house, the home she had grown up in save the time they had lived in Germany and Morocco. She moved back into her old room. It smelled a bit old and musty, but all of her childhood things were still there, even the flimsy narrow shelf rack with her horse and doll collection. One tall dresser, two single beds one on each side of the room with a nightstand next to each, and a small desk crowded the room. The sun poured through one of the windows. A large shade tree darkened the other, bringing down the temperature in the little bedroom. She and

Jill slept together in the close quarters. Drab brown bedspreads had been thrown onto the beds in preparation for their arrival. Two fluffy pillows that smelled like the fresh outdoors were at the heads of the beds. Effie had aired them to dry outside no doubt and had washed the pillow cases, hanging them on one of the outdoor clotheslines like she dried all of her clothes. Bobbie set down her suitcases and slipped off her shoes. She felt the familiar shaggy off-white carpet under her feet. Jill ran through the house happily inspecting each room and searched for Effie, but Effie had already gone back to work after picking them up from the airport.

It was during this time that Bobbie's condition declined steadily. She was seeing another five doctors now: Dr. Abel, Dr. Demmer, Dr. McCafee, Dr. Hadley, and Dr. Zikler. Her daily planner was filled with doctor appointments. Dr. Zikler had studied under Freud himself. Dr. Hadley, Bobbie wrote in her diary, helped her out of a deep depression. Dr. Zikler used to end their sessions by saying, "See you next week, if you're still here."

Bobbie went home after one of these visits and decided to write in her journal. She picked up a pen from the small desk in her room. One of Jill's toys, a jack-in-the-box clown in its little tin can and wind up handle were on the desk. Two small piles of folded laundry Bobbie had washed the day before were next to it. She opened the bottom drawer and got out her journal. Jill was still at preschool and Effie was at work so she had the house to herself. It was quiet. She sat on the bed with one knee bent half Indian-style and leaned against two pillows propped against the wall. The sun hit her outstretched leg that dangled off the bed. She could hear the clock ticking from her mother's room.

Bobbie thought about her old friends, how they had graduated from college, were working now, had families of their own. She thought about how she had dropped out of college because she "didn't need a piece of paper" to show herself and others. She didn't think it proved anything. She thought about her own life, her failed marriage, her child. She thought about the cakes she had baked for dinner parties with friends and neighbors, gaily celebrating in a picture perfect home. She had spent hours madly cleaning before they came so they would see how nicely they lived and what a perfect family they had.

She wrote in her journal:

"1970: I know that there are many young people whose ideals are closely similar to mine and yet they still can somehow compromise and join in with others, unlike though they may be (one is false one is sincere). I can't do it – I just cannot reconcile to the standards ...

Even though I feel this way I can equally say that I experience many beautiful and lovely things temporary and fleeting as they come. I feel as if I am more in touch with beauty and love for all my suffering. It's like I'm drifting endlessly and powerlessly on some certain course. For this feeling I am grateful – it helps me to endure my psychical tortures that rage in my head and stiffen and make sore my back by enabling me to see blindly beyond.

Myself: alone, make myself happy, have a job, go to school, work for teach cred, have VA, I'm seeing still Dr. Hadley who has helped me out of a serious depression and able to be independent. I think I have a lot to offer and live for and give to my child."

Bobbie continued to sink deeper and deeper into depression and was eventually admitted to a hospital. One hot sunny day Effie and Jill went to see her. "Get the picture you drew," Effie said to Jill. "We're going to see your mother." "Mommy?!" "Yes! Mommy," Effie said. Jill jumped up and down. "Yay!!!" and she ran back in the house to get it. Effie grinned, but her face was sad at the same time. There was always a cloudiness that hung over her eyes. Effie was dressed in her very best. She wore a white tailored suit, including a straight skirt and jacket with a pale blue silk blouse. She wore high heels as usual, and her hair had been teased and curled into a bouffant style. Her makeup was delicately vogue, applied first thing in the morning before she came out of her room. It was part of her morning ritual: take hair out of rollers, face cream regime, tease hair, paint eyelids, lashes, cheeks. When she walked out of her room it was with the air of a princess, even her nose was elevated a little higher than everyone else's.

They walked to the car and got in. Jill rode on the passenger side. Her hair was brushed and a small portion pulled back into in a ponytail on top of her head. Effie had put Jill's hair up earlier that morning. She was dressed in a small skirt with tights and boots, and a matching cardigan. The two were dressed in style, like two ladies going to tea. Effie would have it no other way. Jill held her drawing on her lap. "Did you remember your picture for mommy?" "Yes." She pointed to her lap, admiring the colors she had chosen to draw the stick figures of herself, her Mother, Effie and her father. Even their dog Mala was off to one side. Effie smiled. "That's a good girl. We'll just go in and say hi briefly. Your mommy is tired. Ok?" Jill nodded and kicked her feet. She barely heard what Effie said. All she could think about was seeing her mother.

Effie pulled into a parking space at the hospital with her large car. She was a conscientious and slow driver. She turned to Jill and said, "Ok. We ready?" "Yes!" Jill answered, hopping out of the car. "Now you wait there for me, ok?" "Yes, Granny." Effie made her way unhurriedly to the other side of the car. Effie never rushed. It would have spoiled her air of elegance and poise. Effie gracefully took Jill's hand in hers, slowing down Jill's hopping and skipping. They walked across the parking lot to the hospital entrance. They were almost there and Jill could barely contain her joy. Effie had let go her hand by now and she bounced into the elevator imploring her Granny to hurry up.

By the time they found Bobbie, lunch was being served. Bobbie sat at a long table with several other patients. Trays with cafeteria-style food were placed in front of each person. Bobbie wore a loose sweatshirt and slacks. Her face had the look of someone who had just woken up out of a deep sleep. She wore no makeup and her hair was casually messy, like it had been brushed, but nothing else. She looked the part of a sick hospital patient minus the hospital gown. Her movements were mechanical and pensive, like someone who was fragile and unable to break through some sort of barrier to herself. Bobbie glanced up from her tray and saw Jill immediately. A tired smile spread across her face. Jill ran to her and Bobbie had to twist in her chair to reach her. She held her arms open for her daughter to run into. "What's that?" Jill asked, pointing to the oddly colored orange and beige lump on her mother's plate. "That's a good question." A tube dangled from Bobbie's wrist. "And what's that?" Jill pointed to her arm. "Oh it's fluid being pumped into my arm, see?" She pointed to the pole next to her with a bag of fluid in it. "Why?" she asked. Bobbie explained. Effie bent over to give her daughter a hug. "Don't you have something for your mother?" she reminded Jill. "Oh! Yes!" She'd almost forgotten. "Here! It's for you mommy!" "Well what do you have there?" she asked. Jill put it in front of her, a big smile on her face. She stood at her mother's side with her arms and hands flat against the bottoms of her skirt, bobbing up and down, waiting in anticipation for her mother's response. "Oh! It's beautiful!" she said. Jill bounced even more. She beamed at her mother, and proceeded to explain each detail. "That's you. That's me." She pointed everyone out. "It's so nice Jill. Thank you!" her mother said. Jill smiled. She was pleased with herself.

Effie sat down in a chair next to Bobbie. They had walked to her room by now. She noticed the big bags under her daughter's eyes. "And how are you doing sweetheart?" she asked. Effie's brow wrinkled and she placed the palm of her hand on Bobbie's forehead and smoothed her hair. "I'll be ok, mom. I think I'm doing better. I'm just so doggone tired all of the time. Tired but I can't sleep, and yet not enough energy to actually do anything." "It's hard ..." Effie's voice trailed off and she glanced around the room, the white walls, the single window at the corner, the small table next to the bed with one bouquet of flowers in a vase. Effie couldn't help think to herself, "Why on earth would someone send flowers on an occasion like this?"

Effie and Jill visited Bobbie several times during her month and a half stay in the hospital. When she returned home, James, Bobbie's brother, and Effie watched as she steadily declined. They saw how she lamented the failure of her marriage and her disappointment at losing Paul and how he had hurt her. Effie and James felt let down too. When Paul came into their lives he was like a savior to them all, not just to Bobbie. Paul had taught James how to fly, even though he quit one solo short of getting his license. James bought a boat just like Paul's. James put a hitch on the front of his car so he could drive forwards to back his boat into the water – just like Paul. James looked up to Paul like the big brother he never had, maybe even the father that left his life when he was only nine. That is why when they watched Bobbie suffer, it was easy to blame Paul.

The failure of her marriage destroyed her. It was difficult to tell if this is what led to her severe depression or if the condition existed long before her marriage and was bound to surface eventually regardless of the situation that set it off.

On the day it happened, Effie got ready for work as usual. She woke up in bed with Jill next to her. Jill slept with Effie most nights now. "What shall I wear to work today?" "Hmmm," said Jill. This was an important question and required great consideration. "Oh here, I have my outfit picked out from last night," Effie remembered. "Now the big question is, which purse do I use? Which one do you think best matches my outfit, Jill?" This was Jill's favorite; she always got to choose the purse. Jill studied the purses that were stacked on top of and underneath the table next to Granny's make-up stand. "That one," Jill pointed with certainty. It was a pale pink one with a small strap. "Good choice," said Effie, "I'll take that one." Sometimes Jill even got to choose the shoes.

Effie finished getting ready for work. She had a foreboding feeling that day. She worried about Bobbie and had a nagging instinct that told her something bad was going to happen. Effie walked to the door of Bobbie's room and knocked. "I'm getting ready to go. Are you going to be alright?" Bobbie groaned and got up out of bed. There were dark circles under her eyes and her hair was tangled from the night's sleep. She stepped into her floppy slippers and shuffled to the door and opened it. "Yeah, I'm fine mom," she answered in a detached sleepy voice. She stared into Effie's eyes but wasn't really looking at her at all. Effie shivered inside and her forehead wrinkled in concern. "Are you sure you're ok? Should I stay home?" Bobbie snapped out of it long enough to convince her mom she would be fine. "Well, Jill has had breakfast and she was just waiting for you to get up before going in to find an outfit for school." Effie tried to put some order in the day.

"Yeah, ok," answered Bobbie. She was really down and Effie could tell. "Bobbie you know you can't go on like this. You need to pull yourself together. You have a child. You need to take care of her. Why don't you …" Bobbie cut her off curtly. She was getting annoyed. Moodiness came with the depression. It was difficult for Effie to have compassion for her when she was so short all of the time. Bobbie hated her mother's nagging. "Stop telling me what to do mom, I know what I have to do. I know she's my daughter." "Well then why don't you get out of bed and take care of her once in a while?" "I'm up aren't I?" Bobbie rolled her eyes and let out a dramatic sigh. "Yeah you're up alright," Effie said. "Why don't you brush your hair once in a while and put some makeup on? Maybe you'd feel better if you looked better." "Not everyone can live up to your cookie cutter perfection, mom." She said this in a provoking and sarcastic way. Effie'd had enough. "Ok, bye," she said. She had only wanted to help her get back to a normal life but her attempts always backfired. She knew she always did it in the wrong way. Effie's interactions with those closest to her were a confused game of generosity intertwined with control-laced pity and guilt. She had had her own bout with depression after her husband died. Too easily she fell into the lap of her ever comforting and prematurely mature daughter, Bobbie. It was a big burden for a young woman. And now the burden was manifesting the toll it had taken on Bobbie's mental health.

As Effie got into the car to back out of the garage, she felt the foreboding feeling again. She hesitated in the driver's seat, pausing before continuing to apply pressure to the gas pedal. "Something tells me I shouldn't go," she said to herself. But then, Bobbie had shouted for her to leave … "It would end up being another day of bickering between us and that's no good either," Effie thought. Despite her deeper sense of dread, she had no logical reason to stay. She backed out of the garage and drove down the length of the front yard driveway that led to the road.

Bobbie stumbled down the hallway and opened the medicine cabinet. She pulled one of the bottles down and twisted the cap open. She took one pill. Jill was already in the room looking for clothes to wear. Bobbie went back down the hall to oversee the selection. "How about that one?" Bobbie suggested standing from the doorway. Jill turned around. "No. I like this one." "No. Not that one, that won't do," Bobbie answered. Even if she was out of control over the rest of her life, she was at least going to control the selection of her daughter's outfit that day. "How about this one?" "I don't like that shirt," Jill said. "Ok," Bobbie compromised. "You pick out the shirt, but you wear that frock." "Okay," Jill agreed sulkily.

Before long, they were in the car. Bobbie had her hair up and half way decent clothes on. On the surface, she looked presentable, however, she wore dark sunglasses to cover up her sunken eyes. Once in the car, she lit a cigarette and it hung out of her mouth as she drove down the road. The conversation was minimal. Jill did not act excited exactly to be going to school, but she liked it okay. Her mom got her lunchbox and Jill climbed out of the car and walked into the building and disappeared. Her mother called after her reminding her she'd forgotten her hug. Jill came back and put her arms around her mother's neck and said, "I love you mommy." "I love you too sweetheart." Jill disappeared down the hall again and Bobbie got up to leave.

Before getting back into the car, Bobbie lingered at the schoolyard fence and leaned over the top of it with her elbows while she smoked another cigarette. The fence only reached mid-chest level. Bobbie stood there for some time until Jill came out to join the other children. She watched Jill get on a horse that swung on springs and she knocked it back and forth with all her strength. Bobbie remembered standing at this very spot with her mother one day some time back watching her play. She had commented to Effie, "Jill is different than the other kids isn't she?" Effie gazed intently at her granddaughter and agreed, "Yes, there is something unusual about her." Bobbie stood there watching and trying to think what it was that seemed different. She couldn't put her finger on it.

Bobbie went back home and slumped at the kitchen table that formed the breakfast nook, smoking another cigarette. She rolled the pencil shaped tube of tobacco back and forth between her fingers before lighting it. She breathed the smoke deeply into her lungs and exhaled one long puff that was warmed by her mouth before it escaped her lips. She watched it. Feeling something tangible gave her a sense of interacting with the physical life that was her existence now. "Mom would be mad if she saw me smoking in the house," she thought to herself. But she didn't really care. She got up and went back to the medicine cabinet. It was a cupboard in the kitchen but Bobbie had claimed it, making it into her personal pharmacy. She reached up and pulled several bottles down, examining each one, trying to decide which one she needed to pull herself out of her gloom today. She rolled them over in her hand and set them down on the cold white counter. Minutes passed before she made a decision. "This one," she said to herself and popped one in her mouth. It was Valium. A glass of lukewarm water was on the counter. She picked it up and took a large gulp, washing the pill down her throat. She began to put them back up but paused. "Hmmm," she said, "Maybe one Tuinal too. That should do it."

An hour later she continued to feel miserable. All she wanted was to feel better. She opened the medicine cabinet again. She took two bottles of medication out of the cupboard. She poured another tablet from the bottle of Tuinal and one from the bottle of Darvon into her hand. She popped them in her mouth and went to the garage to put the laundry in the washing machine. There was some wet laundry in the machine that had finished washing, so Bobbie pulled it out and piled it into the cloth bag strapped to a folding metal frame attached to wheels. After getting the other load started, she pushed the little cart with wet laundry to the clothesline in the yard and clothes-pinned it up to dry. They didn't have a dryer. Her mother didn't believe in them. Bobbie could hear her mother's words ringing in her ears, "What do you need a dryer for when you have wonderful fresh air and sunshine?" She could picture her face, stern and indignant as she said it. And that was every single time the subject came up. Which was every time she did the laundry. Effie's parents had immigrated from Poland and this particular Eastern European habit stuck.

Bobbie became fidgety and anxious. She threw the rest of the clothes over the line quickly and haphazardly and went back inside. It was getting hot and the desert sun was intense. Bobbie busily flitted from one thing to the next, too anxious to concentrate long enough to complete even one task. Her anxiousness continued and she resigned herself to the fact that this medication had over shot her goal. She walked once more to the medicine cabinet and took out the bottle of Valium. It would calm her nerves and bring her down a notch Bobbie thought. She popped two into her mouth impulsively and sat down at the table nervously smoking another cigarette. By the time she finished she had less anxiety but it was not gone entirely. She got up from the table and paced up and down the hallway before deciding to lie down in her bed and to try to relax. The dark room helped and the calming effect took hold of her. She dozed off for some time and woke up groggy for the second time that morning.

She felt sad as she dragged herself out of bed and sat at the kitchen table again. This time she did not pull out a cigarette. She stared at the wall in front of her with her chin resting on her hands as if she were praying. She was thinking intently and it was about the usual subject: her failed marriage and her broken family. It had been well over a year since she'd packed up and left Paul, and despite a brief attempt to date other men, she continued to turn it over in her mind again and again. Tears welled up in her eyes as thoughts turned to a time when they were so happy and in love and full of excitement about their new life together. And then she looked around at her reality and the contrast made her feel even more miserable. Today was the day her divorce would be final. She broke down sobbing, and to comfort her broken heart and in an attempt to break out of this miserable feeling of despair she could barely tolerate, she walked to the cupboard again. She barely recollected let alone kept track of what she'd already taken. And she didn't really care. She just wanted to make the feelings go away. She reached up to the shelf and pulled all of them down. She attempted an accurate diagnosis and the corresponding remedy that would bring about the desired result. She hardly recognized the drug-induced haze that clouded her mind; she had long been numb to it. She passed the drugs along in a line from one hand to the other as she read their labels. "This one and this one," she decided to herself. She opened the bottles and took a couple of each.

She nearly achieved the desired effect. She was numb to everything, but she thought with a distant fuzzy awareness about her dilemma and decided to put on a Jack Jones record. She slid the wide disc out of its cardboard sleeve and placed it on the turntable. She turned it on and when it was spinning, picked up the needle and gently placed it on the edge of the record. The music filled the room, and she sat on the aqua blue couch and leaned back, allowing her head to rest against it. Looking up at the ceiling she allowed herself to float with the melody of the music and be carried away to a place where everything was ok.

Suddenly, a thought popped into her mind. She had an idea. It was a good decision she thought to herself. She sat on the couch in the living room mulling it over in her head, feeling the warm feelings of comfort that she imagined came from this idea, but may have in fact been a result of the multitude of medications she had taken.

She got up off the couch and walked over to the phone and dialed Paul's number. He answered the phone and said, "Hi." She talked happily like she once had done when they were still in love with each other. As they spoke, Bobbie slouched down in the hallway and rested her back against the wall. They were on the phone for some time and somewhere in the middle of it, the topic of getting back together came up. Although Bobbie couldn't see the grin that spread across his face and the dimples that formed, she could feel the warmness in Paul's voice as he answered, "Well," he began, trying not to act too excited, "I have a trip there in four days. How about we talk then?" "Okay," agreed Bobbie. She felt happy for the first time in a long time. They chatted happily with the anticipation of a renewed attempt at their relationship. They finished their call and Bobbie went unconscious for the last time.

Was her real reason for calling Paul to say her final "goodbye?" She still loved him though and wanted desperately for things to work, but it would never happen. She died that afternoon with the phone in her hand.

Her death was labeled "suicide" caused by barbituate poisoning in the autopsy report, but there was no suicide note found. A single bottle of Darvan, prescribed by Dr. Demmer was found sitting by the sink. There were two tablets remaining in the bottle. Darvan was introduced into the market in 1957. Fatalities were common within the first hour of overdose and there were numerous accidental deaths from it at the time. One research group called it the deadliest prescription drug on the market. It was definitely not indicated for patients with a suicidal past it was later found. It was ranked the most popular prescription drug behind Valium. It was banned from the market in 1991. Tuinal was found in her blood and gastric content too. Tuinal is a downer and has been found to have a high risk of overdose. It promotes physical and psychological dependency. It was a widely abused street drug. There were multiple names for it: Rainbows, Christmas Trees, Beans, Nawls, Jeebs. It was introduced as a sedative but has now been banned from the market too. The last drug found in her system was Valium, the most widely prescribed drug in the world since it was introduced in 1963. Adverse effects from it are: sedation, excitement, rage, worsening of seizures in epilepsy, can cause or worsen depression, cognitive deficits up to six months and physical dependence with long term use. It is now called Diazepam and is used to treat anxiety, panic attacks, insomnia, seizures, muscle spasms, tetanus, alcohol and opiate withdrawal. It can also be used in surgery in place of anesthesia.

Effie phoned the house several times that day, still sensing something was wrong. From eleven a.m. onwards, Bobbie did not answer the phone. When Effie couldn't get through, she called Mrs. Bookher, their next door neighbor. They were good friends, and she asked her to check on Bobbie. Mrs. Bookher did and that is when she found Bobbie sitting against the wall in the hallway with the phone still in her hand. She was unresponsive so she called for help. By the time help arrived, however, it was too late.

Chapter 3

Shadows in the Dark

(1980 – 1986)

Each day of my life I become more and more convinced that there is not a place for me to fit comfortably in the pattern of this society. So I am driven into being an isolationist. I don't ask for this, because just like any human being I need people – but I have no choice. There is, deeply and firmly incised in my character, that which will not let me accept the trivialities, the pretense and the sham acted out in the roles of daily living. I have never been able to "act" in the way that they "act" – so, possibly, at a very tender age I was rejected by them. But also, I have, at one time, tried to be like them, and with moderate success; but with growing distaste for myself for betraying my truer nature.

Continued and ever present sadness, mild and often violently intense, is my condition for accepting (or not accepting) my associations. It is a lonely cause. I love companionship, laughter, light-hearted fun and amusement as a much as any 20 year old young girl would – even more, I think, because I am one who completely revels in an emotion and exploits it. So my pains are the sharper for it.

I know that there are many young people whose ideals are closely similar to mine and yet they still can somehow compromise and join in with others, unlike though they may be (one is false one is sincere). I can't do it – I just cannot reconcile to the standards one must lower him self.

Even though I feel this way I can equally say that I experience many beautiful and lovely things temporary and fleeting as they come. I feel as if I am more in touch with beauty and love for all my suffering.

It's like I'm drifting endlessly and powerlessly on some certain course. For this feeling I am grateful – it helps me to endure my psychical tortures that rage in my head and stiffen and make sore my back by enabling me to see blindly beyond.

Bobbie, 1963

It was dark when the alarm went off. A feeling of dread sank into the pit of her stomach like a bag of rocks hitting the bottom of a lake. It constricted her lungs causing her to breath deeply in order to make it go away. Jill pulled the covers back and got out of bed. She made her way to the green-carpeted kitchen, feeling its short bristly fibers on her bare feet. She focused on each individual task as if she were carrying out a ritual. It helped her maintain control of her thoughts and the heavy feeling in her stomach. She flipped on the light switch so that only the kitchen was lit. Bright yellow wallpaper decorated with bamboo plants animated the otherwise dark house. It was so quiet she could hear the parakeet next to the kitchen sink sleeping. She lifted the towel to his cage to make sure he was still alive. She reached into the cupboard and took a bowl and a box of instant oatmeal off the shelf. It was a new box so she got to choose the flavor. She decided on maple and brown sugar and ripped open the paper packet. One wasn't enough. It hardly filled three quarters of an inch at the bottom of the bowl. She could eat that in three bites. So she took one more packet and ripped it open. The bowl was nearly half full now. She decided she'd better add a third to make it a reasonably meal sized portion so her stomach wouldn't growl before lunch. She filled a pot with water, put it on the stove and waited for it to boil. When it did, she put her hands over the hot steam to warm them. She finished fixing breakfast and sat down to eat. It took about three minutes. She got up from the eat-in counter and washed her bowl. It was a habit of hers to leave no trace of her existence in the kitchen. It wasn't because she was afraid of getting in trouble or because she had to. It was a game. She did it with everything. Leaving nothing in her path that would indicate she'd been there. Sometimes she would imagine she was a detective or a spy and that it was imperative not to let anyone know she had been there. It had more to do with a feeling she couldn't escape, that she didn't belong. She inspected the countertops and put each utensil and dish where it belonged before heading for her room.

She took a hairbrush from her old fashioned off-white vanity and closed her bedroom door so she could look into the full-length mirror on the back of it. She brushed her long fine hair in short gentle strokes, holding a section of hair at the top of her head with one hand and working her way to the ends with each motion. Once through a section of hair she brushed the entire length of it in one long sweeping stroke. It took several minutes to get all of the tangles out. She lifted the curling iron that was plugged in at the wall and began curling her hair. It took painstaking patience getting each and every piece to go into the crab like clamp and roll it before the ends slipped out. She wound the hair around and around the iron, holding it vertically until the iron was near her scalp and she could feel its heat. When she released the iron, a long spiraled ringlet bounced at the side of her neck. After every piece of hair had been forced into an unnatural curl, she brushed it out, fluffing it so it feathered at the sides just right. To hold the feathers in place she sprayed it with awful smelling aerosol hairspray.

She picked up her books and headed for the door. It was about a mile and a half to school. She didn't mind the walk. She had done it for as long as she could remember. She walked past the lonely ranch houses on either side of the road shaped in the same uninteresting rectangles as all the rest. They were old but well taken care of and the lawns were well manicured. The thing that bothered her was the coldness she felt as she walked past them. She imagined the houses harbored fugitives and she made up stories in her head, imagining what their lives were like.

The air was cool. There was a slight breeze that caused the feathers formed in her hair to fan out in one stuck-together wing, flapping at the sides. It was quiet because it was so early in the morning and because the lifeless houses never made any noise. The sun was out now. Jill breathed in the delicious cool air. The rustle of the leaves in the trees made her happy. She savored the moment. There was no thought in her mind about the long school day ahead of her. Wind had that effect on her.

She made it to the busy road that separated her neighborhood from the school. The speeding noisy cars abruptly jolted her out of the dreamy tranquility of her private inner world. It was an unpleasant reminder she was about to enter the real world. She watched a pair of brothers she'd known since elementary school come out of their house. She walked past them and crossed at the crosswalk before they did. The younger of the two was the same age as Jill and had been in every one of her grade school classes. He wore a large red and blue striped shirt that was far too big and had a tear in it. His hair was scraggly and a bit too long, like he hadn't had a hair cut in a long time. "Hey! Give me that shirt back!" The two brothers fought like usual. Jill smiled to herself watching them. The boys never said "hi." They acted like they didn't know her even though they'd spent years going to the same school. Jill ignored them but wondered if she was the only one curious what had really become of them, what their lives were like now. They had known each other so well, and then one day it was as if everyone had swallowed an amnesia pill and they'd never known each other at all.

She was halfway there now, and the closer she got, the more cars and kids she saw making their way to school. Cars raced up and down the road and kids shouted back and forth to each other. She was sweating slightly. The sun was beginning to beat down already and it was like she'd already had a workout before even arriving to school, carrying all those books. She couldn't wait to set them down. She passed the large field with the football stadium and dirt track. The grass was still a bit wet with dew. She walked along the fence until she arrived at the edge of the school property. By then her shoes were damp all around the edges and a bit of morning dew leaked in around her toes.

The buildings were dirty and ugly. They were made of shabby old bricks and white stucco and looked as if they had been there fifty years. They were shaped like large square blocks absent of any trace of architectural creativity. There was nothing attractive about them. Malls and restaurants and shopping center buildings had physical appeal. But this school? None. How could anyone feel enticed to go to school when it looked like this? This was her seven to two o'clock prison.

She headed for the outdoor lockers. The metal door to hers was cold when her fingers touched it. She turned the dial to her combination lock and opened it, pouring her books inside. It was a relief to get the weight out of her hands.

She was happy when the bell rang. She could pretend she didn't care about the glass that still surrounded her since as long as she could remember; she had someplace to go. She went straight to class and took a seat at the side of the room. There were few students. Not many kids were interested in philosophy apparently. Jill loved it. It was her favorite subject.

Mr. Coffman sat in a student's chair at a table shaped like a trapezoid, same as the rest of the students. Only he sat at the front of the class. He looked like a college professor with wild grey hair and spectacles that consisted of two tiny glass circles strung together with a thin piece of metal. The room was small and intimate. The walls and floors were white, and overhead lights glared down on them. The subjects Mr. Coffman taught were electives and not many students chose to take a difficult class if they didn't have to. Jill took all of them.

As Jill took her seat, Mr. Coffman called her name and motioned for her to come to the front of the room. Jill got up and walked to his table. Mr. Coffman handed her the essay she had thrown together in about ten minutes two nights before and cringed at the anticipation of the grade she probably received for it. However, to her surprise Mr. Coffman leaned towards her and mumbled quietly as he handed her the paper, "Good job. This is the best paper I've seen you write. Now you are finally starting to think." Jill was shocked and slowly walked back to her seat, puzzling over the high mark on her paper. She had spent hours on all of her other essays, carefully extracting quotes and concepts from the text, restating their meanings and her interpretations and organizing them in a logical fashion. The thing she'd forgotten to do was completely contrary to everything she had learned in school. She needed to think.

Jill loved her philosophy class, so much so, she signed up for international relations as well. She was intrigued by Mr. Coffman's passion. He was incredulous over the growing apathy and ignorance of her generation towards events unfolding around the world. She remembered when he'd stood at the front of the room with his afro-like grey hair that surrounded his head with several inches of frizzy tight curls giving him the appearance of a wild, mad scientist. His arms flailed in emphatic gestures and his eyes popped out like ping-pong balls. He shouted, causing Jill to jump in her seat. "WAKE UP PEOPLE! HOW can you NOT KNOW about the SANDANISTAS???!!! It's happening right HERE only a short ways from where we stand!!!" It was as if the survival of the world depended on his words getting through to them.

Jill went to her next class and then the bell rang for break. She dreaded break. It meant forced conversation and pretending she was a typical teenager. The thing was, Jill felt anything but typical. She headed straight for her small group of friends. There were only two she felt close to, and they were twin girls she had known for a long time. The two sisters were split into two separate groups, however, so Jill wandered from one to the other from day to day depending on who was easiest to locate. It was a large school.

The forced conversation was misery to Jill. Having to follow the train tracks every single day that led to the same place, the same routine, the same group of kids she could have cared less to talk to was dread beyond imagination.

Inevitably the tiny outliers would flit by and make the same annoying comments. It was always the same question, "Why are you so tall?" Jill always appeared taller than she was because she was so skinny, an attribute that seemed gangly in high school but admirable the rest of her life. In answer to the question, she would think to her self, "I don't know, why are you so short?" But she never said it because she felt it would have been terribly rude. It never occurred to her that the question endlessly posed to her was irritatingly rude too. Later in life when Jill was much older her uncle who had the same tall skinny features magnified by ten, told her the same thing always happened to him. She laughed uncontrollably when he told her that was why he never held back asking fat people why they were fat. Jill had watched him do it and thought it was inappropriate and embarrassing. His explanation, however, made sense in a backward kind of way. She sometimes thought about history back a hundred years or so. Fat was voluptuous and admirable. It was good to be born in the right generation.

Jill endured the daily monotony, the awkwardness and the torturous repeat of barely tolerable interactions. She felt trapped. She wondered when it would ever end. It seemed like forever, the end of high school. She was the opposite of her classmates; most kids couldn't wait for break, lunch, to run away from class. For Jill it was the reverse. She thoroughly enjoyed class. It felt comfortable, safe, structured. And it was interesting. It accommodated the glass wall that surrounded her very well.

"Hey" Jill said as she caught up to one of her friends. It was Michelle. "Hey," she replied, "Lisa's coming." "Ok," Jill said. "It's fish and chips today." It was the only lunch and the only event that actually excited her. Lisa arrived out of breath. The Friday fish ritual had caught on, but only to Lisa. "It's fish!" she said. "I know! Come on!" They raced to the line. When they sat down to their lunches both girls ate with enthusiasm pouring tartar sauce on everything including the French fries. Jill had taught Lisa that too and she now loved it just as much. Jill took for granted that she would. Who wouldn't? She couldn't understand why the rest of the girls didn't partake in their enthusiasm. It was one small luxury in the otherwise dull existence of high school.

After eating lunch, which ended too quickly since they ate the fish so fast, they walked outside and sat on a small brick wall in the middle of the quad. "What happened to Jeremy?" Lisa asked. Her question was directed at Michelle. "Oh we got together last night. We were alone and we both drank schnapps." Michelle proceeded to describe in detail every sexual interaction that occurred including the act itself. The girls were thoroughly enthralled and in awe at how she was able to meet these older college boys. Every lunch was filled with this racy entertainment.

The lunch period was too long, however, to fill up the empty space with enough words. Jill tilted her head back and felt the hot sun on her face. Her attention drifted. Other kids clung to their own circles of friends. "Hey you" one boy yelled to another. A girl who was obviously going out with one of them folded her arms at her chest, stuck one leg out and leaned back on the other while sticking her nose in the air. She loved the attention. Everyone looked at her. She was one of the popular girls in school and was quite attractive. She always wore the latest fashions. Jill watched with boredom. Everything was so trite and contrived.

School ended and Jill walked along the outdoor hallway towards her locker. She turned the dial and it made a clinking sound as she opened it. She sifted through her books. It always seemed like she might need them all, but there was the long walk home so careful consideration had to be made as to how much of a workout she wanted carrying them home that day. Besides, she had gotten much of her homework done sitting in the classes that were too slow. Inevitably the school day ended as it frequently did in a meeting with the ever-irritating two boys she knew from the fourth grade. The amnesia pill didn't work with them. They happened to live in her neighborhood and she could never seem to get away from them. Lucky for her, despite the school holding around two thousand students, her locker happened to be right next to theirs. Jerry and Wayne were their names. Jerry had straight yet strangely fluffy blonde hair, and Wayne had dark wavy hair. They weren't scrawny boys, yet they weren't large either. They were the same height as Jill. It had been their pastime for as long as she could remember to taunt and egg her on about everything and anything. For some reason, it continued right on through high school.

"Hey, how many books you got there?" Oh here we go, Jill thought. "Gonna study tonight? How much do you study?" Why is it wrong to do my homework, it's like you're a nerdy scientific intellect if a person studies and all I'm doing is high school homework, she thought to herself.

The incident that evolved into the current situation happened back in elementary school. It was during a silly chasing game between the boys and the girls. There was a heated disagreement between Jill and Wayne that had to do with kicking each other's shins, and who had started it. The incident led to a war between the sexes. Jill wouldn't back down and it escalated into the challenge of a fight. The rest of the boys turned to walk away assuming the whole thing was over. However, Jill couldn't stand giving Wayne the glory of winning the battle. He was so amused he jokingly played along. She wondered what she'd gotten herself into. The boys came back and gathered around. "Meet behind the swings at the far end of the playground after lunch," he said. His eyes were gleaming as if in a fever. Jill was taken aback by the force of his confidence. Things had suddenly gotten out of hand and she didn't know how to reverse it. There seemed to be no way to turn it around without admitting defeat and there's no way she'd have done that. The duel was to take place in only a couple of hours. She felt dizzy and began to sweat as she faced the boys, but she tried to appear confident. "You are all so stupid!" she said. "We're stupid, we're stupid," they mocked. "You gonna be there?" a boy taunted. The others laughed. "I'll be there," she said with her hands on her hips and her nose in the air. "Really?" Several of them raised their eyebrows;

they smiled irritating clownish smiles, taunting her. She wanted to slap the smiles off of their faces. She thought by now they would have let it go seeing she wouldn't back down because she was a girl, but it didn't seem to be working out that way and she could feel herself being sucked into their growing appetite for entertainment at her expense.

Yet she wouldn't back down. Her pride wouldn't allow it. "Yes." She couldn't believe the word had flown out of her mouth. The girls gasped. She turned and walked away while the boys laughed after her and shouted, "Yeah, meet at the far corner! We'll be there!! Dumb little girl, you'll learn your lesson, you really think you can beat him?" "I can't wait to see this!" They laughed even harder. They continued to laugh long after she had gone. Laughing had never seemed more terrifying to her.

Stubborn and willful, Jill stuck it through and met at the designated meeting place where the boys gathered and snickered. The girls gathered around the other side, offering support and shouting their disapproval. "You shut up!" one girl said. "Shut up, shut up," a couple of the boys chanted and laughed. A couple of the girls took her aside. They walked to the edge of the swing set pit. "It's not too late to back out." Jill shook her head, "No, they'll never stop laughing. He'll back down first, you'll see. I'm going through with it." The other girls weren't so sure. Jill faced Wayne off and he glared her down. He taunted her and said, "Oh you really gonna fight, are you?" Jill didn't answer. "Come on then, take the first hit." She couldn't imagine he would actually hit a girl and she definitely couldn't fathom hitting someone, but he wasn't backing down like she had thought he would. She was terrified he may actually hit her. She was waiting to call his bluff. Instead, he called hers. "Come on, take the first punch!" He grinned and bounced around with his fists in the air like he really was planning to hit her back. Wayne danced around in the dirt, dust flying up around them. The boys got louder and more excited with every passing second. He could read her faltering confidence and he taunted and dared her to take the first punch. Jill suddenly felt extremely hot and wasn't sure if it was the sun or her nerves. She felt faint, and finally she caved. She stomped her foot and walked away. The boys laughed and laughed. The girls turned their backs indignantly and walked after her. It was the worst possible outcome ever and she would never live it down. She had made a fool of herself.

From that day onwards, those two boys, Wayne and his sidekick Jerry who seemed like a permanent appendage, never let go of a chance to bully her. In hind site, she wished she'd had the nerve to swing a punch at him on the playground that day. Her future may have been much different. Be it as it may, it was staggering that an incident from the fourth grade could hang on so long. It was one last dreary event on top of a dreary high school day to deal with those two boys. She never saw them during the day. It was always at the end of it. It was like some higher force was going to make sure to give her one last kick on her way out of the school grounds to finish it off and reinforce with double surety Jill's hate of adolescence. Only it didn't feel like a little stage of life at the time. It felt like it would drag on forever. So as usual, she endured it like everything else in her life.

Wayne turned to Jerry and said, "She probably has straight A's." Jerry laughed and asked, "Do you?" She did actually. "I have a couple B's," she lied. "Ohhhhh!" they put their hands over their mouths in a pretend gesture of mock disbelief. "Oh my God! Did you hear that Jerry? A couple of B's!" They laughed. "Go home and study, Brain." They walked away, laughing. She couldn't seem to shake that label from way back either. Why had she acted like such a know-it-all? Why did she bother giving them answers to everything? Why did she beat everyone at those fourth grade math games? She should have pretended she was a little more stupid when she had the chance.

Jill arrived home and put her key into the lock of the green painted door with white trim and turned the handle. She walked into the dark cave, her home, absent of words but one that heaved with the life of a thousand. The air was thick and it breathed heavy emotions that lingered even after everyone had gone. No one was home as usual. Her Father was in the garage working on something. He wouldn't come inside. He never did, so she had the house to herself. She set her books down in her room on her small worn-out desk and enjoyed having free reign of the house, even if she had no one to enjoy it with. She walked through the dark maroonish-brown carpeted halls and rooms that suited the cave's heaviness.

She headed for the kitchen. Food was top priority and it was the highlight of the day. This was the reward for enduring all the misery. She raided the cupboards and freezer for anything she could find. She opened the door to the freezer, a swirl of ice-cold air hit her face: ice cream! She pulled it off the shelf and set it on the counter. She found a bowl and a spoon and tried to spoon it out of the container, but it was rock solid. She decided to leave it for a moment to defrost despite her urgent desire for it. She walked back to the refrigerator and opened the door. There were fried chicken leftovers from the night before. "Yes!" she said. She placed them on the counter. Before closing the refrigerator door she spotted the bowl of mashed potatoes. She pulled those out too. She scanned the shelves for anything else. She opened one of the drawers and spotted the cheese. One could always count on cheese. She and her Father loved it, and Carol, her stepmother, bought a lot of it. She put it next to the fried chicken. Not seeing anything else worthwhile, she went back to the chicken and placed it in the microwave. She turned the timer for about a minute, listening to the soft buzzing sound. She walked over to the cheese and took a sharp knife from the drawer. Peeling back the plastic wrap she dug the knife into the large block of hard cheddar, pressing with all of her weight to get a slice. She took a bite, savoring the saltiness, letting it melt slowly in her mouth.

The microwave was still buzzing so she went to the garage to scavenge what she could find in the outside refrigerator while she waited for her chicken to warm. Every shelf was full of case after case of soda, every imaginable kind. She took an orange soda and closed the door. It was nice and cold. She peeled back the aluminum tab and took a nice long sip then and there. The icy coldness drew her attention to the cold cement of the garage floor under her bare feet. It was refreshing. She walked back inside. The chicken was ready so she pulled it out of the microwave and took a fork from the silverware drawer. She pushed it into the chicken and lifted the entire drumstick to her mouth. She pulled pieces of the crunchy skin off the outside of it. It was still crunchy from the night before. The meat itself was tender. It had been fried in Crisco, the southern way. Carol was from the deep south. Savoring every bite she finished the remaining two pieces from last night's dinner and started in on the mashed potatoes. She retrieved the butter from the fridge and piled it onto the creamy heap of whiteness. They were still hot so the butter melted quickly.

Then she remembered the ice cream. She walked to the other counter where it was, took the large spoon and dug into it. It went in easily now so she took a big spoonful. It melted and slid down her throat with all the pleasure cold melted goodness can bring. It was chocolate chocolate-chip.

She dug around for the chips creating tunnels in the tub of frozen cream. The sweetness was delectable and she loved chocolate. Before long she realized she had eaten nearly all of it … and she had forgotten to use the bowl. She decided she'd better not eat all of it and put the lid back on even though there were only two bites left. She placed it gingerly back in the fridge feeling a little guilty she hadn't left any for anyone else. Funny thing was, she never saw anyone but herself eating ice cream in her house. Her stomach was bulging and satisfied but she still felt like eating. She picked up her soda and took a few more sips and opened the cupboards to see what else there was. Lucky Charms cereal! She pulled it out and separated the wax paper lining, exposing what was inside. Rather than get a bowl, she probed into the box with her bare fingers, searching for the pastel colored marsh mellow charms and ate only those. She finished her soda and decided to get another. She went outside. This time she got vanilla. She walked back in trying to think what else there might be to eat. Then she remembered the secret hiding place above the stove in a small cupboard where the silver exhaust pipe for the stove was. Carol often hid special things that she liked to save for herself there. She opened the door to the little cupboard and jackpot! She took the can of toffee-covered peanuts from the shelf and ate a few. They were crunchy and sweet. She loved toffee. She ate them one by one and slowly so she wouldn't eat too many and so she could savor them. Mostly she knew Carol was saving them for herself. She put them back exactly as she had found them and shut the door. She picked up her can of soda and decided she had found all the good stuff. She departed the kitchen feeling stuffed and happy, and a slight bit guilty. Her favorite part of the day was over.

She walked to her room and took out her mathematics book. Sitting on the edge of her soft worn bed she opened it to the chapter she was studying. The subject was easy but she decided to pretend she didn't understand so she could ask her Father for help. She longed to be close to him. She got up from her bed and walked to the garage. Math was his passion. He once said if he couldn't get to sleep, he would do math problems in his head until he did. Jill held her book open to the most complicated problem she could find. She opened the door to the garage and stepped down onto the cold cement for the third time that day. She walked past the workbench that was covered with projects. The front nose of an airplane lay in pieces with the propeller on the floor. She never knew what she might find in that garage. Nothing surprised her anymore.

She stepped around the pieces of the plane to get to the little room her Father had built into a private office for himself. There was another workbench there, covered with more intricate electrical circuit boards and wires. There was a coolness about the room, in both temperature and atmosphere; it felt calm, if not a bit sterile in a mechanical kind of way, completely unlike the tension inside the house. The walls had fake wood panel board on them and the same short green carpet with little squares as the kitchen. There was a door leading from the garage and a window that looked out over the backyard.

Jill's stepmother had long given up hope for a normal relationship with her husband. There had been too many disappointments. The anticipation of airplane restaurant dates were usually met with scattered airplane parts spread on airport tarmacs. Jill couldn't remember a time they actually followed through with the plan, save one occasion. The plane was usually not put together in time to go. Paul always said cheerfully, "Oh it'll be done in nothing flat. Just give me a minute." It was hard to imagine that many parts could jump back together that quickly. Carol would ask, "Exactly how long?" He'd answer, "Oh in a jiffy, a couple minutes." And she would reply "Yeah right, no I mean *exactly.*" He could tell she meant business so he would come up with a number that he thought would buy him time: "About 15." She would reply with "Hmm." In time she learned better. She shook her head and mumbled to Jill and her brother, "He has no concept of time. This will be at least two hours. Come on kids, let's go to Carl's Junior." The one occasion the plan actually worked, they never made it to the restaurant. They had flown to a little island off the coast, but there was no way to get from the airport into town. They hung out at the airport on Catalina Island while her Father visited with everyone and checked out interesting facts about the airport.

Today he was bent over a circuit board at his garage desk with wires and pieces coming out from all sides. Small metal objects were strewn over his work area. The back to a computer hung open exposing all of its parts and an old keyboard lay next to it. Computers were something new and hardly anyone had one, but Jill's Father was determined to put his own together with used pieces from other old computers. His credo was, "Good inventions are great, but there's always a way to make them better." Mainly, he just wanted to see how it worked.

When Jill approached him and tried to get his attention by saying his name, he didn't answer. Jill was worried he would be mad that she was disturbing him. He might turn around and angrily reprimand her as was the case a good deal of the time. One could never tell from one day to the next what to expect. He was unpredictable and she had experienced his wrath enough times to know she was stepping into a minefield whenever she tried to approach him. He was deep in concentration as he went back and forth between the graphing pad next to his work and what he was doing. It was so silent that she could hear her dog breathing just outside the door that was slightly ajar. It was hard to imagine he didn't hear her walk in. Jill timidly called his name again, but no answer. Now she knew he hadn't heard her, but, on the other hand, did he? Maybe he heard her and was just finishing up what he was working on, so she continued to wait. Several minutes went by as she awkwardly loitered behind him. The hairs on the back of her neck stood on end as she braced herself for what was to come. She was afraid to say his name again because perhaps his absence of reply meant he did not want to be disturbed. Against her better judgment she ventured another attempt, slightly raising her voice. He turned with a start, wearing one of his typical looks like he'd just woken from a long night's sleep, his eyes wide and surprised. "Huh?" he answered. He was truly startled. Every time this happened, Jill never failed to be surprised he hadn't heard her, even though this too happened a good deal of the time. She was relieved. This meant he was in a good mood. "Um," she began, holding her book out. "Do you think you could help me with my math?" "Uh, oh math?" he answered with budding enthusiasm. "Oh, yeah, let's see what you got there." She handed the book to him and he looked at the problem she pointed to. She relaxed into the comfort of being close to him. "Oh, this is easy, simple as pie. What'd'ya have so far?" She timidly stepped closer and showed him the half-started problem she had carefully contrived to contain one simple mistake. "Oh well, look here. Let's begin over. These teachers. They skip far too many steps. Keep it simple, one step at a time. Like this." Jill took note. She skipped too many steps and that wasn't the teacher's fault. He took the pad of paper with Jill's work and wrote the first line of the problem. "Now give me step one," he said.

Jill gave it. "No, now you skipped several steps. Not like that. You need to be methodical, same way every time. Try again." Jill backed up. This was going to be very tedious, but at least she was with her Father and they were having an interaction. She relished the moment together with him. She pretended to falter a couple of times in order to convince him she was stuck. Her Father proceeded to illustrate where she'd gone wrong. Jill half-listened. She already knew the answer, but that didn't matter. It wasn't the reason she was there.

They finished the problem and her dad said, "Well, is that it?" Jill lingered realizing their session had all too quickly come to an end. She fumbled with the book searching for a problem that was different than the one they'd just worked on, but unfortunately, they were all the same, only easier. Slowly and with hesitation she said, "Uh, no, I guess not ..." She continued to linger and Paul looked at her puzzled. "Thanks Dad," she reluctantly turned to leave. "No problem," he turned back to his work with the hint of a smile on his face. Jill dragged her feet towards the door leading to the kitchen and walked into the cold quiet house that was a different kind of cold and quiet from her Father's garage office quiet. Unlike the peace she felt in his office, the house was a stony indifferent kind of cold. And yet it was loud at the same time, even though there was no noise and no one spoke. It felt stifling. The walls spoke a million unspoken words, communicating what no one dared say, words that bulged at the seams because they were so overwrought with the intensity of frustrated angry emotions that came from years of unexpressed thoughts.

These odd exchanges with her Father were all Jill had to hang onto, and they were few and far between. She longed to be closer to him, but it was nearly impossible. One time, long after he had gone through rehab, he came to her. Jill couldn't remember another time that had happened. Carol and her little brother, Robbie, were gone for the summer, and the house felt warm and different. Jill actually felt at ease, like it was ok to just be. Paul seemed less uptight. They even let the dog in the house, Jill's beloved Mala. Paul seemed happy about that and Jill certainly was.

Harriott pulled up one day during that time in her long wide red and white Cadillac that took up most of the driveway. It was a peaceful day until she arrived. Harriott had a way of taking the peace out of everything as far as her son was concerned. One day dragged on into many. Three days after she'd arrived, she went into the garage, oblivious of the disturbance she caused Jill's Father, violating the unspoken law of sanctity that presided over his office. Somehow, she commanded his attention with a nails-on-chalkboard effect, and it was impossible for him to ignore her. Jill marveled at Harriott's ability to do that. "Paul, where are your tablecloths?" Paul turned his head and rolled his eyes. For some reason she was the only person he could not tune out. "Mom. How would I know?" He wondered what on earth she needed a tablecloth for. "Mom, we don't need anything fancy. There's no need to make a big deal out of dinner." He hated big fusses over nothing. Harriott was fidgety and her forehead was furrowed in consternation, her eyes narrowed and her thick fingers wove themselves nervously around each other. "Well I need that tablecloth. Never you mind what for. I just need it." "Mom, I just don't know ok? Can you leave me alone? Can't you see I'm in the middle of something?" Harriott opened her eyes a little wider and looked around as if she was noticing the workbench, the tools, and everything around him for the first time. "Oh oh oh! Of course, you go back to work then, I'll find it!"

Paul entered the kitchen and passed through as quickly as he could. His mother was at the sink but when she noticed him, she turned towards him. He tried to escape before she could ask him to do anything. He almost crashed into Jill as she approached from the other end of the hallway and he bent down to ask her. "Please will you follow me to the garage? I need to talk to you." The intensity of his green eyes and the panic in his voice told her it was something urgent. She was perplexed and curious at the same time. This was highly out of the ordinary. She wondered what he could possibly need her so badly for.

In the cool garage office her father said to her, "Jill, I need you to do something for me. I can't do it myself. I just can't." The desperation with which he pleaded startled Jill and she wondered what on earth was the matter. She hung on his words, her heart beating a little faster. The room suddenly felt small and familiar, like she had been injected into this particular space and time and she belonged in it. She leaned forward so she could focus. "I need you to ask my mother to leave." Jill hesitated, waiting for the real reason. "Is that it?" she said to herself, the words did not actually come out of her mouth. "I have never felt closer to the urge to drink since I stopped. Until now." He spoke in a quiet nearly inaudible voice. He looked at her intensely, waiting for the words to sink in, waiting until he knew she understood exactly what he was asking of her. Jill nodded her head as she became aware of the gravity of the situation. A warm feeling of purpose surged through her body. Jill's heart swelled with the trust he was placing in her. "Can you do this for me?" She nodded her head. It was the first time he had ever mentioned his drinking problem to her. It was the first time anyone had. Not even during the duration of the two months he was in the hospital and everyone pretended nothing was amiss had anyone explained anything to her. He had acknowledged the truth to her about what happened in a few brief seconds. Even if it was years after the fact, she felt like she had momentarily synced with the universe and she had a firm place in it. "Of course I can," she said. "Oh thank you Jill. Thank you."

It was such a silly thing and yet it was like something huge had moved into her being, reminding her of something, reminding her she was significant. It was a feeling of inclusion, like her mind was inside her body for once and the two were aligned in a rare moment of connection.

She went into the kitchen and walked straight up to Harriott. "Grandma? I need to tell you something." Harriott looked at her, waiting for her to speak. She sensed the hesitation in her own voice. "It's ok. Whatever it is, it's ok," Harriott assured her. "Well Grandma, I need to ask you to leave. It's Dad. He is feeling very close to the urge to drink. He feels stressed and pressured to have you here." Jill looked up at her grandmother, with a sorry look in her eyes. "Oh, oh oh ohhhh. Of course, I'll pack my bags this instant. I would never ever in a million years wish for that to happen." "I'm so sorry Grandma." Jill felt badly it had to be this way. Her grandmother looked at Jill in the most stoical way, Jill thought. "Don't you feel one bit sorry. I'm not in the least bit worried about my feelings. This is more important than that. We can't be worried with feelings. I'm leaving right now, honey." "Ok Grandma." Jill watched her grandmother, impressed with her strength and lack of self-concern for the greater good of the family. She thought her grandmother was a saint in that moment.

Jill didn't wonder why her father couldn't simply tell his mother it was time to go. Speaking straight forward in their family was as impossible as a lizard trying to fly. Their communication swam in circles of mismatched actions and words.

Harriott packed her bags and left that very hour. Jill's father walked into the kitchen, his eyes sparkling and a relieved smile on his face. Jill felt the love from him pouring out to her. He said, "Thank you," in the most heartfelt way Jill had heard him speak to her since she was a little girl. What her father didn't know was that it was Jill who had asked her grandmother to stay in the first place. It hadn't been Harriott's idea at all. Jill only wanted some company, but discovering the hardship it was on her father, she quickly obliged him. She hadn't realized her grandmother was such a burden on him.

After the unneeded math help but the much-needed interaction with her Father after school that day, Jill went inside and sat in front of the TV. It wasn't long before Carol pulled into the driveway. Jill got up and went to her room. She could hear the commotion of everyone pouring into the kitchen and then into the den. The sounds were muffled and she couldn't make out what anyone was saying. Their presence was like a shifting chunk of earth breaking loose from the San Andreas fault, sliding into the house like thick goopy mud, shifting the terrain, pushing her into her corner of the house. She got her homework out and placed it on her desk, turning on the TV that sat on an old metal cart. It was an old and large rectangular shaped box that played black and white. It had been Carol's. It was a good "stay-in-your-room" device. Jill knew that was the underlying motive behind allowing her to have it in her room and she easily fell prey to it. She turned the bulky round dial to the channel playing "Charlie's Angels" and half-heartedly worked on her homework. Her homework was hardly begun, but she flipped on another show as soon as "Charlie's Angels" finished. This time it was "Bionic Woman." Again, she only got a fraction of her work completed, mostly watching TV. Carol called from the kitchen, "Dinner's ready!" Everyone came to the kitchen except Paul. They sat down and waited for him. He didn't come so Carol got up from the table and shouted from the kitchen door into the garage. He didn't answer so she said it again. He glanced up on the third time with those eyes that looked as if he'd just woken up and had only heard her voice for the first time. "Uh, ohhh. Yeah."

She sat down and said, "Let's eat," with tightly pursed lips that formed a straight line and eyes that seared into her food. Jill thought if her eyes were lasers, she could have sliced her meat into very neat slices. She was focused on her food as if it was her only chance at controlling her angry laser eyes. Dinner consisted of chicken fried steak, mashed potatoes, a big mushy pile of spinach out of the can and burnt rolls. It was a good dinner aside from the spinach and only one edible side to the rolls. They started eating and ten minutes later Paul walked in and sat down as if the world waited for him to grace it with his presence. Jill already had a crunchy piece of meat in her mouth. He spoke a few disjointed sentences about the food and random inconsequential phrases. It was communication void of any real content. They were mostly comments mimicked repeatedly every night. It was as if he was trying to make light talk for the rest of the family, but he had no idea how. The dinner consisted of this jibberish and mostly silence interrupted intermittently by Robbie acting up at the table. This always caused a great deal of entertainment. Apparently the same bad behavior was funny every night. Jill didn't think so, but she never said anything.

After a long period of silence Jill finally opened her mouth to speak but was greeted with uninviting silence. "We had a race at the lake last weekend." Despite the stony cold response she elicited, she continued. "It was so funny, Fred fell in the water and had to drag his boat clear across the lake." She inserted qualifiers to justify what she had to say. "Then all of us girls were in the K-4 and we fell in too! We were laughing so hard!" It was a one-way conversation, but she was used to it. It was the only kind of interaction she ever had with her family, and there was no other way to have a conversation, despite the fact there never really was one to begin with. "Coach was so mad we were goofing around … and –"Her father glared at her intolerantly. She became nervous and spoke more quickly to finish the story. She never was really sure why she did this. Maybe it was because to abruptly stop in that moment would have exposed the obvious, that what she had to say was unimportant and she wanted to pretend that wasn't the case. "It took us even longer than Fred to right our boat and drag it across the lake because it's four times as big-" In the end, Paul cut her off anyway. "Be quiet. No one's interested." He said it with such finality she knew there was no arguing and put her head down. She spoke not a word the rest of dinner.

When Paul was done eating he got up, leaving his dirty plate on the table, and headed straight for the garage. Jill washed the dishes. She was particular and cleaned everything just so. When she finished, she passed through the family room where Carol sat on the couch with her glass of wine staring at the TV. Her brother played on the floor. Jill hesitated, longing to join. It seemed Carol hardly noticed her, but Jill knew as soon as she tried to sit down, she would tell her to leave. She had tried it once. It ended badly.

Jill resigned herself to her quiet refuge, her bedroom. She did not feel dejected. In fact, it was the opposite. She felt nothing. She longed to feel a part of the family, but it was impossible. Words didn't form in her mind to try to make sense of it. They fell off somewhere over an invisible cliff. It didn't matter. She remembered the time she had pushed the boundaries and forced her presence with them. Her skin had buzzed with the excitement of injecting herself for a moment into their lives, like a flower jumping off the wallpaper. Her skin was prickling with aliveness at her effect on people around her. She was real. But she was forced to recoil back into her shell because it didn't work. It was ok. It was comfortable there.

Her brother came to join her in her no-man's land. He was fuming that day she had tried to join them in the living room after dinner. All she had done was sit down on the couch, but it was an unspoken violation. His cheeks were red and his words came seething out of his mouth. "I can't believe her. She is so impossible." Jill adored him and found it admirable the way he fought so hard on her behalf. "It's ok Robbie." She tried to calm him down. He said, "No! It's not! It's not!" "It's just the way it is." Jill had a way of imparting tranquility to him even if she lacked the wherewithal to stand up for herself. "This is how it's always been. Things aren't going to change, and it's ok. I've accepted it. I don't even know why I did that tonight. I guess I just thought one more time I'll give it a try and see what happens." Robbie sat down on the worn out and way too soft couch bed that was part of a set with a table that joined another bed in the corner. They were in style. Hers was so ugly she liked it. She loved the softness and that trumped the putrid mustard color mixed with brown and imitation wood table. He was so cute, trying so hard to be a man, Jill thought. He was barely seven. He stared at the shaggy maroon carpet and shook his head. "It's ok Robbie. Really, it is," Jill said. "Come on. Want to play a game?" That always cheered him up. He looked up at her with his short straight brown hair and warm brown eyes. A little bit of something had bubbled to the surface that night, but perhaps the realness of her connection with Robbie was the only part that mattered.

Jill went to bed thinking about the next day. It was kayaking practice and something to look forward to. It was an escape from the strangeness of her life at home.

She woke the following morning to the same humdrum day of school as usual but as the day wore on, she looked forward to practice after school. "You coming today?" One of the twins asked. "Yep," Jill replied. "Why don't you come straight to our house." "Ok!" Jill loved going to their house. The bell rang and Jill poured her books into her locker. There was too much walking to do today to bother with carrying books. Wayne and Jerry didn't bother her. She ignored them and hurried to the other side of the school so she wouldn't miss the twins walking home. Jill went with one of them while the other went with a friend. They walked separately the several blocks to their house. The walk gave them time to talk. Conversation was light and easy with Lisa. She talked about her horse accident. She had broken her hip two years previous and had missed months of school. Jill listened and when she spoke about her Father thinking horses were a waste of money and time she stared at the ground with a frown on her face. Jill replied, "Oh I don't think so. I think it sounds exciting and fun. You should've kept doing it. Who cares what your Dad thinks? Or are you afraid now after your accident?" Lisa replied, "No, I'm not. I would still do it, but my Dad won't let me anyway. It's ok. I just won't do it." "I'm sorry," Jill answered. "Yeah," she said. Jill hadn't realized how important horses were to her. They talked about trivial events from the day the rest of the way home.

Turning the last corner to their street Jill could already see the little yellow house and unkempt yard with boats strewn everywhere. It was a wonder the neighbors didn't complain. The garage door was open and coach was barking orders to the new recruits, middle school boys from the math classes he taught by day. Coach made all of his boats out of fiberglass right there in his garage. It was a regular workshop and with the promise of becoming a kayaker came the responsibility of becoming an apprentice boat maker, but only the boys were taught how to make the long narrow boats. He rarely recruited girls, and the ones that were there or did come by way of some other means than his math classes, were not taught the boat making trade. The girls didn't care; they saw it as a blessing. The boys complained about the fiberglass burning their skin.

The girls stepped inside to a room full of people. There were other kayakers hanging around waiting for practice to begin. Jill never knew whom she would meet when she walked into that house. Coach was renowned for his coaching abilities and he constantly had a stream of visitors from all over seeking his expertise. He welcomed them wholeheartedly. He loved the commotion and giving advice and helping people. A tall blond haired teenage girl stood up as they walked in and introduced her self. "Hi, I'm Ingrid. I'm visiting from Sweden. I came to practice with your Dad." "Hi, I'm Jill." "I'm Lisa." Some young men in their twenties and some in their thirties sat sprawled all over the long low-lying blue couches that were merely boards covered with foam and blue cloth sewn around, supported by cement bricks on either end, a simple yet resourceful way to decorate. "Hey," they said one after the other. Jill lost track of their names. They all sounded so foreign and combined with their heavy accents, she couldn't make out what they were anyway. Lisa walked straight to the kitchen and came back with snacks. She handed some chips and a drink to Jill and said "Come on." She followed Lisa into her room that was painted a deep navy-aqua blue. Jill had helped her paint it several weeks back and you could still smell the paint. Jill couldn't understand why on earth she picked that color. She thought it was hideous. At least it sort of masked the disaster of a mess. Sort of.

The girls walked out of the bedroom and back into the kitchen to search for more food. By then the kitchen table was surrounded by several tall gangly high school boys. It was the regular bunch, Coach's long time math class recruits who had stuck around for the long haul. They mostly ignored the girls. One of them walked in and said "Hey! What's the deal?" They were always saying that.

Coach was in the dining room with a big smile on his face, and in his deep voice announced, "Hey look at this. Looks like everyone's here!
Ok, listen up. All of you get your stuff together. Then come outside and help load the boats. I'll be out there telling you which ones. And we've got some visitors today, so let me introduce them." "We already did coach," one of the regular boys told him. "Yeah, yeah," another couple of them confirmed. He ignored the commentary and said "Well I'm gonna introduce them

anyway." He went around the room and made the introductions and then said sharply and with a clap of his hands, "Alright. Let's go. Everybody outside!" Coach was social but he didn't like to mince words or dilly-dally. Jill always marveled at his ability to command a big group with such ease. There was something comforting and inclusive about it. She felt like she belonged. Her parents thought the sport was silly and something only to pass the time and figured Jill couldn't possibly be serious about it. She played it off as if it were so. It was easier that way. But she really did like it. A boat of her own would have been incredible, yet unfathomable. The thought never really occurred to her since it wasn't a possibility.

Everyone piled into the van. "Load up!" Coach called several times. "Whoever's riding with me, the bus is leaving, so get out here!" A red white and blue trailer held all of the boats. Many months earlier they had hauled it to a big field where Jill and the entire team had spent the day painting it into three separate sections of red, white and blue. It was hitched to the VW van. It was a very long configuration. Three rows of boats could fit end to end. The van was a yellow dilapidated vehicle with rusted holes, but Coach didn't care. He thought it was perfect.

Coach always carried a roll of duct tape everywhere he went, and he stopped the van in emergencies such as rain and people getting dripped on, which happened regularly. He duct taped the holes, and inspecting his handiwork was always saying, "There! Good as new! Duct tape, best invention ever. There's nothing it can't fix. Coach would climb back into the driver's seat to head off, shouting back now and then, "Girls, how's that duct tape holding up?" It always worked. Contentedly he nodded, "Yep, what'd I tell ya?" The girls piled in the back of the van and sang songs like "Happy Trails" over and over on long road trips. Coach usually had to tell them to stop. There is only so much of the same song any adult can tolerate. These were some of the best memories Jill had.

Jill got into the van and squished in between everybody. It was different on these rare occasions to leave straight from the house; the usual routine was for Coach to swing by from the main road where Jill would be waiting on the corner. Since the road was busy, Coach didn't like to stop, so he'd keep rolling and yell "Hurry up! Jump on, I'm not stopping!!" The door would slide open by whoever was sitting on the floor next to it and wait for her to run and jump in, and then the door slammed shut. It was a miracle if she didn't fall over somebody throwing herself in like that week after week. She didn't care. Her only goal was to make sure she made it inside.

The van smelled like musty old socks. It was about as messy as Lisa's room and the garage combined. Old food wrappers and t-shirts and clothes various people had forgotten over the weeks littered the floor. Jill was smashed between four people and that was one person more than the bench was made for. Ashley said, "Come on, sit on my lap." She bent her head so it didn't hit the ceiling. The high school boys joked around as usual as they drove the fifteen-minute ride to the lake. They were silly boys and Fred with his curly brown messy hair asked, "Hey Coach, got any jokes?" Coach always had a joke. "Yeah," he began. Jill leaned forward as did the boys to listen.

"You know why Cynthia's mom insists everyone call her by her full name?" They were a large and very strict Catholic family and Cynthia and her brother were on the team. Everyone asked, "No, why Coach?" "Because she's afraid everyone will start calling her 'sin.'" There was a chorus of "ahhhhhs," after a bad joke. Coach laughed. "I thought it was a good one!"

They pulled into the marina on the outskirts of Westlake Village. Coach parked the van and announced, "Alright. I don't want to see any messing around. I want those boats in the water as soon as we get out. No standing around talking." Fifteen paddlers spilled out of the van.

"Ok, gather around everybody. Fred, you and your brother take C-1." It was an Olympic flat-water canoe for one person. It was a difficult boat, shaped like a steep "V" on the bottom, making it impossible to balance without hours, even days of practice just to stay upright. However, they'd been doing it for years. "You two together, C-2, and the both of you, Joe, Ed, C-2." "Jill, Lisa, Ashley, Becky, K-4." A K-4 was a flat-water kayak for four people. They were the same ages so they were a natural foursome or doubles in the K-2's. The K-4 was the most stable of the kayaks. Regardless of stability, it required concentration to keep even a K-4 from tipping, and precision was necessary to coordinate four paddles to match the headman who set the pace.

"We'll begin with three laps around the island for a warm-up. You boys, do four." He pointed to the oldest and most serious of the group. They went fast, and ended at the same time as everyone else even when they did more. "After that, meet at the top and we're doing sprints. Ten one-hundreds, timed, and four five-hundreds, timed." Everyone moaned. "Ahhh, Coach." "Yeah, yeah, I know. Alright come on! Let's get those boats in the water!" The older boys joked, "What don't kill ya, make ya stronga." The new junior high recruits gathered around Coach and were given an introduction to the sport.

"Grab your boat, I want to see everyone in the water within ten minutes!" The paddles and seats were unloaded from the paddle box and carried to the docks. "Hey! That includes you two over there. Go get some paddles, stop goofing around!" Coach didn't let anyone get away with sitting around. Happy chattering passed through the team as they scattered, gathering the equipment. "Hey, stop talking and get to it already." Slackers looked his direction. They knew who they were. Two minutes later, a small group was off task again and Coach got after them too. Math teaching skills came in handy managing the unwieldy bunch.

One boat after the next dropped into the water. The fastest paddlers were off the dock in minutes. Jill's group fiddled around getting everything together. Their boat was heavy and awkward, not to mention tremendously long. It required all four of the girls to manage the boat off the trailer and into the water. "Hey watch it!" Coach yelled. The girls almost knocked him over swinging the big red boat around to get it headed in the right direction. "You go there, No! back up everyone." Becky naturally assumed the role of leader. No one could see where they were going so everyone fumbled backwards and forwards, sideways and in opposing directions. "All together now, move forward, now left a little, I said a little! Stay together, don't drop it!" She was the only one that could see since she was at the front of the boat and the one leading it towards the ramp to the dock. There was an edge to her voice. She was getting irritated. "Yeah well, she's the only one that can see where she's going," Jill mumbled. Lisa looked back at her and rolled her eyes. They were tired of being yelled at all the time. However, they frequently goofed around and did not pay attention either.

The ribbed cement ramp was covered in duck droppings so everyone wore flip-flops, peeling them off just before jumping in the boats. "Ok, 1-2-3, in the water, ready go!" The girls dropped the boat into the water carefully despite its weight. Jill and one of the twins forgot their paddles, so they ran back up the dock for them. Someone always forgot something.

After an interminably long period of time, the girls held the boat steady for each other while they climbed into the boat one-by-one. It was the only way to keep the boat from tipping over. They did this until everyone was in.

All four of them gripped the dock until they were ready to go. Finally, the girls coordinated their push-off. Without the support of the dock to hang onto, paddles slapped the water and dug in with deep powerful strokes to stabilize the boat before they could get moving. Jill always found this moment exciting, the smooth flow of the water as they glided through it. Their seats were so narrow that Jill could put her hand two inches on either side of her hips and feel the water. It was cold and made Jill shiver all over. She took a deep breath in anticipation of the power and speed of the boat that was about to happen. It always took some time coordinating their balance and synchronizing their strokes until they got moving. Everyone continued slapping the water on either side to brace the boat from tipping over while they got it turned towards the island. Slowly the boat picked up momentum and the icy wind whipped through their hair. Even though it gave her more goose bumps, she knew in a matter of minutes she would be sweating. They worked together. Their paddles matched up as they reached with a nearly straight arm on the side they were pulling, twisting at the waist to maximize every stroke as Coach was forever instructing them to do. Jill could hear his voice ringing in her ears, "Reach!!"

Once in a huge while, mostly when they were goofing off, they would roll over into the water. It was easy to do. It required constant attention to keep these boats upright. The boat would have to be righted quickly before filling up with water. These were not white-water kayaks, and they were not made for rolling. When this happened swimmers dragged and pushed it to the nearest dock or bank. It was not possible to re-enter the boat from the water.

Jill usually took up anchor in the K-4, so she was the wettest. Since they paddled in winter and cold months too, and even in the rain they usually finished practice numb, wet and cold. Jill hardly noticed when they were out on the water. It took so much energy and sweat to keep the boat moving and in unison.

The girls finished their three laps despite joking around. The only teammate that kept them halfway focused was the leader, Becky. She was serious and the most responsible of the four. She often set the pace so fast and hard that she made it nearly impossible to goof off. In fact, the more any of them did goof off, the faster she would make them go. This shut everybody up.

Jill enjoyed the sport, but mostly the camaraderie. She was not too competitive or interested in breaking records. What frustrated Coach was that she and one of the twins were fairly athletic and had the potential to be much better than they were. Unfortunately they were also the two least serious of the four.

When the girls rounded their third lap and entered the line of paddlers at the top of the island, waiting to begin the second half of the work out, Jill breathed a sigh of relief. At least she could shake out her arms for a minute. Jill's tandem-lazy partner invariably did the same. Becky scowled because this meant the rest of them had to work to keep the boat steady while they took their break. They had to take turns getting a rest and the two back people snuck theirs in first every time. Coach lined everyone up and had each group go in waves according to boat size and type. The K-4 went last since it was so big and could go the fastest. Coach looked at his stopwatch and shouted, "Go!" The girls dug deep into the water, heaving the boat forward with a great deal of effort and seemingly very little result. It took tremendous force to get this big boat moving. In a few brief seconds, however, the girls sank into a natural rhythm and the boat glided through the water smoothly. The energy was good today and they were focused for once. The boat picked up so much speed that it sliced the water like a knife through melted butter. Coach came up from behind as the girls tried to halt the boat at the finish line. It was equally difficult to bring so much force to a halt as it was to get the momentum going from a dead stop. They went quite a ways across the marina before it was stopped enough to make the sharp turn.

Becky shouted out the commands. The two people at the front of the boat reached way out to the left with their paddles, dug in and pulled hard. The two at the back, including Jill, pushed away from the edge of the boat and outwards with equal force. Then they switched to their right side and drew their paddles towards the boat to swing the back half to the right. The boat pivoted around and the girls headed back for the finish line. All the while, Coach shouted excitedly, "You girls were flying! Look at your time!! I could enter you into the sprint race coming up! I think you could win if you keep this up. You were perfectly synced. See?! That's what I've been talking about! This is what it takes!! Why don't you do this all the time?!" Coach was far more excited than they were, and yet, they had felt the satisfaction of ease and speed that accompanies a perfect moment of synchronicity as surely as they felt the cold splash of water flipped up onto them by their teammates with every stroke.

They completed the end of the workout, heading for the dock. The girls were tired, wet and cold. They climbed out the boat a little less carefully then they'd gotten in. The worry of tipping out of the boat had long gone. No one cared if they fell in. They just wanted out. Quietly and with less enthusiasm than they'd begun the workout they pulled the heavy wet boat out of the water. They tilted the boat upside down and lowered one end to drain out water that had splashed in during practice. "Hey, no wonder we went so slow! We were lugging a couple dozen gallons of water!" Everyone laughed. "Hey yeah!" They loaded the dripping wet boats onto the trailer, fastening them in place before heading to the docks for the paddles and the rest of the soggy wet gear. There was considerably less goofing around than when they'd arrived. Exhaustion and the idea of getting warm and dry was good motivation. Jill always brought a dry sweatshirt to put on afterwards, and nothing felt better than that after a good hard workout. Today, someone forgot theirs, and pleas for charity went around, but the snug and warm dry-sweatshirt clad paddlers would not give theirs up to the mournful forgetters. The best part of paddling for Jill was the steaming hot shower when she got home.

Traveling across country to the Nationals each year in the beat-up VW or sometimes the Winnebago that smelled like a locker room from the pack of wet paddlers that loaded and unloaded for practice at every place they stopped along the way contributed to the experience. Coach somehow had every lake across the country scouted out so they could manage their once a day practice leading to the biggest races of the year. Getting dripped on when it happened to rain during their journey across the U.S. coming through the rusted out holes in the roof of the VW van while Jill and her boat mates sat cross-legged on the floor in the back, singing and playing games the entire way, she would never forget. Good thing for duct tape.

Jill walked home in the dark, cold, wet and tired, and a little bit numb, but with a happy smile on her face. Entering her lonely home didn't even bother her after a day out on the water. She walked in with a bounce to her step and disregarded the silent deafening scowl on her stepmother's face. She sat transfixed to the TV with the remote in her hand and a glass of wine sitting next to her. For Jill, being a member of the paddling team was like being part of a family, almost.

If a great deal of the year was filled with kayaking, another hobby took over the fall. For as long as she could remember she had twirled a baton. When she was old enough, she joined the band during football season, parades and summer twirling camps. She spent hours in front of the house practicing.

One cold fall day she went to the street at the end of her cul-de-sac with two batons in her hand. Robbie followed and sat on the curb to watch. "Do the knee one!" he said. Jill smiled. "Ok. For you." She bent one leg in the air and rolled the baton over it, catching it in the crease of her knee and guiding it between both legs. In one smooth motion, she flipped it out the other side and bent the other leg up catching it in the crease of the other knee and knocked it into the other hand. Her brother clapped, his eyes belayed his delight. He never tired of watching his sister. They were nearly nine years apart. They had a relationship that held no disagreement or adversity. Jill couldn't even remember one fight in their childhood. "Yay! Do it again!" Jill did. She would do anything for her little brother. "Again!" he said. "Ok, one more, then time for a different one, ok?"

She picked up a second baton. "Oh yes! Two batons!" Robbie leaned forward, anticipating what she would do. Jill winked at him and he smiled. Throwing one after the other in the air, she spun around and caught the first one, and then the second after spinning around again, ending backwards, catching it behind her back. "Another one!" He asked. "Ok, I have one." She'd been working on it for a long time. She twirled both batons horizontally, one in each hand, and tossed one of them in a horizontal throw into the air and let it fall onto one extended outturned leg. It fell still spinning flat onto the upper lateral muscle of her calf and bounced off, popping up, still twirling into the air. She spun around before catching it. "Whoa! When did you learn that one?! Do it again!" She wasn't sure she could. It was still a hit or miss, even after all the practice. "Ok, I'll give it a try, but no promises." This time she threw both, first one and then the other into the air together. Up they went. She caught the first one and when the second came down she let it fall and bounce onto her leg, only this time it missed the hard muscle and landed square on the bone. It had to hit just right or … well there were many bruised shins to be had before this one was mastered. Jill looked down at all the bruises up and down her shins. She breathed into the pain until it went away, then tried again. She could never let a move go without ending it right.

"There's a parade tomorrow." "Really?!" "Mmm hmm." "Want to see my routine? I need to practice it anyway." "Ok." Parades were Jill's favorite and it was their hometown parade this time. Jill practiced the entire thing five times and her brother got up to leave. "I'm going to play," he said. Jill was tired and ready to quit too.

The next morning Jill found herself at the parade with the two other girls on the team. They were bent over their shoes in front of the bus at the staging area, making sure their socks were rolled down just right and their tennis shoes perfectly white. They fussed with their hair, neatly pulled back in tight buns. "Be still, you have some loose strands falling down. Let me fix them," Jill said. She smoothed them back, tucking the loose strands to her head with a bobby pin and uncapped the hairspray. She sprayed long and hard until both girls were consumed in a massive cloud of fumes and her teammate's hair was hardened to a shellacked smooth veneer. "Perfect," Jill stepped back to inspect. It was an immovable mass. The third teammate inspected as well. "Hmmm, looks good." Jill checked her other teammate's hair. "Here, bend down. You need some too." One could never have enough hairspray. She paused and closed her eyes, adding some aerosol to her own head. "Hopefully my hair doesn't crack in half trying to get this out later." They laughed. "You know, Patty heard you can hairspray your shoes and it will keep them from getting dirty." Patty was an old team member. "Let's try it!" They put their feet out for Jill to spray. The girls coughed and choked, but Jill continued. They would endure anything for a competition.

The band conductor blew the whistle for everyone to line up. The twirlers took their places in front of everyone. They were a bit nervous as usual and warmed up practicing a few of their most difficult tosses. The sun caught the silver sparkles on their black costumes, sequined straps and sparkling tiaras as they spun around and twirled their silver batons. "Shall we practice one exchange before we begin?" Jill suggested. "It's going to be a while before the band gets themselves in order." "Sure, which one?" Sherri-Jo asked. "How about the aerial one? Julie, you gonna do it?" "Yeah, I'm ready." The girls lined up. "One, two, three …" Someone let theirs go too soon. "Sorry." "Ok let's try again," Jill said. There was no way Julie could have made the toss for the aerial in time to catch an early throw. Jill caught the girl's baton and tossed it back. "Ok we ready?" "Yeah." "One, two, three." Up went all three batons. Jill had to gage exactly where Julie was going to end up so her throw would fall in front of her when she landed. As soon as she tossed hers in the air she looked quickly for her partner's throw coming at her, keeping an eye on it as she spun around twice and caught it behind her back. Julie landed her aerial in front of them. When it was in her hand she glanced around to check the timing and see if the three of them caught at the same time. "Nice!" Jill said. "Ok, let's go back to the elbow rolls and do the exchange from there and see if we can do it again." "Ok, go!" They stuck their elbows out and rolled their batons over one and then the other, turning in a circle to catch it as it rolled around their necks and shoulders and over another elbow again before going to the next move that led to the exchange. The girls had their eyes on each other to time their throws just right. One girl slowed down, another sped up to synchronize. All batons flew in the air and the girls did their moves and caught them perfectly. "Ok! Let's do that when we're out there!" said Jill. The girls smiled. "We're ready!" said Sherri-Jo. They assumed their positions, doing a few more warm-up stretches in place. The whistle blew and the conductor yelled, "I said no moving! Everyone should be at attention." The girls knew that meant them too. The conductor turned around, "You guys ready?" "We're ready," answered Jill. "Ok, let's go!" Slowly they made their way to the entrance of the parade, waiting once again to begin moving in line with the procession.

The signal was given and the conductor waved his baton for the music to begin. The drummers gave a cadence for the group to march in time and slowly they moved forward. When the rhythm to the cadence altered that was the sign that the music was about to start. The three twirlers glanced at each other and lined themselves up. The very first few onlookers were ahead and Jill could just make them out in the distance. It only took a matter of minutes to arrive where the first people crowded the street sides. They were well into their routine by then. There were many skipping moves and cartwheels and spinning around while the batons were in the air in order to keep the momentum moving forward. The batons had to be carefully launched at an angle so they would fall where the twirler needed to be when it landed several feet ahead. It was a dynamic movement of many parts.

Jill caught the looks of surprise every now and then of onlookers and small children pointing at them when she and her teammates performed an impressive move. As they reached the first crowded corner, it was perfectly timed for their first exchange. The girls breathed in and took one last look at each other to coordinate their timing for the throw. Everyone concentrated hard. All three batons went into the air. Julie moved out front and performed her aerial as the other two spun around. The three batons came down in succession, one, two, three, not at the same time like they were supposed to, but they pretended that's how it was meant to be. There was an unspoken rule to go with it if they messed up. The audience didn't know the difference. Each twirler caught theirs and the kids shouted, "Look mommy!!!" and everyone clapped. The girls smiled and continued past their ever-changing audience. Jill would never forget the sound of the bellowing tubas as each new round began. Just closing her eyes and imagining it made goose bumps run up and down her spine.

When they arrived at the starting line to the judges' stand, they came to attention. This was the big moment. Everything had to be timed just right. The dance, the tricks, the exchanges had to be perfectly spaced so they would land at the precise moment directly before the judges; this is where the imperative and elaborate "salute" had to be made. Every parade required its own tailored salute as an honorary gesture towards the judges. The music began and the girls were a bit nervous. Julie's baton slipped in her hand because they were so wet from nervousness, but she held onto it. Jill was nervous mostly about the exchange. It was a difficult one as it was but it was more imperative than ever that they nail it because it was right in front of the judge's stand. As the batons flew into the air Jill could see that her partner had overthrown. Jill lunged and jumped several feet out of line. They would be marked down a few points for an inaccurately placed throw but Jill caught it anyway, even if it wasn't entirely graceful. A drop, however, would have cost them a lot, so Jill smiled big at the save. Jill met eyes with one of the judges smiling back at her. Jill sometimes thought the judges were just as ambitious as they were for them to catch it. Now they were right in front of the judge's stand. They reached it first since they were in front of the band so it was early on in their routine they made their salute. Jill's typically entailed a string of twirls, spinning around, ending in one bent leg and one leg outstretched while the baton ended at the bottom of her foot and her head lowered into a bow. When each girl rose, direct eye contact with the judges was a formality and one never to be missed if an impression was to be made and hope for top placement and a ribbon or a trophy. Big smiles spread across their faces because they knew they'd done well, and despite their minor mistake, it was a difficult maneuver and complex exchange and they knew they would be scored high for attempting it. The judges smiled back and picked up their pens to mark their scores. The girls relaxed. The hardest part was over. Now they could have fun! They bounced and skipped and twirled the rest of the way.

Jill's Dad came to watch the parade that day. That morning he had told her he was coming after she informed everyone it was her last parade ever. Jill had always hoped someone would come, but no one ever did, not even to one performance or one kayaking race. When he told her he was coming she thought she would have been more excited since she had wished for so long he would, but instead she didn't feel anything. She thought it was strange he wanted to come finally, but why now? It hardly seemed to matter at this point. Later at the parade however she did spot him in the crowd with her brother on his shoulders and a huge smile, pointing and shouting. "There she is!" Jill thought it was amusing. She realized she was happy they were there. Even though he rarely showed it, she knew he loved her.

While in the throws of her activities, Jill could be completely absorbed and distracted from her strange life at home. But those activities were seasonal, and kayaking was only three times a week, barring the lead-up to Nationals. Even when activities were in full swing, evenings always came. Again the confines of her room were her life in-between. The stark reality of her home life was always waiting like a dark shadow.

On the days of her activities she walked home, quiet as if in preparation for the impending silence. The lone journey back each evening paved the way. It was a good transition into the ever so quiet house she would enter each night, into her secret life. Jill and her brother rarely if ever brought friends over. They never explained nor discussed it, and they couldn't have if they'd wanted to. They didn't understand it themselves. It was more of a feeling, an unspoken rule the way things were. Things were off, but one thing was certain. They were embarrassed to bring outsiders into their house. They never told anyone. It somehow seemed imperative to keep it hidden. It took a great deal of effort to conceal their inner life, and they didn't even realize it at the time. Is it even possible? Is anyone really able to hide anything?

Her family had an odd way of communicating. It entailed elaborate self-control. Jill was on constant alert. Someone could come storming down the hall any moment like a raging bull charging through the house in a fury. Tiptoeing around the moodiness was required of Jill to navigate the tiny fragile eggshells that if cracked could unleash a time bomb. It was tricky terrain. Jill didn't want to make a false move.

Because of all this, Jill realized she needed to put herself aside. Jill willingly did this. It was like they were constantly in a state of emergency but no one knew what the emergency was. Although the minor episode that set it off, if there even was one, was usually not it either. It was generally an emergency without an emergency. It was somehow a condition of uncontrolled rage inside of rage. No one knew how it was unleashed or were even aware if they were the one unleashing it, so it came out in bits and pieces and without warning.

The best Jill could do was not to add to the situation and that meant quiet retreat. She was good at that. It didn't matter how much effort it took, even if it widdled away at her spirit, yet no matter how dull the flame of her soul became it was impossible to extinguish it entirely. The candle still flickers and yearns for oxygen no matter how weak it becomes. In the gentlest and subtlest of ways, Jill strove to earn her parents' attention. First, she was always happy; she figured a happy face could at least divert a small measure of the sadness. She, of course, was not generally happy. But since she mostly pretended anyway, pretending to be happy was not a hard thing to do. Masking her sadness was a minor sacrifice.

No one did this on purpose. In fact, it was unlikely anyone was even aware of their part in it, let alone took responsibility for it. It was like they were marionettes in a puppet show but no one realized they could take over the strings anytime because in reality, they controlled the puppets. Everyone was caught up in the show, under its spell, trapped in the illusion that this story was true. Funny thing is, they could have changed the story anytime if they'd wanted to, but no one realized they could.

Jill continued her strict regime of discipline, leaving the kitchen without a trace of her existence, departing for school without a sound or sight, and cleaning as meticulously as possible so as to hopefully make her family happy. It entailed an odd requirement that she do it silently and invisibly. Part of the inherent goal was to leave no trail of her presence; that way they couldn't be mad at her for being there. This regime however, cancelled out any chance of discovery and the recognition that she craved, but somehow this never occurred to her. The goal contradicted the method, and so it was of course, impossible.

One day after years of this long-indoctrinated practice, her Father came into the living room while she was cleaning. He caught her. She was startled. This violated her code not to be noticed and yet wanting to be noticed. Her Father watched her and said, "Wow, you're cleaning the living room!" as if it were the first time she had ever done that. It was remarkable for two reasons. First of all, her father usually never noticed anything even if it was right in front of him. He was usually caught up in his own world. That he happened to catch her and notice what she was doing was highly out of the ordinary, especially given this was the first time he found her doing it. Jill nodded and timidly replied, "Yes," and she ventured further realizing in that moment a tiny hole had opened in the vortex of this rare moment and if she ever wanted to reach out, this was it. "I clean the house every week." He answered, surprised and half asking, "Really?" He was truly impressed. "No, you don't, do you? Not the whole house?" as if he didn't believe it. "Yes, the whole house, every week." Even Jill was surprised at herself. Her self-defeating desire was truly invisible. "You didn't know?" Jill questioned, realizing this sad truth. "Wow, that's really something, I didn't know you did all that." He left the room with a smile and Jill thought she ought to have felt something different than she did. It was all she'd ever sought, recognition. And yet now that she had it, it felt like nothing.

Jill and her Father had been through so much together, and yet each of them traveled down their own paths separately and alone. Because of this, Jill thought perhaps she was the only person who truly understood her Father. They say tragedy brings people closer; she wasn't sure if she and her

Father were, at least not in a normal sense, but she imagined they shared an understanding in some way that there were no words for.

She wasn't entirely sure what she felt; her own feelings were something that eluded her. As far as her Father was concerned, she was sure it was sadness. Something was missing and there was a void where that something should have been. Somehow Jill always knew that.

Even though he was not emotionally present, he was present in body. He didn't notice things. That's true. She could've been angry at that. Or she could have looked past it, which is not the same thing. Mostly she observed and tried to make sense of him and herself and where she fit into his life. Nobody could understand her Father. Jill was perplexed by him too in many ways. Even so, there was a quiet sort of connection between them. They rarely talked but there were a few rare occasions she could count on one hand that might have been considered real exchanges. They were always halted and broken, unexpected and in such low quiet voices it took Jill by surprise every time; she had to strain to hear. The most significant was when he began talking about a freighter. Jill was barely listening. They were at her brother's house. They had both long since grown up and were adults by then.

Jill and Paul were in the kitchen. Others were there but they were in the dining room that opened out from where her Father and she stood. The others were wrapped up in their own conversation. It was late at night. Paul seemed to feel safe then. It was like the darkness was a cloak of comfort he could hide behind. The coffee pot boiled in one corner of the kitchen and filled the room with its bold aroma. Robbie and Paul drank coffee all hours of the day. Her Father spoke quietly, and suddenly she was aware he was speaking about the night of her mother's death. This account came out of the blue and unrelated to anything in that moment. It was the first time Jill had ever heard him speak about that night. She already knew he had been on the other side of the country, in New York when it happened. Harriott had told her that. He spoke of how flustered and confused he was; he didn't know what to do. A roommate finally told him, "Well you get on a plane and you go to her." He said, "Oh yes," as if the thought had not occurred to him. He jumped on the "freighter" as he called it, and recounted how he proceeded to throw up the entire five-hour trip back to the west coast. That was all he said that night.

Later Jill got up the nerve to ask him if he really was the last person to speak to Bobbie before she died that day. He said he was. Timidly, she asked him what they spoke about. His face lit up and he said they talked about getting back together again, and he told Bobbie he had a trip in four days back to the west coast where she was, and they could talk then. She had died with the phone still in her hand.

Other than this rare exchange, and a few brief encounters, true communication between them was nonexistent. Yet whenever his eyes fell on her, she could sometimes see and feel a love in them deeper than words, and really, what else was there? Small things he held onto after Bobbie died: Mala, their dog, who stayed with friends of the family until he remarried and Jill and he were together again, and the boat that held so many memories at King's River where he loved to go even after she was gone. Jill never realized at the time why that river meant so much to him, but she always knew it did. She could see it in his face every time they were there; it was a tribute to her, being where they shared so many happy memories. He seemed so at peace.

The loss of Bobbie was an unbearable one for Paul she concluded. He never talked about her while Jill was growing up, even when she asked him questions repeatedly. For so long he shelved his feelings. When he retired, the time and the silence forced him to examine them. Was he really able to shelve them completely? Is that possible? When feelings go underground they seem to emerge in other ways. Jill sometimes wondered how it was for him to look at her, growing up, a constant reminder of Bobbie. Jill was always told she looked just like her. Things must have been teetering on the edge of the shelf ready to fall at any moment.

When Jill was an adult, Effie finally parted with a small album Jill had never seen. In it were pictures of Bobbie and Paul and herself when she was a baby. At the time, it was a rare piece of the past for her that she was a part of, something that placed her squarely in the existence of a different life that Jill had been jerked out of and sometimes doubted had ever happened, and she treasured it. She brought it with her to show Robbie and his family, but mostly to show her Father. Robbie and his wife commented they had never seen Paul look so happy. Jill realized they were right. The grin that spread across his face, the big dimples that formed at the corners of his mouth were in every picture. They were candid and genuine. The happiness and hope caught in every frame were disarming. Later in the evening Paul came to her brother's house to see Jill, and Jill held the small album up for him to see. He did not take it from her hands. She had thought he would be as excited to see it as she was. She opened some of the pages and held them up for him to see. She was a little baffled at his behavior. He looked at a couple of the photos without lifting a hand. It was like he was frozen stiff to his chair, and a frown formed on his face and he looked away. Jill continued to hold it up for him to see, confused he did not enthusiastically take it from her. "Do you want to look yourself?" she asked. "No." He said it with such finality that Jill knew she'd better not ask again. He had only seen a few of the pictures. Jill looked at him and she saw the look of pain in his face, the sadness, and she saw what her brother had seen: a different man before her than was in the photo album from way back then, when life had been full of promise and love and everything life had to offer. In that moment, Jill realized a part of Paul had died the day Bobbie left their lives. It was a loss no one had completely recovered from, if at all. She started to think maybe it was the reason no one could talk about her, tell her who she was, what she was like. It gave her a tiny sense that there was something more to her Mother than she knew, but she still didn't know what. Seeing Paul like this gave Jill a glimpse, in all its intensity, of the past. Words were absent. They had always been. But this was a moment of something real, a tangible feeling, an expression of truth. Jill still didn't entirely understand it, but she could feel something underneath it all that gave a certain depth to everything. Its escape was an expression that validated the past, a tiny thing to grasp and hang onto, to verify something happened that got her and all of them to where they were now.

Her dear Father, Jill didn't think anyone had ever understood him. She didn't think he ever tried to understand himself. She did think he gave what he could at least as much as it occurred to him. People always referred to Paul as special or unusual. Jill didn't think so. Aren't we all? Jill spent so much time trying to figure things out when she grew up and sometimes wondered if he even knew her, or if he ever even tried. If he did, he sure kept it secret. Could it be they were simply too focused inward, selfish, insensitive to others, but overly so towards themselves? Jill wondered if she wound herself into a fantasy of similarity to him in order to help herself feel closer than they actually were ... although, the likenesses she attached to the pair of them are ones that by definition estranged them both.

Jill considered the idea that there was a difference between sensitivity towards oneself and sensitivity towards others. She thought about it and came to the conclusion that sensitivity towards her self was an illusionary attempt to protect her own ego, an endless quest, like reaching for fog. She was protecting nothing. Sensitivity towards others, on the other hand, was reaching out to others, an acknowledgment of someone outside herself. Like her Father, she had trouble with that.

Jill reached a point where she felt so alone most of the time her latter half of growing up. There was no one there. No one she could talk to. She felt like there was no place she belonged. She felt nothing except the torturous loneliness. She stayed in her room nearly all of the time when she was inside the house where she spent her teenage years. When she stepped out of her bedroom she felt uncomfortable, like she had no right to be there. This would propel her back to the room. She felt like a stranger. She was a ghost. The one thing about ghosts is they can watch from a distance without being noticed. They can look from the outside in. There were advantages to that. She didn't think too much about it. It just was the way it was and she kept it to herself. And it's good that she did. To admit this would have been to admit that her existence was meaningless. Sometimes she wondered how her life may have been different had her mother still been alive. She sure could have used her advice.

As it was, she put a fake smile on her face and continued to pretend she was happy. Inside she felt anything but. Thank goodness for her outside activities, even if they weren't every season or every day. At least she had that.

Eventually towards the end of high school she pushed everyone away. She couldn't explain why. It just happened. It was like a giant tide was pulling her out to sea and she was powerless to do anything about it. When she went to college she kept herself at bay. She would drift from one group of people to the next, not getting too close. That's when she withdrew completely. Jill wondered if she would ever come out of it but the further into her self she retreated the more impossible it became.

Jill functioned enough to get to her part-time jobs and to classes, although her grades plummeted eventually despite having straight "A's" her first year. She barely graduated. She kept all of this to herself and told no one. She remained in this place for quite some time. She tried to pull herself out, but something was holding her back. It was like an invisible thread wove its way around her feet and kept her tangled.

She could not have lasted much longer this way. Something had to give if she was going to survive. She needed a big change to jerk her out of it and something eventually did. It happened one day towards the end of college. She saw a table and a woman who spoke at a job fair and Jill listened to her story. The story spoke to Jill and she couldn't stop thinking about it. She knew this was it. She decided to become a Peace Corps Volunteer right then and there. Once she'd made her final decision, all she could imagine is what her life was going to be like. She waited for a response and an invitation, and finally she got one. She accepted her invitation to Nepal, and this was where she began her new life. More than that, this was what brought her back to life.

Chapter 4

A New Beginning
(1967-1968)

The more I live, the more strange! And me, what an odd creature I am. I guess that's why – I'm the world's filter for me and that I am so complicated, so the world goes.

I feel like different people – or do I feel at all – I act at everything stimulating me this way or that, turning and twisting, pushing and pulling; laughing … fighting. I'm such a puppeteer for myself!

But all of this for what? Why act – which is, after all, how we "try?" What will be different in the end – just what---why the pain and the hurt always … both real in my body and my heart, I can bear it less and less the more I try. And no one really knows, ha! What one good thing I can do – act. What is, really isn't at all, but it's contrary. But who cares.

Bobbie, March 1964

. . . . .

June 15, 1968

Dear Mom and Dad,

I'm sorry for not writing earlier, but it's taken us a while to unwind. I, for one, was very glad to be back in our own home, as much as I did enjoy our visits. Thank you, especially, for making our time with you the more pleasurable, and for all of the helpful things you did for us. I know it must have been difficult for you never knowing for sure just what was going to happen –

Bobbie put her pen down when Paul walked into the room. He was excited it was plain to see. He paused at the door, looking at her. "You're writing a letter? Now? We're about to leave!" "I know. I was just trying to get this off in the mail before we go and are gone for such a long time. I don't want to forget to thank your parents for the wonderful time we had with them. I'm almost done. Promise!" She scribbled a few last words and quickly stuffed the letter in an envelope that was already addressed. She grabbed her bag and went to the front door, reaching around to the mailbox attached to the house and clothes-pinned it to the side for the mailman. Everyone was waiting by the side of the car.

Bobbie, Jill and Effie got into the station wagon. It was loaded with all of their luggage, camping gear and two dogs. The trailer with Paul's boat was hitched to the back. Paul climbed behind the driver's wheel and started the car. The anticipation of a road trip across the state of Washington filled them with excitement. Jill squealed and one of the dogs barked as they pulled out of the driveway. The sun was out and everything was bright green after a long dreary wet spring. It was summer in Renton.

"We got everything?" Paul asked Bobbie. "Yeah, I think we got it all." "I even have some sandwiches for later so we don't have to stop for lunch." Paul nodded. He stepped a little harder on the gas pedal as if that would get them to their destination more quickly; he was looking forward to some good fishing and water skiing with his newly formed family. "But we'll probably have to stop anyway to give the dogs water and change Jill now and then," he pointed out. "Yeah that's true," Bobbie said. "But at least lunch will be one less stop, and that much less money to spend." Paul looked at Bobbie and smiled, nodding his head in approval. They were constantly on a budget and always looking for ways to stay within it.

"We're off!" Bobbie said loud enough so everyone in the car could hear. "We're off!" Effie echoed back. Effie sat in the backseat next to her granddaughter. She crooned over her first grandchild and enjoyed every moment with Jill. "To the East!" Effie said. "To the East!!" Paul and Bobbie sang out together. The dogs danced on the seats and wagged their tails with their heads hanging out the windows, ears flapping in the wind. The joy was contagious. Even Jill and the dogs could sense the excitement.

The first two hours of the trip went smoothly. They stopped for gas and got out to go to the bathroom. Paul gave the dogs water and Bobbie took Jill to change her diaper. Effie helped her. "Paul is just perfect isn't he?" Effie slid her daughter a sideways glance as she washed her hands at the sink. "Oh yes," answered Bobbie. "He is wonderful." "You two are truly happy aren't you?" Effie had to pinch herself to check if this miracle was really happening. "What do you think, Mom?! I have a handsome husband with a job and dreams for an even better one, a baby, a house, and now a vacation with you! How could life be any better?" Effie smiled. Her eyes sparkled and her face radiated with happiness. "Indeed, all of my prayers have been answered!" she said.

When the women came out of the bathroom, Paul was leaning against the car smoking a cigarette, waiting for them. Bobbie handed Jill to Effie and pulled out a cigarette too. She joined Paul and after a few puffs asked him, "You doing ok? Are you tired yet?" Paul inhaled and let out one long puff before answering. "Nope. I'm good." He looked into the distance as if the meaning of the universe lay out there. He thought about the logistics of the trip but also considered two of his latest projects sitting on the garage workbench at home. Bobbie stood next to him, silently savoring the moment and thinking about their perfect life and their perfect family. Paul's fingers that gripped the cigarette were oil stained and black around the nail beds like usual, but he didn't notice. Bobbie didn't mind. She held her cigarette in her soft clean and newly manicured hands. As they smoked, the dogs ran from one patch of grass to another, searching for a place to relieve themselves. They were happy to be out of the car and to explore new places and smells.

When Paul finished his cigarette he went to gather the dogs. Bobbie finished hers and dropped it on the ground, snuffing it out with the ball of her shoe. She got back in the car. Jill and Effie were already settled in the backseat, waiting to leave. Bobbie leaned over the front seat to look at Jill and asked her mother, "Everything ok back here?" "Good as punch," Effie answered. Jill's eyebrows were becoming tinged with red. That's how Bobbie knew she was tired. "Jill will probably be irritable in a minute or two, but she will be asleep just as quickly." Paul opened the door and let the dogs in before climbing into the seat behind the steering wheel. "Ready?" he asked. "Ready!" Bobbie and Effie answered. "Ready for take off!" Effie teased. Paul was a pilot accumulating hours so he could work for the airlines. Paul looked over his shoulder at Effie and grinned, dimples forming around the corners of his mouth.

The further east they traveled the more arid the landscape became. "This is a far cry from the lush wet green side of Washington." Bobbie said. "Yeah, you said it," agreed Effie. "It's getting to be like dessert out here." "And it's getting hot." "Paul, can we pull over soon?" she asked. "I need some water." "Yeah, soon as I see a pull off," he answered. A few miles down the road there was a large dirt shoulder. Paul swung the car around and came to a stop. Dust swirled up from the ground forming a little cloud around them and it drifted into the car through the rolled down windows. Everyone squinted their eyes and covered their mouths with their hands to keep from breathing it in. As soon as the dust settled, they got out of the car and stretched their legs. Jill whined. Paul opened the trunk to pull out a jug of water. The dogs ran out of the car and looked around. They were not as full of energy as they had been when the trip began. They were feeling the heat too.

Bobbie put her hand up to her forehead to form a shield from the sun and looked around. There was not a town in sight and the flat dry ground that rose into small rolling hills here and there stretched on forever. "Not much out here, huh?" she remarked. "Nope. Not much," Paul said. "Boy it's hotter than Haites." Effie dabbed a hankerchief around her face and patted it under her arms. She wore a scarf around her hair to hold it in place against the wind blowing through the open windows while they drove. She was not about to have her hair messed up. She'd just had it done.

Jill's whine turned into a cry. She'd had it. Bobbie got Jill out of the car and gave her a sip of the water that she had poured into a cup for herself. Jill gulped the water and squirmed in Bobbie's arms, obviously disgruntled by the uncomfortable heat. The car had no air conditioning so they drove with the windows down, allowing the hot air to blow into the car.

That was the first of many stops under the hot desert sun before they arrived at the lake to put up camp. Each stop became progressively hotter and more miserable than the last. By the end of the day it had become unbearable. Paul resorted to throwing water on the dogs to cool them down because they were so hot and he was worried they may have a heat stroke with all their panting. At every gas station, he filled the water containers and off they'd go again.

They had decided they could not tolerate camping that night. Paul found a cheap hotel and by the time they arrived, all of them were like wet mops. They were drained and exhausted and they couldn't wait to get to their room to absorb the cold air-conditioning. Even Jill settled down and became visibly less irritable. Bobbie took Jill in the shower with her and turned the cold water on. She stood under the water and let it run over them. Jill reached up towards the shower nozzle with her small hands to feel the water spraying down on them. Bobbie smiled and held Jill close to her chest. Jill touched Bobbie's nose and laughed as the water poured over them. Despite the cold shower, their bodies remained warm; the water sizzled over their hot skin, slowly bringing their body heat to a reasonably comfortable level.

Effie was next. She untied the scarf and put a shower cap over her head to prevent her hair from getting wet. She patted her face with an astringent, carefully removing her make-up. Effie was not about to let her hair and beauty rituals be compromised even though they were on a car trip that imposed hardship. She turned the water on and placed the plug into the drainage hole of the tub. She tested the water first to make sure it was the right temperature and dropped a few drops of bath oil into it. She never took a stand-up shower. She gingerly stepped into the tub and sat down to soak. Very gently she rubbed glycerine soap over her body.

Paul was patient. He understood the importance of Effie's beauty rituals. He waited for her to finish. He wasn't too inconvenienced; he was used to being filthy and full of car oil and grease. He had put himself through school working as a mechanic. The way of life followed him out of school and he never let anybody work on his cars. He even replaced engines and took the time to do even the smallest jobs just to keep from spending unnecessary money. He could do the job better anyway. If he wasn't busy working on a car, it was something else. The more intricate the task, the more absorbed he became, and the more oblivious he was to minor details like black finger nail beds and hands full of dirty crevices.

Effie stepped out of the bathroom tucking the last of a small tuft of hair into a curler for the night. She always slept with the curlers in her hair in order to keep the poof and bounce in her hair fresh for the following day.

Paul headed for the shower. Finally it was his turn. Though it was ladies first when it came to cleanliness, Paul couldn't wait to cool off. He stepped into the shower and felt the cold water pour over him. He closed his eyes and let out an audible sigh of relief. It was a welcome end to the tiresome and trying day. He was still motivated by the idea of fishing and skiing, but the heat had chipped away from the excitement the day had begun with.

Everyone slept well in the cool air-conditioned room. Jill was the first to wake the following morning. She was consistent with her early rising routine no matter where she was. No one wanted to wake up that early, but Jill was so pleasant and cute, it was difficult to be annoyed with her. Bobbie got up and began taking care of her. She got Jill dressed and walked onto the balcony with her. It was early enough that the sun hadn't come all the way up and therefore it hadn't had time to reach the scorching temperatures that would heat up every surface it touched in a mere matter of hours. They enjoyed the short reprieve of the cool morning air.

Bobbie came back into the room a little while later, giving everyone, and especially Paul a chance to sleep in. She spread a baby blanket on the ground, placed a few toys nearby and put Jill on it to play. She unpacked the box of stationary that was in her suitcase and pulled a chair up to the desk. Taking one piece of pink paper from the box she took up a pen and continued to write where she had left off the day before. She decided to take advantage of the quiet early morning to write a sequel to her letter she had already sent off to her mother and father-in-law.

We began our trip to Eastern Washington and it has been very nice – but it is terribly hot. Paul doesn't mind hot weather, but my mom, Jill and myself (and the dogs) are not too enthused. We had to stop & wet down the dogs every so often. Jill didn't care at all for the hot driving although she was pretty good most of the time.

Bobbie put her pen down to shake out her hand and get a glass of water. She glanced at Jill who kept her eye on her mother to make sure she didn't go anywhere. Bobbie sat down again.

> *I'm sure you want to hear about Jill! She's grown so much … she's 19 lbs and 27" at 5 mos. She can almost sit up and she rolls over all the time. She talks and squeals with delight about everything – and smiles and laughs when you just look at her! Everyone comments on how pretty she is, and it's true! She is just getting to be prettier every day and her personality is disarming. She's still a good baby but she does not like to be left alone – she gets so excited when you pick her up and she really adores her daddy – and vice-versa!! She's teething, and it's hurting her a lot more now – she gets spells where she is intolerably fussy … I put a soothing teething gel on her gums which slightly numbs the pain and she settles down. She chews on everything her little hands grab. She's not the least bit afraid of strangers, charms them! She's so cute, it's the cutest stage so far … She is plump but solid, and it's a pleasure to hold her and she notices everything responds to you talking – pipes up immediately if you happen to look away. She's entranced by our neighbor's puppies – she'll have her own to grow up with one day.*
>
> *Paul has been working very hard – he has been teaching steadily and working on Saturdays too. Also, he's re-hauling the V-8 so he's tired but he enjoys all of it. Especially the warm weather we've been having … We've gone boating & fishing & it was beautiful.*
>
> *Thank you for the darling blue dress for Jill, blue is really her color, her eyes are so blue … she looks precious in it. As*

soon as I get more film, I'll send pictures. – Thank you for Paul's baby pictures ... it's Jill all over!!

How has the weather been down there? It has been 75 here. Everything is so green and flowers blooming everywhere. I've got so many letters to write yet – and I know I won't – for awhile ...

Thank you again for everything –

Write soon,
Love,
Bobbie, Paul
and Jill

Bobbie finished the letter and stuffed it in an envelope. She put a stamp on it along with the address and left it on the table.

Paul opened his eyes and looked at Bobbie. She looked at him and said, "Hey sleepy face, you finally awake?" "Yeah ... what time is it?" "Time to get up," she said. "Aren't we going to make it to that lake today? We'd better get moving." "Yeah, how about some coffee?" he asked. "Ok," she answered. She got up from the edge of the bed and opened the top to the cheap hotel coffee maker and filled it with water. She put the grounds in the filter and waited for it to boil.

When the coffee was ready, she brought a steaming cup of it to her husband. "Here you go," she handed it to him. The aroma of coffee filled the room. "Thanks," he replied. He took the warm styrofoam cup into his hand, feeling its warmth. He took a few sips, and said "Hmm, not bad. A bit weak, but not too bad." He was beginning to wake up. Looking around the room he asked "Where's Jill? I can hear her but I can't see her." Jill made noises, hearing her Father's voice. She was always excited at the sound of her Father and she looked around for him too. Bobbie picked her up. "Here she is." Bobbie set her on the bed next to him. She chirped happily at the sight of him, and he to her. Her immense pleasure at seeing him gave him just as much joy. "Hey there Jill! What are you up to this morning?" She grinned and answered in her own baby language. Paul pretended to understand and proceeded to carry on a conversation with her, imagining what she must be trying to say. Bobbie watched the exchange between them and smiled. "She's been up since the crack of dawn like usual. I'm surprised she didn't wake you up. Guess you were pretty tired. I'm going to make Jill some oatmeal. Paul, can you watch her for a minute while I do that?"

Effie stirred in the bed next to them and rolled over just in time to see Jill and her Father talking to each other. Effie smiled and remembered where she was and how happy she was to be with her family. Her daughter was married, she had a grandchild and Bobbie was happy too. She couldn't have asked for more.

"Hey over there," Effie said. "Yes Mom," Bobbie answered. "Got any more of that coffee?" "Yes, I do. I'll give you some of this and put a new pot with just water on to boil for Jill's oatmeal." While Bobbie tended to the beginnings of a breakfast in the mini makeshift kitchen, Effie pulled herself up in bed and tugged at her curlers. Most of them had stayed in for the night.

"So guys, what's the plan for today?" Effie was not one to sit around. Once she was up, it was time to get on with the day, that is, once her makeup was on and her hair was fixed. Effie needed plans before she did anything. Bobbie smiled and asked Paul, "So, what's the plan Stan?" Bobbie relished the fact that they had the means to take care of her mother. It made her happy to be able to give her mother the support and attention she missed not having her own husband.

"Well," Paul climbed out of bed. "Let's get packed and get the show on the road. Then we can stop for breakfast somewhere. After we've eaten, we'll drive straight for the lake. How's that for a plan?" "Sounds fantastic!" Effie agreed. "I'll start getting ready right now captain." Effie was reserved and flamboyant at the same time and there was an air about her that some could call a bit snobbish. But to those she got to know well and liked, they were treated with the hospitality of a close family member. She had grown up in a Polish household and somehow had acquired the dry humor of close extended family members, all of whom were a collection of characters. Her father had been a drunk, albeit a friendly one. The paddy wagon had come to their home regularly to pick him up for drunkenness. The policemen always apologized, telling him, "Sorry Aleksy, we're going to have to take you in again. You should be out by morning though." He spent all of the money he earned on alcohol unless Effie's mother could get a hold of it first. She regularly sent Vivian, Effie's sister, to grab the money from him when it was payday and before he could spend it. Vivian always knew where to find him: at the local bar, usually buying drinks for everyone. One time he told Vivian, "Come on my Vivianka, sit up on the stool here with me and I'll buy you a coke." Vivian did and she waited for her father to pull out the wad of money. As soon as he did, she swiped it out of his hand and ran out of the bar without looking back until she reached home and promptly handed it to her mother. "Good job," her mother would say. To supplement their income, Effie's mother was a bootlegger as well. Between it all, they managed to make ends meet.

Effie and Vivian got along like typical sisters. Every conversation turned into an argument eventually leading to a digression into their native tongue, Polish. Their personalities were opposite in every way. As much as Effie was flamboyant and dramatic about everything, Vivian was equally pragmatic. Effie's middle name was Polish but it was spelled the American way. Effie was indignant that the proper way to spell her name was "Karolinka." Vivian heard this one time and told her, "Oh what nonsense. That's not what it says on your birth certificate. Your name is Caroline, and it's spelled with a 'C'." "Well, it is most certainly spelled correctly with a 'K'," Effie argued. "Your name is spelled with a 'C' and that's how it is." Vivian loved getting one up. She would prod Effie until she engaged in a fight.

Paul got out of bed and went to the bathroom. Fortunately there was a large mirror above a vanity with a sink just next to the bathroom, so Effie could take as long as she wanted putting on makeup and teasing her hair. Bobbie fed Jill the oatmeal she had prepared using hot water from the coffee maker and began packing their belongings. Bobbie was already dressed. After she finished feeding Jill and changing her diaper, she joined Effie at the mirror. She quickly put a bit of makeup on herself and ran a brush through her hair. Effie looked at Bobbie to inspect the product of her efforts. "You really should have put it up before we left for the trip. It's going to be a disaster by the time were through here." "Mom, we're going camping and water skiing. I don't think it matters." "Well. I think it does," Effie said. "A woman must always look her best. You never know when you may run into someone. You don't want just anyone seeing you look like you just rolled out of bed, do you?" "Oh Mom," Bobbie caught herself. "Well, at least I'm putting a bit of makeup on. That'll have to do." Effie made a smirk and turned back to the mirror. "I guess," she said, in her guilt-provoking way. Paul came out of the bathroom, threw his jeans on, but thought twice about it. He took them back off and pulled on a pair of shorts. He put his clothes into the suitcase along with his toothbrush and he was done. He didn't bother with shaving. "We about ready to hit the road?" Bobbie replied, "Yep. I am in about two minutes. Let me just brush my teeth." Effie didn't answer. Bobbie rolled her eyes at Paul and gestured towards her mother behind her back. Paul nodded his head discretely and grinned. He picked up the suitcases that were ready to go and walked to the car.

He found the dogs that he had tied to a tree for the night with two very long ropes he normally kept in the boat. They wagged their tails when they saw him and he untied the ropes as they jumped all over him, licking his face. "Alright, alright!" he said to them, laughing. He let them run around while he grabbed some dog food out of the car. He poured it into two separate bowls and walked over to the tree where the water bowl was. It had been knocked over during the night so he brought it back over to the car and filled it again. The dogs ran to the water and drank all of it, then ate their food.

Paul opened the hood to the car and poked around at the engine, checking the oil and fluids. He left the hood open while he pulled out a cigarette and made his way around the boat and the car, inspecting the tires and the tarp that was tied down over the boat to hold all of the camping gear and ski equipment in place. He leaned one arm over the hull as he finished the cigarette and looked over the arid landscape. "Soon we'll be at the lake," he thought to himself. "Then we can set up camp and I'll get the boat in the water." He imagined himself performing each task. "First I'll pull all the skis out and set them up on the bank so they're ready to go when we're ready to use them. Then I'll set up the grill and put the cooler with the beer under a tree." He pictured the dogs swimming happily in the water, throwing sticks for them to play fetch with. He pictured Bobbie in her swimsuit smiling and holding the baby while she set up the playpen in the sand. He imagined himself finding a place for a campfire and searching for kindling. He remembered how he had proposed to Bobbie while searching for kindling way back at King's River and smiled at the happy memory. He saw in his mind Effie sitting in a lawn chair with a big hat and sunglasses and a pair of fancy flip flops, trying not to let the sand touch her toes and he laughed out loud at the thought of it. Effie hated sand. He envisioned her sipping a nice cool drink of iced tea with lemon. He had watched Bobbie make sun tea in a couple of large glass jugs the day before they left home. She had specifically made it for her mother because she knew it would make her happy.

Paul heard the women coming out of the room. The door opened out onto a walkway. The women headed towards the stairwell that led to the parking lot, carrying what they could. Bobbie had Jill in her arms. Paul snuffed out his cigarette and ran to help them. "Go sit in the car ladies and I'll get the rest." Paul walked back to the bedroom and picked up the remaining two large suitcases the women had left for him. He inspected the room one last time to make sure they hadn't forgotten anything. The women were busy getting Jill settled in her car seat and situating themselves. Paul walked to the back of the car and put the suitcases into the space he had left specifically for them, but it was filled haphazardly with the smaller items the women had tossed on top of everything. He shook his head and pulled them back out so he could repack. Paul had a careful system; he organized by visualizing in his mind where each item should go. He knew how to make it all fit.

Paul walked to the front of the car and looked under the hood one more time. Everything seemed in order so he closed it. He climbed behind the wheel and asked, "Everyone settled?" "All settled," Bobbie answered. "Ok then, let's go," Paul said.

Paul drove for several miles before he spotted a small breakfast diner. Bobbie saw it at the same time. "Hey, there's a place. What if we stop here to eat?" she said. "Just thinkin' the same thing," he answered. Paul swung the car around and took the turn off for the diner. His stomach was growling and he became more aware of it the closer they got. He could smell the breakfast smells coming out of the little restaurant and he imagined the big plate of over easy eggs, bacon and pancakes he would order. He parked in the back of the parking lot so he could take up more than one parking space for the trailer and boat to fit. Everybody got out of the car. "Time to eat!" Paul said. Breakfast was his favorite meal. He waited for his wife and mother-in-law to get Jill unstrapped from her baby carrier. He thought about lighting a cigarette but resisted the urge. He didn't want to waste any time getting to the table so he could order his food. He would have a cigarette inside the restaurant while he waited for the food to arrive.

Jill fussed while the women tried to get her out of her car seat; she was getting tired for her morning nap. She had been up five hours already. The women struggled with a wiggly baby who did not want to cooperate. Bobbie lifted her out of the carrier after prying her loose from the grip she held to the sides of it. Effie had been trying to distract her by making silly noises and speaking nonsense to her. Paul patiently waited for them. They finally got her out of the car and shut the doors. They walked to the entrance and Paul held the door open for the women to pass through.

The waitress seated the small group and asked for their order. When it was Paul's turn he listed off his order with enthusiasm. It included a bit of nearly every item on the menu. "Oh, and uh, a cup of coffee too please. Black."

Jill continued to fidget. Bobbie pulled out some crackers and put them on the tray of the high chair. Jill picked one up and pushed the entire thing into her mouth. Bobbie said, "Wait Jill! You're going to choke!" She tried to retrieve what she could from the toddler's mouth but Jill shook her head and pushed her mother's hand away. Bits of cracker spilled onto the tray and Jill made a screeching sound, clearly communicating her dissatisfaction. The waitress brought her some juice. Bobbie lifted the cup to her mouth, holding onto it as she took a couple of sips from the straw. Jill was stubborn, however. She latched onto the cup tightly and tugged trying to get it from her mother. Bobbie tried to reason with her, but the more she did, the more Jill tugged and the angrier she became. Jill began banging on the tray. Her eyebrows were becoming red. "Let me go get her carrier. I think she's about to go to sleep. Paul, can I have the keys to the car?" "Oh, uh sure," he reached into his pocket and handed them to her. He hadn't been paying attention to their interaction. He smoked his cigarette imagining the breakfast that was on its way.

Bobbie returned with the baby carrier and lifted Jill from the high chair. "Let me just take her outside for a minute." She excused herself. Bobbie took a bottle with formula she had mixed at the car and walked up to the register of the diner. "Would you mind warming this for me?" "Oh sure, no problem," the waitress replied. "Not too hot please." "Sure thing," the waitress answered over her shoulder. Bobbie waited with her fussing baby until the waitress returned with the bottle. "Oh thank you ever so much," she told the waitress, and she went to the door leading out of the restaurant. Bobbie gave the bottle a shake and took the lid off the bottle to test the temperature on her wrist. The smell of milk reached Jill's nose and she wiggled and cried even more. Bobbie put the lid back on and gave it another shake. Jill was livid by then. Bobbie turned her onto her back, cradling her in her arms and put the nipple to her mouth. Jill grabbed at it pinching and pulling at it with her little fingers. Bobbie fought with her to release her grip and quickly slipped into her mouth. Jill sucked at the nipple as if she hadn't eaten in weeks. In minutes, the bottle was empty and Jill was asleep.

Bobbie walked into the restaurant with her sleeping baby and went back to the table. "Everything good?" Paul asked. "Good." Bobbie said. "She's out like a light." Bobbie put her in the carrier and set it on the bench next to Paul and then proceeded to get herself seated once again. Paul glanced down at his little girl and grinned. "She is so beautiful, isn't she?" "You bet," Effie agreed. Bobbie sighed and forced a tired smile.

Breakfast came and Bobbie and Effie wondered where it all was going to fit in their stomachs. "You gonna eat all that?" Effie asked Paul. "Where you gonna put it? In a wooden leg? Good heavens!" Paul had ordered two eggs sunny side up, a platter full of bacon, biscuits, and a stack of pancakes. "Wowwwww ..." Effie couldn't get over it. Effie on the other hand, was given her small plate with a piece of toast and a tomato sliced in quarter inch round slices. It was what she ate every morning. Effie asked the waitress for more coffee, handing her cup still two-thirds full over to her. "It's cold," she said. The waitress apologized. "Just make sure it's good and hot, very very hot," Effie told her, followed with a smile and stern eyes that communicated her demands in a kind yet authoritative way that let the waitress know she meant business. "Yes ma'am," the waitress replied. As she walked away from the table with the cold cup of coffee in her hand, Effie shook her head and wrinkled her forehead, muttering, "I can't stand cold coffee, or luke warm for that matter. A cup of coffee should be hot." Bobbie looked down at her food and tried not to laugh. Paul looked at her from under his eyelids as he sipped his own coffee. Bobbie knew if she looked at him, she would laugh. "I don't know how a restaurant can't manage to serve coffee hot like it should be," Effie continued. Bobbie couldn't resist Paul's gaze. Their eyes met and Bobbie pierced her lips, trying to keep from laughing. Paul's eyes sparkled and if she could have seen his lips that enclosed the side of his cup, she was sure they would have been smiling. Nearly every restaurant outing included this scene or one similar.

Bobbie ate two eggs, a biscuit and two slices of bacon and fruit. Paul asked for another pot of coffee. "Make sure it's hot," he glanced at Bobbie. Bobbie looked down at her plate and choked down a laugh with a bite of egg in her mouth. The smell of bacon and syrup mingled with the coffee. The table was silent. Forks lifted to mouths stuffing eggs and bacon into them. Glasses from other tables clinked and utensils met ceramic plates, scraping, magnifying the sounds as if in a theater. Paul's "Mmmmm, Mmmmm's," dominated the lack of chatter. And with each new bite, the "Mmmm's" began all over again.

Paul polished off every crumb from his plate while Effie watched. "I never knew one person could eat that much food in one sitting." "I never saw someone eat so little." He gestured towards her half-sized plate that contained the rest of an uneaten tomato. "You gonna finish that tomato?" "Oh no! I'm full." Paul shook his head. "Really?" he asked. "That wasn't enough food to feed a fly." "Oh ho! It was plenty," she said. Paul couldn't understand how that was possible.

Paul paid the bill and they left the diner. Bobbie struggled carrying the awkward baby carrier with Jill sound asleep in it. Paul opened the door and took the baby from her.

Lake Wallula was only a short distance away. They had covered most of the distance the day before but enduring even one more second of heat had made the last leg of the journey impossible. If they hadn't made so many stops the day before, it may not have stretched on so long. With a good night's sleep, however, the rest of the drive seemed like nothing.

Pulling into the entrance of the park they noticed the visitor's center and stopped to ask for information. Paul picked up a map and stood outside the car analyzing it while having a cigarette. Bobbie got out of the car and breathed in the cool air and outdoor smell of pine mixed with cigarette smoke. She looked at the map with Paul. "See any campsites we can stay at?" she asked. "Uhmmm hmmm," he pointed to a few. "The ranger suggested this one." He pointed to a spot on the map. It was partway around the lake and down a section of the long corridor that wove its way through the park. The lake was quite large. In fact, it was the largest in the county. "The ranger indicated that this is a good one for us since it is where a lot of the recreational boating and skiing takes place. We can fish anywhere we please." "I see," Bobbie replied. "Well, let's go then!"

Paul pushed his cigarette into the ground with his foot and hopped into the car. "Ok! Let's find ourselves a campsite!" He was happy they had finally arrived. Now the vacation was about to begin and he could hardly wait.

Paul weaved around the curves of the road around the lake. "Hold up there cowboy." Effie complained. "My stomach is not feeling so hot. Can you take those turns a little more slowly?" Her stomach churned and ached from the cramps of carsickness. Paul drove slower until they arrived at the campsite the ranger suggested. There were a few trees past a clearing and he could just make out some wooden posts marking the campsites. He pulled in and drove down a ways. Paul searched for an out of the way spot. He liked privacy. He and Bobbie discussed the pros and cons of each camping space.

"How about that one!" Bobbie pointed to a bend in the road where the landscape jutted out into its own little peninsula. "Oh yeah, that's the one!" Paul agreed. It was perfect. He pulled the car into the dirt parking space with Jill, the dogs, boat, trailer, wife and mother-in-law in tow, waiting for directions. Everyone got out of the car to breath in the fresh lake air and to inspect the grounds that would provide their lodgings for the next couple of days. Even Jill squealed with delight.

Paul walked to the end of the peninsula and gazed out over the water. The sun was nearly midway up the sky. He watched a small fish jump to the surface of the lake. He glanced around at the beach and the trees surrounding their site. He had already chosen the location of their fire pit. Further back he eyed a nice bare patch of ground for the tent. He walked to the water's edge where the water met the small beach. He looked for a good spot to moor the boat. Slightly left of the place he had chosen for the fire pit there was a thick wooden post that looked like a remnant to a former dock. It would make as good a post as any to tie the boat.

Paul walked back to the car where Bobbie, Jill and Effie were. Bobbie had let the dogs out of the car to run around. They raced from tree to tree and to the water, sniffing everything. "Well, this is it! Let's unpack and I'll take the boat back over to the ramp and put her in. I found a perfect mooring post right there." Paul pointed to where the post was. Bobbie nodded her head. "That's perfect," she said.

Paul went to the back of the car and unloaded the equipment onto the ground. Next, he began on the boat. He untied the tarp he had so carefully attached earlier the morning before, and spread it on the ground. The skis and gear were inside the boat. He unloaded it neatly onto the tarp and when he had a fair amount of gear stacked on it, he grabbed the four corners of the tarp and carried it like a rucksack over his back with all of the equipment inside and made his way down to the edge of the lake. It was heavy and awkward, but Paul carried the load with a smile on his face.

After several trips back and forth, the car and boat were emptied. He organized all the skis neatly in the sand just a few feet from the water's edge while the dogs ventured into the water. The dogs went as far as to get the bottom of their bellies wet. Paul picked up a couple of sticks and threw them across the water. Both dogs barked and wagged their tails and when Mala finally decided to go, Paige took off after her, both chasing the same stick. Paul found another stick and threw it so they would see. Mala saw it and immediately dropped her stick and went for that one instead so both dogs still went after the same stick. Paul shook his head and laughed. "Ok, I'm off to the loading ramp," he announced. "Ok," Bobbie answered. Paul got in the car and carefully backed the trailer out of their campsite. He drove down the dirt road to the ramp they had passed earlier and stopped in front of the boat launch. He unhooked the trailer from the station wagon. Paul had a hitch on the front of his car as well as the back. He turned the car around and hitched the trailer to the front of the car. This way he could push the boat into the water while driving forwards rather than trying to maneuver the car and a swerving trailer into the water backwards.

He cranked the heavy wire at the nose of the boat attached to the trailer, slowly releasing it as he backed the boat down into the water. He pushed the boat the rest of the way until it was floating freely and jumped in. He put the key in the ignition and lowered the engine into the water.

Paul had spent hours the week before running the engine in a large trash can full of water to make sure it was running properly. He tied the boat loosely at the dock and parked the car and trailer before going back to the boat. He pulled the rope off the dock as he hopped onto the deck and jumped into the driver's seat.

The boat sliced through the water forming waves on either side of him all the way to the little peninsula that formed their campsite. He searched for the small post sticking up out of the water that he had spotted earlier and slowly made his way to it. He looked for objects poking up out of the water too; the last thing he wanted to do was damage the bottom of his boat.

Once he had the rope tied to the post, he climbed out and waded through the water towards the beach. Bobbie had heard the boat coming and stood on the water's edge with Jill as he brought the boat in. "See Jill? There's the boat!" She pointed to it. Jill pointed too and said her dad's name in her infant babble, "da da." Jill was fascinated with the sights and sounds.

Paul walked up the beach and poked his finger into Jill's belly button. She giggled. Paul grinned and told Bobbie, "Ok, I'm off on a walk to get the car." "Sounds good," Bobbie answered. Paul retraced his steps up the dirt road. It took him a good fifteen minutes to reach the car where he had left it. He wasn't in a rush. He enjoyed the fresh air, the smell of the trees, the sound of the water lapping at the beach. He pulled out a cigarette and smoked it as he approached the boat ramp. When he arrived at the car, he stopped and took in the view over the lake and observed for a good long while. He thought to himself, "This is spectacular. It is so beautiful and peaceful. This is going to be a good trip."

Paul dropped his cigarette on the serrated cement ramp and stepped on it. He walked the rest of the way down the ramp towards the water and looked off to either side, searching for any sign of wildlife. He spotted a small school of fish, and he tried to figure out what kind they were. He knew there was trout in the lake. He was hoping to get some good trout fishing in so they could have a fish fry one night over the fire, and hopefully even catch enough to lay over ice and bring home with them. He smiled at the thought, then got up and walked towards the car.

Paul unhitched the trailer and left it there. Driving back to the campsite he noticed a pair of men walking along side the road carrying fishing poles. Paul slowed the car and leaned his head out the window. "Do you gentlemen know where the good fishing is?" he inquired. The two men walked to the driver's side of the car where Paul's elbow rested. "Yeah, we're headed down the path here to that small bend in the distance." One man pointed ahead. Paul nodded his head. "But I hear there is a spot loaded with fish on the other side of the main part of the lake, northwest side I believe. If you have a boat, you would be able to get over to it easy." Paul nodded in a way that appeared as if he had been given the secret to a coveted treasure. "Hmm. I see." He made a note in his head picturing exactly where that would be.

"You got a boat?" the other man asked. "Uh, yeah, I got one." Paul answered. "Just got done putting it in the water as a matter of fact." "Where you keeping it?" he asked. "Over by our campsite." Paul pointed in the direction he was headed. The man nodded his head. The men were quiet for a moment. "You know," Paul slowly pulled out another cigarette and lit it as he spoke. "I have no one to fish with. I came with my wife and daughter, and my mother-in-law. I wouldn't mind having a couple of fishing partners," he told them in between inhaling puffs from his cigarette.

The two men were obviously happy at the idea. "Sure, that'd be just swell!" one of them said. "Yeah, sure would," the other agreed. "Hey I'm Paul by the way." He pushed his right arm out the window towards the men. One of them reached out to take his hand and replied, "Nice to meet you Paul. I'm Harold. You can call me Harry." "Hi Harry," Paul said. The other man put his hand out. "And I'm John." Paul shook hands and said, "Hi John, nice to meet you." "You too," John said. "Well, we're going to do a little water skiing tomorrow with the family, have a cookout and whatnot. Maybe the day after?" Paul suggested. Harry told him, "Yeah, that could work. If we get an early start, we might get some really good fishing in." Paul didn't need much convincing. He immediately agreed. "Yeah, let's do it. What time do you think? About 6:00?" Paul hated getting up early, but when it came to fishing, nothing was an inconvenience. "Perfect," Harry replied. John chipped in, "Maybe we ought to say 5:30 leave here by, that way we can be out on the water and in place by 6:00." John was a serious fisherman. "Ok," Paul replied, slowly drawing another puff from his cigarette.

"You know," Paul said, "You're welcome to join us for our cook-out tonight. It's just hotdogs and hamburgers, but we'd love company." Paul relished the idea of males to converse with. "You could meet my wife and family." John and Harry were camping alone without their families, and the thought of some good old burgers and hotdogs was too good to pass up. "That's swell!" Harry answered for both of them. "Great!" Paul pointed out the way, "So we're on that little peninsula. Come on by anytime. I got a cooler with some beers too." The two men nodded their heads with thoughts of cold beer and hot barbequed hamburgers as they said their goodbyes. "Better get to fishing now," one of them said. Paul could see they were itchy to go. Harry held one hand up and turned to leave. "Nice meeting you. See you tonight then," Paul said. "Yeah, we'll be there," and they walked away.

Paul smiled as he drove to the campsite. Things were going even better than he'd expected. He parked the car and got out. Bobbie was doing what she could with one hand, carrying Jill. Effie dragged small items from here to there, not really knowing where things went. Paul walked over to them. "What ya doing there?" he asked. Effie replied, "Oh we're just gettin' things set up here," she replied, as if she knew exactly what she was doing. "Well, how about you sit down Effie, and let me finish up." Paul suggested with a voice that said "I'm taking charge." It was the gentlest way he could think of to remove her from the set-up efforts. He really preferred to do everything himself. He could do it much more efficiently alone and have everything the way he wanted it. Effie sat down with her drink and said, "Ok boss, whatever you say." It didn't take much persuading. She knew she was simply shuffling things from one location to another. Effie had a slim figure with a slight frame that she carried with an air of nobility, and it was difficult maneuvering around with her designer sandals without getting sand in them. Camping really wasn't her thing and she certainly had no idea how to set up a tent. Having been the former wife of a Colonel, Effie was accustomed to having things done for her. Her husband never let her lift a finger when it came to outside men's work. When they lived overseas, they'd always had servants. Her husband treated her like a princess when he was alive. Effie never stopped playing the part.

Paul was fast. He had the campsite set up in no time. He put the large green army tent in the foreground nearest the road and next to the picnic table. Paul faced the opening towards the lake. It was an arduous process laying out the awkward poles and putting them in the correct places to form the frame. An awning stretched out over the door. A barbeque grill was next to the table. Bobbie had Jill in the playpen and Effie sat next to it in her lawn chair. Bobbie sat on the beach.

The fire pit was the next item on the agenda. Paul walked closer to the water's edge and dug a shallow hole in the sand, spreading it over a three-foot diameter. He scouted the area for large rocks to form a ring around the hole. After that, he walked over to the women and stood with his hands on his hips, proud of his efforts. "Hey there Bobbie, would you like to help me search for kindling?" Bobbie looked up and held back a grin. Paul's eyes sparkled. The task held significance for them; it's exactly what Paul had asked her to do when he'd asked her to marry him. Bobbie got up from the table and said, "Sure, of course. Mom, you mind if I leave you with the baby for a bit?" "Oh no, of course not! You kids go on."

Bobbie followed Paul down a path that ran along the edge of the lake. There were trees lining the path moving inland. A scarce smattering of spindly trees separated the walking path from the lake. Paul led the way. Bobbie straggled along behind him carefree and playful in anticipation of what may come. "How far are you going?" Bobbie finally asked him. "Is there some secret place where kindling grows in abundance that you know about?" Paul glanced behind him at her, pretending not to smile. "Oh you'll see. I saw something on the way driving in and it's full of the best kind of kindling." "I see," Bobbie said, playing along.

They continued down the path, walking in silence and reached a small clearing that was entirely enshrouded with dense foliage and stopped. He turned and looked out over the water, as if performing an inspection. Bobbie stopped next to him. "This it?" she asked. "Yep," he answered, seriously. He continued looking out over the water as if he were studying something important. Bobbie suppressed a smile. "I don't see any kindling," she said. "Hmmm?" he answered absentmindedly. He glanced behind them at the small grove of trees and then at Bobbie. "Oh, will you look at that? I guess you're right. Nothing." "Mmm hmmm," Bobbie replied. "You don't believe me? You don't believe I saw what I saw earlier?" Bobbie looked at him, as he looked out over the water, pretending to be serious too. "Nope." "Ahhh. That's not demonstrating much trust in your husband." "Oh I trust you," she answered, "I trust you found a spot alright." "I see," he said. "Well, now that you mention it." He turned to her now and drew her towards him. "I really just wanted to get you away from everyone so I could be alone with you." Bobbie looked up at him and he down at her with love in his eyes and he kissed her. "I love you Paul," she said. "I love you too Bobbie." In that moment, their world couldn't have been more perfect.

A little while later Paul and Bobbie entered the camp holding hands, chatting happily. Effie looked up and smiled. She was happy to see them so happy. "You two lovebirds find what you were looking for?" Paul suppressed a small grin and so did Bobbie. "Yeah Mom." Paul glanced at Bobbie and realized they hadn't even picked up any kindling. "Well, I'll go look over here for that kindling," Paul said. Bobbie laughed. As he walked away he called over his shoulder, "Hey, when I get back, shall we take the boat for a spin?" "Ok!" Bobbie said. "I'll get my suit on now and get Jill ready." Paul gathered kindling and threw it in the fire pit so it would be ready for the evening and headed back to the tent. He took the sleeping bags out of the car and threw them in the tent to unfold later when it was time for bed. Then he unpacked the three cots and put them in the tent too. His suitcase was at the back of the trunk of the station wagon. He pulled it to the front and unlatched it. He took his bathing trunks from the suitcase and headed back for the tent a third time to put them on. He emerged wearing his dark blue skin tight and very short trunks, ready for a ride in the boat. "Ready ladies?" "Almost," Bobbie called out. "Give us a minute. I'm still getting Jill ready." Effie already had her one-piece suit on and a broad rimmed sun hat, her large round-lensed sunglasses, as well as large flowered plastic flip flops on her feet.

Bobbie came out of the tent with Jill in her sunbonnet and a pink ruffled bathing suit. She smiled and waved her arms up and down excitedly. She knew something fun was about to happen. Paul tied the dogs to a tree and placed a large bowl of water near them. He went to the boat first and unhitched it from the dock. The boat drifted into shore. The women waded through the water. Effie was first to be hauled into the boat. Paul lifted her in and then took the baby and handed her to Effie. Bobbie was last.

"Ok!" Paul said. "Everyone seated?" "Seated!" Effie answered, as if repeating a military command. She saluted Paul with her hand at her forehead. "Aye Aye, captain." Paul placed the key that hung on a chain with a miniature floaty into the ignition. The engine sputtered into motion. It hummed. "Sounds smooth as can be!" Paul was pleased with his work. He lifted the engine in and out of the water several times, turning it on and off one more time. "Everything's working fine!" He backed the boat away from the dock.

Once out on the water away from the shallower depths, Paul increased the speed, careful to obey the shoreline speed limit. As they gradually moved further away from the coastline, he increased the speed. The engine got louder and pretty soon the wind whipped through everyone's hair. No amount of fussing with her hat would keep Effie's hair from blowing all over. She held it tightly, trying to keep it from blowing off. Bobbie handed her a scarf and Effie shouted out to Paul, trying to be heard over the sound of the roaring engine. The boat was moving so fast they hit breaks in the small waves created by the stronger wind that had picked up in the middle of the lake. Paul turned around only after the third attempt by Effie to get his attention. "What?!" he yelled back to her. He bent down to hear. "Can you slow down a minute while I tie my scarf around my hat?" "Sure," he replied. He pulled the lever down and brought the speed to a mere five miles per hour. "Wow!" said Effie. "That is some kind of wind!" She tried to sound cheery but the grimace on her face said otherwise. Effie hated the wind. It messed up her hair and she didn't like it blowing in her face. "Are you in some kind of race?!" She always tried to be funny yet a bit sarcastic to make sure everyone knew when she didn't like something, and in an attempt to hopefully alter the situation in her favor. She pulled the scarf around the hat and pulled the sides down tightly, tying the ends under her chin.

Paul waited patiently but said nothing. Female pleasantries did not interfere with his passion for speed. He had been a racecar driver in his younger days and he wasn't about to compromise this rare pleasure. It wasn't that he was not trying respect his mother-in-law's wishes. He simply saw the division between man and woman as such that Effie was on male turf when it came to his boat.

Effie tolerated the boat ride, but this would be her last she decided. Paul raced around the lake, inspecting the far end of it and entering one of the long arms that stretched out of it and down one end for quite some ways. He took note of what would make ideal waterskiing runs. He swung the boat around, having made his way partway down the length of it. He slowed the motor to an even speed and happily skirted the shore between two arms that extended out. He reached the second one and entered the opening. Effie made a comment that clearly conveyed her lack of enthusiasm for a ride that seemed would never end. Paul heard her but pretended not to. He increased the speed to create more engine noise. Effie pierced her lips together and turned her head, resigning herself to the fact that the ride would be continuing far longer than she would have liked.

Paul raced through the corridor, standing at the wheel so he could see over the hull. The wind whipped through his wavy brown hair and the look of delight was visible not only on his face but rippled through his body. He slowed the engine to turn the boat around and Effie took advantage of the opportunity to ensure Paul knew she was done. Paul glanced back quickly with a look of disappointment his fun was coming to an end sooner than he wished, but he realized he couldn't disregard Effie any longer. "Okaaaay," he said and it sounded more like a sigh than a reply. "Back home," he answered like a little boy who had been told he had to stop catching tadpoles and come in for a bath. He had gotten a good first ride, however, so he was not disappointed.

Paul did not compromise speed as they raced across the lake towards the campground. Effie held the gutter to the boat for dear life trying to keep her balance while holding fast to her hat all the while. She had had it. Water gushed up and down the gutters, splashing over her hand that gripped it. Effie sighed in exasperation. Paul slowed the boat fifteen minutes later as they entered the slow zone, quieting the roar of the engine, forcing him to endure Effie's remarks. Paul kept his gaze focused straight ahead as if his direction required every bit of his attention, and pretended not to hear her. He couldn't wait to dump her off at the dock. Bobbie put her hand on her mother's lap and told her to relax. She reminded her that they were camping and nature sometimes entailed some minor inconveniences. "Minor?!" Effie said with contempt. Bobbie ignored her mother. She was used to her air of entitlement and what really amounted to nothing short of acting spoiled.

Paul lassoed a post on the dock. He had a good aim and landed the looped end of the rope to it on the first try. "Will you look at that!" he said. He pulled the boat in to the dock slowly until one side bumped. He instructed Bobbie to push against it while holding it at the same time to keep the boat from being scratched. He was not about to have his boat dented. Effie was already standing in the boat long before they'd approached the water's edge. She was ready to get her feet on dry land. Paul helped her out of the boat. He raised his eyebrows and lowered his head as he looked out to one side at Bobbie as if he were questioning someone's judgment that more than lacked his approval. Bobbie put her head down and muffled a laugh. Effie disregarded both of them. "Good to have my feet on solid ground," she announced. Her spirits had risen the moment she had stepped off the boat. "Enough of that," she said. She was fully aware their smirks were at her expense. Paul thought to himself, "Thank God." He figured women just weren't cut out for roughing it. At the same time, he thought, as he looked at Bobbie, "What a good sport she is."

As Effie stepped off of the dock heading straight for the campsite, Bobbie apologized. "I'm sorry about my Mom." "It's alright," Paul accepted the apology. He knew it wasn't her fault. "She just isn't cut out for it. I understand," he said. She nodded her head and let a sigh escape her lips. "Uhhmmm, hmmm." She lifted Jill into the air, trying to change the mood. "But Jill on the other hand, she LOVES it, doesn't she?" She half said to Jill and half to Paul. Paul took her out of Bobbie's hands and lifted her up and down in the air as she squealed. "My little girl is going to be a water baby, isn't she?!" Paul giggled in delight at her. Nothing could dampen his enthusiasm for too long, not now anyway.

At the campsite Paul and Bobbie began the preparations for dinner. "I'll grab the meat." He reached into the cooler where the hamburger patties were. They had been neatly wrapped in foil, ready to put on the grill. "I'll take care of the cold food and the cutlery." "Sounds good." Bobbie put the tablecloth on the long wood picnic table and looked for the paper plates and plastic utensils. She reached into the cooler, shifting its contents around searching for the container that held the potato salad she had prepared at home before the trip. "Can I help you with anything?" Effie asked. "No I got it Mom." Effie was already in better spirits, having gotten to reshape her curls, finding the damage to her hairdo wasn't that bad after all. Paul ran up the beach to the car to look for the bag of charcoal. "Guess I need charcoal if I'm going to make this work!" He smiled at the women. "Yeah I guess so," Effie said.

Paul stacked the charcoal bricks into a small pyramid and poured liquid kerosene over it. His fingertips were black and he smeared some of it onto his pants as he reached into his pocket for a lighter. The smell of the kerosene was strong. He stood back from the grill as he ignited the fluid. It caught immediately. He stood back and observed. Once it was going he pulled the metal rack down over the bricks and adjusted it so that the burgers would cook at the right height.

He walked to the edge of the lake and looked out over the water, grabbing a beer on the way. The sun was beginning to hit the horizon casting brilliant colors over the lake. He took a deep breath, breathing in the smell of the burning charcoal. He waited for the bricks to turn grey and hot before carefully laying each round patty onto the grill. It was then he remembered he had forgotten the spatula. He shouted up the beach, "Hey Bobbie, you got the spatula for flipping the burgers?" "Yeah I'll look for it." A moment later she jogged down the small hill, her feet sliding in the sand. Paul watched her and couldn't help but admire her beauty and how happy he was that she was his wife. He took the utensil from her, and slid an arm around her waist and swung her around to look at the sun setting over the water. "Look at that," she gasped. She leaned her head against his shoulder and he hugged her tighter to his side. "Isn't it beautiful? Look at all those colors." Effie came up from behind unannounced and startled them. "What are you two lovebirds doing over here? I don't see any work getting done. Do I need to step in and supervise?" "What are you talking about?" Paul said, ready to defend himself. "Do you not see meat sizzling on the grill?" "Oh well there," she said. "Guess I'll have to give you that. Thought I'd better come break up this little rendezvous at any rate," she said.

Effie noticed they were watching the sunset and looked out over the water too. "Will you just look at those colors?!" "Wow! Yellow, orange, pink, red. Just gorgeous." "The way it reflects off the water is absolutely breathtaking." Paul nodded. "Sure is." The three of them stood side by side, silently watching as the water lapped the shore.

"Ok well I guess I'm not going to get anywhere with this meal preparation," Effie said before climbing the sandy hill with her big flowery sandals. She struggled as her feet sank into the sand with every step. She let out a little groan as she glanced down at the sand creeping in between her toes. "Oh good gracious," she said quietly as she made her way back to the campsite. Bobbie and Paul laughed.

From across the campsite two men approached. "Who are they?" Bobbie asked. "Oh those are the two men I met earlier. Remember, I told you? I invited them for dinner, hope you don't mind." "Oh, not at all!" Bobbie answered. She was used to lots of people and entertaining, growing up with a mother like Effie. "Hello gentlemen." Bobbie greeted them. Paul introduced everyone. "Bobbie, this is John." He extended his hand. "I'm Bobbie". "Yes, hello, your husband told us about you." "And I'm Harry." Harry put his hand out to her. "I hope we're not intruding," he said. "Oh not at all, we love company. So nice to meet you," she said. "Come on fellas. Have a seat." Paul pulled a couple of chairs up for them. "Can I get ya both a cold one?" He was already headed for the cooler he had placed next to the fire pit earlier. "Sure! I'll take one!" Harold replied. "Make that double!" John answered. "Sure thing." Paul reached into the cooler and took out three cold beers and closed the lid.

"So ya have any luck with the fishing today?" Paul asked as he passed out the beers. "Oh, I caught a couple," John said. Harold's face lit up. "I caught five." He tried to play it cool as he said it but everyone knew it was something to be proud of. "Five? Wow!" Paul said. "That's real good." Paul looked over the water, imagining how many fish were waiting out there for him to catch. The sun already sank behind the mountains.

Paul got up to finish the burgers and handed them out to everyone as soon as they were done. "There are chips and condiments on the table here so help yourselves," said Bobbie. The evening went well, everyone chatted, and Paul even built a fire as night fell. Even Effie seemed to enjoy the evening despite the sand between her toes.

The next morning Effie and Bobbie woke up to the smell of bacon. Bobbie poked her head out of the tent and Paul said, "Oh, there you are sleepy head." Paul was busy flipping pancakes and Jill was on the table in her carrier next to him gurgling inaudible sounds that if Bobbie could have translated would have been, "Mommy! Good morning! Here I am! Aren't you happy to see me?!"

"What time is it?" Bobbie asked, rubbing her eyes. "It's 7:00!!" "Oh, is that all?" "Yeah the sun's been up for two hours already!!" "Uh huh," she answered. "Thanks for letting me sleep in." Bobbie walked over to Jill and gave her a kiss and rubbed her cheek against Jill's before getting her formula ready. "I thought you'd be long gone fishing with the men by now," Bobbie said. "I decided to put off fishing until tomorrow. I thought it would be nice to spend our first day together, water skiing." It was difficult to decide which he wanted to do more, fish or ski. He loved them both. Effie poked her head out of the tent and said, "Well hello there!" She was talking to Jill. Jill squirmed in her seat and gurgled to her Granny like she wanted her to pick her up. "Let me get my sandals on first," she said.

The four of them sat down to a feast of pancakes and bacon and Paul talked about the day that lay ahead. "As soon as we get breakfast cleaned up and everyone finishes up with a bathroom run, we'll start getting the boat loaded for skiing." Paul knew this would be at least another couple of hours and this is why he decided early on to outline the day so he could get a head start and possibly be in the boat ready to go by 11:00.

Bobbie walked back from the bathroom and the water pump with her arms loaded with the washed cookware from breakfast. "I met a nice couple just now as I was washing dishes and I invited them to come skiing with us." "Oh that's great." He was thinking about Effie, and a diversion with some extra young people was a perfect solution to dampening her influence on the boat. "Yeah, they both ski and seemed real excited at the offer to join us." Paul's face lit up. "Well that's just swell then!" When it was time to get in the boat and load up, the neighboring campers Bobbie had invited appeared. "Hi, my name is Larry." He extended a hand to Paul. "And this is my wife Martie." "Well it's great to meet you! I'm so happy you could join us. The more the merrier! I'm Paul." The men got to talking while the women ogled over the baby. Paul interrupted after about twenty minutes. "Hey, enough socializing. We'll have plenty of time for that on the water. Let's get the show on the road. Everyone come on over and lets size up some skis." Paul always had extras and he always brought all of them just in case. Skiing was a social sport. They sized up and carried their skiis to the boat. Paul climbed in and let everyone pass their skis to him so he could strategically place them out of the way between the sides of the boat and the seats. "Hand those up here," he told Martie and Bobbie. "Can I give you a hand there, Paul?" Larry asked. "No. I think I got it."

"Ok, I think that's everything." Paul said. He hopped out of the boat. "Let me just grab the cooler with the beers." Effie walked out of the tent with her wide brimmed hat and a scarf and a new pair of sandals with sparkles on them. She had a book in her hand and told everyone, "You kids go ahead. I'm going to sit here and enjoy the beach with my book." There was a beach chair to the side of them with a towel on it, and another cooler next to it with a drink on it. "Are you sure Mom?" Bobbie asked. "Yes I'm sure! You kids go on. Enjoy yourselves. I have a small bottle of daiquiri mix, so I'm going to be enjoying some quiet 'wind-less' time to myself." Bobbie and Paul laughed. "Ok we'll leave Paige with you." Effie loved her big beautiful German shepherd. "But we'll bring Mala with us. Mala was swimming in the water clear past the boat. "Come on Mala! Let's go girl!" Mala paddled over with her front paws to the edge of the boat making circles trying to figure out how to get in. Paul waded through the water and gently scooped her up, dripping with water into the boat. Mala shook her black and white coat tinged with yellowish-brown around her snout and legs as soon as she was in, covering all four seats with water. "Well I guess we're all going to be wet soon enough anyway." Paul laughed.

He followed the soggy wet dog into the boat and extended a hand to the women. "Here, grab my hand," he said. He pulled Martie into the boat first and Bobbie handed the baby to him next. He handed her off to Martie and pulled Bobbie into the boat. Larry was last. "Everyone have a seat." Paul started up the engine. They waved goodbye to Effie who was already in her beach chair with her drink in her hand sipping out of the straw and waving back at them. Paul taxied out of the low speed zone and as soon as he had cleared it, he cranked up the engine and soon the boat was hitting the water with a big slam each time the boat came down onto a big wave. Water sprayed in at the sides and the sun beat down on them. It was a fantastic day of skiing. By the end of it, they were the best of friends.

It was a memorable trip. They enjoyed themselves and even Effie made the best of it. Paul never got any fishing in. They were too occupied with their new friends and skiing and Larry didn't fish. When it was time to leave, relaxed and sun-tired, they packed all their gear into the car and the boat the same way they'd arrived and began the long drive home. Even though it was just as hot on the return home, the four of them noticed it a lot less. Vacation-drenched sun and relaxation soaked their bodies through and through.

Martie and Larry lived near Bobbie and Paul and they got together often after they'd returned home from the trip. They went to Lake Sammamish for more skiing and Paul even talked Larry into learning to fish. They went to the many nearby lakes to catch trout and other fish in the Sound. Paul even learned all the tricks from old-timers in the area so they would be ready when the salmon started to run.

That fall, when the festivities of summer came to a close, and fall set in, Bobbie sat down at the table, pen in hand and a leaf of stationary paper in front of her, to write a letter.

November 18,1968

Dear Mom and Dad,

Mala had her puppies! Jill adores them but it is quite a lot of work. Taking care of a nine-month-old baby requires all of my time. Feeding 11 puppies four times a day is double time. Mala is ravenous because of the strain but I feed her about five pounds of food each day plus vitamin supplements. Not to mention taking Mala out for runs since I can't let her run loose anymore. Mala has turned into a garbage pail outlaw going right into other peoples' houses!

I managed to save the littlest one who we really thought we'd lose. He was so weak he couldn't even open his mouth to eat. I had to force the milk down. I had to go to a dog breeder for supplies and help. Often the mother will reject the weakest puppy, but Mala did not. Mala has turned out to be an exceptionally good mother.

The breeder says I will be able to cover my expenses because she is sure she can sell them for me at $25 a piece, and she is doing it for nothing. She is right about the fact that asking money will insure good people who will take good care. We'll see! I sure hope they sell! I'd be content to know they had good homes.

Here are their names: Chip, Chap, Chicco, Toby, Mickie, Mandy, Candy, Cocoa, Ginger, Cindi, and Chance.

Otherwise, Jill's been fine. She's been doing patty-cake and "peek-a-boo." She's settled down to her regular schedule and is good as gold. She walks all around the tables and couch so she should start walking alone soon. There's no hurry.

Though our Xmas will be a little poor this year, it will be a pretty one, and I wish you could arrange to come and share it with us, but don't feel badly if you can't, and please don't buy extravagant gifts – you've given us plenty already – I will feel badly that we cannot give as nice gifts.

The weather has been dreary but our warm fires are very comforting, the smell of wood, the fall colors giving way to winter is all very peaceful.

Thank you for the album. Let's see how many little ones will show up in this album over the years – and may Jill always be something special for filling our stockings and being our first and bring you many happy moments as we send you pictures watching her grow.

I will try to get those pictures to you as soon I can.
Thank you more than I can say for everything.
Write soon,
Love, Bobbie, Paul & Jill

Chapter 5

Jhapa

(1989 – 1991)

Chasing those silvery, shimmering bits of gloss – run hard, stop for breath – bear down again – but look! You fall, get up fool! On the path and chase else you'll lose sight; see, they've blurred in the distance; do you know which you're after? Can you distinguish? Get closer, run, run, run – never mind for fatigue and ability – take it on the chin, like a good person. Oh yes! Now you can see! How clear and beautiful – how harmonious! Don't faint from joy for you'll lose them again. Ooohhh!!! They've jerked up and away; well take the one you have, at least, it's nearly strangled, you've held on so hard. Poor thing, it's all you have – but don't leave it there half dead on the wayside, take it, nourish it. Maybe it can help you capture what you're after. Come, pick HOPE up again and get along. Hurry, hurry, hurry …!!

Bobbie, March 1964

Jill graduated college and went home for three weeks before departing for Nepal. Carol told her "No sitting around. Get a job." Jill wondered who would hire her for three weeks. Carol had an answer for that. "Go to a temp agency." Jill still needed to gather the few required supplies that would fit into precisely two bags that were the allotment for the two-year service as a Peace Corps Volunteer. This meant shopping with very careful selection. A little mental preparation would have been good too. At this point in her life, it almost felt comical that a requirement to work was imposed on her for this short period of time. Carol needed her out of her life even for a mere three weeks. This was how Jill interpreted it. She could have been wrong. Perhaps there was some other reason. Jill didn't really care anymore. To the contrary, she found it amusing and a bit trite.

Jill obliged the insistent request. She found a three-week job at an insurance office where she worked in a filing room. Of course it was mundane. Jill quietly observed office politics, everyone vying for a way out of the file room and into the real office and to a real desk. Jill found it absurd, the idea of fighting for a desk. The people that had succeeded in breaking free of the file room and sat at a hard-won desk did not appear any happier, but they did seem to take joy in gloating about the elevated status over their once equal peers. All Jill could see was the insignificance of the contrived office environment. She felt so removed that inside her mind she laughed. She was far away lost in thought, thinking about the adventure she was about to embark on.

When it was time to board the plane for San Francisco to begin her volunteer training, Carol was the one to take her. It was a one-man send off. Jill hugged Carol goodbye with watery eyes and walked down the ramp to the plane. She turned one last time to look at her stepmother of the past thirteen years and tears streamed down her own face. Jill loved her despite everything and had only ever wanted her love in return. Carol looked back at her without expression. Jill didn't find it unusual. She was caught up in her own emotions. Tears ran down her face throughout the entire take-off. Jill did not notice anyone around her. She allowed her emotions to flow freely, and she realized in that moment, it was something unusual for her. It was a relief. She allowed herself to feel what she felt.

Jill's Peace Corps volunteer group, Nepal N-168, took off from San Francisco after three days of training and introduction to the fifty-some people she would be spending the next two years of her life with. They stopped in Thailand for a layover and due to a bomb scare, remained there for an additional three days. When a decision was finally made and the arrangements to complete the final leg of the journey, they boarded a plane bound for Kathmandu.

They got off the plane carrying large backpacks stuffed with sleeping bags and essentials unavailable in a developing country. Each person had a different idea of what was crucial and that they considered impossible to do without. For Jill it was toothpaste. In her bag she carried fifteen tubes of Crest.

The air outside the airport was cool. Everything felt fresh and open. A large bus waited for them and they climbed on. As the bus wound it's way from the airport to the city Jill marveled at the beauty of the landscape. It was intensely green everywhere and varying shades of it, adding dimension to the exotic picture before them. Tiered rice patties wove in and out of small hills. Occasionally a brightly dressed Nepalese woman passed on the road carrying a basket on her head. They were fascinating too; their eyes were a blend of almond-shaped Indian and Oriental, their faces resembled that of a Tibetan or perhaps Mongolian, but not quite. They wore long cloth skirts from the waist down that wound their way around their legs like a saari. The shirt was called a "*chobundi*" Jill came to learn. It was part of the traditional Nepalese dress. It was a small red and white print and made from a sort of flannel type cloth that suited the cool mountainous region. It was short, at or above the belly button and wrapped tightly around their upper torsos and tied at the sides. A final long piece of contrasting and brightly colored fabric wound it's way several times around their waists and formed a sort of bulge that tied the ensemble together. The bold colors were stunning. Jill thought it was perfectly exotic, the scenery and these beautiful women with long dark hair tied into long braids that hung down their backs and over their shoulders. She was entranced and pleasantly surprised by the sights and sounds of such a remote and mysterious place. To Jill, it was absolutely magical.

After a greeting from the Country Director of the Peace Corps program in Nepal, the entire group was escorted to their lodgings for the next couple of nights. When they arrived Jill was appalled at the condition of their small hotel. The walls were jail-blue and cracked. The ground was a slab of dirty cement. The shabby wooden framed beds were covered with equally shabby and well-stained mattresses. The mattresses were bare of linens of course, as Jill would come to get accustomed to. Guests were expected to provide their own. Everyone pulled out their sleeping bags and laid them on the mattresses. Jill thought the place looked like an absolute prison. She sat on the dirty mattress and looked around. Everyone had already left the room. Some of them called to her from downstairs. They were about to leave for a walk. Jill resigned herself to the fact that this was where she was going to have to sleep.

She got up from the bed and joined the others, trailing along behind. They rounded a bend in the narrow dirt road only large enough to walk and Jill eyed a little hovel that sunk down below street level. Entering required stepping down a few steps to get inside the small shop. It had a wooden sort of patio-type awning that stretched out over the dirt path. From it hung a goat's head. The neck dripped with blood and its eyes stared blankly ahead. Jill's throat tightened. She tried to gulp. To say she was repulsed didn't come close to what she was feeling. Her heart dropped into her stomach. She gasped and called to the others. They turned briefly to see what it was and she pointed. They brushed it off informing her, "Yeah, we saw that earlier," and continued walking. Jill felt dizzy and stumbled over a large stone in the road. Everything was spinning, the little hovels that formed the tiny shops and sunk down into the ground, the sharp smells of sickening incense mingled with the rancid smell of sewage. She imagined this must have been what medieval times were like.

She stopped where she was, turned around, deserting the others and ran all the way back to the room. The hotel suddenly seemed like a haven compared to all of that. For five long minutes she wondered if she had made a terrible mistake and didn't know if she could live like this for two long years. She sat on the edge of her bed, overwhelmed by her overloaded senses. Gradually she came to the conclusion that she was here, and she had already made the decision to be a volunteer. She had made a commitment and she was determined to follow it through. She decided right then and there, "Alright. This is how it's going to be. I will just have to put my chin up and bear it." Every time she passed the goat head's stall, however, she closed her eyes and looked the other way.

A mere two days later they were on the bus again, this time winding their way through the lush green Nepali hills. The Nepalis called them hills, but to anyone else they surely would be called steep mountains. They arrived several hours later to a little village called Trisuli. It sat next to a large river and it was beautiful. The riverbanks, the roads, and the farmlands were composed of a rich red soil. The contrast of rich bold colors painted a stunning landscape. Once again, however, after so recently having come to terms with the first set of accommodations, she was confronted with a whole new level of squalor. Jill walked into a dark dank room. There weren't even any beds. Another girl walked in and said, "Yes there are, see? Those are them, on the floor." Jill looked down and there they were all right. Four thin foam mattresses lined the walls. "Oh," Jill said. There were no windows but there was a small bathroom that was a pit in the ground. At least it had a door. "Ok," Jill said as she walked around inspecting the hovel. She walked out thinking to herself, I won't be spending much time in there. And this was how she came to realize it was a good technique Peace Corps used; gradual submersion into worse and worse dilapidated living conditions.

There was one more shock left for Jill before she was fully indoctrinated. One night as she lay sleeping on her piece of foam on the floor, something woke her. Whatever it was pulled at her long blond hair. She reached back and felt something furry was caught in it. It took a moment to realize that the little claws she was feeling belonged to a mouse. Instead of falling apart she reached back to untangle him. He was all wound up in her hair. It's amazing how the mind and body can detach and endure momentarily a horrific event just to get through it. Jill carefully pulled strand by strand out of the small creature's claws. Finally he broke free. He must have been just as terrified as she was.

As soon as he had escaped, Jill sat bolt upright in the middle of the bed. What had happened was only beginning to sink in. She pulled herself away from the edges of the mattress and made herself into the tightest ball she could and shook muttering silently to herself, "Oh my God, Oh my God, oh my God." After sitting for several minutes like that, she remembered her flashlight in her bag. She left the safety of her island mattress to look for it. After finding it she ran back to the bed and turned it on. There were small noises all around her and pretty soon she saw that there were several little mice running in circles around the room. She shined her light on them every time one came near. She noticed that the head of her bed lay right along their running path next to the wall. She sat all night like that, jerking from side to side, intensely alert to every movement they made.

When morning finally arrived after hours of torturous torch duty, Jill marched straight for the training room to inform the staff. They howled with laughter. Jill stepped back in dismay. It wasn't the response she had hoped for. When they stopped one of them said, "Ok, ok. We'll find you a mosquito net for tonight." The same man turned to ask her, "Just where is your bed?" "Well, in the room of course," Jill answered. "No, I mean where in the room?" "Next to the wall," she replied. "Well why is it next to the wall? Of course the mice are going to run over your head. That's where mice run." "Oh," she said, trying to see the logic. The teachers grabbed the opportunity to make a language lesson out of the experience and taught her to say, "Mousa cha, mero kopal ma." "A mouse is in my hair." They told her that her assignment that day was to tell the class about what happened in Nepali. "Great," Jill thought, "Maybe it will help me get over my trauma to talk about it."

From that night onwards, Jill pulled her bed into the middle of the room and tucked her mosquito net in tightly. She pulled herself up into the middle of it to make good and sure absolutely no part of her body touched the sides. Every now and then throughout the night she would awaken and check the edges of the mosquito net to make sure it was still tucked in. She kept the flashlight with her at all times.

Training continued in this way and the volunteer trainees were slowly immersed into the culture. The training was divided into three parts. The first was language and that took up most of the time. It was six days a week and four to six hours each day. Second was technical training to learn the specific job each volunteer was to do, and third was cultural training. Cultural training was the most amusing. Each session began with the day's observations. One time someone offered this: "I've noticed that clothing is optional under the age of six." Everyone laughed and the trainers joined in even though one had to wonder if they really found it funny or if they only laughed to join in with the volunteers.

They continued to learn things like how to use the *charpi,* a toilet. They learned that water was used in place of toilet paper and the *lota,* a pitcher of water, is poured only into the left hand and that is why the left hand is always considered *"jutto"* meaning "forbidden." It would be extremely disrespectful to shake someone's hand with anything but the right, nor offer a gift with it. They learned all of the "do's" and "don'ts" and what was respectful and what wasn't. They also learned the correct way to speak in levels according to your elders and your inferiors. Children were addressed in a certain way. Elders, on the other hand, received an entirely different verb tense and how they were to be addressed. There was another and quite lengthy collection of verb endings reserved for the King's family. No one had to worry about that of course.

The training continued in different locations as well. They traveled in a large caravan of volunteer trainees and training staff moving to three separate villages during the three-month training. The first stage involved a heavy concentration of language. The second mostly consisted of language too in addition to increased time for technical training. The third was only technical. During the second stage of training each volunteer lived alone with a family. Jill was assigned to the best family of all. The small home was very neat and clean, a big step up from Trisuli. It had little gardens of flowers and the floors were neatly "*lipnoo'ed*" every morning, smeared with mud and cow dung. When it was dry it had no odor and left a smooth cool surface. Delightfully, the home consisted of nine sisters! They were the most pleasant and adorable girls ever. They were at Jill's every beck and call and never left her side. The youngest daughter was nine. Jill even had her own bed, complete with blankets and sheets! The training staff's strict instructions to the families were to speak only Nepali. Jill rarely left the house. She spent all of her time with them, talking endlessly. When it came time for the oral language evaluation, to everyone's surprise, Jill was rated highest!

Towards the beginning of her time with the family the father of the household took her into his garden and told her to sit down on the stone bench. Very gravely he informed her in Nepali, "We are extremely concerned because you are not eating your *dahl bhat* "(rice and lentils). Jill was so sick and tired of rice and lentils she couldn't eat it. What the family didn't know was that everyday when she went to training, she ate as many eggs and peanut butter as she could from the training site provisions. That was the only thing left to fill up on. The father continued to inform her what they had decided to do. "Every night, we will fry up some *roti*, flat bread, and eggs along with *dahl fry*, a thicker version of *dahl* because we've noticed you like those things. But in the mornings, you must eat your rice, because how can anyone begin the day without rice?" "Tik Cha, buje," (Ok, you understand?) Jill agreed and realized how seriously they were about her welfare and that they were putting a great deal of effort in on her behalf. She was touched and made an equal effort to oblige them and eat the food.

The village of Ghorka was beautiful. Poinsettas grew in the wild and lined the trails leading to the top of the mountain where a view of the Himalayas waited. Jill enjoyed this village and the family almost more than her own. A family of nine daughters almost seemed to be a sort of premonition to the family of four daughters Jill would later create for herself.

Woven into the training were day trips to the capital for immunizations. These were usually done on days off. On such days, everyone boarded the bus and the driver sped through the mountains that were even higher and with more winding roads than the drive to Trisuli. It took several hours during which time a good percentage of the volunteers became motion sick and stops along side the road were frequent. Post injection, side effects from the immunizations added to the array of symptoms along with the carsickness on the windy fast speed trip back up the mountains to their training site. Eventually they realized Dramamine was the only way to make it to Kathmandu. Since dysentery was common in Nepal, those lucky enough to be saddled with that had even more to contend with. Hopefully no one had all three at once.

The final segment of the training was interrupted by a "survival visit." Each trainee took the bus, a small plane, or a hike as the case may be to get to the place that would be their village for the next two years of their lives. They had to travel alone and make it back in ten days, surviving on the language and cultural skills they had learned. Jill's village entailed an eighteen-hour night bus ride. She later found out that eighteen hours was the optimistic projected timeframe. This happened only if the bus did not break down, and that was rare. One time Jill noticed her bus had no headlights, and so quite resourcefully, the driver had taped two very large torch lights onto the hood of the bus. It was quite ingenuous, Jill thought.

The volunteers accompanying her found that riding on top of the bus was much more desirable than sitting inside of a packed interior with four times as many people as the bus could hold. The small group of them were headed to the same district and they fanned out from a central village once there to what would become their permanent villages for the rest of their stay in Nepal.

Jill arrived at her village and met the headmaster of the school she would be working. He introduced her to some of the teachers. He showed her the Indian Roadside Project where some barracks stood next to the school. There were several small apartments made of shabby wood with planks that barely met together forming many cracks through which children could peek through quite easily Jill came to discover. It was decided Jill would live there for the time being once she arrived to live for good. One of the teachers lived next door, so, thankfully, she wouldn't be alone. This teacher always wore a furry Russian hat regardless of the often one hundred-degree temperature. Once permanently in her village she asked him if he was not hot and he always replied, "No." She wondered if he was lying.

She was taken to the local teashop where they drank tea and ate chickpeas mixed with hot spices and onions along with *singatas*, a fried potato pastry, as a snack. They walked across the dusty road that served as the east-west highway. Jill's village fanned across both sides of it. The sun was unbearably hot. Sweat trickled down her back and at her sides and little droplets formed on her forehead. "Here, have a seat," the Headmaster said. The benches and tables were made out of rustic old wood and the floor out of dirt. It was dust really. The entire village lay on a sheet of dry dust, and it made everything feel even hotter. The building itself was nothing more than a wooden shack opened at one side. Some of the teachers had followed them over and the Headmaster introduced Jill to all of the villagers that happened to come to the teashop that afternoon. "We'll have *chiya, singatas and chana chura*," he said. Jill realized later that the *chiya pasal* (tea shop) was a sort of safe haven from all of the staring any place else she went in her village. Eating seemed to be off limits for staring. The people eating with her, however, engaged in a great deal of constant questioning.

Arrangements were made for Jill's classes. It was decided she would teach the science class of eighty fifth grade students as well as two forth grade math classes that were divided into fifty and forty students each. The headmaster insisted she teach English for the rest of the classes. It was a large number of students, but the children were so small and the rooms so tiny, it didn't seem like there were so many of them.

After tea the headmaster walked her to the school to show her around the classrooms and as a show of respect the students of each class sang and danced traditional Nepali folk dances for her. She was touched. The classrooms themselves had dirt floors and scratched blackboards. Steel bars ran through the windows that had no glass in them. The roof was made of tin, and Jill would later come to find this made teaching impossible when it rained. It was far too noisy. However, since the rain came in the monsoon season, there was no school anyway. Prior to that, the class sizes dwindled progressively as farming season approached and the school days grew shorter and shorter.

When Jill came to live in her village permanently, she noticed school began at a different time everyday. This was confusing because she wasn't sure when to go or when to get ready. She tried to pinpoint the time school was meant to begin. "Kamala, what time does school start?" She asked one of the teachers. "Ko ni," she said. It meant "who knows." She was in the teachers' lounge so she turned to the rest of the teachers and asked them. They all looked at each other and started laughing. "Will someone give me an answer then?" One of the male teachers told her "Ko ni." She asked the students. She asked the peun, (janitor). She even asked the neighbors. The answer given to her question was always the same. "*Ko ni.*" Most of the teachers had watches, but none of them worked. They dangled from their wrists like a loose bracelet. It was more of a status symbol or an adornment Jill observed. Time seemed to have no relevance she was beginning to realize. Finally one of the teachers suggested an answer. "Look out the window and when you see the students coming to school, then you'll know it's time." Jill could see the school from the window of her *dhera*, (apartment). She was satisfied with this solution. School began anywhere from 10:00 to 11:30 a.m.

The closer it came to farming season, the later school began and the sooner it ended. The *peun* (janitor) rang the school bell between periods at shorter and shorter intervals. On some days, school would end abruptly for no apparent reason at all. When Jill questioned the headmaster about this on one occasion he eyed her precociously and walked away with two other men. But she was determined to know the reason why; she thought maybe she was missing some obscure special holiday and wanted to know what it was. Finally he turned to her and said, "I don't feel like having school today." Jill said, "Hmm."

Jill arrived back to the training site successfully after the survival visit to her village. Where she would be living for the next two years was no longer a mystery. This provided everyone with a great deal of relief. The unknown is always more stressful than the actual thing. The last segment of training consisted of hikes to various villages of two to three volunteers. Trainers accompanied each group so they could observe the trainees during student teaching at the schools in those villages. When the posting was put up, the volunteers raced to choose theirs. Jill and the small group of volunteers who had travelled with her to their district during the survival visits hung back wondering why there was such a rush. What possible difference could it make what village anyone went to for the last phase of training? By the time they made it up to the board they realized they were left with the most remote village and it required nine hours of walking to get there. What they later discovered was that compared to all of the other volunteers, their minor eighteen-hour night bus ride was a piece of cake compared to what everyone else had gone through to get to theirs. Some had to take a plane flight that landed on a small patch of dirt high up in the mountains in the middle of nowhere and flew out only once every one or two weeks. Then they had to hike for days to get to their village.

Jill and her small group, three in total, walked all day, carrying all of their things on their backs. The trainers carried the supplies and very small bags with their own personal belongings. Eventually Jill learned that most of what she carried was unnecessary when she trekked anywhere. She realized she could take one small backpack and that she could fit everything she needed.

They arrived at the training village and Jill found she was to stay in a very small room with a very poor family. Fortunately one of the older volunteers who had already been in Nepal for a year and was there to observe student teaching would be staying with Jill. She was relieved on account of the number of children that swarmed around her to stare. The older volunteer knew how to handle them. It was a bit overwhelming.

Taking baths was an ordeal. Jill dreaded it so much she waited three days between, and this was unthinkable for her. She never missed her showers, ever. They were her ritual daily reward. Hot baths were the answer to every problem, sickness, and heartache. However, circumstances can alter the most solid of habits. Her first attempt was a disaster. Jill gathered her things quickly before the children could figure out what she was up to. It entailed careful planning, waiting for a brief lull in the amusing activity of constant staring. Jill figured the villagers must have needed to work or eat now and then forcing a break from their amusement at her expense. As soon as it did, she made a run for it. She grabbed her things and dashed out the door for the trail that led around the village along the edge of the mountain that looked out over more mountains below.

She could hear the kids behind her shouting to the others to gather up. The stranger was on the move. Jill sighed but continued walking quickly for the public tap that came out of a stone wall. There was a stone platform where the water poured out and Jill pulled out her *lungi,* a long piece of fabric sewn along one side forming a sort of tube.

Jill stepped into the tube of fabric and pulled it up over her chest. It hung down past her knees. A *lungi* was always a dark color. Hers was deep purple with black and various shades of more purple swirly flower and paisley designs. She tied it firmly at the top into a knot. She tugged hard at the clothes beneath to pull them off. She took out her shampoo and soap. Her *chapels* (flip flops) were already on her feet and ready to go. She turned on the water. It was ice cold. There was no time to hesitate. She could hear the crowd gathering momentum as they came down the trail. She took her *lota,* a small plastic pitcher and filled it quickly with the icy water and poured it over herself. She started at her neck. She would leave her hair for last so as to be cold and wet for as short a time as possible.

She applied the soap through the thin course *lungi* fabric and vigorously scrubbed using the *lungi* itself as a sort of washcloth. The soap easily passed through the fabric as did the water she used to rinse it off. She moved down her body quickly but the crowd had already formed. They stood in a ring around the tap, two layers deep and growing. Even grown men and women gathered to watch Jill take a bath. It was miserable. She wondered if getting three days worth of grime off of her was worth it. She still had her hair to go. She turned around to face the crowd and desperately tried to think of something to say in Nepali that might make them go away. They stared back at her blankly. They understood nothing she tried to say, or at least they pretended not to. They didn't turn away out of embarrassment or shame even though Jill knew perfectly well it was "jutto" (taboo) for them to do it. Jill realized she was simply going to have to endure it.

"Doggone it, I still have my hair to go," she thought to herself. At this point, she figured it was as bad as it could get. She may as well follow through and feel the pleasure of clean hair. She bent over and poured a *lota*-full of icy water over her head. She cringed when the icy water hit her scalp, chilling her to the bone. It made her head numb it was so cold. She shivered and shook like a leaf. Every inch of her was covered in goose bumps. She still had to put the shampoo in, let alone rinse it out. The crowd continued to grow. It was several layers deep by now and it nearly surrounded the tap, forming a long crescent from one wall of the tap to the other. She figured the number didn't matter at this point. There were so many of them.

She completed the final rinse. Her head was throbbing and numb. Why this village decided to put a tap on the shady side of the mountain was beyond stupid, Jill thought. Now for the drying and putting her clean clothes back on. There was no room to slip up. Jill was new at this and it was tricky sliding clothes beneath a clinging wet *lungi* without exposing body parts. What was worse, the careful procedure took a great deal of time. Jill finally finished. The torture was nearly over. She picked up her bag and turned to them and spoke in English, "There. Are you happy now? You got a good show." Walking away she added, "You people are utterly devoid of respect."

She walked quickly as the crowd parted to allow her to pass. This time they didn't even bother to follow her. It was as if they were as dumbstruck as she was. It must have been unfathomable to see a white woman taking a shower in this unbearably cold weather in this remote village that had probably never seen a westerner in their lives. When she arrived home, a member of the family that she was staying with came up to her and said, "You shouldn't take a shower. You're going to get sick." Jill looked at her with her long tangled wet hair before going to her room to brush it all out. The older volunteer asked her, "How did that go?" Jill replied, "Miserable." "Yeah, that's why I don't take one," she said.

The women in her own village later informed her that all she had to say was, *"Costo jhutto"* (how taboo) when people were doing something unacceptable. These words held the power to turn staring heads in shame and move them away. Jill wished she'd had this word power in her practice teaching village. The water tap in her own village that would be her permanent home was pleasantly and surprisingly enjoyable. It was a meeting place for the women. Women and girls would gather around to do their washing and bathe. They would ask her all kinds of questions and giggle at the answers. They would usually tell her why and explain the differences in their own culture and that would lead to a big discussion.

One day at the tap several women whispered among each other and Jill couldn't stand it any longer. She knew it was about her. Finally she asked and one of them timidly stepped forward. "Why don't you dye your hair black?" Jill was puzzled and answered, "Why would I do that?" The woman looked back at the other women for support and they urged her to go on. "Because your hair is ugly," she replied. "What?" Jill said. "It's ugly," she repeated, as if Jill hadn't understood the first time. "Really? You think my hair is ugly?" Jill asked. "Yes," she said. She looked back at the other women and all of them nodded their heads. Another woman stepped forward and walked up to Jill to feel her hair. *"Costo raamro."* It meant "how nice." "It is so soft," she commented. The other women came to feel and a murmur passed through them. "Ohhh. How nice," they agreed. "Now if you only dyed your hair black, it would be absolutely beautiful," they said. They nodded their heads again in agreement. One of them spoke up, "I'll run to the store to get you some black medicine, ok?" This is what they called hair dye. She said this enthusiastically several times and turned to go anticipating a positive reply. Jill laughed and asked, "But why don't you like the color of my hair?" Bashfully one of them put her head down and quietly said, "Because it looks like a *budi maanche*," (an old person). They equated her blond hair with the grey hair of an old lady. Jill laughed. They looked at each other puzzled and forced a laugh in response. Now that they had worked up their courage, another spoke up and said, "And your eyes. They're ugly too. They look like an old person's. They're blue, like a *kweedy."* It was a derogatory word the volunteers and other Westerners were sometimes called by gangs of unruly boys if one happened to be so unlucky as to pass a gang of them. "Really?" Jill asked. "My eyes too?" Ohhhh, because some old people have blue eyes when they have cateracts or eye diseases?" Jill asked. "Yes," they said. Well there was nothing she could do about that. As far as the black hair, she informed them she would not be dying hers black. They sighed in disappointment.

Nights in her village were warm and comfortable. It was a welcome cloak hiding her from the constant staring. It always felt intimate and comforting walking with her friends in the dark to the tea shop for dinner. Back at her *dhera* she used a lantern for light. Sometimes she would sit up and write letters, and even though the evenings cooled off somewhat, her little room somehow managed to contain the heat from the day despite all of the cracks in the walls and floor. Writing always proved a challenge. The lantern attracted hundreds of little bugs and mosquitoes. On top of that, in order to see, she needed to put the paper close to the lantern where all of the bugs were. Bent over her writing, sweat dripped from her arms onto her hands and from her head, resulting in a soggy piece of paper covered in bugs by the end of it.

It wasn't until towards the end of Jill's time in Nepal that an older volunteer came to visit her village. She went with Jill and the rest of her teachers to the teashop for lunch and a long discussion took place. The topic was Jill's blond hair again. That day this volunteer informed all of them that in our country blond hair is considered beautiful. The astounded looks and gasps of surprise passed through the little teashop. "No?!!" one of them asked, "You have to be kidding, right? Really??" "Really," she replied. It took a great deal of convincing for them to believe it.

Another event took place at the tap. It was among the little girls this time. Once again the girls whispered among themselves wanting to ask Jill something. "What is it?" Jill asked. One little girl named Januka stepped forward. "Miss?" she began, "Where did you come from? Did you come from Kathmandu?" "No no, much further away than that," Jill told her. Their eyes grew wide. "Further than that?" They looked at each other. "Yes, much further," Jill answered. Januka looked at Jill intensely. "Where then?" The girls hung on every word. "I come from America." "Ahhhh, America," they nodded their heads.

The girls spoke quickly and whispered between themselves. "Miss? How did you get here? By bicycle?" Jill laughed and they laughed too, not really knowing why. "No! You can't ride a bicycle across the ocean! I flew in a plane!" One of them said, "Ahhh! A plane!" They became still, looked at each other speaking quickly and then asked, "What's a plane?"

Jill tried to explain but they still looked more confused then ever and then suddenly Januka seemed to know. She spoke rapidly to the others, trying to explain. Januka pointed to the sky and put her arms out. Jill said "Yes! That's it! A plane in the sky!" The confused little girl slowly nodded her head, looking as if she was trying really hard to understand. They were silent again until they couldn't stand it any longer. One of them spoke up once more. "Misss? Where is America?" Januka's eyes were glued on Jill, wide with curiosity. "It's across the ocean, very far." "Oohhh," they said. "That's very far." The two girls looked at each other in awe and nodded at each other as if they understood.

The food in Jill's village was plentiful compared to most of the villages around Nepal. It was the flat jungle lands just at the foot of the mountains beneath Sagarmartha as the Nepalis called it, or Mt. Everest to the rest of the world. On a clear day and a bit further back from the small hills where Jill's village was, Jill had a perfect view of it.

Jill knew she had it good regarding food. Back at the village of her final phase of training the food was meager in comparison. Her family was poor and the food reflected that. She stayed at their home for three full weeks. The Nepali trainer staying with Jill told the mother, "This is deplorable. There are three beans floating around in water. The only substance to the meal is a big pile of rice." "Peace Corps is giving you money to feed us. Where's the food?" He picked up a glob of saag (spinach) with his bare hand to show her and slapped it back down on his plate. Jill tried not to laugh. He said, "There isn't even any *achaar*" (chutney). "And no spices either." He was right. The food was bland unlike the typically spicy food of Nepal. The woman stared back at him as if she didn't hear. He said to us in English, "She's saving the money so she doesn't have to spend it on us." It was unusual and the only time Jill experienced this for the rest of her time in Nepal. Nepalis were typically extremely generous and always overfed their guests. Jill felt badly that they must have been extremely poor. Who knew what circumstances she was enduring. Perhaps her husband was abusive in addition to the harsh living conditions, it could have been anything. Simple living was difficult enough.

The other two male trainees stayed at the headmaster's house and his beautiful wife cooked gourmet Nepali food. They came walking down the mountain talking about the *kier,* rice pudding with raisins and nuts and spices she made. Jill glared at them. Everyday they went on and on about their delicious meals.

At break time each day the three of them, the other two male volunteers and she would sit on the wall in front of the only store in town. They had eaten every packet of biscuits and snacks the store had within three days of their arrival to the village. The boys, despite getting fed well were still hungry, and Jill, who wasn't fed so well, now stared longingly at the store the remainder of their three weeks there. Jill's stomach growled for the duration of the time. It was a relief when it was finally time to pack their bags and leave despite the fact it was a nine-hour walk carrying all of their belongings on their backs. Jill could feel her clothes hanging off of her loosely she'd lost so much weight and she couldn't wait to eat. It's a good thing Jill was not posted in one of the remote mountain villages like a lot of the volunteers were.

Fortunately when it was village-choosing time Jill did not get the village she wanted. She thought she wanted the most remote far west village she could get in order to have the most intense authentic volunteer experience possible. However, five other volunteers had also bid for this village, probably thinking the same thing. The trainers' method of handling the gridlock was to leave it to the volunteers to sort out among themselves. There was a fair amount of discussion and Jill decided early on to back out and let the others fight over it. She figured none of them really knew what any of these villages were like anyway, so she would take what was left, the only one of which was at the opposite corner of Nepal, the far southeast. As it turned out, the poor girl who ended up with the highly sought after village had a metabolism similar to Jill's, the two of them being the only two girls in the group that did. Fast metabolism does not hold well on a rice diet, and even Jill dropped weight despite the wide array of fruits and vegetables available in her village. For virtually the rest of the females in the group, the opposite was true, and they put on weight accordingly. This unlucky girl became so skinny the medical unit had to fly her in to the capital regularly to check on her. They had to send her very large supplemental cans of powdered milk and peanut butter too. Jill breathed a sigh of relief she didn't end up in the poor meager village everyone fought so hard over. And anyway, it was in her region that she met her future husband whom she might not otherwise have met.

It was in this way that Jill was indoctrinated into a life completely opposite in every way to the one she came from. Not only was daily living and physical hardship a sharp contrast to her old way of living, but the social environment and the supportive, loving and hospitable people were too. It was this latter element that acted as a balm to her soul. It was warm and sincere. The Nepalese people were genuine, kind and generous (most of them). In addition they were also brutally honest nearly to the point of annoying. However this was the honesty Jill needed. Their words were penetrating and curious. They told it like it was. They wanted exact details. If Jill's answers were vague, the Nepalese villagers pressed her until they were satisfied they had gotten an adequate answer. If Jill hesitated between her words and her actions, the Nepalese called her out on it. They weren't ones to let things slide. This was good for Jill. She hadn't acquired this skill growing up.

When Jill arrived at her village to stay, even tougher challenges lay ahead, but she witnessed beautiful moments too. For instance the day one of the teachers she worked with walked to the bazaar after having received his monthly salary. A man approached him and said, *bai,* meaning "little brother," though he wasn't really his brother. "I need some money." He never explained why. The teacher pulled out the entire wad of bills in his pocket and handed it over to him like it was only a small favor, like asking for a piece of gum. The villagers were so poor. Most of them owned one pair of clothes. And yet, if there was a friend in need, no one asked questions, and no one ever said no. The lack of attachment to everything was staggering. In this way they were richer than the richest man on earth, Jill thought. She decided too much money often made people forget what is truly important.

The Indian Roadside Project Jill lived in happened to house the cabinet that contained all of the village's family planning supplies. Five robust women were in charge of the family planning committee. Every so often they came bustling into Jill's dhera without knocking, chatting happily as their saaris swept around the floor, brushing the ground as they walked. They went straight for the cabinet and pulled out the necessary supplies, stopping only to chat with Jill for a while. The routine question was, "When will you wear a saari?" After many months Jill finally agreed. The women were elated. Jill had bought a long piece of saari fabric and she pulled it out. Two of the women grabbed one end while another tied the petticoat tightly. Tying it tightly was necessary to hold it in place. It was the only thing that held the entire outfit together. The women proceeded to tuck the beginning end into the petticoat and wrap it around two or three times, tucking all edges in along the way. After that, using one hand as an anchor one woman flipped the next section of fabric back and forth several times like a fan and tucked it in. It looked like a pretty little ruffle at the front. The remaining fabric was then draped over the top of the small and very tight top that exposed her middle. Jill felt very exposed. Contrary to the Western way of thinking, it was the ankles and the shoulders that are the most risqué area of a woman's body to show and one would never do so. Exposing the belly was okay though.

Jill learned you never lock your door in Nepal. She tried it a couple of times coming home after a long day at school with a splitting headache. Trying to think and speak Nepali for hours was grueling. The neighbors and other teachers came to her *dhera*, (apartment) frequently and banged on the door. If she didn't answer, they banged harder. She had no choice but to answer. They were alarmed and concerned for her. "Why was the door locked? What's wrong? Are you okay?" Jill laughed, resigned to her new way of life in the village. She invited them in. Several of them filed in the door and sat down wherever they could find a seat. The endless questions and discussions began all over again, and Jill sat patiently answering and trying to politely converse with questions of her own. She had to pay close attention because the Nepalis were attentive and determined to obtain accurate information from her, and this required intense concentration, and she was still learning Nepali. One missed word and the entire meaning of the conversation was lost. A cat and mouse game would follow with circling attempts at an explanation to guess the meaning of the missing word. It would sometimes take minutes for that one word. It was painstaking. Eventually, after several months, Jill's language improved enough to converse without so much headache-inducing effort and life in the village became pleasant.

For some time, she remained slightly annoyed and perplexed at the intrusion on her every personal detail. The question whenever she left her village was this: "What will you be doing?" and "Did you eat your *dahl bhat*?" (rice and lentils) for which she was not released until a thorough explanation was given. The question on return was invariably the same. "What did you have for breakfast?" and "What were you doing?" At one point another older volunteer explained that the *dahl bhat* question was equivalent to "How are you?" Knowing this minor detail made a big difference.

There were numerous unexpected adventures that took place during Jill's stay in Nepal. One was the day her village friends took her to the county fair. Five teenage girls from the high school that loved to hang out with her arrived at her house. The girls accompanied her next door neighbor and teacher-colleague with the furry Russian hat. They picked her up and the girls surrounded Jill, walking hand in hand, discretely vying for who would get to hold her hand next. They walked in a horizontal line, reaching onto the East-West Highway, which was nothing but a big dirt road with a lot of potholes. It extended from Kathmandu, through the hills out of the valley and down into the flat jungle plains, bordering India and nearby Bangladesh. The highway even reached beyond that across the border into India and to Darjeeling only a mere few hours away from her village.

As they approached the small incline on the highway the fair appeared below. Jill halted and the girls asked what was wrong. Jill realized too late that this fair consisted of villagers from miles away adding up to thousands of people. Already Jill could not stand at her bus stop in her own village for too long or she drew a small crowd that would multiply in a matter of minutes. The fair was so big that it was impossible to see a single patch of dusty soil from the river to at least a mile in the distance and it littered the entire area from the highway to the base of the foothills. The girls held fast to her hands and urged her forward. Jill resisted, pulling back telling them, "I don't think I'll be able to do this. Look how many people there are." They replied, "It's ok. It's no problem at all. Don't worry. It's great fun. You'll see. Come on!" Jill planted her feet squarely where she stood and slowly shook her head with an obvious look of immense dread. "Please," they pleaded. "We promise. It will be just fine. There's nothing to worry about." They tugged and tugged at her hand. The looks on their faces made Jill relent. They appeared so disappointed. They had been so excited to show her this big fair that was the most exciting thing to happen all year. Jill went.

As they drew closer to the fair, more people noticed the tall white foreigner with white hair and *kweedy* eyes. Their group got larger as more people gathered around and joined them. The further they went, the bigger the crowd that surrounded her grew. By the time they reached the fair, their group extended clear into the highway. Jill felt like Jesus in the multitudes. A policeman appeared and pushed through the small crowd to tell her she was going to have to move off the highway because the crowd she was attracting was blocking the road and the buses couldn't get past.

When they got to the actual fair the girls and her furry Russian-capped friend pulled her through the throngs of people. There were so many of them that she had to squeeze through and there was something good about this; only the front row of people could see her, and this prevented her from attracting as many stares. The girls and her teacher-friend continued to pull her through the crowd. Jill couldn't understand why they had to rush through the mob. What could they possibly do on the other side of it that was different from the side they were on? The girls assured her it was something wonderful.

When they reached the other side of the fairgrounds the wonderful thing appeared. It was a *ping*. Jill looked at it, trying to show excitement at their surprise for her. She nodded and said, "Oh yeah, wow, you have a ferris wheel." They said, "No. It's a *ping*." Before she knew what was happening she was dragged to one of the hanging benches and pushed on. She said, "Wait a minute, who's going with me?" "No one," they said happily satisfied that they were giving her a ride and so excited at the anticipation of her reaction. Jill could have fought her way out of it, but it would have required physical force the way they all pushed her on and stood in front of the bar preventing her escape, plus she saw all the effort they had gone to and couldn't deny their generosity.

One of the girls ran to get a ticket and returned. She gave it to the ferris wheel operator and the gate was slammed shut. It was already beginning to move. Jill glanced around and saw there were no other people on the ride. "Great," she thought. Up and up she went until she was high above the crowd. Little by little, a ripple of heads turned in her direction and looked up. They pointed at her and she cringed. To her it felt like a horrible dream she wished she could escape from. She wasn't sure if it was her imagination, but throngs of people began pushing towards the ferris wheel. They crept ever so slightly forward. She was horrified, imagining what might happen if that many people pushed around the ferris wheel at once to look at her. She imagined the entire carnival ride getting knocked over. But then an idea occurred to her. The crowd was so packed they could barely move. This small fact alone, she realized, was what saved her that day. The crowd continued to sway in her direction in waves, but the waves swayed back every time it moved forward; it was a stagnant wave that could not actually go anywhere.

Eventually, Jill settled into life in the village and her teaching position at the school. She found her classes enjoyable. She was charmed by the row of five girls in her math class that crowded onto the bench at the very front of the room every day. The benches were made from old course wood and similar benches several inches taller served as a long desk they could lean their elbows on. The row of small girls at the front of the room looked up at her all prim and proper and with the intensity of an adoring puppy. Looking up at her with their large brown eyes, they hung on her every word as if she might say something profoundly significant and they didn't want to blink an eye for fear they might miss it. One of the girls wore a large sunbonnet rimmed with big gaudy flowers every day to class. Her little head was a fraction of the size of the large white rim that framed her face. It was endearing and comical at the same time. The contrast between this absurd and completely out of place hat and the little girl's seriousness made it difficult for Jill not to laugh.

One day, a group of boys acted up. During break she discussed the problem with the other teachers, not wanting to take action until she verified what the school procedure was for bad behavior. The teachers described to her the typical protocol and Jill looked at them in disbelief. "Are you sure?" she asked. "Yes yes," they answered, "That's the way we do it." "Does it work?" Jill asked. "Oh yes, it works," they assured her.

Jill walked back into the classroom and as soon as the naughty group of boys started in she called them to the front of the class and said, "Come on boys. We're going outside." The rest of the class crowded around the doorway, but there were so many of them that by the end of the ordeal, the entire class of fifty kids were outside with them. Jill instructed the boys to do what the teachers had said. The boys lined up against the building and got down on their knees. Next they put their hands behind their heads.

Jill said, "Go!" And they began to shuffle across the grassy schoolyard on their knees. One of the teachers came out of her classroom and stood in the doorway nodding her head in approval and then went back inside. One of the boys had a bit of trouble and Jill encouraged him saying, "Ok, just do your best." The class watched intently to see what else their strange white teacher might do.

As the boys shuffled across the schoolyard Jill thought they looked a lot like chickens and swallowed a giggle. Jill's students were far too observant. Even though Jill tried to cover it with a cough, the students saw it and one shouted, "Miss laughed!!" A couple of them timidly began to laugh. Jill let another laugh slip out. Then the chicken-walking boys began to laugh. Pretty soon the entire class was laughing and so was Jill. Only one naughty boy vigorously reached the other side of the schoolyard and respectfully called out, "How many laps, Miss?" Jill laughed even harder. This boy did not laugh. He was the only one. Jill finally answered, "Ok, enough, come on back to class." Jill muttered to her self, "That has to be the stupidest punishment I ever heard of." The boys did stop acting up though.

The women worked so hard in Nepal. The men, Jill observed, seemed to drink a lot of tea and do a lot of sitting around while the women served them. The women reaped the rice and then pounded it with giant mortar and pestle type contraptions that pounded the rice. A large log-sized chunk of wood served as the pestle. The women cooked all of the food on mud stoves, using cow dung as fuel. They did all of the dishes, washed all of the clothes and took care of the babies. Everything was washed at outdoor taps. Clothes were beaten or pounded like kneading a piece of dough to get the soap and water through, then hung to dry.

Jill asked her Russian fur capped friend one day why the men didn't help out more. He answered it was because the men did the "hard" work. She asked what it was because she never saw them doing anything. He said they did the work the women couldn't do and that was to plow the fields with the water bison. Jill agreed she had seen them doing this, but then thought some more about it. "But how many months do they plow out of the year?" Her friend replied, "Oh about two." Jill nodded her head. "So … the women do the cooking, the wash, reap the rice, pound the rice, take care of the kids all year, every day … while the men … have one task which is to plow two months out of the year?" He said, "Well yes." She asked him, "Don't you think that's a little unfair?" He answered proudly, "Well, like I said, they do the work the women can't do and it is really hard work. That's the way it is." She thought about this and asked, "What exactly is it the men do when they plow?" Jill had observed the men standing on the backs of the ox carts while the water bison pulled. He looked at her as if he wondered why she asked such an obvious question. Jill continued, "Don't they only stand on the ox cart while the ox does the work?" The teacher looked at her sideways and let out a huge laugh. "Ok, ok, ok, you're right, you're right!"

Jill's teacher-friend added to the conversation, "But there are men who have office jobs and work all day." He looked at Jill with raised eyebrows like she had to give him that. But Jill had an answer for that too. "Except the office workers, they drink tea all day too!" He laughed even harder, saying, "It's true, it's true!!"

Going to dinner each night with her Russian fur-capped friend and Kamala, her teenage friend who came to her house regularly became Jill's favorite part of the day. It would be dark outside by the time they arrived to her house. The darkness provided a protective cloak, disguising Jill from all the stares. It felt easier and like she could almost fit in as one of them. There was also something familiar and intimate about the dark, Jill thought. They would walk together in the warm comfort of it, talking all the way to the *chiyaa pasal*. Gas lanterns lit the teashop and once there, the waitress, who was Kamala's sister, would ask, "What would you like?" One day Jill said as usual, *dahl bhat*, (rice and lentils). The waitress looked back at her and asked, "What?" Jill replied again, "*Dahl bhat.*" Jill couldn't understand why the confusion. Finally Jill answered with the proper aspirated "h's" trying to annunciate each one and the waitress answered, "Ohhhh, *dahl bhat!*" "Yes, *dahl bhat*, that's what I said." Jill asked her, "Do you even have anything else?" She looked at Jill blankly. Jill wondered why anyone would even ask. There *is nothing* else to eat.

Kamala's sister was so skinny and overworked. She couldn't have been that old, but she looked haggard. Little ones hung at her sides. She cooked and waited on people at the teashop that served as the main meeting place in the village. She did all of this single-handedly all day long on her small mud stove with cow dung for fuel. Jill always wondered where her husband was. He was probably out drinking tea, or standing on the back of a plow.

Keeping in mind the latest medical reminder to drink boiled water and to take better responsibility for volunteer health, Jill asked the skinny waitress for a cup of boiled water. She stared at Jill with a funny look on her face and asked, "Why?" Jill explained, "Because I want to have clean water." "Oh our water is clean." The young woman assured her. "You don't want hot water in this heat. You need some nice fresh *chiso pani*," (cold water).

Getting her boiled water was going to require some effort, Jill realized. "The reason I would like *umaleko pani* (boiled water) is because I want my water with no bugs." Jill didn't know the word for "amoeba" or "microscopic organisms" and she wasn't sure if the uneducated waitress would have understood the meanings of the words anyway. She answered, "Oh we don't have bugs in our water." "Well, I don't mean bugs exactly." Jill tried to explain. "Well, what then?" the waitress asked. Thankfully Jill's Russian furry-capped friend joined the conversation and tried to bridge the gap. "Ok, yes they are bugs, but they are tiny tiny little bugs, so tiny you can't see them."

The teacher said excitedly, "Oh! I know what she means!" "Like amoebas?" he turned to Jill for verification. "Yes! That's what I mean!" she answered. He was educated so he understood. Quickly he tried to convey what Jill was trying to explain to the waitress. However, she blankly stared back at him too. He waved his hand and said, "*Na bujne,*" (she doesn't understand). The waitress walked away and Jill called after her, "Don't forget my *umaleko pani*!"

The waitress returned with a tall metal cup and placed it in front of Jill. In it contained the boiled water. Jill asked to be sure, "*Umaleko pani ho*?" She nodded her head, but in the waitresses opposite hand was a pitcher of cold water. She picked up Jill's cup and began adding the cold water into the rest of the cup. Jill said, "Oh no! That's not boiled water! What are you doing?!" The waitress replied, "I'm mixing nice *chiso pani*," (cold water). "You can't possibly drink that hot water in this heat." Jill said, "No! I can't have the cold water! Only boiled!" "What's the matter?" she asked. Jill tried to explain again but the waitress answered, "Yes, I gave you your boiled water and I mixed some cold water so it's not so hot." Jill's furry Russian-capped friend laughed and shook his head, "*hoina, hoina!*" (no, no!) Jill picked up the water saying, "It's ok, forget it."

The waitress came with the large metal plates partitioned off into sections. However the plates were still wet. Once again, attempting to follow Peace Corps medical unit advice Jill informed her that she would need a dry plate. The waitress looked at Jill with a puzzled look and picked up the plate. She walked over to the doorway and began drying it on the grimy curtain that looked like it hadn't ever been washed and was so dirty the color was indeterminable. Jill shook her head in disgust and said, "Never mind, can I have another plate? I don't care if it's wet." Her Russian fur-capped friend laughed even louder. The waitress walked off with the plate wondering why Jill had so many odd requests tonight.

The *dahl bhat* arrived and the waitress spooned large portions into the different sections of the metal plate. The food was steaming hot and smelled of spicy curry. A few villagers had stopped by their table inquisitively asking questions. Jill pinched four fingers of her right hand against her thumb and used her hand in this way to pick up a mouthful of food. There were no utensils and this was how the Nepalis ate. After the first bite, Jill's eyes watered as usual because the food was so hot. Her mouth burned and she sucked in air breathing quick breaths to try to cool it down. Now it was the waitress's turn to laugh, and like usual she ran to get the *chiso pani*. Everybody in the tea shop seemed to have comments. "Our food is hot, *hoina?"* Jill couldn't speak. She nodded yes. Her nose began to water too. Her head was on fire. Every taste bud in her mouth burned. It took Jill a good year to get used to the spicy food. Nobody seemed to tire of the entertainment watching Jill's eyes water and liquid dripping out of every orifice at every meal from the hot spices. It was a topic of discussion every night, and so was her blonde hair.

It was during Jill's time in Nepal that she met the man that would become her husband. He lived in another village several hours away, and that, by Nepali standards was a very close neighbor. He had arrived as a Peace Corps volunteer one year earlier than Jill and with another group. She met him for the first time briefly during the survival visit to her village. The older volunteers had come together from their various villages for a day to greet the new volunteers and show them around. Jill's husband-to-be seemed aloof and did not talk much. He leaned against a railing of the porch to the wooden stilted little shack one of the volunteers lived and where they had decided to meet for that brief night and a day. He appeared to be observing the new volunteers, Jill thought, like he was trying to decide if he liked them or not. Either that, or he was trying to be cool. It was hard to tell.

The bungalow they had gathered in for the night did not have enough floor space for all of them to pull out their sleeping bags and so Jill and Michael offered to sleep on the porch. They barely spoke a word to one another and went straight to sleep. Later he would always joke that the first night they met, they slept together, and then they'd have to explain the whole story.

It took several months before the two of them became better friends and eventually showed interest in each other. The real spark seemed to come during a volunteer conference in a remote village. There were over one hundred volunteers gathered together and after one of the sessions, a trainer asked, "And who would like to cook dinner for everyone tonight? We have cooks but we need someone to direct them. We've been requested to make an American dinner, and they don't know how." No one raised their hand and everyone glanced around the room at each other. No one wanted to speak up. Michael raised his hand and volunteered Jill. She was sitting far in the back and hadn't been listening but suddenly realized the entire room was staring at her. "What?" she asked. The trainer said, "Great! Thanks for offering to cook us dinner Jill!" Jill wondered what had just happened. The trainer announced, "And we will be having spaghetti tonight. That's what everybody has been requesting." The person sitting next to Jill whispered, "Looks like you're making spaghetti for everybody." Jill said quietly, "But I don't know how to make spaghetti." The trainer was already on to the next subject and she did not have the chance to protest. She caught Michael's eye, and he was grinning mischievously. Jill glared at him. The last and only attempt she had ever made at spaghetti was a disaster. The pasta came out in a big sticky clump and she had used spaghetti sauce in a can. She went down to the kitchen and the first thing the cooks asked was "What spices do we use?" Jill replied "I don't know." She thought to herself "Well this is going to be fun." Jill ran outside the kitchen asking everyone and anyone if they knew what spices to use for spaghetti. No one knew. Finally a person answered, "Basil, oregano." "Oh thank you, thank you," she said. She ran back to the kitchen and told the cooks. They gave her a blank stare. "What's oregano?" Jill said

"I don't know." What's basil?" "I don't know that either. The head cook said "Well we don't have anything like that." "Well what do you have?" she asked. They looked at each other and said, "We have *jira and dunya."* That was cumin and coriander. "Do you have anything else?" "Nope," they answered. "Well I guess that'll have to do." As the preparations went along they kept bringing samples to Jill as if she were an expert to see if it was ok. "Well it's not quite right," and they would go back to the pots and suggest adding more *jira* or more *dunya.* After about twenty repetitions of this Jill finally gave up. It wasn't getting any better. In fact it was pretty awful. The volunteers complained about dinner that night and Jill couldn't wait to give it to Michael.

Somehow this event led to dates to each other's villages, and those consisted of three bus rides, biking four hours down dusty roads, crossing rivers and navigating narrow rice patty paths to visit each other. If it was monsoon, it was a different story. In that case, the rice paddy paths were slippery and muddy too. The only consolation to the miserable trip was the *pasals* (shops) along the way that sold *jard.* Jard was a type of millet beer that was thick and milky but surprisingly good. It gave a slight buzz but not enough to get a person drunk. But it did make the unpleasant bike ride endurable. She would drink one at each village she passed until she arrived to Michael's village.

Jill's newly formed relationship with her husband-to-be filled her with hope. It was exciting and new. She felt close to someone like she never had before. They spent hours talking into the night beneath gas lit lanterns and candles by dark. He would bring his small speakers and plug them into a battery powered small cassette player and they would listen to Van Morrison. They became very close and looked forward to any opportunity to spend together. Jill was happier than she had ever been.

The most romantic gesture he made was to hang a screen on the ceiling where a bat lived inside her attic to catch the poop that fell on her bed each day. Until then, Jill brushed it off before climbing into bed each night.

Despite their happiness there was a brief period of time that Jill rejected Michael. There really was no good reason for it. She pushed him away just before he left for a training in the mountains. Michael was very sad and Jill immediately regretted it. She had become cold and distant, and barely talked to him. She really didn't understand why she did it, but she wrote him a long letter that muddled through even her own understanding of her past and her fears and insecurities. She tried to make sense of her own behavior but it was hard. It was like there was something deep inside of her that didn't trust anyone, or herself. Maybe she didn't think it was possible to be this happy, or that she deserved it. The letter arrived on the worst day of a very difficult training. The trainees in this particular village resisted cooperating, there was mud everywhere and Michael actually fell in some and got stuck. The toilets were a massive dump pit behind one of the buildings. Even by Peace Corps standards, it was deplorable. Jill's letter arrived on this day, and after Michael thought the relationship was surely over. Her letter expressed the opposite, how much she loved him, and she truly did. Even Michael's worst day turned into the best after receiving Jill's letter.

The two of them had many adventures in Nepal before they decided to get married. One such adventure was a trek across the eastern hills. The goal was to reach the conference site where Jill's group was to meet after a teacher training she had given on the other side of the mountains. They had decided they were not going to take the dirty crowded buses around to the south and all the way back up again to get there. They inaccurately thought that a small trek would be much easier and also miscalculated that it would take a shorter time than the bus.

First off, they were given poor information. Every person they sought directions from told them something different. In Nepal, one can never not have an answer even if it's the wrong one. The original projected trip time of six hours turned into three days and that had not been *anyone's* projection. They had also been assured there were plenty of villages along the way, lodging and places to eat. There were none for nearly two day's walking. They had planned for such an emergency. They carried one can of tuna between the two of them.

To make matters worse, the water system had broken at the first village they came to after two day's of arduous walking and to the top of a mountain. They had eaten fried green bananas they'd scouted out at the river below the night before and they were sticky and pasty. Jill couldn't eat it. They slept on their sweaters for the night and hung a sheet of plastic above their heads between two trees. The following day's walk began on an empty stomach and one bottle each of water filled from the river below.

Their endurance and stamina waned. They didn't eat until the end of the second day's walk. *Dahl bhat* never tasted so good.

The most harrowing part of the trip was crossing a very long rope bridge that spanned the width between two mountains and contained rickety and rotted wooden slats to walk on. It must have been some five hundred feet high. Jill hesitated at the start of it while her fiancé dashed across at one go. He was over the bridge in minutes. Jill carefully put one foot on the bridge and tested the strength, stomping on it. It held, so she took another step. Noticing some missing planks and seeing through to the bottom below made her stomach drop. The wind picked up and the bridge began to sway back and forth but she was already a third of the way across. Jill held fast to the ropes on either side that formed a sort of railing. The problem was, as she neared the center of the bridge, the ropes went higher and higher until they were out of reach. There was nothing to hang onto. Jill got down on her hands and knees to crawl, testing the steadiness of each plank as she went. The wind picked up and the bridge tossed from side to side even more. Jill's nerves were so wrought and her heart beat so hard she didn't know if she would make it without fainting of fright. Her fiancé sat on the other side against a rock laughing. Maybe that should've been a premonition. Jill inched her way slowly across one plank at a time until she reached the end. She scowled at his lack of chivalry. Michael thought it was hilarious.

At the end of three long days, they reached their destination, a small village called Hile, pronounced *Heelay.* Hile was having water problems too. It was this day that Jill had a "shower in a cup." It was an unimaginable feat, but one Jill was proud of for years to come. They would not give her a bucket of water to take a bath because of the water shortage, but she was determined after that harrowing three-day hike to have one. She was full of dust and dirt. Since the restaurant owner would not give her a bucket with water she asked for a cup of water. She was in the back of the restaurant where the work was done and where the toilet and a closed-in empty stall was for taking showers, so the restaurant owner eyed her suspiciously. He had told her there was absolutely no possibility for him to spare water for a bath.

It was difficult, however, for a man to deny a woman a cup of water. He brought her the cup of water and he watched her head for the shower stall. He shook his head and walked off. Jill set the cup down carefully and got out her small washcloth. She wet her soap and one corner of the washcloth and proceeded to scrub, using only enough water to cover the soap; she needed to save the majority of the water for the rinse off. Jill took an ever so slight dab of shampoo and applied it in the same way to her hair. After scrubbing and scrubbing for some time, she picked up the cup of water and gingerly poured a bit over her hair. Rinsing her hair required most of the water. Since she used very little soap, she was able to manage with the small amount of water. She moved on to the rest of her body and dribbled water ever so sparingly on the rest of her body until all of the soap was rinsed off. She was cold, but it didn't matter. She was clean, sort of. She put her clothes back on, including one fairly clean t-shirt and one clean pair of underwear and headed back to the restaurant where everyone waited. Her hair was wet and tangled when she passed the man who wouldn't give her the bucket and he glared at her. She didn't care. She was clean and that's all that mattered. She could sit down and enjoy her *momos and tumba* (Tibetan dumplings and millet beer) in comfort. The *tumba (pronounced toomba)* came in a large wooden barrel with a wooden straw that fit down through the center. Metal stripping held the barrel together. The yellowish-brownish millet beer filled the barrel and every so often the waitress came by and poured boiling water over the remaining millet enabling the beer to last a long time even though it gradually became weaker. It gave an ever so slight and relaxing buzz, but no matter how much one drank, it was impossible to become drunk. After the harrowing trip, a clean bath and good food was an excellent reward. Other volunteers joined them as they poured into the village for the upcoming conference.

Jill thoroughly enjoyed her experiences in Nepal even if a bit rough sometimes. She was curious to learn all she could. She felt alive in a way she had never felt before. Life was real. It was course and rough and rugged, that's true, but it was real, and Jill needed real more than anything.

As much as she loved the beautiful rugged country and it's people, it was difficult in ways hard to explain and yet the Nepalese were charming. It was the more difficult situations that provided the greatest experiences, and yet the hardships of living in Nepal were completely opposite the difficulties she had faced at home. In some ways, the psychological torture of loneliness and dysfunction outweighed the physical and cultural challenges of Nepal. Meeting her future husband changed everything. He showed her love, and that was something she desperately needed.

Chapter 6

King's River
(1966)

"You shall above all things be glad & young
For if you're young, whatever life you wear
It will become you, and if you are glad
Whatever is living will yourself become."

EE Cummings

Bobbie sat at the kitchen table with a smile, staring out of the window over the fields and canyon below. Her light blonde hair fell around her face in sweeping wavy curls like the sage weed that swayed in the wind. Everyone was dancing in the eye of Bobbie's mind. She held her pocket calendar in her hand and flicked it between her fingers. In it was written all of the dates and outings she had had over the past month with the man she imagined spending the rest of her life with.

She was deeply in love, but was it infatuation? Bobbie couldn't fathom it. In her love-soaked mind she quietly said to her self, "Loving with all of your heart, seeing only the goodness and the brightness of a man's soul, this is seeing truly." Light cast out the shadows that hid his flaws. Bobbie admitted it could be blissful naivety. But, on the other hand, maybe not. Maybe it was a beautiful innocence, seeing a man for the first time, with the freshness of a new relationship, seeing him with a true heart, open to all of him, with unconditional acceptance. "Perhaps the flaws are the illusion and it's love seen through forgiving eyes that is real," she said to herself.

Bobbie drove to Big Bear, a small mountain town, one morning two months earlier, to spend the day with her cousins. James was with them. They were six in total. The twins, Jim, John, and Patrick Jr., were brothers. The three of them along with James, Bobbie and a friend of theirs, Clark, bantered around at the log cabin where the three brothers lived. "Bobbie, will you type my paper for class?" Clark asked. He was always flirting with her. Jim called out from another room, "Yeah, Bobbie, can you do mine too?" John added, "Since you're doing theirs, how about mine?" The boys always took advantage of the chance to get Bobbie to do work for them. Bobbie sighed. She had really wanted to relax, breath in the fresh mountain air and the pine trees. She had been looking forward to going outside and doing something with the boys. Instead Bobbie acquiesced. "Ok, hand 'em over," mumbling to her self, "Guess I'll spend the next couple of hours typing."

Bobbie typed away. She wasn't too upset once she set to work. She could hear the boys goofing off in the living room. Two of them were socking each other while the others egged them on. It sounded as if it might turn into an all out brawl if Vivian, the three boys' mother and Bobbie's Aunt, hadn't walked into the room just then. "Boys! Not in my living room! Take it outside, you're going to break my things!! What have I told you before? You boys are too big and my little house is no place for that!!" Nobody messed around with Vivian. John said, "Hey guys, let's go outside." John was Vivian's favorite. Vivian could always count on John, Jim's twin, to be responsible.

Vivian walked into the back bedroom and found Bobbie typing. "They got you typing again, eh?" her Aunt asked. "Oh yeah," Bobbie answered. She turned around to acknowledge her favorite Aunt. Vivian inspected the number of pages she had completed, and how many there were to go. "Maybe one day you'll get to come over and have some fun." Bobbie laughed and said, "Ah, it's ok. I'm glad to help out. They don't know how to type and I do." Bobbie got up from her chair to give her Aunt a hug. "It's nice to see ya Aunt Viv." "It's always great to see my favorite niece too!" Vivian hugged her back. "I believe I am your only niece," Bobbie reminded her. The two of them had had many long talks together over the years, and

Bobbie was grateful for the close relationship they had. Bobbie always felt she could talk to Aunt Viv about things she could not with her mother. Mainly they would talk about her family and the difficulties Bobbie was having since her Father died and dealing with her own mother's depression because of it. Often Bobbie felt the burden of holding the family together. Effie, Bobbie's Mother, had never really gotten over the death of her husband. She went back to work because she had to, but emotionally, she was unable to be present for her children in the way that they needed. As a result, James got away with everything, doing whatever he pleased and got into all kinds of trouble. Bobbie, on the other hand, took responsibility for everything, including supporting her mother emotionally. She encouraged her mother, telling her to have confidence and listed to her all of the things she could do. She told her she needed to pull her self out of her depression. She also told her she needed to discipline James once in a while. Aunt Viv was a good listener. She loved Bobbie and enjoyed spending time with her. As far as Bobbie's mother and Aunt Viv were concerned, however, they mostly argued.

Bobbie sat down to type again and was sitting at the desk working away for another hour before she was finished. She got up from her chair and looked for a stapler. She organized the three separate essays and stapled them together. She walked out of the bedroom and found the five boys lounging around in the living room. She passed the essays out and the boys thanked her profusely. "You're welcome," she answered. Clark slid his foot out in front of Bobbie as she walked past. She tripped and looked back at him and smirked. Clark pretended he didn't have the slightest clue what happened. Bobbie had a small crush on him and she always looked forward to seeing him. She had been disappointed to be stuck in the bedroom all that time typing instead of spending it with Clark.

Bobbie let herself drop onto the couch with a deep sigh and leaned back. Aunt Viv brought her a glass of water. "Thank you Aunt Viv," Bobbie said and took the glass from her. She was tired after sitting at the desk for nearly two hours. James asked, "Where's our water?" "Go get your own you lazy lump." "Ahhhh," James said, shaking his head. "What?" Bobbie asked him. "What d'ya think? Someone's gonna wait on you after all you did was sit here all afternoon?" James shook his head in mock disbelief. "Whatever."

"What are we gonna do now guys?" Bobbie asked. "I don't know," Jim said. "Let's go to the bar downtown," John suggested. The five of them were old enough now and enjoyed this new privilege. "Great idea!" Jim said. "Yeah! That sounds great!" Bobbie agreed. James whined, "No! Let's not do that! Then I can't go!" James wasn't old enough to drink. He was four years younger than Bobbie and three years younger than the rest, and he hated not getting to do what the others did. He wanted so badly to go to the bar with them. Everyone ignored him. Clark said, "Well you guys go ahead. I gotta get home." He got up to leave and said, "Thanks a bunch for the paper, Bobbie," He tapped her on the head with it.

"Well, shall we go then?" Bobbie asked. "Yeah!" Jim answered. John said, "Yeah," too. "Ahhhhh," James whined, and he stuck out his bottom lip. "Come on guys, can't you stay here? We could play some baseball or something." No one listened. He thought of another idea. "Hey, how about you try to sneak me in guys?" Bobbie looked at him and said firmly, "No James. You just stay here. We're not doing that." James slumped back on the couch and let his feet fall hard on the ground. The boys and Bobbie continued to ignore him.

Bobbie and the twins arrived at the bar and went inside. They found a nice table at the side of the room and sat down. John got up and asked the bartender for a beer. While he waited a young man a little older arrived and did the same. "Hey, I haven't ever seen you up here before." Big Bear was a small town and the boys knew everyone. "I'm from L.A. I live in Westwood." "Oh groovy," he said. Before long, the two of them struck up a conversation and their beers were half finished when John asked him to join their small group at the side of the room. Bobbie and Jim had ordered drinks by then and were having their own conversation. "Hey guys," John said to get their attention. "This is Paul. He's up from L.A. Lives in Westwood." Bobbie and Jim greeted him and held out their hands to introduce themselves.

Bobbie felt a tingle all over her body. He was absolutely handsome she thought to herself. Jim made room for Paul to sit down. John pulled out a fourth chair and sat down with them. The four of them talked and it seemed to Bobbie Paul fell right in with them as if he had known them his entire life. They laughed, told jokes and ordered more beer. Jim and John were a pair and Paul was easily entertained by their typical banter. They were twins and it was nearly impossible for them to have a conversation with someone else unless they were together; they spoke as one, completing each other's sentences, telling the same stories, as if on cue where one left off the other picked up and vice versa until the story was complete. Bobbie was used to it, but for Paul it was something he'd never witnessed before, and it was quite amusing. Bobbie had a lot of fun with them and they always had a good time together. Paul was drawn to Bobbie's twin cousins and their lighthearted company. Bobbie's extended family was a tightly knit one. There was a warmth and humor that made it easy to be around them.

Two hours went by and John looked at his watch. "We'd better get going Jim." He looked in John's direction. "Yeah, we better," replied Jim. "Well, it sure was swell meeting you Paul," John said. "Yeah, it was great," Jim added. "Come up any time. You got a place with us whenever you need one." Paul shook their hands and said, "Thanks!" with the most sincere grin and dimples that melted Bobbie all over … and those sparkling green eyes …

Paul got up from the table and looked at Bobbie. "Well, I better get going too. I've got a long drive ahead of me." Bobbie nodded, trying to keep her head down so he wouldn't see her blush, "Yeah, I gotta get back to my little brother and drive him home myself." They walked out of the bar together and Paul commented what a beautiful place it was. It was dusk and the sun was falling behind the trees. Bobbie said, "Yes." She tried to think of things to say but her knees felt weak and she was too shy. She could feel Paul looking at her. "He is so handsome," she thought to herself. She stumbled over her words, unable to pick out the right thing to say. Before Paul left for his car he asked, "Would you like to go out sometime?" Bobbie's heart gave a leap. "That would be grand," she answered. "Ok!" Paul said. He looked at her with his sparkling green eyes, disarming grin and those charming dimples. Bobbie thought she might faint. "Well then, how about we go to L.A. for dinner? Next week?" Paul suggested. "Ok!" she said. "Great! I'll come pick you up. What about 5:00? That'll give us time to drive back to L.A. from your house and still have time to eat." "Perfect!" Bobbie agreed. They exchanged information and he walked away. Bobbie was tingling with excitement. She walked with a little skip back to the car smiling the entire way.

The twins waited in the car for her, and when she climbed into the backseat, Jim twisted around to face her and grinned. "So? What was that about? Seemed a bit long for a goodbye." "Oh nothing," she said. "By that smile, sure doesn't seem like nothing." She smiled more and blushed. "Ahh, I knew it! Someone got asked on a date! Great Bobbie, good for you! I approve!" By the time they reached home, Aunt Viv was putting dinner on the table. "Why don't you two stay for dinner before you head back? That way you'll start off with a full belly and give a little time for that beer to digest." "Oh that sounds great" Bobbie said and she bounced into the kitchen to help her Aunt put the food out. James was starved as usual and ran to the table, forgetting his miserable afternoon being left alone. He always missed out on everything. Bobbie's eyes twinkled and she couldn't stop smiling. Aunt Viv asked what was up. Jim answered for her "Oh she's all twinkly eyed because she got asked out on a date." Aunt Viv observed the radiant smile on her face. "…by the most dreamy man in the world," Bobbie added. "You've said that before. Like about a dozen times." "Oh! But no! This time it's truly a dream! He's taking me to dinner in L.A. next week!" "Oh," said Aunt Viv, eyeing her niece skeptically, "Well that changes everything." What she was really thinking was "Young people. Every new encounter is so exciting." "It's our first date but I can tell this may really be something." It was Saturday, July 9th, 1966 and Bobbie marked this day in her calendar: "Met 'P'."

Paul arrived at Bobbie's home the following week on a Friday to take her to dinner. Paul knocked on the door and Bobbie let him in. Paul was wearing nice pants and a decent shirt, and that was unusual for him, but Bobbie and her mother didn't know it at the time. His normal attire was a white short-sleeved t-shirt and jeans. His wavy dark hair was neatly combed and he was on his best behavior. "I'll be just a minute," she said. Effie sat on the big chair in the corner of the living room with a magazine. She looked over the tops of her reading glasses and said "Won't you come in? She motioned to the couch and stood up to introduce herself. "I'm Effie, Bobbie's Mother." "Oh, how do you do? I'm Paul." Effie eyed him up and down trying not to be conspicuous. "And what do you do Paul?" "Oh I'm in college studying for an aeronautical engineering degree." Effie raised her eyebrows, "Oh? Is that so?" "And … I work as a mechanic on the side to make ends meet." "Really?" Effie's interest was piqued. Bobbie came back with her handbag. "Was it a long drive?" she asked. Then she noticed her mother and made a grimace and said "Oh come on Mom, you're not interrogating him, are you?" "Oh no, we were just having a little chat, weren't we Paul?" Paul smiled. "Yes we were. And in answer to your question, the drive was not so bad." Bobbie wore a pretty blue dress, and it made her eyes look all the bluer. Paul couldn't take his eyes off of her. "Do I look alright?" she asked him bashfully. "Oh beautiful," he said. Effie smiled in delight. "I like this one," she thought to herself. "Shall we get going?" Paul put his hand behind her back and led her to the door and opened it for her. Effie thought "What nice manners this young man has." Bobbie thought he was a perfect gentleman.

Paul's car was parked at the curb. It was a shiny beige-gold color. He waxed it and worked on it constantly. He was proud of his Falcon. It had wings that jutted off of it at the corners. He opened the door for Bobbie. She had to balance on the curb between the evergreen bushes and the car that was a bit too close. She awkwardly crouched down to get in. Once in the car Bobbie asked, "Where are we going?" "We're going to Bing's." He seemed excited. Bobbie had heard of the place before. "Oh that sounds terrific!"

They had a great time that night. Paul took Bobbie to Venice Beach and they walked on the boardwalk holding hands afterwards. They talked and talked and laughed together for hours. It was late at night before Paul finally made the long drive to take Bobbie back home only to turn around and repeat the drive back to L.A.

Five days later, Paul called again and asked her out. After that, they were constantly on the phone together. Paul asked Bobbie to join him at King's River one day with a group of friends. He had a speedboat and loved to go camping and water-skiing. Bobbie did too once Paul taught her how. He could ski endlessly. "He is quite the athlete," Bobbie thought. "And a bit of a clown too."

One of his favorite stunts was taking a large round disc, setting it on the beach and placing a tall stool on top. Someone would hand him the rope with the handle attached. The other end was attached to the back of the boat. The first time he ever took her, Paul performed the feat like usual but mostly to impress Bobbie. He climbed on top of the stool and sat down on it. A friend took the driver's wheel and when Paul yelled "Hit it!" the friend slammed on the accelerator and somehow dragged the disc with the stool and Paul on top off of the beach into the water, keeping all three parts in tact.

Gliding over the water Paul turned in circles, skied backwards, held the rope with one hand, and anything else he could think of. Everyone on the beach laughed and cheered when the boat sped past pulling Paul from behind. He searched for Bobbie each time to see if she was looking and if she was, he made sure to do something impressive, grinning all the while. When he was finished he signaled to the driver and as soon as the boat made a last pass by the beach, the boat turned in the opposite direction and slowed down. Paul let go the rope and surfed towards the beach, waving at Bobbie as he sank into the water three feet short of reaching the exact spot he took off.

"What a goof!" Bobbie said to herself. Bobbie enjoyed the attention and the social atmosphere with all of his friends. Paul ambled up the beach, wet and sunburned, still grinning. Bobbie suggested it was time to get the food ready. "I think everybody's getting hungry." Paul agreed and got the grill stoked. He made hamburgers and hotdogs and Bobbie passed them out to everyone. When nighttime arrived they built a fire on the beach and sat around drinking beer, laughing and talking late into the night.

Bobbie learned to ski quite well through all the visits to this favorite river of Paul's. Bobbie thought, "We're sure having some fun times." He always insisted on King's River. It was a place of happy memories. He loved everything about it: setting up the tent on the beach, sitting outside talking by the fire into the night and waking up in the morning to flip pancake after pancake with that great big silly grin of his. Yes, Bobbie was definitely in love. Those were great days.

It was August 19, 1966 and Bobbie, Paul and a group of friends found themselves at King's River once again. However, this night was different. It was dark already. The tents were set up and a few people bumped around inside of them while a few others searched for wood and began the evening bonfire by the beach. Paul asked Bobbie to go with him to look for kindling. Bobbie smiled happily and said, "Ok." Paul walked for some ways and Bobbie called to him, "Why are we going so far up the beach? There was plenty of kindling back there." "Oh, I want to get a few big logs so the fire will last longer," he said. She did not know he was making excuses to get her away from the rest of the group. He made his way to a small clearing in front of a patch of trees by the edge of the lake. The moon glistened on the water. He waited for her to catch up. Bobbie said, "I seriously doubt there will be any logs here." "No," he said. Bobbie looked at him puzzled. "Well then why are we here? I thought you said we needed logs."

Paul put his hands around her waist and told her, "I wasn't looking for logs." Bobbie looked up into his eyes and quivered, wondering what was coming next. "Bobbie," he began. "Yes, Paul. What is it?" Bobbie began to get nervous at what was coming next. "Will you marry me?" Bobbie's head felt dizzy and it took a moment for the question to register. "Marry you?" she asked. "Yes," he replied. His eyes were twinkling more than ever. Bobbie thought she may float away she was so elated. He waited for her answer as she looked down at the ground and out at the water and finally up at him again. "Yes," she said. Her blue eyes sparkled too and Paul grinned bigger than ever. He took her in his arms and he kissed her, pulling back to pause in between so he could tell her, "You've made me the happiest man on earth." "And you, me," she answered. Her chest was filled with so much happiness, she thought her heart may burst.

They had only been dating one month but were certain this was it. They were the ones for each other. When they told Effie, Bobbie's Mother, she was all for it. She was so excited she pulled out the Martinis and toasted a toast to anyone who was there. Effie called the neighbors, her friends, anyone who cared to come and served out Martinis and whipped up snacks faster than anything. Even James got a Martini that day. In fact, there were many toasts that evening. Each time a new visitor arrived at the door, Effie raised her glass with all of them and made another. She was quite tipsy by the end of night.

Paul's parents were not quite as excited. Harriott was slightly troubled and hesitantly gave her blessings. Louie tried to be excited but felt his wife's tugging ambivalence. Paul and Bobbie, however, were brimming with love. Bobbie couldn't believe it was happening to her. Paul felt a renewed purpose in life to achieve his goal to become a pilot. Bobbie's goals were equally contagious to him, as were his to her. Bobbie wanted lots of children to create a big happy family. Bobbie could have said anything and Paul would have made it his goal too as if it were his own. And Bobbie was willing to sacrifice anything it took to help Paul achieve his. She knew it was his dream to become a pilot. It was easy for Bobbie to fall in with this dream because Bobbie had made it a goal way back as far as she could remember to marry a pilot or a doctor. It was written in her high school book of memories.

The wedding was planned immediately and happened just as quickly as the courtship leading to it. Bobbie penned in each task in her planner in preparation for the wedding. Sept 13: Jo & Dale's dresses, Sept 16-17 parents' dinners, Sept 29: material, Sept 5: 5 weeks to plan the wedding, Invitations, Oct 5: L.A. Paul & Aunt Viv, Oct 7 – 8: shopping, fitting for me and bridesmaids, Oct 10: dinner with relatives, Oct 19: organist, Oct 21: Faculty shower, Oct 23 – 24: look for apartment, Oct 28: rehearsal dinner at Phil's, Oct 29: 9:00 hair appointment, pick kids up, 2:00 wedding, 3 – 5 reception.

Intermingled with all of the plans were her continued psychiatry appointments. She saw three doctors: Dr. Gaines at the Norton Air Force Base, Dr. Jablon, and Dr. Zernlick in San Diego.

Chapter 7

I'm so Darn Unstable

(1992 – 1998)

What's the matter with me lately? I'm so darn unstable, unreliable (to myself), undecided, unconfident, and unhappy. Is it "senioritis," I wonder? Whatever it is, I wish it would go away. One minute I can be in the happiest mood, and any little disturbing thing that comes along switches me off and I'm in a blue, blue mood. I feel explosive most of the time, like a bomb. I have to be "handled carefully" or I feel crushed and hurt. I am constantly thinking pessimistically. Of course, the only time I show it is at home, but why?

I guess the only thing to do is psycho-analyze myself. One reason I think I feel this way is because I'm basically insecure. I miss my dad more than anyone will ever know. That expression "Time heals all wounds" is a phony, time makes it worse. All the problems I face, I say to myself: "If Dad were here I'd know what to do, he'd be able to help me," but Dad's not here, and it's a hard fact to get straight, even after 2 ½ years. Sure, Mom helps me, but often not the kind of help I need. She's fundamentally a weak person; every time we discuss any problem of mine, she brings up her own, and we both are trying frantically to get our problems solved. She doesn't understand me at all. On account of this I've become nervous, tense, and frustrated, which I never was before.

Another reason is trying to choose the right college. That's an awful big order, considering you'll be living there for four of the biggest years of your life. Mom doesn't want me to go up North, but something inside me keeps instilling the desire to go.

Bobbie, November 19, 1960

Jill and Michael departed Nepal to begin a new life together. They traveled through Thailand, Malaysia, Australia and Hong Kong. It took them three months and they budgeted on a shoestring using a portion of their readjustment allowance allotted by Peace Corps. They stayed in questionable hotels and yet they were several steps up from the housing of their villages in Nepal. In Thailand they put up lodging in thatch-roofed bungalows on the beach at two dollars a night and in Australia they stayed with a family on a sheep farm and road horses all day through Eucalyptus forests and fields of kangaroos and emus.

On the way home Jill became pregnant with their first child. Jill was sure her daughter was conceived in a bungalow in Krabi. She could feel it. They called her their bungalow baby. She also knew she was a girl. She had a dream about it.

They packed Jill's car with every belonging she owned and drove across the United States, stopping to see relatives and camping at national parks along the way. The heat of Jill's non air-conditioned car combined with morning sickness and constant driving was miserable. Camping in the cool beautiful forests, however, compensated for it.

The destination was Philadelphia where Michael's parents lived. Their daughter was born there as well as their second. They went to graduate school on a Peace Corps Fellowship and lived in row houses that bordered the ghetto and the Italian neighborhood. They did not have a TV, however they didn't need one. Sitting on their tiny balcony that overlooked the street below provided all the entertainment they needed. A brothel occupied the row house two over from them. A constant stream of traffic flowed from it. An alcoholic who instigated dramatic explosions from the family regularly and that usually propelled them outside for some reason, lived on the other side of them. Police cars filled the end of the cul-de-sac nearly every night. Evel Knievel clad attire adorned a very large young man who lived on their street too. He road a tiny dirt bike and wore a brightly colored skin-tight suit. Michael called him a "monkey humping a coconut," whenever he drove past. But the most interesting one was across the street. Jill and Michael would observe the events at this apartment with keen interest and they fabricated all kinds of stories. Jill's favorite was that the overweight middle-aged man was a record producer in New York and that was why he only made his appearances occasionally. His being a record producer was why the pretty young woman who lived there sung her lungs out morning, noon and night. The record producer wore a velvet red robe and smoked cigars on his patio. He also parked a Lamborgini, a Rolls Royce, and a Jaguar on the side of the road in front of Jill and Michael's row house. The reason for the random location was to mask their relationship, the pretty young girls' motivation of which was to break into the record business and for the man, to hide his illicit affair. It seemed like as good an explanation as any.

In order to budget efficiently on their poverty level graduate student income, they did their shopping in Lancaster County where the Amish lived in the countryside. It was a beautiful drive and much of the food was locally produced by the Amish. The store was called *Shady Maple.* They went once a month. For a treat, they went to the beer outlets and bought a case of *Rolling Rock* for $11.00. The single case of beer was allotted for one month. It provided beverage accompaniment for their evening balcony-neighborhood entertainment.

Jill was overjoyed with a fulfillment unmatched by any other with her new husband and her first child. She imagined she would do everything right. She would be the best mother there was. She now had the chance to give to her daughter the traditional life she hadn't had. Jill loved her with a love unmatched by anyone she'd ever loved. Now she truly understood the meaning of "a mother's love" being unlike any other. Jill read dozens of books on parenting to try to find answers. She wanted so badly to do a good job, but Jill felt like a fish out of water. The examples she had growing up were a far cry from her expectations. It's difficult to teach what you don't know.

Jill and Maya took regular spring walks to inspect the tulips and daffodils popping up when Maya turned five months, and that's when Maya spoke her first word. From her stroller she pointed at a small brown furry squirrel and said, "quirrel!" Jill could barely believe her ears, but her baby was pointing right at it. She had been working on da-da but it came out as more of an indecipherable "duh" like she was really trying. But squirrel??! Of all the words, that was that one!!

It was not long after the birth of their first child that Michael came home for dinner one night. He got home late. He was gone from 7:00 a.m. until 7:00 p.m. every day. He taught English classes by day, and went to graduate school in the evening. They had both started out in graduate school, but when the baby came, there was no reliable babysitter. There didn't seem to be any question as to who the person to drop out would be. It was Jill of course. This left Jill alone all day with the baby, and due to the danger of gunshots going off at regular intervals in the park behind their house, and the long periods of inclement weather, she went long stretches of time without getting out at all. They had one car and Michael needed it. Jill tolerated it well for some time, but the realties of motherhood and marriage and sleepless nights and the barely endurable stretches of isolation caught up with her. She sought for things that she didn't ask for, didn't know how, or even think that she should. She thought her partner should have noticed on his own if he really cared.

"Hey, I'm home." Michael walked in the door expecting to find the same smiling face greeting him as usual. Jill was quiet as she set the table. Michael walked in, put his things down and walked straight for the bathroom and then the bedroom. He came back and asked her, "So … everything ok?" "Yeah," she looked up briefly from what she was doing, but turned right back around saying nothing. "Oh, ok," he said, not pursuing any further. He walked over to Maya and picked her up. "How's my baby??!" He poked her in the belly button playfully and sat on the couch, holding her little hands to play patty-cake.

"It's ready," Jill said flatly. "Oh?! You hear that Maya? It's ready! Come on, let's go!" Maya smiled and giggled up at him. He put Maya in her high chair and found her bib. He fastened it around her neck and pulled out a chair. Jill put the food in front of him without a word. "Something wrong Jill?" "No," she looked up with the same blank look as if she had no idea what he was talking about. "You haven't said a word since I walked in the door." "No everything's fine, just tired is all." That was supposed to be his cue but instead he said "Oh good," and turned his attention towards the food. He helped himself. Jill was annoyed. He was supposed to sympathize with her, and what she was looking for was some kind of acknowledgment, like, "Aww, I know how hard it is staying home all day. You must be lonely. I appreciate everything you do."

Jill sat down and stabbed at her food a little angrily. Michael munched happily and the happier he was the sulkier she became. Forks clinked plates and glasses knocked together. It was so silent they could hear each other chew. When they were finished eating, Michael asked again, "Are you sure something's not wrong?" "No of course not," Jill replied, this time with an angry edge to her voice. Then he knew something was wrong. "Do you mind telling me instead of banging dishes around? Why do you have to act like that? Why can't you just tell me?" She whipped around and told him "If I have to tell you then that's exactly the problem!" Michael was confused and perturbed, "Oh come on, why are you doing this?" Jill spat back "Come on, can't you see?" To her it was plain as day is night. "No. No I don't." She let out a big sigh and pulled Maya out of her chair and huffed off. "Ok, go, just don't talk about it, run away. That's great."

Jill was mad. She didn't get what she wanted and was frustrated he didn't understand. She changed Maya's diaper, getting her ready for bed, and shut off the light. Michael came to the door after she was already sitting in the rocking chair with the baby in the dark. "Mind telling me what's going on?" "There's nothing. Forget it," she said. "Well I'll be waiting in bed if you want to talk about it." "No, there's nothing to talk about." "Fine," he said. "I'm not waiting up for you then. I'll just go to bed." Now he was for sure not going to give her whatever it was she wanted and they were both mad.

Jill came to bed a full hour later. She put her nightshirt on and climbed in, careful to stay on her side of the bed and trying not to move too much so she wouldn't wake him up so she could avoid him. As soon as the bed stopped moving his deep voice said again, "Do you mind telling me what this is all about?" She was turned away from him and shook her head, not saying a word. "Oh come on Jill, knock this off!" That was her opening. She was waiting to be provoked so she would have justification for laying into him. She whipped around. "I have been alone all day. Do you have any idea what that's like?! I take care of Maya, and I'm completely alone. I can't even go anywhere!!" "Why didn't you just tell me?" he asked. "I shouldn't have to." "Well how am I supposed to know if you don't tell me? I'm sorry it's so hard." Those were the words she wanted to hear, some affirmation, some validation, but she wanted more than that, much more. "Well what can I do?" He tried to put his hand on her shoulder but she pushed it away. He was perplexed. He didn't know what to do. "I didn't know you were so unhappy." She wasn't really. It was a little hard, but mostly she just wanted acknowledgment for something, anything, her contribution to the family. Deep down something was churning inside of her but she didn't know what exactly. It was some kind of indistinguishable disappointment in life, disappointment that this was the reality of the fairy tale dream marriage and family she'd dreamed about. She felt let down, and she felt something else that she couldn't put her finger on, a slowly brewing resentment. Resentment that she didn't get to stay in school, that she had to give it up, that Michael got to get out every day, make friends and have all of the experiences while she stayed alone at home, not experiencing the outside world at all.

"There's nothing you can do," she sulked." Honestly, she loved being a mother, and she adored Maya and loved being with her, but she was torn between this dichotomy of feelings she couldn't understand. It was like a primordial mourning for the death of the maiden's lost freedom of independence and feminine power deep within that she hadn't gotten to express the loss of on her wedding day. A tradition replaced by overly elaborate and fanciful wedding planning. The bride is happy, everyone smiles at another cap to place on the container of a sealed union, a dream come true and happily ever after. It is the time lost tradition of mourning the loss, and being neatly placed inside a glass bottle, for everyone to look through and see her pretty perfectness that she tries so hard to uphold. The force bubbles inside of her no matter how much she tries to suppress it. Men know this power, because it's one to be reckoned with but women acquiesce to men's egos. No one wants them to feel a diminished sense of their strength and power, outwardly bold, but inwardly hollow. Yet this collective feminine power, if unleashed could change the course of humanity because the very nature of it strives for equality, tenderness, deep care of everything, and disregards the masculine ego that is destroying it. Instead, women get married, pretend they're happy, when if they only looked within, they would find it, still sitting there, waiting to be expressed.

It leaks out in the form of frustration at tiny things towards husbands and resentment of the freedom that men still have. It's a covering up of the sadness, suppressing it, and not even being aware of it. Perhaps this was what Jill lost, and what every married woman has lost. And men have no idea how much energy is drained from the serving of their egos.

Most of the time, they were happy and things went well, but every now and then, one of these eruptions would happen and they'd move through it using the same script each time. After their second child was born, they moved away from Philadelphia. Michael was to begin his first real position as a manager.

They left their little car in Philadelphia and flew to Melbourne, Florida, their new home. They traveled by plane with their two little girls and after settling into their hotel, they went the very next day to buy a car. They took out a loan and signed the papers, then drove straight off to look for an apartment to rent. They found one quickly. It was on beautiful grounds with little lakes scattered around the property and large spaces of green grass. Each of the lakes had a little bridge and in the lakes were alligators. They drove around in a golf cart with the property manager looking at the various models. They decided on a two bedroom where the girls could share a room. The living and dining room were large and bright. The apartment opened onto a spacious screened in patio.

They adapted quite easily. The warm climate and nice conditions made it very easy to take care of the girls. They took walks every day to all the little lakes. They made friends with another family and had picnics and play dates. They went to library story hour weekly and frequented the large pool on the grounds. It was quite agreeable living. Time went on. The girls grew rapidly, and they were happy.

One day Jill got the girls ready to go on their daily picnic. This did not entail too much effort since they usually picked out their own clothes. Jill had a large basket filled with collected old dress-up clothes from her grandmother and thrift stores. Some things she made herself, like a Tinkerbell costume from Halloween one year, Pocahontas another. She made tutus and braided flower and ribbon garlands for their hair. Maya walked down the hall in a gown that dragged on the floor behind her as she walked. It was light blue and hung off of her shoulders. "Maya, get your shoes on, we're going on a walk to meet your friend Zac." "I'm not Maya,

I'm Esmerelda." "Oh excuse me, Esmerelda." Every day she was someone different, and Jill had to keep in character the entire day or be reprimanded for it. "Is Esmerelda a princess?" Jill asked. "Yes, of course," Maya had a bit of an air about her as if her mother should have known that. She was four now and had a mind of her own. "Well, get your shoes on princess." "My name is Esmerelda." "Yes, Esmerelda. Shoes on, now." Madeleine came down the hall wearing nothing but a tutu. "And who are you, pray tell?" Jill asked. "I'm Jasmine."" Well Jasmine, it's a beautiful tutu, but how about a shirt with that?" "No. I don't think so," she replied carelessly. Madeleine often wore her tutu like that, and without anything underneath as well. Jill usually let her if they were staying around the house. The little old ladies strolled across the street from the condos frequently to tell Jill she was not dressing her children properly and mostly for not making them wear shoes. Jill just laughed. She didn't care. "Well, we're going on a walk this morning to go play with Zac, so we need to put a few more clothes on, ok?" "Ooooohhhh Ok" she said." She was nearly three, and followed whatever Maya did.

They started their walk, wearing their costumes. Maya and Madeleine ran ahead of Jill, Madeleine chasing her sister trying to keep up. When they reached Zac's house the girls were already knocking at the door before Jill arrived. His mother opened it and said "Well, hi everyone! Hey we're just on our way out the door. Zac's grabbing his shoes." "Come on guys, let's wait out here so they can finish getting ready," Jill told them.

Two minutes later they walked out. "So how are you guys?" "Oh we're good," Jill answered. The two women started talking and the kids ran ahead. "Hey, that's as far as you go guys, wait there for us to catch up." The kids stopped and waited until they thought they could get away with running on. "Ok, that's far enough," the mothers yelled after them again. Zac became distracted and wandered off towards one of the ponds where he'd spotted a turtle. When the two women caught up, Madeleine was laying on the grass and Maya was standing over her with her hands on her heart saying "Oh Romeo, oh Romeo, where fore art thou?" Madeleine lay still for a moment and peeked out of one eye. Maya whispered "No, not yet." Madeleine shut her eyes and kept still. Maya bent down and whispered some other directions and then ran away. Madeleine jumped up and went running after her. "No, not yet! Wait for me to lay down!"

Madeleine turned around and dawdled for a moment or two. The moms watched in amusement. "Ok now!" Maya instructed. Madeleine came running and knelt down beside her. Now it was Maya's turn to lay perfectly still. "Oh Juliet, my sweet Juliet, oh what have you done?" Madeleine lamented over her until Maya peeked an eye open and told her to go. The moms were laughing and both girls looked up and said angrily, "No, don't watch." The moms turned around and said "Oh no, we're not watching." "Go further away," Maya told them. "Ok ok, we're going." The women took a few steps away and pretended to resume their conversation, but they were dying to watch. They waited until the girls didn't notice them looking, pretending all the while to be engrossed in a conversation. Maya caught them again and hollered, "Hey, you're looking!" "Oh oh oh, sorry, we're not really looking, we were talking and not paying attention."

The girls we're reenacting Romeo and Juliet, one of their favorite pastimes. Michael and Jill finally had a TV, but they kept it in the closet to encourage themselves to choose their shows carefully. Jill liked to have the girls watch Shakespeare and classics and sometimes they watched a family movie after much deliberation and thought as to exactly what movie the would be. Then they would go to Blockbuster and carefully make their selection.

It was in this way that the girls and Jill spent their time until one day Jill found out she was pregnant again. Marley was born a bit premature and was a tiny baby. Her head was the size of Michael's fist when she was born. Her middle name was Maris and meant "by the sea." Michael and Jill thought it was appropriate since Marley was born near the ocean. It was interesting that Marley grew up to love and study the ocean and everything in it. She was passionate to save the whales and dolphins well into her adulthood. The girls adored her. By this time Maya was already five and Madeleine, four. It appeared their little family was destined for girls. It was like Jill was being rewarded with the love of and for her three daughters, filling the empty space of the one female she wished she'd had growing up. Little did they know, there would also be a fourth. Many years later Maya once said, "Wow Mom, you were four when your mother died, and there are four of us. It's like there's one of us for each year you were with her, all girls, to replace the mother you didn't have the rest of your growing up. You get to have us now." Her words touched Jill deeply. It was true.

Not a great deal of time went by after Marley's birth before Michael was offered a job overseas. Soon they would be packing their bags and moving to Bangladesh. Jill lived her life vicariously through her daughters, like many parents do, but for Jill it gave her life, meaning, structure, and a place to belong. Her world had been expanded by her experience in Nepal and completed by a perfect family, and yet there was still something missing. It was something at the very core of her being and she didn't know what it was. Jill wasn't really sure what she wanted, but she wanted it desperately and Michael wouldn't give it to her, but to be fair, Michael didn't know what it was either.

Later, and perhaps much too late Jill realized what it was. It was an empty hole of not knowing who she was that she tried to fill with being a mother, a wife, roles to fit neatly into the scheme of life. But it didn't really work. Those weren't who she was. The more she embraced these roles, the more covered up the "real her" became. She chased the shimmering beads of thread that wove their way through their lives to find happiness. She cooked elaborate meals like a Betty Crocker Mom, only to be exhausted and dinner out way too late. Practical reality wasn't her thing so average didn't really happen. Daily life teeter tottered between extremes. Consistency was a challenge. Plus she was searching for something. Recognition? Acknowledgment? Practical wouldn't have done it. The thing is, elaborate didn't either! She sewed many dresses for the girls, and she loved doing that. But it didn't fill the hole either, only distracted her momentarily.

She sought every quintessential, traditional, unique and world-wise experience she could find for the girls, thinking all of these things would keep the hole from forming in them too. And most of all, she thought her efforts would somehow sum up to the perfect life, the monumental task of turning out beautiful girls, her girls, human beings who would not have that hole, even if she couldn't fill her own. But it didn't really work that way.

Jill was lost, but for a long time she let herself be caught up in the whirlwind of family. The closer the end to that chapter in her life came, however, the more she retreated behind her girls. She was afraid of who she was.

Chapter 8

Nig & the Maryknoll Priests

(1964)

Where will it ever end, this troubled troubled state of things. I can see the good & beauty and I can try for it … but … alone, I must always try alone. Why, oh, why cannot someone understand my purpose and join me – together it would be so much less difficult.

- Bobbie, February 1964

Bobbie packed her bags and headed off to college. She decided to go to San Diego State University to study French. She loved the language and had been studying through private tutors ever since she lived in Morocco. She moved into the dorms and made new friends and immersed herself in college life.

Bobbie closed the door to her brick walled room that looked like a cross between a dank prison cell with its adjacent blue walls, and a medieval fort. This was one of the older dorm buildings. She walked down the long carpeted hall and out the door at the end, leading to the common area. There, a gang of students lounged around the pool table, the couches and the resident assistant's office. This was where constant watch was kept over the rowdy young freshmen. Alcohol was strictly forbidden. One time the

RA caught someone with a bottle of beer and Bobbie watched as the RA poured the contents into a drinking fountain. An onlooker sang out "one dollah, two dollah, three dollah" as the beer trickled down the drain. Everyone laughed.

Bobbie's small gang of new friends sat among the loungers near the black and white TV. She walked into the room. "What took you so long?" Justin asked. "Hey, looking like that doesn't happen at the wave of a wand," Liz informed him. Bobbie was dressed up to go out. "Let's go," Randy said. "It's time to party!"

The five of them walked out the door and around the building along the cement sidewalk that led to the football field. The football field sank down several flights of stairs into a massive pit-like arena surrounded by bleachers that ran just as many flights up from where they entered it. The group of them began the long descent into the arena. This was the only passageway to the rest of the campus around which most of the sorority and fraternity houses were.

It was a long walk, but they talked the entire way so it didn't seem so long. The sun was beginning to set and the night about to begin. As they entered the frat house-filled neighborhoods, other small crowds of college students appeared and collections of good-looking young men loitered the lawns in front of their houses, some of them holding beers. Most of the houses already had someone sitting at a little table ready to collect fees for entering. Girls were granted free entrance of course.

"Here's the one," Randy announced. The five of them stood at the front of one of the fraternity houses. "I heard this was going to be a good one. They're having a band." "Ok, let's go," Marge went up the front walk to the money collector's table. The young man at the table said, "No charge for you honey. Go on in and grab yourself a beer." Marge smiled sweetly. Randy stepped up next and walked towards the door to the house. "Hey, not you man," he said. "That's one dollar for you." "Ahh man, why'd she get in free?" he complained. "She's a lot prettier than you." There were enough guys in the house already, it being a fraternity house. Bobbie stepped up next and he said, "Definitely no fee for this one." He winked at her and yelled towards the door of the shabby little house, "Hey John, get this young lady a beer!" Bobbie smirked at him.

The other two went in, paying their dues accordingly. Inside the dingy living room young men loitered around in small groups. One of them approached the three girls and handed two of them a drink. A different boy quickly appeared to hand out the third. Randy and Justin stood empty handed and were directed outside to stand in line to get their own.

While Randy and Justin walked outside to get their beers, three fraternity boys approached Bobbie, Marge and Liz, swarming around them like flies until more girls arrived. The swarm of flies moved towards each successive wave of incoming girls. Bobbie saw a man in the back of the room holding a clipboard. He looked to be surveying the growing crowd of people. He noticed Bobbie looking at him. He walked over to her and explained what he was doing.

"Hi, my name is Peter," he introduced himself. She said, "I'm Bobbie." "Nice to meet you," he said. "What's the clipboard for?" "Well, let me explain," he began. "You came on a special night. Tonight is 'Little Sister' night. We are looking for our 'little sisters' who will join our fraternity." He held up the clipboard to indicate there was a process and this was serious business. "Only certain girls will be selected." He said this as if it were a competition and a privilege. "I am making notes and deciding who will be asked to go back for an interview." He pointed to a back room where several young men waited for their applicants. Two girls walked out of the room with smiles on their faces. Apparently they were among the special.

Bobbie asked what the criteria were and he told her. "There are many qualities we are looking for." He said it as if it were a privileged secret and that was all he was willing to divulge. Bobbie wondered why the mystery. "Can you list a few of them?" She was curious. "What exactly do 'Little Sisters' do?" Marge asked. "They hold a special status in our fraternity. They are like our own little sisters and they are invited to many of our functions and given special privileges. He left out the details, including the highly sought after qualities, leaving plenty of room for interpretation.

Liz had gone outside to search for Justin and Randy. The man with the clipboard walked outside and Bobbie saw through the sliding glass door Liz turning her shoulder inwards and slightly tilting her head as she smiled flirtatiously with him. Something was marked on the clipboard and Liz was escorted to the back room. "Hmmm," Bobbie observed, "I think I've discovered one of the 'criteria.'"

Bobbie and Marge were skeptical, however they mingled with the 'brothers' of the fraternity. Somehow every girl at the party was inaccessible. There was a frat boy or two even, to match every female present. Marge and Bobbie stuck together, forming an alliance. They weren't about to be separated, and they kept their eye on the door where Liz had disappeared, to make sure she came back out. Bobbie tried to relax and enjoy herself. Justin and Randy returned to join them and were immediately intercepted by three of the fraternity men. It was about this time the clipboard man reappeared. "Bobbie, you have been selected for an interview." Apparently Bobbie had satisfied some of the criteria too.

Bobbie glanced back at the room. A small part of her felt flattered and curious. But then she looked about the room and her greater common sense took over. "That's ok. I think I'll pass." Clipboard man was appalled. He hadn't encountered rejection from anyone that night until then. "What?" he asked. "I don't feel comfortable going into a back room with a bunch of boys I don't know," she replied. "Oh!" he said. His confidence returned and he explained, "You needn't worry! They are only talking to the interviewees. It's perfectly safe. I promise. I'll even walk you back personally." "No, that's okay," Bobbie answered firmly. The man was perplexed. "Are you kidding?" The expression on his face clearly showed his dismay. Bobbie laughed. "This is an honor and a privilege," he continued. "It's one you don't want to miss, I assure you."

Bobbie stood her ground. Marge did too. Bobbie wasn't fooled by flattery. "It's plain as night what's going on here." Clipboard man said, "Ok, your choice." He walked away and did not return. From that moment on, none of the boys came to talk to them. They stood alone, the two of them, as if they had been ostracized. They served no purpose now. Justin and Randy rejoined them when they saw the two girls standing in the middle of the room alone. No one spoke to Randy or Justin all night.

Liz was inducted into the 'Sisterhood' that night and she was elated. She had attained the coveted 'special status.' She walked home with a bounce in her step and a smile on her pretty face.

Later, Liz attended her first 'closed' party with the fraternity as a "Little Sister." She came home that evening frustrated. Bobbie and Marge asked her how the party was. "Oh, it was fine." She had gotten plenty of attention but the other girls and she were overwhelmed by the suggestive pushiness of the fraternity boys. The next party she went to, which was also 'closed,' the boys became even more aggressive. Several of the girls were pressed to go into back rooms and were pressured into more than they anticipated. Liz was pursued by one of them and struggled to fend him off. He pushed her to the point that she feared the worst. She ran out of the house terrified. Liz discovered too late the real purpose of 'Little Sisters.'

For a time, Bobbie was happy. She relished being away from home and her newfound freedom. Included with her initial experiences attending many of the parties and gatherings off campus, she attended some of the sorority gatherings too. A few of the girls asked her to join, but after observing the superior attitudes of many of them, she decided against it. From her observation, the fraternity and sorority scene was superficial and a bad excuse to act out of order.

Slowly, she pulled away from the college scene. College life had drawn her into the circles of friends she had made. Without the motivation to lead this social life, she eventually withdrew from them too. Whether it was a self-righteous perspective or simply a movement in a different direction in her life at that time is perhaps beside the question. It may very well have been simply that her mind, her predisposition, and the genetics of her brain caught up with her.

She moved into an apartment by herself. She decided she didn't care for party life and the immature behavior of many of her friends. She also needed a job as the veteran's affairs check that she received each month was not enough to cover everything and she needed to make up the difference. She had long since changed her field of study first to art, something she had done regularly growing up, and something she fell back on as a means of expressing and working through her emotions. Later, she switched once again, this time to teaching. It was about this time she got a job as a hostess at a restaurant and became close friends with the owners. She also worked part-time as a teacher's aid in a classroom while building up the necessary credentials to be a teacher. She adored children and one day wanted to have many of her own.

Living alone she spent time writing. Her problems resurfaced and she struggled with depression. She had always battled the ups and downs of her moods, but it was during this time that they became even more acute. She saw several doctors by this time in an attempt to remediate her struggling.

One Valentine's day she sent a letter to her mother in an effort to help her understand what she was experiencing.

Feb. 16, 1962

Dear Mom,

Thank you for the Valentine. I'm sorry I didn't send one, but I just wasn't in the spirit so no one got one from me.

Ever since I left home I've been worrying. Mom, you just don't realize how much I worry about you and James. I can't seem to tell you in person, in fact I make it worse. But if anything ever happened to either one of you, I'd kill myself. In fact, I have nightmares about that very thing.

I know you've been through so much and I'm proud of you and admire you for all you stand for. It's just with little things that we can't seem to meet – the little things that mount up to volcanoes. I don't know why, I guess I'll never understand what happened. We're both applying completely different experiences and points-of-view to our interpretations of the problems, maybe that's one reason. I think TIME is all that will help. Too much has been said already, too many wounds ripped open again and again. It's almost habit, the only common thing we have to discuss.

I don't want to go on hurting you, or James. I don't want to argue or fight and disagree anymore. I take most of the blame on myself. I should have been a better person; but my intentions were always out of love besides being deep and from what I thought was right – you've got to understand that. I can't say that there weren't times that I was unreasonable, probably many, but I'm not infallible, none of us are.

I'm a very complex person, no one really thoroughly understands me. Maybe if you saw what went through my mind and my heart you would be able to see another person. Everything that is a problem I take very deep and search for profound answers. But even the closest to me don't know these things, no one does. That's because I prefer my external life to be as simple and beautiful as possible. Of course it can't be entirely so, or you'd have to commit me to an institution for being a psycho living in his world of fantasy. But I am sensitive to the deeper more beautiful meanings in life, which are, ultimately, the simple things. My Art teacher knows this, that's why she's giving me special consideration with my portrait drawings. My English teacher knew this, that's why I got an A.

Being this way, I can't stand to hurt people. And the ones I love most, I hurt most. That hurts me too, I just can't take it. So, I better avoid these occasions by not being there.

I love you both very much and I have a deep ache in the pit of my stomach being cut off from you, but it's best. I'll have to do it alone; live, that is.

I pray for you every night and hope that you'll be happy. I can't bear to see you unhappy, that's another thing. Sometimes I lay in bed crying for you. I wish I could help you, but I can't, I just can't.

James will grow up into a fine man. He has many wonderful qualities. He'll be a great athlete, certainly! I wish we could have a closer sister-brother relationship; I'd like to share his growing up.

Our wires are too crossed; I'm the element that has to untangle them by elimination.

I appreciate more than you know & more than I can express in person everything you've done and are doing for me. I hope my job angle pans out so I'll be able to help out more.

The V.A. office is going to pay for last semester, in case they haven't notified you yet. That should help.

I'll leave you with a sincere "sorry" for all the mean and nasty things I've ever said or done – they can't be righted, but they can be forgotten and anguished.

A Belated Happy Valentines!
Love,
Bob

One year short of graduating, she dropped out. A piece of paper did not matter, she reasoned to herself. She didn't care. She continued to work for Lila and Grant at the restaurant, picking up as many hours as she could manage and she continued working in the classroom as well. She was barely able to make ends meet, but her good friends, Lila and Grant helped a great deal by feeding her many meals from the restaurant. They knew how much she struggled.

Along with the downs she was facing in her life, she also experienced up moments. San Diego, being the port town that it is, welcomed an abundance of military men from the Navy. She met one of these men and his name was Nig. He was out to sea a great deal of the time. Much of their relationship consisted of exchanging letters.

Friday April 17, 1964:

Dear Bobbie,

Honey I'm about to die now. I know how you felt when you didn't get a letter from me. I'm so terribly lonely for you anyway. I just hope and pray with all my heart that everything is OK there. You are <u>everything</u> in the world to me. Tomorrow is Saturday and I've just got to get a letter from you. I can hardly wait until we're together. It will be November or December no matter where I get stationed. Just as soon as I can get to San Diego I'll be there. In my dreams I picture us walking along hand in hand on a street, on the beach and most of the time walkin' by a little stream in the mountains.

I got a letter from a girl back home today. I grew up with her. She is like one of the family. She is goin' to marry Jay I guess. She's graduatin' in June. I told her all about you in the last letter I wrote. She wants to meet you. I think you saw a couple of pictures of her one night up at your apartment. Her name is Marcella or Cella for short.

It's 13:49 in San Diego and I wonder what you're doin' now. You better be and your lips better be just waitin' for me.

I got a day watch tomorrow so I gotta hit the hay darlin'. I'll get this in the mail in the morning.

Remember I love you – I love you.
All My Love,
Nig
P.S. Write to me soon, honey I need you!!

Nig came home from one of his assignments and went straight to Bobbie's apartment. He came a day earlier than originally scheduled. Otherwise, Bobbie would have been there to meet him. As it was, Nig surprised her instead. Nig knocked on the door and waited for Bobbie to answer. Bobbie came to the door in her pajamas. It was 8:00 am and she hadn't gotten out of bed for the day. When she saw Nig she screamed. "Nig!" "What are you doing here? I thought you weren't coming until tomorrow!" He picked her up and swung her around. They hugged and he gave her a big kiss as he pushed his way through the door, still holding her. He set her down and reached back to close the door.

"I can't believe it!" she said. "Well, here I am! We pulled in early to port. We got in last night, but I couldn't come until I was released from watch duty." Bobbie smiled. "Come on! Sit down! Tell me everything. How was it? How was it sailing all around the sea?! What adventures did you have? How are you??!" "Ok, slow down, I'll tell you everything!" Nig said. "Do you need something to drink, to eat?" Bobbie asked. "Oh, a cup of coffee would be fantastic," he answered.

Bobbie went to the kitchen and boiled some water. The coffee filter sat over the pot. She put the roasted grounds into the cylindrical funnel. When the water boiled she poured it over the grounds and the coffee dripped out of the bottom. She opened the cupboard and got two ceramic mugs and put them on the counter. She waited for the coffee to finish dripping and poured it into the mugs. "Do you want milk or sugar?" She called from the kitchen. "No," he answered from the living room. "I like it good and black. I was up all night. I need caffeine." "You got it." Bobbie finished pouring the black coffee into the mugs and got a bit of sugar for herself. She placed one small teaspoon into hers.

"Here's your coffee," she handed it to him. "Wow, thanks, you're a sweat heart." Bobbie sat down on the couch next to him and they sipped their coffee. "I just can't believe you're here!" she said. "Yeah, it seemed like forever, didn't it?" Nig finished his in nearly three gulps. "How did you drink that so quickly?" Bobbie asked. "You'd be surprised how fast you can eat and drink when you have to. In the Navy they sometimes only give you minutes to eat, and if you don't … well, you ain't eatin.'"

Nig leaned back on the soft green sofa and waited for her to finish. She was so slow he finally took the mug from her hands and set it on the coffee table in front of them. "Hey, what are you doing? I wasn't finished with that yet." "I don't care," he said, and he grabbed her arms and pulled her to him. With her face close to his, she could feel his hot breath and he said to her, "I've missed you so much and I've been waitin' a long time to do this." He kissed her. Then he kissed her again. His hands moved around her and one slipped under her top. She pushed it away and he asked, "What's the matter?" "Nothing is the matter. It's just that I think we should go a little slower. I'm not ready for that." She was thinking about her Father. She had sworn to herself and promised him when he was still alive that she would always live up to his expectations.

Nig sat back and said, "It's ok. I get it." "You're not mad are you?" she asked him. "I do like you a lot," she told him. "I understand. You come from a military family, and you are your Father's daughter. Father's protect their daughters and they hold a high code of honor, and your dad was an officer. It's ok Bobbie. I respect you for that. Why don't we go out for breakfast?" "Sure you're not mad?" She asked him again. "I'm sure. Come on. Go get dressed. Let's get outta here."

Bobbie went to her bedroom to pick out something to wear. She came out dressed, her hair up and a small dab of makeup on. Nig waited for her to lead the way to the door. He reached his arm around her and opened it and closed it behind them. They went to Denny's and had a very big breakfast. They talked for hours, and laughed and joked and caught up on everything that had happened since they last saw each other.

Nig was in love with her, and perhaps she him. However, Nig was out to sea a great deal of the time, and it was easy to conceal what happened during his long periods of absence. The brief interludes between his long assignments were exciting. The excitement of reuniting provided fire for their romance each time he returned. It was easier for Bobbie to pull out of her moods with the stimulation of each long awaited encounter while he was there. What he did not see were the times in between.

They were together for two weeks before Nig set out again. This time he was bound for Greece. He was to be there six months. They stood on the docks and she hugged him goodbye, pushing a letter into his hands. "Something for you to read once you're out to sea and you're missing me." He started to unfold it. She grabbed his hand and said, "No. Not now. Once you're on your way." He smiled. "Ok." He pushed it in his pocket. "For later." The ship's horn blew signaling it was time for all to be aboard. "That's me, gotta go." They hugged one last time. "I'm sure going to miss you," she said. "I'll sure miss you too. Ok! Time to go!" He walked quickly up the ramp to the ship with his rucksack over his shoulder. The men below were yelling and throwing the ropes onto the ship that held it to the dock and it began pulling away. Nig stood at the railing closest to her and they watched each other for as long as they could. He blew her several kisses goodbye and she watched the ship disappear into the distance.

Prior to his return home after the long absence he sent to her a form letter that was more of a sort of a joke with his fellow sailor mates. It was sweet nonetheless, and it conveyed his excitement at coming home to see her.

To: MISS
BOBBIE
ISSUED IN SOLOMN WARNING THIS DAY OF 8 AUG 1964 TO THE RELATIONS, NEIGHBORS AND FRIENDS OF ONE NIGEL M FRAZER, RATE: RM3, SER. NO. 5929893

FILL UP THE ICE BOX TUNE IN THE T.V. PUT GAS IN THE CAR
BREAK OUT THE CHECK BOOK

----CAUSE----

VERY SOON THE UNDERSIGNED WILL BE ONCE MORE IN YOUR MIDST, DEHYDRATED, DEMOBILIZED AND

DEMORALIZED, TO TAKE HIS PLACE ONCE AGAIN AS A HUMAN BEING WITH FREEDOM AND JUSTICE FOR ALL, ENGAGED IN LIFE, LIBERTY, AND THE SOME-WHAT DELAYED PURSUIT OF HAPPINESS. IN MAKING YOUR JOYOUS PREPARATIONS TO WELCOME HIM HOME, YOU MUST MAKE ALLOWANCES FOR HIS CRUDE ENVIRONMENT WHICH HAS BEEN HIS LIFE FOR THESE LONG MONTHS. IN A WORD HE MIGHT BE CONSIDERED "EUROPEAN". THEREFORE SHOW NO ALARM IF HE PREFERS TO TAKE A HORSEDRAWN CARRIAGE, OR A SHAGGY MULE INSTEAD OF A CAB. KEEP COOL IF HE TAKES "MOUSSAKA" OR A PLAIN PIECE OF STALE BREAD TO A T-BONE STEAK, AND TAKE IT ALL WITH A SMILE IF HE INSISTS ON SLEEPING UNTIL 3 PM. DON'T LET IT SHOCK YOU WHEN HE IS TALKING TO SOMEONE AND SAYS "KALIMERA" INSTEAD OF GOOD MORNING AND "ANDIO" INSTEAD OF SO LONG.

NEVER ASK HIM WHY THE SMITH BOYS HELD A HIGHER RATING THAN HE DID AND NEVER MAKE FLATERING REMARKS ABOUT THE ARMY, AIR FORCE, OR THE MARINES. (ESPECIALLY THE AIR FORCE) AND ABOVE ALL NEVER MENTION "ROTATION", AND WITH GOOD REASON.

FOR THE FIRST FEW DAYS (UNTIL HE IS HOUSE BROKEN) BE ESPECIALLY WATCHFUL WHEN HE IS IN THE COMPANY OF WOMEN, PARTICULARLY YOUNG AND BEAUTIFUL SPECIMENS. AFTER MANY MONTHS OF BEING AWAY FROM BEAUTIFUL AMERICAN WOMEN, HE WILL NOT KNOW HOW TO ACT IN THEIR PRESENCE. BUT, IT WON'T TAKE HIM VERY LONG TO GET USED TO BEING WITH WOMEN WHO SPEAK THAT LITTLE KNOWN AND SELDOM HEARD LANGUAGE CALLED "AMERIEEKEN ENGLIEESH."

KEEP IN MIND THAT BENEATH HIS PALE AND WORN EXTERIOR THERE BEATS A HEART OF GOLD. (???) TREASURE THIS, FOR AFTER LONG MONTHS OF CONTINUOUS WATCHES, WATCHES, AND WATCHES, CARD GAMES, CARD GAMES, FLICKS, AND MORE WATCHES, AND MISSING THE PEOPLE HE LOVES SO MUCH, IT WILL PROBABLY BE THE ONLY THING OF VALUE HE HAS LEFT. WITH KINDNESS, TOLERANCE, AND OCCASSIONAL

BOTTLE OF FIX YOU WILL BE ABLE TO REHABILITATE THAT WHICH IS NOW A HOLLOW SHELL OF THE "ONCE HAPPY SAILOR" YOU KNEW.

HOPING TO SEE YOU VERY SOON,
Nig
P.S. DO SEND MORE LETTERS IN CARE OF NAVY NR. 577 NEA MAKRI, GREECE AND ALSO GET THE DOGS, CATS, AND KIDS OFF THE STREETS, BECAUSE .... ;------//DAMN IT!//----- "THE KID'S COMING HOME"-----

Despite her brief love affair, Bobbie had withdrawn from many of her relationships. Her relationship with Nig ended eventually too. A longer protracted time together after he returned from Greece proved to reveal the differences between them and their true characters to one another. Nig went his own way.

Bobbie continued with her doctor appointments, trying desperately to get to the bottom of her ailments, to figure herself out. She felt so trapped and so confused. She wrote to her mother, making an attempt to explain to her what she was feeling. She didn't know if her words fell on deaf ears, but one thing she did know. Her written words took time and were deliberate. She felt she was more accurately able to convey what she was going through this way. On one occasion she wrote in an attempt to help her mother understand:

November 16, 1964

Dear Mom,

I just barely made it on Friday. In fact, I was 10 minutes late. I stopped by my apt for only 2 minutes to pick up my books. I was sweating my car making the trip.

My hair lasted until Saturday night. Everyone liked it. Some said it looked much better up than down – but others still like it down better. Anyway, it was fun for a change, thanks.

It's been awfully cold here, I guess there too. It feels good, I think, but all the natives complain. However, I did catch a cold again, but not bad.

I found myself a cat. It's a big fluffy furry calico cat and very lovable. I don't know who it belongs to, and it only comes around once in a while.

I told the doctor all about last week and he said it sounded like a lot hit the fan. From my point of view, it did, anyway. But it was good, it was brought out in the open. I'm not only talking about Wednesday night, but Tuesday night, too.

I would like to talk to you more about our sessions, and I always intend to, but I just can't seem to when the time comes. What I have told you is only part of it. It's never just one answer, anyway, it's very compound and it takes a lot of serious and painful discussion to unravel. People who get hurt easily (which is nearly everyone, but some feel it to an unsensibly high degree) have a way of covering up or hiding until the real feeling is indistinguishable anymore. It's a horrible and confusing way to feel, and that's why I've acted in such bizarre ways. I thought I was protecting myself, but I was only making matters worse.

Now that I realize this, you yourself can see that Dr. Zemlick has made a great deal of progress. Very subtlely, and gently, he's made me see it in myself, without coming right out and saying the words. However, at this point, I'm not quite through draining away all what's been harmful, and at the same time, what I have gotten rid of needs to be replaced – and it'll take some time to discover myself in myself. It makes me very vulnerable and, for the lack of a better description, rather naked. Do you see what I mean? To get stronger, first I have to be very weak and unsure – experiment – probably still get hurt because life still goes on. It's like learning years and years of faulty building and clearing it all off the lot before you can rebuild a new and stronger edifice.

Thank God for everything – and for letting me have a mother who helped me. Otherwise, and it was inevitable,

I would have completely destroyed myself in one way or another. To me, this type of education is far more important than college – it's not money wasted. It's investing in a life of a person, keeping it alive and finding a way.

That's why I can't even think about school. It's hard enough to sit in that one English class and try to concentrate … I find myself thinking about all kinds of things rather than listening.

What college I had is not wasted, either. It's part of me, and has shown me many things, and it's been an important part of my personality. And it will, even though there is no degree attached, put me ahead of a lot of others job-wise; three years of college is nothing to sneeze at.

Well, I've at least attempted to explain, Mom. I know you are entitled to that because I've caused a lot of strife. But, I am mending, and the wounds will heal. And I'll go on searching, because, for one thing, I was taught and brought up with the right values and ideas – it was me who thought along too extreme lines.

I have so much to be thankful for, and I am – and proud of – precisely, my family. Nothing in life means more … family and good friends …

So, whatever you decide about your life, if it makes you happy, do it. If James feels so strongly about leaving, you can hardly blame him. I'm old enough and have proven my capabilities in carrying a lot of responsibility. I can stay in with James and we can manage quite well, we're both quite self-sufficient. I'm sure James is old enough, now, where he can adjust to the situation. And, gratefully, he's far more adaptable than I was … I'm confident he would not get into any trouble.

And, Aunt Viv is not that far away. Plus the fact that we do have good friends. It'll all work out – God is good, not wrathful.

You never did say if you wanted the picture. Lila and I are going down to Tijuana early Thanx morning and we can check on the frames.

Lila just called and they're taking me out to dinner tonight. They took me already last Friday. They're so darned nice, and you can never repay them.

My phone bill was outlandish – but ... words are important and money is just a means.

So looking at life day by day and trying to reach some sort of balance even though the future is shaky and dim, but believing that through all the confusion there is something and someplace for us all, I will send this letter off to you with lots of love and thanks.

Love, Bob

Two weeks earlier Bobbie found herself at her apartment. She had just been to the store. She turned the key to unlock the door to her apartment. She held a bag of groceries in the other hand and struggled to balance it along with her purse. The apartment was dark. The curtains were drawn. She didn't bother to open them. A dreary plant sat in one corner of the living room. It looked half alive and like it hadn't been watered in weeks. Dust lined the shelves, and clothes were strewn around the chair and couches. A magazine and some unopened mail sat on the coffee table. She set the bag of groceries down on the kitchen counter and the telephone rang. She took her purse off her shoulder and answered it. It was her friend Lila. "Hi Bobbie, what are you up to tonight?" She had no plans. She lied, "Oh I have someone coming over, why?" "Oh nothing, was just going to invite you over for some dinner if you were free." "It's so sweet of you, but I can't tonight. And anyway, you've done so much for me already." "Oh we don't mind. We love having you over anytime. Well you have fun tonight and stay out of trouble. I'm so happy you are getting together with people Bobbie, I really am." "Yes, well," said Bobbie, trying to act cheerful. "Ok, well I'll see you at work tomorrow. You're coming in at 4:00 right?" "Yes, that's right. I'll be there." "Ok, talk to you later then." "Yes, talk to you later. Bye."

Bobbie walked back to the kitchen to unload the groceries. She was on a tight budget and her meager bag of groceries did not consist of anything too enticing to eat. There was a can of sphagettios. She put that aside and figured that would be dinner, with a sigh. She looked at the dirty dishes in the sink and noticed the dank musty smell in her apartment and it made her sigh again. She felt sad and didn't know how to shake it. She opened a cupboard and stared at a couple of bottles of medication that her doctor had given her. She reached for one and decided to take a tablet, and then changed her mind and made it two. She found a clean glass and filled it with water and swallowed the two pills.

She pulled her shoes off and left them right where she'd been standing before reaching for the can of spaghettios. She searched for the can opener and opened it. She poured the spaghettios into a pot on the stove and turned up the heat, stirring until they were hot. She pulled the pan off the stove and found a bowl to put them in, grabbed a spoon and plopped down onto the couch, sitting on top of the clothes that were there. She pulled a jacket out from under her and tossed it on the floor while putting her feet up on the coffee table and sat back to eat her dinner.

She reached for the TV remote and turned on the TV, flipping around for something interesting. There was an old western playing so she decided to leave it on. She sipped her glass of water and ate her pasta dinner half-heartedly. It wasn't too appetizing. Everything tasted bland when she was in this state. She set the bowl of partially eaten noodles on the table and left it there. The western movie did not grab her attention, yet she felt too tired to do anything else. It wasn't a physical sort of tired. It was a tired of life sort of tired, a tired that zapped all of her mental and emotional energy. She was so sick of feeling this way.

She got up and walked back to the kitchen, shuffling her feet along the way. She opened the cupboard with the medications and pulled out a different bottle this time. She read the label but stopped partway. It hardly seemed to matter what it said. She popped one in her mouth, hoping this one would do the trick. She sat on the couch in front of the TV. The drab western was still playing. The medication made her drowsy and soon she was asleep. She woke up two hours later and it was already getting dark. The TV was still playing and she drowsily reached for the remote to shut it off. The silence was so loud it sent a surge of dread to the pit of her stomach. She pulled herself up off the couch and realized she had one of those too much sleep headaches. She felt groggy and not tired at the same time, and more miserable than ever. The sun going down darkened the room, signaling the impending nightfall. The weight of it bore down on her shoulders. She took a bite of the unappetizing and now cold spaghettios and forced it down with a gulp of water. She sat back down on the couch staring at the wall and wondered how much more she could endure.

She decided to get up and take a hot shower. That always made her feel better. The hot water poured down her face and back and warmed her through and through. Running the soap over her arms and legs followed with a good scrubbing with the washcloth was invigorating and brought the blood to the surface, turning her skin pink and making it tingly. She stepped out of the shower when she was finished and slipped on her robe and slippers and crawled in bed. A pad of paper and a pen were sitting on the nightstand and she reached for them. She began a letter.

October 29, 1964

Dear Maryknoll Fathers,

I am a new subscriber to your very illustrative, and, I must say, eye-opening magazine. For many years, I have been skeptical of "good-workers" in other lands. As a Catholic, to a Catholic, working in this area, this may sound a bit audacious. But let me also explain that I am twenty years old and my learning processes take on many hard and bumpy rides before I feel satisfied or, at least, on the right track with the answers.

I might also add that I have been, myself, to places of grievous poverty and painful suffering – pictures very remindful of those sad, pitiful faces you portray in your magazine. This was North Africa, Morocco.

I have been attending college for three years trying to win that "cherished" degree – the badge of honor, so society can see I've achieved. I thought, then, I would join the Peace Corps. I am a teaching major. This is my first semester cadet-teaching.

I elected to be placed in an area where conditions were poor because it offered a teacher-assistant job that enabled me to earn money as well as help get experience for fifteen hours during the week. I also have a night job: I work as cashier-hostess at a very nice Chinese restaurant where I have made the most wonderful friends in the world in the Chinese proprietors.

I try to hold up my share of expenses in my college career as much as possible with these jobs. I also get money from the U.S. govt. They class me as a war-orphan, because during our stay in Morocco they were having considerable trouble with brush fights (etc). And all the while my father was deathly ill (unbeknown to any). He died of cancer at San Diego Naval Hospital a year later.

I live alone in a charming apartment, quaint and situated I can look out at trees and greenery rather than houses and big buildings. I can't share my apartment with anyone; it's in the lease. Anyway, I'd rather choose it this way because I had a very unfortunate experience with a roommate. And, I have a very hard time adapting to the social patterns of college life. I attend San Diego State. I can find no enjoyment in any of the parties or get togethers; to me, it is frivolous and non-meaning. I tell you, Fathers, it is hard being a "rare-bird" for three years through the misinterpretation of "no care, & when deep in my heart there is bleeding for those people I have purposed myself to help. I have talked to and become fast friends with Father Merybach. What an interesting person! He's a German, Jewish on one side, who has been all over the world. He fully understands my attitude & believes in me. If you care for his reference, it is: St. Catherines Church, Kealia, Kauai, Hawaii.

He was transferred from the University of San Diego over the summer. Another reference is a good friend of mine also:

Father Glazier
Immaculate Conception

2540 San Diego Rd.

The reason for this letter is this: I have decided to drop out of school. There are simply too many non-sensical demands that bear no essence to the profession I proposed to embark upon. I think you understand; social status is big everywhere. I find living alone is impossible – I have so much to share and yet I isolate myself because what I want to share is twisted and contorted by my peers. People deal with, take things for granted and what they want is usually for some selfish and, not any real need or sincere need. Not all the people, Fathers, I'm not quite that cynical! There are many wonderful, kind, good people here, and I cherish their friendship.

Thirdly, I have faith in your organization, mainly because it is through my religion, and because Father Glazier endowed it. Please, will you find a way to help me attain my purpose? With so many areas in need, I know there is a place for me. Whatever it is I need to learn, I will learn. I have a good record. I am strong, healthy, able, and willing to work hard and for nothing at all if it will relieve the pain in any way for someone.

I am in deadly earnest over this, Fathers. It is no sudden whim or means of escape. I feel it in my heart, and I know God wants me to follow this path.

Will you be so very kind to reply as quickly as possible. I would greatly appreciate a personal meeting with one of your missioners and I will be happy to come to Los Angeles if you can arrange such a meeting.

Thank you very much,

Bobbie

Bobbie never had an interview with the priests. In fact, she never even sent the letter. She continued working for the next two years and struggled with her condition. It wasn't until these two years passed that she met her future husband.

Chapter 9

Mogul Land

(1998 – 2001)

If a man does not keep pace with his companions, perhaps it is because he hears a different drummer … Let him step to the music which he hears, however measured or far away …

- Henry David Thoreau

Maya and Madeleine went up the stairs that led to the rooftop of their apartment. They went there nearly every day, in fact. Sometimes their youngest sister, Marley went with them. It was common to use the rooftop as a patio in Bangladesh. All of the houses and buildings had them. They were ideal for throwing large parties. The rooftops were always flat and they often contained a built-in railing or small cement wall that went around the edges of the building. There was nothing fancy about it. Everything was cement, but the apartment was six stories tall. There was a great view of the city of Dhaka.

Jill knew about the coveted rooftop hangout but she didn't think it was safe for them to be up there alone. The problem was there wasn't a whole lot to do in the overpopulated dirty city. Going out onto the streets was not practical or advised for several reasons. One, the streets were crowded with every imaginable vehicle that could move on wheels: baby-taxis, small black triangular scooter type vehicles that three people could fit into. There were rickshaws, a sort of bicycle-like contraption with a carriage on the back with enough space to fit two people and driven by a rickshaw "wallah." Street vendors sold chickpeas, onion, curry and other spices rolled up inside of newspaper cones. Mini produce stalls, pedestrians, cyclists, trucks and plain old cars littered the roads too, filling in every bit of space. Another important reason was that it was culturally not acceptable for females to be out on the streets or out in public without a man; Bangladesh was ninety percent Muslim, and though for the most part it was a liberal Muslim, there was a thirty percent faction that were extreme. Regardless, the culture did not welcome the idea of women roaming about alone. Harassment, bullying, getting followed, jeered at, and in the case of Jill on one occasion, a stone thrown at the back of her head, were regular occurrences.

Activity options were limited. This is why the two girls would sneak out onto the roof even if against the rules. Being trapped inside of an apartment for hours on end was intolerable for a seven and an eight-year-old. It was for this reason Maya and Madeleine found them selves spending a great deal of time at their semi-secret hangout.

From the top of the building, it was easy to see quite a distance out over the city. So many things happened on the streets below. Construction sites were everywhere. New buildings sprouted up over night. So many skinny brown men scurried around in thin worn out clothing full of holes, pushing bamboo sticks into place to hold up each level of the building until they reached the next. Ancient Egyptian Pyramid-building slaves must have looked like these Bangladeshi men, so many of them, working so hard. Many times they would sing what sounded like old pirate songs in Bangladeshi version, if one could have understood what they were saying. That's what Maya imagined, sitting on the rooftop watching them. The work was labor intensive, and they did it together like a well-oiled machine, only they weren't a machine and they weren't well-oiled. They pushed their bodies to the breaking point. They were gaunt and underfed. They would not live long.

The fate of a widowed woman was worse. Left with nothing on account of all of the assets going to the men in the family, widows were cast out to fend for themselves, along with their children. Many of them were left with the most menial of jobs. One of these was brick-breaking, and it was a common one. Since there were no stone quarries, bricks were broken down into small bits and powder to form cement. Women often carried babies on their backs while they squatted on the tops of large piles of bricks chopping away for hours in the hot sun. There was one directly in front of Maya and Madeleine's apartment building, and it had it's own widow breaking bricks, complete with a baby attached to her back with a cloth snugly wound around him.

Maya was eight, and she had already seen a lot for her age. Crowds of beggars chanting "baksheesh" surrounded their car when they went out, mothers holding babies with their hands outstretched, barefoot children wearing pieces of dirty clothing with so many holes it wasn't good enough to use as a cleaning rag in most places. Some of the women had sores and the men injuries. Each had their claim to impoverishment and they utilized it to their benefit as much as they could. Some inflicted the injuries themselves purely for the prospect of better baksheesh. They lived in the slums. The girls drove past them every day and watched as the throngs of people poured out from little hovels and sheets of plastic tarp stretched over bamboo sticks, hanging feebly and providing the only shelter they had. Slumlords ruled their existence and forced them to pay dues. If they were far enough out in proximity from the city center and from the most lucrative begging venues, the slumlords organized vehicles, usually a small truck covered with a shabby blackish grey flap. The beggars piled in and were driven to their designated posts to carry out the duties instructed to them. A percentage of every beggar's wage went to the slumlord.

The most strangely beautiful site were the young and colorfully dressed young women that poured out from the slums every morning, huddling together in large groups like a Greek army in phalanx formation. They were strength in numbers and protected each other from any possible onslaught of harassment, traveling without men. Every morning and every evening, the huddling groups of women brushed through the city from the slums to the clothing factories, working twelve hour days, six days a week in buildings without air conditioning and questionable conditions. They walked with their heads held high. They were genuinely proud of their status. They carried small handbags like a young girl trying to act grownup. Ironically, the purses had to be left by the door to the factory. They were not permitted inside. The flood of color, however, was like a shining bright artist's paint stroke on a canvas with every color on his palate. It was captivating to watch, a rare splotch of beauty in a deplorably ugly grey city. The wage was around three hundred taka per month, equivalent then to six American dollars. Returning from the factories each night, they re-entered their slum-homes and cooked the evening meal together using a large pot over a fire in the open air next to their scant shelters. They pooled their money together to afford food and the slumlord fee for their small slab of land.

Maya stood next to the wall at the edge of their rooftop patio and looked out. There was always something happening on the street below. Today a little man with a basket wandered around, searching for an audience to watch his snake charming skills. There was a cobra in the basket and he knew how to lure it out and back in using his hands. He found a man and set the basket down to begin his performance. From above, the little man didn't see his overhead audience. Otherwise, he would have charged them too. "Madeleine! Come look! There's a snake charmer!!" She ran over. "Where?" "There," she pointed to the spot on the street below where the man with the basket was. He was busy negotiating a fair spectators fee with the man. The performance had already finished by the time Madeleine arrived. The man in front of the snake charmer pulled a couple of "taka" from his wallet and handed it over to him. The snake charmer took the money and bowed his head in thanks and stuffed the money in his pocket. He picked up his basket and continued on. The girls watched to see if the man with the snake in the basket would perform again.

It wasn't long before he located another customer. It was a woman and her child this time. She held a baby on one hip. He put the basket down and began to lure the snake out. The mother looked apprehensive and she protectively looked down at her child and patted him on the head to be still. The child tried to step closer to take a better look, but his mother took him by the sleeve and yanked him back. She flinched at the sight of the sides of the snake's head that were fanned out and the skinny threadlike tongue that whipped back and forth. The snake charmer relished the reaction he elicited from them and he stepped cautiously closer to the snake, bent over, waving his hands to control the snake. He was dramatic and determined to put on a good show in the hopes of a good tip. He commanded the snake back into the basket using elaborate hand gestures and turned to the woman for his monetary reward. The woman pulled back as if she were repulsed by what she had seen. The man was proud of his performance and dismayed at her response. He put his hand out to collect his reward, but the woman stepped back further. The man shook his head and said something to her. Maya nor Madeleine could hear what they were saying but it was obvious the snake charmer was not happy. Guards from the garage of Maya and Madeleine's apartment building came to see what was the commotion. They formed a circle around the woman and the man. The snake charmer and the men and the woman engaged in a community debate over who was at fault. Half of the men thought the woman should pay, the other half didn't. "She got the service, she should pay." The other half maintained that she happened to be there as the snake charmer pulled out his snake of his own accord. He never asked the woman if she wanted to see his performance. She had no choice so therefore had made no commitment. The woman continued to back away from them. She did a bow face and hurriedly walked away. The snake charmer and the other men watched her as she disappeared. The guards walked away too and the snake charmer followed them into the garage.

Maya said to Madeleine, "Come on! He's in our building! Let's go see!" The girls ran down the stairs taking two steps at a time and bolted through the door to their apartment. "Mom! Mom! Give us some money! There's a snake charmer!! Can we go, please?!! He's in the garage right now! Hurry, he'll be gone if we don't go right away!!" Jill walked out of the kitchen where she had been instructing the cook what to make for dinner. As usual it was more of a teaching lesson, explaining each and every step how to cook the meal. Jill sometimes thought it would be easier to just cook the meal herself than have to explain every detail, in her broken Bengali to her cook who understood no English. The task was laborious.

Jill walked into the living room entryway to see what the commotion was. "A snake, a snake," they yelled. "Hurry Mom! We gotta go see it! Please." "What in the world are you talking about?" She was confused and tried to figure out what the excitement was. "A snake charmer!!!" Maya explained impatiently. "Hurry Mom, he'll be gone soon, we have to go now!" "Where do you have to go?" She never allowed them into the garage alone with all of the guards. The girls knew that was absolutely forbidden.

"Please Mom!" Madeleine pleaded, "Please will you come with us?" "And bring some money," Maya said. "A snake charmer?" Jill suddenly became interested. "How fun!" She decided they should go. "What an exotic experience!" Jill thought. It was finally something interesting in contrast to the daily reality of their current living situation. "Ok, let me get Shenoli to watch the baby." Maya impatiently stomped her foot and let out a sigh of exasperation. "Watch your behavior young lady," Jill said as she walked away. "If you don't settle down we won't see any snake at all." That wasn't going to happen, however. Jill was just as excited as they were. Any chance for excitement or an unusual experience and Jill impulsively took it. Marley listened to all of the excitement and was glued to them. She wasn't about to miss out either.

Jill handed the baby to Shenoli and grabbed her wallet. "Ok, come on!" She said and they headed out the door in a hurry. They took two steps at a time, including Jill. They were out of breath when they reached the bottom level that opened out to the garage. The girls ran from one corner of the garage to the other until they found him sitting with the guards drinking tea. "There! There he is!" the girls shouted. They ran back to their mother and pulled her by the arm towards the snake charmer. The startled snake charmer didn't move. He stared back at them. The guards were used to seeing Westerners but he was not. The guards urged him forward. The snake charmer slowly got up. His mouth hung opened and his eyes were wide open as if he'd seen a ghost. He stared at the three white people that had appeared out of nowhere as if in shock. They were more entertaining to him than his snake was to everybody else. The guards told him "Come on, get your basket, they want to see your snake." The snake charmer made his way to his basket not taking his eyes off Jill and the three girls.

He lifted the lid to the basket, moving his hands while the snake rose into the air, all the while not taking his eyes off the white people. Jill had the impression that she and the girls were the attraction and not the snake. The girls watched the basket, trying to hold still and contain their excitement. Jill told them to stand back and not get too close. They hardly noticed the snake charmer's head turned in the opposite direction of the snake basket staring at Jill. Jill was worried how he was able to control the snake without looking at it.

The performance ended and so did the excitement and the girls and Jill went back to the apartment. Maya and Madeleine slipped back out the front door and up the two flights of stairs to their hangout on the roof, hoping their mom wouldn't notice. The event of the snake charmer left the two girls with plenty to talk about. Maya went to the edge of the building and stood close to the small wall that enclosed the roof. Madeleine followed.

"That was so awesome!" Madeleine said. "Yeah, it was," Maya agreed. Maya didn't look at her sister. Her eyes were glued to the horizon and the endless rows upon rows of buildings that were mostly half built, stretching on into the orange and pink smog filled sky. "We can see everything from up here," Maya said. "Yeah," Madeleine agreed, "All the way to the sunset." Madeleine stood next to her sister, enchanted by the city and the clatter coming from the throngs of people that toiled around them.

From their rooftop plateau, they never knew what they would see below. At the moment, they watched the rickshaws ringing their bells, looking for passengers. There were "Baby taxis" teetering on three wheels and letting off far too much exhaust. There were hundreds of people walking, a cow wandered across the road, a goat strayed in front of a truck that swerved to miss it, a little further on chickens scattered and scrambled between moving vehicles while a boy tried to catch them. Dhaka was a city that thousands of villagers from the countryside had crowded into, but they had no idea how to be city dwellers. They looked at the women wearing their scarves over their heads, and their brightly colored saaris – long reams of cloth wound around and around their bodies that covered them head to foot. Occasionally a black ghost floated down the road, completely covered with a bhurka, including her head. All of the women were accompanied by a man, or were with a group of other women huddled close to each other, moving quickly down the road. The sounds that echoed around them were just as chaotic as the scene below. Horns honked, cars screeched to a halt, men yelled to each other from their rickshaws, and fruit and chickpea snack vendors shouted to passersby hoping for a sale. Chickens cackled and goats baaahd, bells jingled from rickshaws, and hammers chopped away at their construction work as well as at the piles of bricks being turned into powder for cement.

As filthy as it was, some things were truly shocking. The cow that was slaughtered right in front of their apartment in the middle of the road on "Eed" was one. "Remember the cow last Eed?" Maya said. The girls stared at the spot where it had happened, vividly reliving the experience. "Yeah," said Madeleine. Blood had poured all the way down the road like a thick flood oozing everywhere. The girls were horrified. If it had happened in a village it would somehow have seemed more palatable, but right in the middle of a city street? It was like a scene from a horror film. "Do you know what happens to the cow?" Madeleine said, "Yes, they have a celebration and eat it." "But do you know that they divide it up into thirds?" Madeleine didn't answer. She knew Maya would answer the question whether she wanted her to or not. "The tradition is to divide the meat of the butchered cow into thirds: one-third to the poor, one-third to their friends and relatives, and one-third to themselves." She thought it was a nice way to live and she told Madeleine, "I agree with this philosophy." Maya was always using big words. "But I don't like the blood."

The sirens went off for the five o'clock evening call to prayer. Men hurried to the temples and poured in, laying on their small mats, bending over in a position that looked like the yoga child's pose. It was a show of submission and gratitude for Allah. The girls grew tired of watching the streets below and walked to their favorite spot in the middle of the roof where the stairs were. They took their places around the little brick wall that enclosed the other three sides of the stair well. They could see all the way down the six flights of stairs to the garage below where the small square opening was exposed. "Hey look! The guards are right there!" Maya carefully pulled out the cups she always brought when they came to the roof just in case and handed them out. Maya gave Madeleine three of them and three to herself. She got out the bottle of water she had stuffed into her other pocket, unscrewed the lid and poured a bit into each of the six small cups and the girls placed them one by one along the edge of the wall. They looked at each other with mischievous grins. "Ready?" Maya's eyes had a gleam in them. "Wait till that one comes back, can you see him?" Maya said. "Yeah! There he is, GO!" "Ok, one-two-three!" They stretched their hands over the wall holding their cups, one in each hand and turned them over. The water fell down the long six flights to the garage. They quickly jumped back and waited for the yelling. It took a few seconds for the water to reach the guards.

"Hey!!!! What you doing?!!!! They spoke in broken English because they knew it was the American girls. "Stop that, who doing that? Watch out! You got us wet!" The guards shouted up at them from the garage. Maya and Madeleine laughed and laughed. They hid behind the wall and waited for the guards to calm down and for enough time to go by that they might forget anyone was up there. Eventually they peered over the wall again, still giggling but taking the risk because they were too impatient to see what the guards were doing. Maya poured water into the cups and handed two to Madeleine. "Ok, are you ready?" she asked her. "Yeah, I'm ready," Madeleine said. They extended their hands over the wall for a second time and tipped the cups over. The water cascaded down the long six flights of stairs and onto the guards that congregated there. This time the girls' curiosity was too great. Two pairs of little eyes peeked over the ledge to see the guards' reactions. One of the guards saw them and started shouting. The girls jumped back and hid behind the wall, giggling hysterically. They looked at each other and laughed even harder.

The girls waited. They didn't hear any voices from below, so they decided to take a peek over the edge. "Shall we look?" Madeleine asked. "Wait one more minute," Maya replied. "Ok, I think it's safe." The girls peeked over the stairwell wall and no one was there. They left their cups near the ledge and walked to the middle of the roof and sat on two of the utility covers that were there. Madeleine swung her legs back and forth as she sat on her makeshift chair. "Sure is fun living here," "Yeah, sure is," Maya agreed. Caught up in the moment it was easy to forget the remaining fifty percent of the time they were bored to death. "What do you like best?" Maya asked her. "I like climbing the jackfruit trees and going on the roof at the American Club," Madeleine said. "Most definitely." "Yeah," Maya said reminiscing the thrill of it with their band of troublemaking friends. The guards would yell at them there too. The guards were constantly irritated by them, but that made it even more fun. "I like the track meets at school and the swim meets," Maya said. "Me too," Madeleine agreed. "Too bad you stopped and stood up before you touched the edge of the pool during the last meet." Madeleine laughed at the memory of it. Maya wrinkled her forehead, annoyed. "I made it to the end," she argued defensively.

"Yeah but you didn't touch the wall, you have to touch!" She laughed even more. "Mom told you before the race to be sure to do that, ya know," Madeleine reminded her. "Yeah, well," Maya said. She turned her head away indicating she was finished with the topic. "But you always know everything," Madeleine went on. "Oh be quiet," Maya said. "I won that race," Maya said stubbornly. "No you didn't," Madeleine said. "You don't win till you hit the wall!" Maya pouted and furrowed her brow even more, crossing her arms in front of her chest indignantly. The ribbon had gone to someone else that day, to the boy who came in just after her. Maya didn't win any ribbon, not even second or third. "Let's talk about something else." "Ok," Madeleine said.

"Should we go check the stairs again?" Madeleine asked. "Sure," Maya replied. She was relieved not to talk about swimming anymore. They went to the ledge and peeked over it. One unsuspecting guard came into view. "Better wait," Maya warned, "till more are visible." "Yeah, we wanna try to hit as many as possible, right?" Madeleine looked at Maya for confirmation. "Yeah, that's right," Maya said.

The girls leaned their backs against the wall facing out over the city. "Sure is dirty here, isn't it?" "Sure is," Madeleine agreed. A thick layer of smog covered the entire city stretching out to the horizon. It was impossible to see past the city's edge. The girls' attention was drawn to a group of screaming children. They were laughing and playing. It was a collection of Bangladeshi street children. The noise came from about five blocks up from theirs. Leftover floodwaters from the biggest flood in ten years that had only recently ended still overflowed from the open sewers and the street kids played in it. The big flood had lasted three whole months, and it was devastating. Many Bangladeshis starved or drowned. Mothers tied their babies to wooden posts to keep them from falling in the water. The wealthier class could not get down the roads with their cars. If the roads were passable, it would take hours to move a mere mile or two. Some areas were so flooded, it was necessary to take a boat, and that was why rickshaws were replaced by boats for a time.

"Yuck!" Maya said. She was referring to the kids playing in the sewer water. "Yeah," said Madeleine, though she looked a little more envious than disgusted. "Shall we check again?" Maya asked. "Sure." She was an obedient accomplice. They walked back over to the ledge to see if any targets had wandered into view. They looked over the wall and their eyebrows went up in delight, "There they are! Are you ready?" Madeleine grinned. "Oh yeah!" Her cups were already poised for dumping. "One-two-three-GO!" The girls dumped their cups at the same time and jumped back. They heard the yells and shouts of the angry guards below. They'd hit a lot of them that time. They knew the guards were probably shaking their fists. They sat down on the ground and leaned against the stairwell wall, giggling louder than ever. "Oh man, is this fun!" Madeleine laughed. "Sure is."

The noise settled down and the girls ventured another peek over the ledge. That was when they saw one of the guards winding his way up the staircase. "Oh no!" They knew their fun was over. They ran for the stairs. Fortunately they only had two flights to go down whereas the guards had four. They ran as fast as they could, trying to beat the guard to their fourth floor apartment.

"Come on!" Maya shouted. "I am!" said Madeleine. "I'm right behind you!" Madeleine never failed to keep up with Maya. If Maya was fast, Madeleine was right there with her even though she was a head shorter. Madeleine was competitive with Maya for as far back as anyone could remember. "Hurry!" Maya shouted, turning the doorknob to their apartment. Thank goodness it was open. They dashed in and pulled the door shut. Their mother happened to be standing right there. "Where have you two been and just what have you been up to?" She eyed them suspiciously. They looked very guilty. "Oh nothing," Madeleine said innocently and out of breath. Madeleine had the ability to get away with anything by looking into her parents' faces with her big blue eyes and pouty lower lip that drove Maya up a wall. At this particular moment, however, Maya was appreciative of her sister's pouty lip. Maya hated how she never got in trouble, but at least now she was working her charm to keep both of them out of trouble, so it was okay this time.

Their mother told them to go take their baths before dinner when the doorbell rang. Maya and Madeleine looked at each other and ran to take their baths faster than they ever had before. Their mother didn't notice. She went to the door, curious to see who would come at this hour. She opened the door and an angry guard stood in front of her waving his fist, trying to explain in broken English what the girls had been doing. Jill tried to understand. "Pani?" she repeated back to him. It meant "water" in Bangla. "Achay. Pani." The guard nodded his head hoping he'd gotten through to her. The guard pointed towards the stairs and up to the ceiling. Jill walked out of her apartment and over to the stairs. She arched her neck and looked up. Then it dawned on her. The girls' "secret" hang out was up there. Jill put two and two together. The guard came to their door upset and the girls had run into the apartment only moments before, and something to do with water. Jill apologized to the guard, and she told him shaking her finger towards the inside of her apartment, that she would punish the girls for whatever it was they had done. The guard nodded his head, appearing satisfied, and feeling Jill had adequately understood and left, taking the stairs down to the garage to resume guard duty.

"Dinner's ready," their mother called. Maya and Madeleine walked out of the bathroom with wet hair, trying to look as innocent as possible. They were careful not to misbehave or to engage in a sibling fight like they usually did. Jill eyed them and raised her eyebrows giving them the nonverbal cue that she knew what was up. Maya and Madeleine's mouths formed into "ahh ohh's," and they crept over to the table like they were trying not to set off any alarms. Their mom continued eyeing them and informed them they would be having a talk after dinner. Maya's shoulders slumped in her chair. Madeleine looked at her sister and slumped her shoulders too.

The girls didn't ask what was for dinner. They knew it would be rice and *biriani*, Bangladeshi chicken with all kinds of spices, and badji, curried vegetables, as usual. "We're having something special tonight," Jill said. "Oh really," Maya answered. "I learned all about the hundreds of different "*bortas*" that are typical Bangladeshi dishes at my Asian Study Group today. We even had a cooking demonstration how to make them." "Oh great, more Bengali food," Madeleine rolled her eyes at Maya. Jill was excited, oblivious to their downcast heads. If she had said 'grilled cheese sandwiches' now that would be something to get excited about. "Yes! I asked Shochana if she knew how to make them, and she said yes, of course like why in the world wouldn't I?!! I asked her why on earth hadn't she told me about these before. She looked at me blankly and asked 'Why in the world would you want to eat borta? That's not food for rich people, that's common food for the locals.' So funny! We got to try them at the demonstration, they had dozens of them and they are sooo good!" "I sure wish she'd stop going to that Asian Study Group," Madeleine whispered to Maya. "Yeah, no kidding." "Although, the trip down the river in the boat to the pottery village was kind of cool." "Yeah, that was worth it," Madeleine agreed. "But this food … yuk!"

Jill continued, not hearing what they said. "And tonight she made *kacha kola borta*, green banana *borta*. So interesting! I can't wait to try it!" "Why does mom get so excited over such weird things?" Maya asked Madeleine. "So they mix whatever leftovers they have to make these different *bortas*, and add fresh coriander and some other things that make it specifically a *borta*," Jill went on as if everyone around her was as interested in *borta* as she was. "Great," said Madeleine. Michael, their Father, had just arrived from work and sat down at the table, listening to the tail end of the conversation. He looked about as excited about *borta* as the girls were.

Marley came to the table, and Jill put the baby, into her high chair. Shochana and Shenoli brought the food into the dining room. Maya and Madeleine looked at the mashed greenish-white *borta* and wrinkled their noses. "Oh look!" Jill said, "Here it is!" "Hmm," Maya said. "Looks like barf," said Madeleine. "Hey, none of that." Their mom glared at Madeleine. "You can't judge something until you give it a try." "They had this one at the demonstration today. It's really good!" "I'm not trying that," Maya said. "Me either," said Madeleine. Even Marley said, "ewww." She made each of them take a small spoonful onto their plates. "More gross stuff to go with already gross stuff," Madeleine said. "Hey, enough of that," their mom was getting angry. "Shochana spent a long time making this, you enjoy it and tell her thank you." The girls smiled their big fake smiles and said, "Thank you Shochana." "You're welcome" she said with her timid smile as if she was delighted everyone was trying something Bengali. "Mmmmm," Jill said, "Oh this is GREAT!" "Shochana! I LOVE it! We're having *borta* every night! "Oh great," Madeleine muttered under her breath. "Yeah, great." Maya wore a look of disgust.

"Ok, try it you guys! You're gonna love it!" Jill tried to act enthusiastic. "She's not going to give this up is she?" They looked at each other as if they were being led to the guillotine. They wrinkled their noses again and slowly spooned up the smallest bite possible. The *borta* was gooey and green. "Come on! Hurry up already!" Their mom was impatient. Maya and

Madeleine pinched their noses and brought the spoons to their mouths. Maya spit hers back out onto her plate. Madeleine put a whole bunch of rice and chicken in her mouth to chase it down. "Did you like it Madeleine?" Their mom asked. "Oh my gosh, Mom is delusional," Maya thought. Maya and Madeleine made such a fuss out of the whole thing as if they had just eaten flies. Their mom was disappointed. "Don't make them eat any more of it," Michael said. "I don't think it would be possible," Jill answered. "You'd think we were marching them to their death by the looks of them."

Jill put a wee bit of *borta* on Marley's plate and she mimicked Maya and Madeleine. "Eeewww, yuck, I won't eat it." She had to copy everything her older sisters did. Poor Marley, the older girls were always running away from her, leaving her yelling and screaming, and pounding on the door after them whenever they played. Maya sometimes felt sorry for her, but not enough to let her join in. As far as the girls were concerned she was just too doggone annoying. A few minutes later Maya saw Marley shoveling the Gosh-awful *borta* into her mouth by the spoonful. Marley was a good eater and she loved hot spicy food; she would eat anything. Their Mom turned to Marley, trying not to grin, "Good Marley?" She could hardly stop long enough to talk, Maya observed as she answered "Umm, hmm" with her mouth full of rice and *borta*. "You like the *borta*?" mom asked. Marley looked with dismay at the little pile remaining, realizing she had eaten most of it. She nodded her head, "Yeah, good." "What a traitor," Maya said. "She even ate Shenoli's badji." Marley ate vegetable curry at lunchtime every day and Shenoli's badji was so hot that when she cooked her chilli, it made Jill's eyes water from clear across the entire apartment, simply from the smell of it. Those were some kind of hot chilies.

Living in Bangladesh was an intense mixture of extremes. On the one hand, it was immensely difficult. The culture was rigid and constrictive, and the depravity of the people and the harsh living conditions was a difficult thing to face everyday. On the other hand, there was a richness to the culture, the language, the music and the art. It was a place where the limits of the human spirit were tested to the breaking point, and where the biggest miracles seemed to happen too. During the floods that occurred regularly, it was a place where famine and squalor should have wiped out millions, but it did not. Somehow people survived; the test of human kindness in the face of disaster was unfathomable. Testimony after testimony demonstrated it. The warmth and the depth of emotion of the Bengali people was beyond compare.

The difficulties in Bangladesh were often overwhelming. However, to compensate for the extreme imbalance between what they had and what most of the Bengalis did not, Jill and the girls ventured out into the streets to make their feeble attempts at doing something good. One such deed they embarked on involved driving their Landcruiser around the city. It was a great big dented up and bright blue dilapidated tank. It was perfect for Dhaka. They also had a driver.

Saju was their driver and he drove the car, the girls, Jill and piles of used clothing. The clothing looked one hundred times better than anything anyone wore on the streets. With the clothes ready to go, Saju drove the car up and down streets while the girls and Jill looked for someone of the correct size for the item they had in mind to give. It was difficult to convey to Saju the gist of what they were doing on the first occasion they did this. At first, he was confused. Jill explained over and over again in Bangla. He drove too quickly to have time to get out and do what they wanted. Saju couldn't figure out why they wanted to stop next to a beggar or a poor person. He sped past them before they could get him to stop. Finally, he understood what they were doing and he took them to a heavily populated beggar hangout. As soon as they opened their car door with the clothes, however, the beggars swarmed the car and grabbed anything in reach. The girls and Jill could barely get the doors shut again. Jill explained to Saju that this wasn't going to work and that she only wanted him to drive down some less congested roads where there were only a few poor people at a time.

Saju thought he understood, so he took them directly into a near-slum neighborhood over narrow dirt roads crowded with people. Saju and the girls and Jill sat inside their enormous Landcruiser that the road barely accommodated. Only one car at a time fit on the road. There was no way to turn around. Jill wondered if they would ever get out. She shook her head and told Saju, "No, we can't do this." "No?" he asked, surprised. He was so proud of figuring out what his "Madame" wanted. He looked heartbroken. Jill patiently explained that it was a compromising situation. They were blatantly on display. It was not at all discreet. On top of that, they were locked in with no escape route if something were to happen, such as a mob attack, and that was a real possibility in Bangladesh. It did happen every so often. If an incident occurred, such as a minor car crash or a street person or a rickshaw getting hit, (and that was not a hard thing to do given the crowds and congestion everywhere) a mob could form in minutes to deliver a dynamic crowd frenzied punishment. Saju understood. He weaved his way in and out of the narrow dusty dirt roads before he could find an exit. The bewildered slum dwellers stared at them in disbelief to see a giant jeep and white people in their neighborhood.

Saju found a wide-open quiet road and drove slowly enough so that everyone had time to look and time for him to stop the jeep if they found someone who was a fit for the item they had to give. Up the road in the distance the girls and Jill spotted a woman and a young girl about Maya's size walking alongside the road. The girls jumped up and down on their seats and pointed, "There, there, Saju go closer!" "I think she's the right size, Mom!" Madeleine said. When the car was only yards behind them, Jill confirmed, "Yes, I think she is perfect!" Jill held up the dress in question. It was simple but well made and in good condition. She handed the dress to Maya. The girls couldn't get the door handle to the car opened fast enough. They ran with the dress in their hands and held it out to the little girl. The little girl's mother looked confused. Maya tried to explain, but she didn't understand English. She made hand gestures pointing to the dress and pointing to her daughter. The mother tilted her head to the side and smiled. She said something to the little girl and the girl's eyes grew big and her mouth opened and formed a big smile. Maya handed the dress to her and she took it timidly from her. She held the dress up examining it. She looked back to her mother and asked her something. Her mother nodded, and the next thing they knew she began pulling the dress over her head and right over the raggedy clothes she was wearing.

Maya and Madeleine got back into the jeep and Saju drove away. The girls watched out the back window and saw the little girl twirling around and around in her new dress. Everyone, including Saju, smiled at the sight. Several minutes later, Maya said, "This is a hundred times better than Christmas."

When it neared time to move home from Bangladesh for good, Jill began allowing Shenoli to take Maya and Madeleine to the road in front of their apartment building. The girls had gotten the idea that they could collect their allowance money to buy small bags of already cooked rice and badji, curried vegetables, from the food stall. The cost was so miniscule that they could buy quite a few, and it was like an entire meal contained into one small plastic bag.

"Hey Maya," Madeleine said on one such occasion. "Yeah," Maya was busy digging in her pockets, counting her change. Madeleine was already handing the food stall vendor one taka. "How much more do you have? Can we buy more?" "Yeah, hang on, I'm counting it," Maya had her head down counting every piece of change she had. "Ok, here, you can buy five. I get to buy six." Maya handed Madeleine her share of the money. "Why do you get six and me only five?" Madeleine asked. "Because I'm older," she said matter of factly. "Hmmm," Madeleine said. Her bottom lip protruded slightly.

Once they'd collected their bags, the girls combed the vicinity for more people to give their bags to. The young mother who looked twice her age and broke bricks on the pile in front of their apartment everyday was obviously top priority. Today her baby was strapped to her back with a large piece of shabby cloth. She was bent over her bricks with a hammer, chopping steadily, creating the familiar and constant tapping sound that reverberated throughout the neighborhood. The sweat poured down her face. She squatted low with her feet planted firmly beneath her and spread a good two feet apart. She nearly touched the bricks in a squatting position, but hovered just above them, balancing on the uneven surface.

The girls walked up to the brick pile and held out the bag of food. She looked at the girls and smiled. She set her hammer on the rocks and stepped partway down the pile and reached for the food. She was used to the token gift from them and was always gracious and thankful. She bowed her head and put her hands together, a warm smile spread across her face. *Dunyabad*, she told them. It meant "thank you." She took the food and walked the rest of the way down the pile of bricks and stood off to one side. She opened the bag and took a bite. Maya and Madeleine watched her until she looked up and realized they were staring. They told the young mother goodbye. She smiled and went back to her food.

Up and down the street they walked, searching for would-be takers. One thing was certain, however. Only females would be given a bag of food. Maya and Madeleine had decided that the women had it worst and so they would be the ones to receive their charity.

The men had it rough too however. Next to the construction workers, the rickshaw wallahs had it worst. They were the rickshaw drivers. The rickshaw wallahs peddled the three-wheeled contraptions, carrying two and sometimes up to three passengers at a time. The amount of duress on the human body by these men was severe. Their legs were like tree trunks. However, they were skinny from lack of nutrition. It was not the kind of skinny that model magazines and the beauty industry portrays. It was ironic to the Bangladeshis that skinniness was a coveted thing in the west; for them, being skinny was a sign of poverty. To be plump was a sign of wealth, and this is what they felt properly deserved admiration.

The rickshaw drivers strained to pull heavy loads of people all day through the crowded streets of Dhaka, narrowly missing recklessly speeding cars. Often, they were forced to come to a screeching halt to avoid near fatal accidents. Regaining the inertia to get moving again required extreme effort. Hour after hour of this grueling work took its toll on their poor engine-bodies. Their lifespan was typically around forty years old, and some less than that.

The realities of life in Bangladesh even for the rich foreign expats that lived there, mostly doing aid work to help the people was difficult. Simply watching the devastation every time they stepped out the door put an ache in every person's heart, constantly. How it manifested itself differed greatly. Some people dug in and gave everything they could. Others turned a blind eye and out of sheer despondency claiming that "the problem was irreconcilable. If you give to one, you must give to all, so why give? It will not help the root of the problem. The solution must come from within the system, from their own government who ultimately determines the class system of the people." Regardless, one thing was certain. Returning to the United States carrying the burden of these experiences made a former foreign resident marked with a tenderness that would stay with them forever. Well paved roads, streetlamps, a police force that is not corrupt, a fire department and education for every child suddenly became gifts beyond compare and one not to be taken lightly. Complaints such as standing in line or not getting a service expected at any level seemed like the mere inconvenience of swatting a fly on the wall in comparison.

So-called poverty at home relative to the poverty of Bangladesh was equal in contrast; the American poverty stricken would be considered wealthy by Bangladeshi standards.

Constantly being around people was difficult for Jill. She felt as if she was being watched much of the time, even in her own house, and she was. Michael and she had their differences. He wanted the helper people they'd hired to be in the house all of the time. Jill realized after talking to other women in the community that just because they were paying them full time didn't mean they had to be in the house full time. Jill wasn't the only woman who needed her space. She went home one day after one of these discussions and told Shenoli she could have afternoons off after the cleaning was done. She also told the two of them, including the cook, Shochana, that they did not need to come to the house until seven each morning. The two women were upset and worried they'd done something wrong and that's why Jill didn't want them there as much. She assured them over and over again that wasn't the case. She told Shenoli, "Why don't you go shopping? Or go see your sister in the extra free time?" just to reassure her. A big smile spread across her face at the thought of it. "Ok Madame!" A couple of times Jill even gave her some extra money to buy some new "*shalwar kameezes*," a long colorful baggy shirt over equally colorful baggy pants and a long scarf to match.

Michael was unhappy about the reduced hours. He liked his coffee made in the morning, and the luxuries that accompanied living in a developing country. Jill told him she would make the coffee. He told her, "No you won't. You don't get up early enough." She said "I'll make it at seven." "No. I like Shenoli and Shochana doing it. They do it early, and I know they'll for sure do it." They argued and Jill appealed to his sense of considering her needs as well as his. She explained, "I don't like strangers walking by our open bedroom door in the morning with me still laying in bed. It feels like an invasion of privacy." Michael was unsympathetic. "They aren't strangers, and anyway what's the big deal? You're being ridiculous," he said. With the new changes, other dynamics happened as well. Jill almost had to laugh at the absurdity of the situation. Shenoli and Shochana raced each other to work everyday to try to outdo each other and impress their boss and madam by arriving early. Jill shook her head at the attempt for privacy. Her husband resisted the change and the two helper women hung out on the stairs half an hour earlier than the designated time so they could vie for the one to be first to walk through the door at seven sharp.

The job conditions in Bangladesh, although including many perks in living style, had its difficulties as well. It was a contract, so when the contract ended, Michael had to search for a new job all over again. The rules for how long it was possible to serve in his position were rigid. When time neared its close for them, Michael felt the pressure and responsibility bearing down on him. He applied for many jobs and none came about before they departed Bangladesh. He was disappointed and angry at the situation. Jill pointed out that they knew the conditions of the contract when he took the position. It was a risk, but together they had decided it was worth it in order to give their girls the opportunity to live overseas, experience a new culture and open their eyes to the reality most of the world lived. Michael was unhappy with his prior job so in addition to providing the girls with this educational experience, she was more than willing to give up stability in exchange for his happiness if this was what he wanted. She felt happiness trumped everything and work and supporting a family was hard enough without being miserable. Unfortunately, he was not happy in this position either.

.....

It was one year before leaving Bangladesh for good that Jill departed from Bangladesh to have her fourth child. The day before she left for Thailand, Jill took Maya and Madeleine out for a special date. She was to be separated from them for one month while she waited to have the baby. She took them to the fanciest hotel in Dhaka, the Shonergon. They had their first manicure and pedicure ever. Jill looked down at her toes and wondered what the big deal was. She thought to her self, "I can cut my own toe nails. And I don't like nail polish." When she stepped off the chair, small circles of blood spotted the floor behind her. Her toe had been cut. Jill thought, "I don't need skin cut off my feet either."

Maya and Madeleine were delighted with the extravagant outing. They held their hands out admiring their freshly painted nails and looked down at their toes protruding from their flip flops. The three of them wore dresses along with their painted nails. Now that they were perfectly beautiful they made their way for the large hotel dining room and sat down for lunch.

Maya and Madeleine felt like princesses. They sat tall and prim, looking at their menus. They were beyond excited to have something to eat other than *biriyani.* The choices were abundant and they couldn't make up their minds. In the end they chose grilled cheese sandwiches. Jill shook her head. This was the dish they ordered every time they went out. The baby that was about to be born would grow up to have a similar fettish. She ate nothing but peanut butter and jelly sandwiches. She would stare at her beloved peanut butter sandwich before eating it and whisper under her breath with sparkling eyes, "Oh I love my peanut butter and jelly sandwich." Maya and Madeleine sat up proudly to the table when their grilled cheese sandwiches arrived and ate them with equivalent satisfaction.

The following day, Jill boarded the plane for Thailand with Marley. Marley was nearly three and Jill couldn't bear to part with her for one whole month at this stage in her life. Once in Thailand, Dr. Nisarat, her obstetrician, made a plan that if she went into labor they would send an ambulance and they would bring Marley with them. The nurses would care for Marley while she had the baby.

As it turned out, this never happened. Bobbie was on time to the day. Michael and the older two girls arrived one week before her delivery date. It gave them time to reconnect and do some fun things in Bangkok. When the night arrived, Michael and Jill went to a nice restaurant and ordered spicy Thai food for dinner. The waiter appeared, looking at Jill's big belly and he said, "Ahhhh, good. In Thailand we have saying, 'hot food, hot bath, hot sex, and the baby will come.'" Jill smiled. "Oh great." She did however, come home and take a hot bath following advances from Michael whom she pushed away because her contractions had begun. She got out of the tub and her water broke. Maybe the saying was true. She wasn't sure if it was dripping bath water or amniotic fluid because she was still wet. A moment later she was sure.

They called a taxi and the three girls and Michael climbed in. Jill sat in the front and gripped the dashboard every time a contraction began. They got stronger and stronger and the taxi driver looked at Jill in a panic that increased with each contraction. His eyes were big and he gripped the steering wheel. He drove quickly yelling at the cars, "Get out of the way!" Despite the increasingly painful contractions, every time the poor driver looked in Jill's direction, it made her laugh. The look on his face was sheer panic. She would have laughed hysterically if she hadn't been battling intermittent bouts of extreme pain, and what struck her funniest came at the peak of it because it was this that induced even more panic for the poor driver.

Two blocks from the hospital the taxi drove down a single lane road. A short ways down there were two large fire trucks blocking it. Men were scattered about dealing with some kind of emergency. The drivers were nowhere in site. The poor taxi driver yelled in Thai and waved his hands frantically. No one heard him so he got out of the car and yelled some more for everyone to get out of the way, that he had a pregnant woman in the car. The men slowly walked to their trucks and moved them out of the way so Jill and her family and the taxi driver could pass. When they pulled up to the front of the hospital, the taxi driver pushed Jill out of the car so fast it made her laugh all the more; he couldn't wait to be rid of her. He opened the back door and pulled Michael and the girls out of the car by the arms and pushed them towards the front of the hospital.

A nurse calmly came out of the door to the hospital and said something to the taxi driver in Thai. The taxi driver appeared utterly beside himself. He pulled at Jill and pushed her back in the car. "We go! We go!" he said. He pushed Michael and the girls back into the car too. He sped around the hospital to a different entrance. Once again, he pulled Jill out of the car and pushed her to the hospital door. A nurse was already there waiting with a wheel chair. He opened the back doors to the taxi and pulled Michael and the girls out. He pushed them towards Jill and the wheelchair swooshing his arms to hurry them up. The taxi driver got in his car just as quickly and began to take off. He hadn't even remembered to collect his fare. Michael ran around the taxi and banged on the window just in time. The man looked like he'd seen a ghost and horrified to see Michael again. Michael handed him a large tip to go with the fare.

Once inside the hospital they were taken to their room. There was a large double bed and a flat couch next to it. Jill asked if she could have a water birth; there was a tub in the room too. They had talked about it. Dr. Nisarat replied, "Honey, there isn't time to fill the bathtub up." As Bobbie's head crowned, Marley hit the walls on either side of the room as she ran back and forth shouting, "It's coming! It's coming! I can see the head, it's coming!" When her head popped out she said, "Ohhhhh, she's so beautiful!!" Michael caught their new baby daughter as she came out and Maya and Madeleine cut the umbilical cord. Marley couldn't keep her hands off of her new baby sister. She stroked her head, her arms, and she cradled her best she could, as much as her mother would allow, saying all the while, "My baby, oh my baby, I love my baby." Jill had to hold on to Bobbie firmly to keep her from taking the baby.

The day the family left Bangladesh permanently Jill took one last ride with Saju, the driver. They took the car to the embassy car lot to drop it off for good. They would wait for a buyer after they had returned home. On the drive there, Jill gave Saju all kinds of advice. "Don't ever act up or steal. Don't do anything unprofessional and you will always have a job. I have you on the embassy list since you have been recommended by me and the regional security office has checked you to make sure you are reputable. If you listen to your next boss and do everything he says, you will be recommended again," she told him. He was young so Jill continued, "Marry a good wife Saju and have a great family. Don't ever cheat on her and be good to her. Remember our talks about how to treat women?" Jill went on as Saju nodded his head and listened. He sniffled now and then. A special relationship had developed between the two. He was like her little brother.

Saju had dutifully taken Jill everywhere she needed to go while she lived in Bangladesh. Every time they drove somewhere, she sat in the backseat practicing her Bengali with him, having conversations about everything and anything. Saju corrected her and asked questions of his own. When they arrived to a destination, Saju would step out and open the door for her and then step in front of her to provide a barrier between her and any loitering men so they wouldn't jeer at her or harass her. While she entered and exited the shop or where ever it was she was going that day, he would stand and lean against the car with his arms folded, glaring at anyone who looked at her. Before Jill entered the car again, Saju would open the door and brush off the seat for her in case it was dirty. In contrast, Saju never did this for Michael nor did he get along or cooperate for him. They were always at odds with each other.

After they dropped the car off, they walked out of the car lot together and stood on the corner of the embassy property. Michael and the girls were waiting with a Peace Corps jeep to take them to the airport. Tears

Chapter 10

Things I Love

(1959 – 1961)

Something deep inside is compelling me to bring to worldly notice those I love and care for so devotedly.

But, first, let me begin with some observations.

Living with people can be such a painful thing; or it can be a rich and beautiful experience. There are so many outside forces existing in society today making people react in their endless variety of ways both to these forces and in their dealings with other people that it is difficult to judge a person for his own character treasure. Society has forced "modern" people to adapt to so many superficial values and possessions in life that the real person is hidden deep down under layers and layers of a barnacle-like personality; one responded to by a host of defense mechanisms or "devices."

That is why I find it so hard to communicate with people. By communication, I mean the highest forms of understanding, sympathy, recognition of like ideals, values, beauties, and mode of expression (semantics). And by highest form I do not mean the ideal, for I am aware that between any two human beings the "ideal" is impossible due to our lack of complete understanding of an absolute interpretation of all things. By highest form, I mean the highest possible form of communication between individuals based on their willingness to express themselves through their most true character and using to their best ability their entire potential of understanding and interpretation of a given thing at a given time. That is what I ask of anyone, anytime; and that is what I, myself, strive always to do. But, I find, people I talk to are not talking to me with this purpose at all – they are talking over me, and themselves, with a motive so inconsequential to what is being said that the whole conversation itself is simply a parody.

And, to my observation at this point, I feel that these ridiculous forms (or vehicles) of communication, these non-meaning, senseless and deceptive misrepresentations of life are due to the complex society whose straining forces condition individuals to respond so falsely and without desire to be "real."

Happily, and to my best fortune, there are many who are trying to be "real" with themselves and to others, despite the hypocrisy, the sham and pretence of a confused society. These are the people who find living most difficult, as I do; for struggling against these undercurrent wills is a hard undertaking and often, a lonely one.

The influence of each of these people I am about to name, has, in some way, some more than others, had great effect on my own character, my own being.

It is to these wonderful unselfish and generous people that I owe much gratitude for the happiness and well being that I have had and still have:

My mother — *My Aunt Viv*
My father
My brother
My Granny R. — *Granddad*
Jr.
Jim
John
Granny A. — *teachers*
Uncle Max — *Miss Paulsen*
Aunt Betty — *Mr. McCoy*
Uncle Bob — *Dr. Shields*
Joyce
Andrea

Friends

Sherline & Dick

Lila & Grant		
Joanna		
Linda	*Nig*	*Father Keane*
Dale	*Joy*	*Father Glazier*
Vince	*Katie*	
Bob	*Shannon*	
Larry	*Kathy*	
Mrs. McCracken		

Bobbie, January 3, 1964

Bobbie, Jo and Lin made their way up the steps of their small town high school. Lin had on her three quarter length and slightly tight fitting aqua blue pants and a white blouse, a paisley scarf and tennis shoes. Bobbie wore a modest skirt and tightly fitting pink sweater and Jo who was forever trying to show off wore a form fitting and daringly colorful short dress and brightly colored stockings with a solid matching straight scarf that held back her hair. Her flirtatious outfit attracted attention and Jo loved it. Girls whispered behind her back all morning. She turned the boys' heads, and some of them commented shamelessly. "Hey baby, looking mighty nice today, how about a date?" More than a couple whistled at her. Jo held her head high and pretended not to notice. However there was a slight sway to her hips as she walked from class to class that day. She knew she looked good and she played it up.

When it was lunch hour, Bobbie and her girlfriends went to Bobbie's house. Jo peeked out the kitchen window, "Is that your Mom's car?" "Um yeah, why?" "Your Mom home?" "No. She's at work. She left it here today." "Hmm ..." "Hmm what? You thinking what I'm thinking?" "Mmmm hmmm, I think I am thinking what you're thinking." "Hey Dale!" Jo called down the hall to the other girls. "Yeah!" Dale yelled back. "You girls up for a little fun?" Lin, Dale and Carolyn came walking down the hall and into the kitchen. Lin asked, "What ya got in mind?" Bobbie leaned against one of the counters jingling the car keys in her hand, smiling mischievously. "And just what are those to, might I ask?" "Oh," Bobbie said as if it was not much of anything, and she spun herself around, taunting them, jingling the keys over her shoulder. "Maybe they're just the keys to my Mom's car …" and again, she flashed her mischievous smile. "Oh ho! We're goin' on a joy ride girls!" said Carolyn. Dale and Lin clapped their hands. "What are we waitin' for? Lunch doesn't last that long! Let's go!!"

The girls grabbed their things and filed out the back door. "You sure your Mom won't come home?" Jo asked. "No, for sure she won't." "She doesn't have a way home!" Bobbie laughed. "Oh right!!" Jo laughed too. They walked out onto the patio. A huge shade tree covered everything. The girls passed under it and the rhododendron bushes that framed the patio. They were in full bloom and bursting with color. Pink and white flowers were everywhere and some dusted the backyard driveway. Once on the black asphalt, the heat of it went right through their shoes. The sun beat down on their necks.

"Alright!" Lin jumped in the car. "Let's get outta here!" Dale, Lin, and Carolyn piled in as Bobbie put the key in the ignition and started the engine. Lin cranked up the music and rolled down the windows and Bobbie sped down the long narrow driveway that led from the backyard to the front of the house, nearly taking out the mailbox at the end of the driveway. Carolyn hung her head out the window and yelled, "Woo hooooo!!" and they raced down the road to town. The excitement of passing by shops and the favorite local fast food hangouts, waving and stopping to talk to friends took more time than they realized. The school bell had rung long before the girls swung into the parking lot. Quite a few kids still loitered around. The girls made sure whoever was there noticed them. A few students were still heading to class, and a few stragglers hung back, smoking cigarettes, leaning against their cars. The girls weren't ready to end their fun.

"Well now what?" Lin asked. "Go back to class I guess," said Dale. No one moved to get out of the car. "Ooooor …" Bobbie said. "Yeah," Jo asked. "Got something in mind?" "We could keep driving …" "Oh yeah, let's keep going," said Carolyn. "Yeah, let's keep driving!" said Jo. "Where to girls?" asked Bobbie. "I'll take ya anywhere you wanna go!" "We could go get a shake," one of them suggested. "Mmmm, I'm not hungry, we just ate," said Dale. The other girls agreed. "We could go back to Bobbie's house and hang out," another girl suggested. "Aww, we were just there, that's boring," said Jo. "Yeah," everyone agreed. "What about …" "Yes?"

Jo asked. "I see that little mind of yours workin' ..." Bobbie had that mischievous grin on her face again. "Whatcha got up your sleeve?" "What if..." the girls hung on her words. "Well out with it!" Carolyn said. "What if we go to Big Bear?" said Bobbie. "Whoaaa!" said Jo. Someone whistled. "Wheeeww!! You really got nerve girl!" said Dale. "Let's do it!" Carolyn said. "Yeah, let's do it!" said Jo. It was unanimous. Bobbie pulled a U'eee in the middle of the road and flipped the car around. They were headed for Big Bear.

The wind whipped through their hair as they flew around the curves that wound through the mountains. They turned the music up even louder and sang with the windows down. The cold mountain air stung their cheeks the higher up the mountain they went. It was a good hour before they arrived at the town of Big Bear. They drove down the main street through town once and that took about five minutes, so they decided to go to the lake. The lake was surrounded by tall evergreens. Bobbie loved the fresh smell of the pines. She breathed it in with one big breath. They parked the car, and ran to the lake, shouting and laughing, slipping off their shoes. They walked barefoot over the thick bed of pine needles to the water's edge and dipped their feet in the icy water. "This sure beats English class fifth period!" laughed Jo. "Yeah," agreed Lin, "poor kids stuck in class with Mrs. Schumocker!" Bobbie laughed at the thought of it. She grabbed both hands of the closest girl, which happened to be Jo, and spun her around in a circle. The other girls joined and the five of them collapsed laughing onto the ground completely out of breath. "Uggh, I'm going to have mud all over me!" Lin said. "Aw you're alright," Jo said. "Hey it's been a while since we ate lunch. I don't know about you all, but I'm hungry! We ought to go grab something in town," Dale suggested. Everyone agreed that was a great idea.

They drove down the street speaking loudly with the windows still down. Anyone walking down the quiet street that day could've heard every word they said. They were a bit of a spectacle. Finally, they arrived at a little deli on the side of the road. It was a sort of convenience and grocery store in one, and it included a sandwich bar. The bell dangling from the door handle jingled as the girls went inside the small store. A man was at the register paying for his items and the clerk said hello to the girls as she collected his money.

Two of the girls went to the deli counter and asked for already made sandwiches from inside the display widow. Lin couldn't decide between a hot dog or a ham and cheese sandwich. "Which one do I want more, hmmm. Hot or cold?" She decided on the hot dog and walked to the register, grabbing a coke along the way. Jo and Bobbie were already at the register finishing their purchase and heading for the door. "Wait for ya outside guys" Bobbie called over her shoulder.

Dale was at the back of the store checking out other snacks. As Jo went to open the door, Bobbie happened to see Aunt Viv who lived in the small mountain town, and she was marching down the sidewalk in their direction. Jo recognized her too. She'd met her once before. She stopped in her tracks and looked at Bobbie. "It's your Aunt, she whispered. "Yeah I see her." "What do we do?" "Come on," she pulled Jo back into the store. "Cover for me. I'm going to slip down one of the aisles."

"What's going on?" Carolyn asked. "Shhh," said Jo. She gestured towards the door. "That's Bobbie's Aunt. She's hiding. We gotta cover for her." "Ohhhh." She whispered the news to Lin as Aunt Viv came right inside the very store they were in. The bells jingled and the clerk said "Hello there Viv, how you doing today?" "Oh couldn't be better," she said. "How about you? How's this fine weather treatin' you?" "Oh it's fantastic, but you know I'm stuck in here most of the day, so can't really enjoy it much. But it's a lot easier to get to work without all that snow we were having last week, so can't complain!" "I hear ya," Aunt Viv said.

The girls at the front of the store kept their heads down and tried to act inconspicuous. Bobbie nearly knocked Dale over running to the back of the store as Dale was coming the other direction. "Hey, what's the rush?" she asked, a little annoyed. "You nearly knocked the food out of my hands!" "Oh sorry Dale, come on, you gotta come with me. Stand in front of me and act like you're picking something out." "Why?" "Because! My Aunt is here. She'll tell my Mom and I'll be in big trouble." She followed Bobbie trying to stay directly in back of her. She held on to her sweater so she wouldn't lose her. "Hey don't pull my sweater out!" "Don't worry, and anyway, what are you more worried about, your sweater or getting caught?" "Good point. Sorry." "The way you're moving I can barely keep up." "Ok ok!" They got to the very back of the store and Bobbie slipped behind the very end of the aisle to take cover. Dale wasn't sure which aisle to stand in to keep her hidden.

Aunt Viv was at the deli. "Well that ham looks very nice, I think I'll take some of that," she told the deli man. "Gimmee half a pound. That oughta do. Will you cut it up nice and thin for me Sam?" "Sure thing. Anything for my special lady." "Oh now, am I special?" "Sure ya are, you're always in here. That's special ain't it?" "Well when you put it like that, I suppose it is," she said. "Give me some of that potato salad too, will ya?" "Sure thing. How much?" "Oh give me a pound. Everyone in the house'll eat that up." Lin, Jo and Carolyn lingered at the door, not sure what to do. "Let's go put our food down in the car and come back in like we forgot something, and at least we can provide some distraction for Bobbie," "Good idea," said Jo. The bell jingled when they opened the door. The clerk said goodbye to them and Lin told her "Oh we'll be back. We forgot something. We're just going to go set these things down in the car first." "Well here, how about you girls just give your stuff to me and I'll hold it up here while you go back and get what you need." "Oh thanks," said Jo. They piled their purchases on the counter. "They'll be just fine right here, I'll keep an eye on them. No one'll bother 'em." "Thanks," they said and they fanned out each in different directions.

Bobbie saw Jo coming up the aisle and said "Come on Dale, this way." She guided Dale from behind, maneuvering her with her hands at her waist so she would go the way she wanted her to go. When the two girls reached Jo, Bobbie peeked around to see if the coast was clear. She didn't see anyone so she pushed past them nearly knocking over a stack of canned tomatoes. Dale caught one that was about to fall to the floor. Bobbie dashed quickly down the rest of the aisle as inconspicuously as possible and crouched low behind a row of macaroni and cheese.

She tip toed around the end of the aisle and did not see anyone there so she made a run for it, but as she rounded the turn she nearly ran right into Aunt Viv. Bobbie froze. It took a moment for Aunt Viv to recognize her. "Bobbie! What on earth are you doing here on a Tuesday?! What a wonderful surprise!" Aunt Viv loved Bobbie. They were very close.

Aunt Viv was aware of the three girls peeping from behind the other isles. It was hard to pull anything past Aunt Viv. "Who are your friends?" She made it clear she knew they were together. "Oooh … we were just hangin' around and I was showin' the girls old Big Bear ..." Bobbie said casually as if it was nothing out of the ordinary. Aunt Viv eyed the girls suspiciously. "Well come on then girls, if you're gonna play hookie, may as well come on over to my house and have a cup of tea and cookies." Aunt Viv was secretly delighted to have a bunch of young girls interrupt her lonely day off work. Having three boys, she quite welcomed the chitter chatter of females.

Aunt Viv finished her shopping and told them to meet her at the house. She put her shopping bags in the car, including a packet of biscuits for the girls to have for tea. She pulled away from the curb and headed for her small cabin in the woods. The girls were already making themselves comfortable in her living room when she walked in the door.

"So tell me girls, how'd you manage getting hold of Effie's car and coming all the way up here without her knowing?" She was quite amused at the stunt. Effie prized her fancy blue Cadillac. Bobbie had a very guilty look on her face and said, "I guess there's no point in trying to pretend she let us do it." It was halfway a question. Aunt Viv laughed. "Nope."

The girls told her all about it and she howled with laughter. She secretly delighted in sharing a secret with her favorite niece. She relished the idea of having one up on her sister. She promised she would not tell. Aunt Viv and Effie had a sister relationship like that of teenagers. All of their encounters ended in a fight, each speaking indignantly and self-righteously until it descended into their native tongue, Polish.

Aunt Viv began in with her stories. She had hundreds of them and endless enthusiasm for recounting each one. Bobbie had to cut Aunt Viv off so they could depart in time to beat Bobbie's mother home from work. She had to do this several times actually. They finished up their cookies and thanked Aunt Viv for the tea and said their goodbyes. Quickly heading for the door before Aunt Viv could start up another story, they made their exit.

"Thank you for coming girls. I really enjoyed meeting all of you. And don't worry, your secret's mum with me." She winked at them. The girls laughed and said thank you and hopped in the car.

They came down the mountain by late afternoon with plenty of time to beat Bobbie's Mom home from work. Bobbie dropped Carolyn, Dale and Jo off at their homes and Lin at school to join her after school sewing club before coming home herself. She carefully parked the car in the garage where it had been and left everything as she had found it, with the exception of the gas gauge that had completely escaped her attention. Bobbie stepped out of the car with wind blown hair and the smell of pine and fresh mountain air still in her nostrils. The adrenaline rush of the day left her pleasantly tired as she walked into the house.

Bobbie's Mom came home and knew right away something was off. She couldn't put her finger on it, but she knew there was something. She went to the garage to begin a load of laundry and peeked into her car for her sunglasses. She'd been missing them all day and was worried she'd lost them. The door was locked and they weren't where she normally left them so she went inside to get her keys. She unlocked the car door and got inside to look around. She found them on the other side of the console from where she normally put them. "Hmm." She slid the key into the ignition, not really sure what prompted her to do it, and noticed the gas gauge was not where she had left it. In fact it was more than three quarters of a tank empty!

She was quiet when she walked back into the house, but it was not the calm sort of quiet. It was the stormy kind. Bobbie couldn't be sure if this stormy quiet was a result of knowing about her ill deed or if it was something else. Guilt has a way of putting one on edge even when nothing is amiss. Poor Effie. Bobbie and James really took advantage of her lonely station as a single parent; one small lady holding down a job is no match for two boisterous and impetuous teenagers.

Their mother paced the house with a look of consternation on her face. Her forehead was wrinkled as if she was puzzling over something trying to make sense of it. It wasn't unusual for her to do this. She frequently came home this way. She marched up and down the hall with her typical quick pace, changing clothes, going through the motions of a normal after-work day, back up the hall, pulling something out to eat, head still bent in consternation. She rather harshly dropped the lettuce on the counter for dinner and a few other ingredients, not looking up. Timidly Bobbie approached her mother, maintaining the façade that nothing out of the ordinary had happened.

"Hi Mom. Have a good day at work?" Effie looked at Bobbie, penetrating her with a gaze that seemed to be able to see right through everything and anything Bobbie was thinking in between. "*I* had a good day. What about *you?"* Bobbie was cautious. Did she know? It was hard to tell. "Oh, it was average." She tried to play it cool. "Is something wrong Mom?" Bobbie asked. She walked across the kitchen and looked up sideways at Bobbie out of the corner of one eye. Her brow was still furrowed like she was trying really hard to recall something she couldn't put her finger on. "I just don't know, something … hmm, not sure what it is, something doesn't seem right." "What is it Mom?" Effie was mad and didn't appreciate being played but she knew someone was playing her.

"She hasn't figured it out yet, but she knows something," Bobbie was sure, but she thought she was safe for the moment. Time to divert her attention, Bobbie decided. "Mom, Marge called earlier and wants to set up a bridge party this weekend. She was wondering if you could have it at our house." It worked! The creases in her forehead slowly smoothed out thinking about her friend and the idea of entertaining. "Hey Mom? Is there anything you need me to do? Want me to do the laundry or something?" A little syrupy sweet helpfulness can go a long ways she figured. "Or I can go water the yard if you like?" "Well, that's kind of you." It took Effie a little too long to answer, and in Bobbie's anxiousness she added "I could even mop the kitchen for you." She made the last offer a little too impatiently and a little too sweetly. As soon as the words were out of her mouth she realized she'd gone a little overboard. That's when Effie cocked her head sideways again, eyeing Bobbie suspiciously. "You're awfully anxious to be helpful today." She didn't take her eyes off Bobbie. She was studying her and it made her uncomfortable. She tried not to fidget and to appear composed.

By this time James was in the kitchen with his gangly legs and arms sprawled all over a step stool that served as the head chair to the eat-in kitchen table. He was stuffing his mouth with whatever he could find. He was amused to see what was going on, because for sure something was. The tension hung like a thick blanket in the air. "Oh, well, you look tired Mom, and I just thought I'd offer to help you out, you work so hard for us kids and do everything all the time …" Altruism is always a good course of action but too much is a sure sign of guilt. What self-absorbed teenager is that helpful?

"Hmmm," she answered. Bobbie's stage performance was hanging on a thread. Effie's head went down again and the wrinkles came back. "Hey

James, what are you staring at?" Bobbie gave him a good slug. Wrong question. His answer did not help. "Oh, I was just sitting here waiting to see what's about to blow." He had that ridiculous irritating grin of amusement on his face. Bobbie tried to ignore the anger rising inside of her and said as convincingly as she could muster, "Hey, wanna play some basketball?" He looked at her slyly, with that stupid grin. Bobbie wanted to slap it off his face. He got up out of his chair about as slowly as humanly possible saying, "Oooookaaaaay, sure." What he really relished was the outcome to the drama he was sure was about to play out. He sauntered towards the door, slowly. Bobbie held it open trying to hurry his slow lanky body along, rolling her hands in emphatic gestures like a valet, and giving him a good shove once he was in front of her.

Before they made it out the door, their mom said "Hey! Wait a minute there." James stopped in his tracks, turned, and planted himself in a comfortable position against the kitchen counter. The inquisitive amused grin returned to his face. Bobbie's hand was still on the doorknob. "We were so close." She kept her back turned, and her head down. She answered with as peppy a reply as she could muster, trying not to betray herself. "Yeah, what is it?" She tried to sound innocent. "Did anyone go anywhere today, Bobbie?" "She knows ..." Bobbie thought. It was a trap and Bobbie had the feeling no matter what answer she gave, it would be the wrong one. She hesitated a bit too long. "No, just school, Mom. Where else would I go?" Bobbie was frozen in the doorway, not sure what to do with herself. She could feel James's penetrating and ever increasingly inquisitive gaze falling on her. Just then the phone rang and Effie said, "We're not done yet," and went to answer it.

James waited for her to speak. Finally she couldn't stand it any longer. "WHAT?" she asked him. She wanted so badly to slap the smug look off his face. "Oh nothing. Nothing at all." He waited. When she did not offer up an explanation, he softened his demeanor and asked in as deep and as reassuring a voice as his newly formed vocal chords could muster, "So what'd you do?" There was a silent code of loyalty between them once a secret had been divulged, and it was obvious one was about to be. It was a pact neither of them would break.

Bobbie didn't know where to begin. He prompted her, "So'd you take the car?" "Yes, I did," she admitted. "Where'd you go?" Slowly she answered, "Big Bear." He broke into a hearty laugh, his eyes watering he laughed so hard. "You went to *Big Bear???"* he asked incredulously. "No! You didn't!" "Yes, I did," she said. "And I'm glad you find this so amusing." "You went all the way to *Big Bear????!!"* He still couldn't believe it. "That's what I said." She had to admit that his laughter was taking the edge off of the intensity of the moment. It was kind of preposterous she had driven all the way there. It was a little difficult to remain mad when he was laughing so hard.

A grin formed around the corners of her mouth despite herself as their mother walked back into the kitchen. Very calmly and deliberately she came towards the kitchen table, raised her hand high above it and let the keys to the car fall dramatically, landing with a loud cachink chang. Bobbie's grin faded but James's did not. He was highly amused and looking forward to the outcome. He sauntered over to the stool again and had a seat. Bobbie looked up at her mother. Effie pierced Bobbie with her gaze. There were daggers in her eyes. "So do you still want to stand there and tell me nothing happened today?" Her eyes bore into Bobbie. Bobbie stammered, "Well, I … I might have taken the car out for a little ride …" "Little? Are you sure about little? Would you like to clarify your definition of *little?*" She laid into Bobbie like a lawyer who had found the last piece of incriminating evidence to win a case. "Well, it may have been a *little* more than *little,"* she confided lamely. "And exactly what does '*a little more than little*' mean? Please enlighten me." "Well … I guess I drove around the town quite a bit … is what I mean …" Bobbie tried to be vague, figuring the less she talked, the less her mom would know and the smaller the infraction. Effie dropped the gavel. "*Well,* that must have been some driving around town to use up *¾ tank of gasoline.*" "Oh ho!!" James bellowed. There was no point in keeping up the pretense. "Alright, Mom, you're right. I'm really sorry, I know it was wrong; I went to Big Bear with my friends."

Although it was Bobbie who suffered the brunt of it, James still had to listen to the screaming angry voice that crashed down as well. He winced as if in physical pain. "And you *missed school too!* A *whole entire day* no doubt! What were you thinking? That is *not your car!*" She yelled. "I know Mom." Effie cut Bobbie off. She was beyond caring what Bobbie had to say. "That's our only car, what if you had crashed it? What if you had been hurt, or worse killed? What if you had injured or killed those other kids you took joyriding with you?? Did you think of that?" "Well, I … no … I guess not …" Bobbie answered meekly. "NO! I didn't think so! It just makes me SICK to imagine what could have happened. I'm so angry I don't know what I'm going to do. You are in such big trouble I can't even see straight!"

"Yes Mom," she put her head down. Effie went on and on and on until even James had had it. He looked at Bobbie because by this time, their mother was ranting and raving, repeating her self over and over again. James winked at Bobbie with one eye and smirked slightly out of one corner of his mouth so their mom wouldn't see. Bobbie tried not to smile. When Effie's head was turned briefly, slamming something down while she went on her tirade, James bobbed his head from side to side mimicking her words in silent mockery. His eyes bulged out like a silly clown and Bobbie couldn't help but laugh. Bobbie put her hand over her mouth to muffle the sound and Effie became more furious than ever. James swung his legs back and forth like a jester miming a play. It was a sharp contrast to their mom's violent gestures. She was so focused on her anger at Bobbie she didn't notice.

James made a head bobble right in front of her, swaying his head from side to side like a singing marionette. Bobbie bit her lip to keep from laughing. But he wouldn't stop. Little by little he dared make fun of their mom right in front of her. He could somehow get away with it; he had long been accepted as the family clown. There was no reining him in. Effie had long since stopped trying. He always got away with everything and this usually annoyed Bobbie to no end. At the moment, however, it was funny. He continued miming, moving his lips as if he were mouthing Effie's exact words, only he was doing it to her. A small giggle escaped from Bobbie and that encouraged him even more. He loved an audience. Bobbie tried to be serious. She turned and furrowed her brow at him with her arms folded across her chest in a pretend show of scolding. He looked back at her and raised his own eyebrows, adding the biggest grin you can imagine, his mouth opened wide in the goofiest expression ever.

Bobbie burst out laughing as she hit him in the arm. He feigned dismay as if it hurt. It was part of the jest and he continued his dancing head mime. Bobbie couldn't hold back. Now she was laughing. Trying not to laugh made it all the funnier. Her brother laughed too. Even he couldn't hold back his enjoyment of the entertainment he had woven into this little family scenario.

He broke into a fit of laughter and both he and Bobbie laughed and laughed right in front of their poor mom. By now they didn't hear a word she was saying. This made Effie angrier than ever. She asked "Oh? You think this is funny? Well we'll see how funny you think it is to be grounded." She picked up a dishrag and threw it at them. After that, she picked up a broom and swiped at them with it. The exchange between them became absurd. "You cut it out!" she yelled at Bobbie's brother. Bobbie and James got up and ran through the house with Effie chasing them with the broom and the rag. Effie wasn't much of a match for the two of them; they were young and strong. She was small and slight and a good two inches shorter than Bobbie and a foot shorter than James.

Effie brought the story up for years afterwards, and retold it, recalling each detail as vividly as if it had just happened every time. Her brow furrowed during each retelling and her voice had an angry edge to it. She would look away appearing as if she could see it that very moment in her mind's eye and it was as if she was reliving it all over again.

Bobbie was tired after the thrill of the trip to Big Bear, and then the letdown of getting caught. She went to her room to write in her journal. It was her last year of high school and she was determined to make the most of it but interwoven with her adolescent escapades and eruptions with her mother were times of reflection. This was one of those moments. She kicked off her shoes and got comfortable on her bed, laying on her stomach, with her feet in the air, leaning on one elbow, a pen in the hand of the other. She began to write, but it was not about the day's events. It was about something entirely different, a quiet moment to reflect on something that had been on her mind for some time and now felt like as good a time as any to write about it.

Nov 13, 1960

"This school is so darn cliche and snobby! It's so darn hard to get in a group of kids you really like and have fun with. I'm not just speaking for myself, I have lots of friends; but for new kids; it's murder. It's a hard thing to explain. Linda & Joanna & I are like sisters; inseparable; we're always together, so we

don't have this social acceptance problem. We're not hermits, we have other friends, lots of them; but we're broad-minded enough to recognize it on the kids who don't have any friends or a "group," especially new kids. We three are kind of nonconformist; we do what we want, when we want, and don't give a damn if the "socies" think we're neat or popular. We don't hate the "socies," some of them we've known for years, but what we hate is the fact that they think they're the "ultimate," the "high society," the "popular ones." They are about the only ones who think this way. Any way, at school, the three of us just mess around with everybody; & not being conceited (just frank) I'd say we were pretty well liked & respected by everyone (including the socies). But it shouldn't be this way. I don't mean the three of us shouldn't be friends; it'd be terrible if we weren't (we're havin' too much fun), but I don't think the school should be divided up in these groups so much. From the socies on down I bet there are about 50 groups in our school. And each group talks about the other and chops it, and gossips about it. That's why we aren't in any one particular group, we just mess around with the kids we like as individuals from each one. It's not a very big school anyway, and I think everyone should be in one big group. Maybe I'm asking for a perfect society, I don't know, but it seems so unfair to new kids who have a hard time being accepted in any one group & maybe winding up with the wrong bunch unknowingly."

Bobbie had a list of all of her favorite things. From time to time she would pull it out and add to it just to make herself feel better. Now was one of those times.

Things I Love:

August 28, 1960

America, the Military, My Family, Sheppy, My Friends, Fresh Air, Nature, God, Water, Beaches, Mountains, Exercise, Sun, Dark Tans, Rain on my Face, Listening to Music, Writing, Reading, Daydreaming, Art, Learning, Wisdom, Respect, To Laugh, Clothes, Individuality, Privacy to Think, To be Mischeivious, To be Mysterious, Moods (not bad ones), To feel Inspired, To feel Secure, To feel Belonged, To be Loved, Compliments, Good Food, Plane Rides (esp. take-offs!), Steaks, Fried Chicken, Salads, Ice Cream (esp. peppermint), Spaghetti, Records by Perey Faith, Arthur Lyman, Billy Vaughn, Kingston Trio, Johnny Mathis, Bobby Darin, Doris Day, Ella Fitzgerald, Edie Gorme,

Ray Conibo, Movies (esp. love stories), Being Impulsive, Mackie (my bird), Getting Dressed Up, Formal Occasions, Helping People, Surprises, Being Tough, Foreigners, Being Myself, Nonconformity, Ambition, Perseverence, Having a Mind of my Own, Being Headstrong, Pine Trees, Big Log Fires, Horses, Horseback riding, Animals, History, Darkness, Romance, Humbleness, Generosity, Westerns, Sophistication, Tactfulness, Carefreeness, Bike Rides in the Country, Sunsets, Sunrises, To Feel Warm, To feel Good, To feel Accomplished, To feel Starry-eyed, Children, Marriage, Youth, To be Free, Independent, Responsibility, Stuffed Animals, Knickknacks, Sweatshirts, Tennis Shoes, Shiney Hair, Unpredictability, Intellect (but even more – common sense), Cities at Night, All the Seasons, Snow, Tobagganing, Log Cabins, Mountains, To be Proud, Quiet Bravery, Meeting People, Family Get-Togethers, Birthdays, Watching People, To be Happy, To Sing in the Shower, To Play Tennis, To Play Volleyball (esp. at the beach), To be Daring, To Understand Myself, To Understand Others, French, Literature, Painting, Drawing (esp. people).

~ Bobbie

On the last day of school before winter break they were full of vacation fever. "Why don't you guys come over to my house tomorrow so we can discuss our plans for break?" Bobbie suggested. "For starters we have to plan how we're going to put on this dinner for our moms." "Great idea!" Lin agreed. "I can come," said Jo. "Good. It's set then. How about noon? Then we can sleep in for our first day of break." "Sounds good."

"I can't wait to go out, sleep in, get together with boys …" Jo said. "Me too!" said Lin. "Oh yeah!" Bobbie said. "I wonder who we'll meet, and where." "Oh we'll have to plan that too. We can do what we want. We're seniors and this is our last chance!!" said Bobbie. "Yeah!" answered Jo. "We'll never get this chance again," "This may be the only time the three of us will be together, young, beautiful, free." "That's right!" Bobbie said. "No responsibilities, no one to answer to" "…except our parents," reminded Lin. "I could do without the parent part," Bobbie frowned. "Oh bother parents," began Jo. "That obstacle is easily remedied. You sleep at my house, I sleep at yours …" "Oh yeah!" Bobbie said with a cunning wink. The girls had that trick down.

The girls stepped down the stairs of the entrance to the school. They got into Lin's car as several boys drove by shouting out their windows, teasing them. The spirit was contagious. The three girls laughed and Jo leaned half way out the window and answered flirtatiously. That was all the encouragement the boys needed. "Be careful," Bobbie warned. "They're going to think you're flirting with them." "Of course," Jo said flamboyantly as if that was exactly what she wanted. Bobbie turned her head and commented to Lin in a secret whisper, "Ok, she's asking for it."

Monday, Lin and Jo came to Bobbie's house for a meeting. They knocked on the door and Bobbie answered. "Come on in guys. Let's get this meeting started. We have a lot of planning to do. Mom works, so we have the house to ourselves to plan the food and mess around" Bobbie told the girls. One by one the girls made their way into the kitchen and sat around the eat-in kitchen nook table that was the gathering place at Bobbie's house. "First off, there will be cocktails," Bobbie stated matter-of-factly. That was a given of course. "Tuesday we'll bake cookies & fudge," Stated Jo. The food preparation planning continued until each course was finalized and the tasks were delineated.

It was at some point during this gathering that Bobbie went and dyed her hair blue. James came home and laughed his head off. Lin and Jo had been trying for a different color, however Bobbie's hair was so blond, the dye took extreme effect apparently and didn't quite turn out right.

Their friend Dave came over to add to the chaos. He thought he was really cool. In he walked thinking he was all that. Bobbie got so mad at him she threw a raw egg on his head. The thoughtful idea to plan a party for their mothers spiraled downward into a playful and rather messy get together.

That night Bobbie and her friends went to the Drive-in show to see "North to Alaska." They left at 5:30 and got grinders on the way. The girls pulled into the Drive-in and into a parking spot almost in the middle and slightly over halfway back from the screen. Bobbie volunteered to get soda and popcorn from the outdoor concession stand. She walked to the car trying to balance everything on the small tray they had given her and handed it out to the girls. She slid in and the three of them sat squeezed together on the front seat to get the best view of the movie screen.

Bobbie wrote in her journal several days later that contrary to what they had told their parents, what they really did after seeing the movie was go to L.A. to see the lights.

Dec 16, 1960-*"We left after the movie and got grinders on the way. We saw the lights, and went to a coffee shop, and went on a high chill, and met some boys from Claremont Mens College; and in that order. We got home at 1:00 and ran out of gas in our driveway! Lin & Jo both spent the night so we could get an early start on our dinner that day. We got up at 1:00 and started at 3:00. We were washing breakfast dishes, vacuuming & cleaning house at 6:00 and were (by some miracle) ready by seven for dinner."*

"Hey Bobbie, what about cocktails?" "Yeah, Jo, got the crème de mint?" Bobbie asked. "Yep. Sure do," replied Jo. "Well then, bring it over and pour it in! I got the shaker." "Next! Who's got the milk and lime sherbet?" "I do!" It was Linda. "Ok, get it shakin' then!" Jo picked it up and did the cha cha around the kitchen shaking the ingredients. "Ok, that should do it. I think we better taste it to make sure it's right," said Jo. "Absolutely," replied Bobbie, as if it went without saying. "It's pretty darn good," Bobbie approved. The girls kept tasting, however, and before they knew it, the shaker was empty.

Effie, Bobbie's Mother, walked in the door first. "Surprise!!" the girls yelled. The table had been set with the formal dinnerware and all the trimmings. "Oh my!" Her hands went to her mouth and her eyes grew big. She smiled and said, "You guys! What have you been up to?" "Sit down, Mom," Bobbie told her. "We have a special dinner for you tonight!" Effie did as she was instructed immediately and Jo put one of the cocktails in front of her. "Wow! What's this?!" Effie acted extra surprised. She wanted to make sure the girls knew how grateful she was.

The doorbell rang and the other two mothers appeared at the door. Jo and Lin let them in and brought them to their places at the dining room table. Their exclamations of surprise were just as elaborate, and they quickly joined in the fun, toasting each other with their exotic cocktails. Effie held her glass high and cheerily said, "Nazdraviya," in Polish. Effie said this at all of her toasts. It meant "To your health."

James walked into the living room to inspect the progression of events. Mostly, he wanted food. He was continuously hungry. James was dressed in his usual sloppy jeans and an old t-shirt. It was in direct contrast to the prettily dressed ladies who were never without their high-heeled shoes and perfectly sculpted hair. "Dinner ready yet?" he asked, walking into the kitchen. Bobbie looked over her shoulder and cringed. "James, if we have to feed you, you'll take half the food. Can't you feed yourself?" "What d'ya expect me to do? I don't know how to cook." "I don't know, and I really don't care," Bobbie answered. "But you're not eating our special dinner for our moms."

Jo picked up a pitcher containing more of the pre-made cocktail drink. She waved it in front of James, raising her eyebrows at him. He asked, "What's that?" "It's our special cocktail," she tempted him. "No, he can't have that," Bobbie abruptly curtailed the offer. "I didn't want any anyway," he informed Bobbie with his nose in the air like he was one of the ladies. "I'm hungry. I just want food," he said. "Come on. Just a bit?" "No." Bobbie was adamant. He poked around the kitchen, attempting to snitch a little tidbit here and there. Bobbie was right behind him, scolding him and trying to kick him out. James scavenged through every dish, successfully getting a few bites into his mouth. Bobbie slapped his hands and chased him out of the kitchen. He meandered back in, poking through the cupboards and anything laying around.

Effie and the other women sat at the table, sipping their cocktails, waiting for their food. Drinking on an empty stomach made the alcohol go to Effie's head. She was of slight build and forever on a most strict diet she adhered to with unwavering discipline. As a result, she was perfectly thin the whole of her life. Effie waved her glass in the air, calling for a refill. "Girls!" she asked, "Got some more of that stuff?" Jo ran over and poured another glass. Happily and with ever-enthusiastic gusto she raised her glass into the air and announced for the third time, "Nazdraviya!!"

James hovered between the kitchen and the dining room like a vulture waiting patiently to drop in and scoop up any leftovers. Effie spied him loitering around the living room and called him. "Come on James, come join us!" "Jo! Get James a glass!!" "Yes M'amm! Coming right up!" She went to get the pitcher and a clean fancy glass. She handed it to James and he held the dainty stem in his big hand. "What do I do with this? I don't drink out of this little tea party ladies stuff." "Get me a real glass," he said, trying to act like the man he was becoming. Jo took the fancy glass from him and got him a new one. She came back with the pitcher as well. Effie held her glass in the air, ready to toast again. "Come on James! What's taking you so long?! Get over here. Let's toast!" James mumbled under his breath, "I can see she's already toasted." Jo grinned. "Nazdraviya!" Effie announced impatiently, a little louder than the last time, and not waiting for James to walk over to the table. Effie held her glass up as she said it. The other ladies drank modestly, and though Effie was a lady beyond compare in every other respect, she could hold her liquor better than a drunken sailor. As the night wore on, she called to the girls and James and anyone who cared to join her, "Come on guys, fill her up. Where's your drink?" She asked anyone who wasn't holding a glass.

The girls pulled the dinner off and everything went better than they could've expected. A few days later Bobbie went to the mountains for some mistletoe and greenery with a few of her friends. That night they made big plans for sneaking up to the cabin to spend the night. They had had another key made, & told their moms they were spending the night with Carolyn even though she was going too. At the last minute plans fell through, but it was a good thing because the weather turned bad and they would've gotten snowed in. They went horse back riding instead. Lin and Bobbie went with a couple of guys, John and Larry.

Bobbie went to the mountains again with her family for Christmas to spend it with Aunt Viv. They arrived at 7:00 pm and went to midnight mass. It was a disappointment Bobbie thought. "The whole thing lacked any spiritual message, it was too business-like. "They had fun at the cabin, even though it was cold and there was so much snow. When they came home they went horse-back riding again and Bobbie wrote in her journal "What a blast!"

After Christmas, parties and sleepovers filled the rest of winter break. One such sleepover was at Jo's but it turned out Jo's mother was out of it and she couldn't have Bobbie over. Jo called and informed her several times, "My brother thought you were coming and got all spruced up." She kept bringing it up and shortly after Bobbie received another call. "Hey Bobbie, how would you like to come to a dance with me?" It was Clark, Jo's older brother. Bobbie had her reservations because she knew his nickname was "Wolf," but Jo talked her into it.

The dance wasn't exactly what Bobbie was expecting. Most of the girls were about as dressed up as she was, that is, they wore "sheaths," a type of form-fitting dress. There was supposed to be a band but they never showed up. There was beer and Clark kept meandering off to get some. The money that was meant for the band ended up being used on more beer so it wound up being a big party.

Clark and a friend tried to get Bobbie to have some beer all evening. "Here Bobbie, I brought you one, now you have to take it." He was polite about it, but she refused. She ended up having a bit of beer eventually but acted like she'd had much more than she had to be funny. She wrote in her journal the following day:

Dec 29, 1960-Clark tho't I was out of it so after the Sheriff broke the party up around two AM he took me to some café for a coffee. I was fakin' him out for the most part. After that we first drove around; I finally got home at 3:00. Mom heard me after I'd gotten all the way back to my room so I told her I was just gettin' up to go to the bathroom & had gotten in at 12:30. Heh, heh. Clark didn't try anything other than makin' out-which he's pretty good at. I didn't have a hangover Saturday, but I sure didn't feel like eatin' anything."

The following day she, her brother and Effie went to the mountains again. She wrote about that too:

Dec 30, 1960-We didn't get up to the mountains till about 1:00 PM. I'm surprised we made it up there at all the way James & Mom were screamin' & yellin' all morning. I tried my darnedest to keep out of it, but Mom always drags me into it. I was so fed up, I almost walked to Big Bear. She just can't seem to realize that James is usin' her for all she's worth. The louder he screams, the more he gets. Well, I won't go into that now.

There were more parties but school started back up and shortly after, she wrote about her reflections of the parties and all of the festivities of winter break.

Jan 5, 1961-I haven't changed, I know that. I had a good time at those parties, sure, but it's not a habit. I promised my Dad, when he died, I would live up to his standards: and I will. Linda and Jo have high standards too, and if we do anything silly, it's just for fun's sake.

Like last night! We went to Palm Springs after the basketball game. We met one of the same boys we saw last time, and asked him if there were any parties. He saw to it there was one. He & his two buddies buzzed us over to their house for some "stuff." (We went in our car, we weren't about to chance it). We had champagne, whisky, vodka, crème de mint-anything or everything. All three of us had some, but not enough to do anything. The boys took us to one of their houses but their parents came home ... and we had to go anyway, we took 'em back to their car and Joanna and I started actin' like we were really out of it. When we got there we (Jo & I) really assed off; we took off down the road at a dead run, laughin' & screamin', with Linda and the boys chasin' us in the car. What a riot! We had all of 'em faked out, they thought we were stoned. After we got into the car & left the boys, Linda blew up – wow! It took us some time to convince her we were sober as the judges and were just havin' a good time. She dropped us off home without too many words; I don't know as we have her convinced yet. I sure hope I haven't just lost a darn good friend. I'll find out later 'cause I called her, had her mom tell her to call me back (she wasn't home, obviously!) Well, back to my good ole' term paper.

Nope, she isn't mad, in fact, she thinks it's funny. I knew good ole Lin'd pull through!"

It was mid-January and school was back in full swing. The excitement of winter break had come to a close and now the contrast between living senior year to its fullest and senioritis kicked in. Riding off the tide of all of the social events, the thick of winter set in, even if it wasn't that cold. January proved to be a time of reflection accompanied by sickness, which afforded even more time for reflection.

Jan 16, 1961

I wonder who I'll marry. I wonder if I'll find someone who is really a person, a good, fine person, the way I see it, a man that is all man, but great in mind, word and deed. Maybe I'm asking for too much, I don't know. Maybe

I'm trying to compare all boys and men with my father. But I know my father wasn't the only man like that, Uncle Bob W. is, I can see similar qualities in my cousin John, and even Jim in some ways. I can think of others, but none in high school or boys I've met or gone out with. There are so few people like that, how will I ever meet one? Somehow, somewhere, I was indoctrinated with a belief (I think it's an inborn truth, that you just know) that there is such a thing as a complete love, almost divine love. That when two people are meant for each other, even if they live thousands of miles apart, some celestial power brings forth circumstances whereby these two people meet, and know they are meant for each other, fall in love, helplessly and forever. I think this only happens to some people, chosen individuals.

Oh, I hope I'm one of the chosen! I'm always dreaming of the day when I'll meet the man for me, when I'll give him all my love, do anything in the world for him, be his completely. It's like something divine and heavenly; the love we will have will be eternal and will make us one; I'll be dependent on him and he'll be dependent on me. We'll have an understanding between us that is like nothing ever before heard of: we'll feel each other's thoughts, emotions and needs, giving all the time. Can it happen to me? Will it? Oh, please, God, make it happen. We'll have lots of children and love them all: and I'll know happiness, full, true, genuine happiness like I've never known it.

What will he look like? He'll be a strong character, I know that. He doesn't have to be handsome … he will be through my eyes anyway … but he'll be verile, protective, gentle, kind, strong, considerate, understanding, knowing, fun, athletic, with firm opinions and ideas. Will he be blonde or dark? Maybe red-haired, oh-no! I wish I could meet him today! I know one thing, when I'm with him, he'll make me feel like the most beautiful girl in the world. He'll adore me, just as I will him, and there'll never be eyes for anyone else for either one of us: ever---

Guess I might as well have my "fun" now. I'll never, ever break my virginity, that's for HIM and HIM alone … but I'll experience all the character types. It seems that that is all most boys think of … sex and sex alone, the heck with the person. I don't see how they get that much from sensualism from just anyone, anytime. From some people there might be something … I haven't even kissed very many boys that have really meant anything. I mean, it was nothing, like kissing my pillow. I have gotten that odd sort of feeling, tho', from some boys not completely, but enough to want to at least. One thing I can't stand is

FRENCH KISSING. What a mess, and how sickening! I get much more out of it, if anything if a kiss is planted squarely on shut lips (closed lips sounds better) and doesn't involve all the convulsions and writhing around. Honestly, that bit reminds me of slinking, slimy snakes, evil, dirty snakes.

One thing I do like, from most any boy I like, is being held. I don't know why, but just leaning on him, pressing near him, does something to me, and smart boys would take advantage of a kiss 'cause in my case, it's a perfect lead up. Fooling with my head (sounds funny) hair, face, etc!, or caressing should I say?, my back, or anywhere (not any!), but you know, is another one of my weaknesses.

Bobbie

Jan 16, 1961-"I've really got the cold today. I have to stay home from school on account of it; one of the few times I haven't had to play the big role.

I make myself sick. I've been tryin' to lose weight for 2 ½ yrs. now, and instead I gain about 5 or 10 lbs per year. Well, I know why. I convince myself that "this is it, I'll lose it or else." I carry out my campaign valiantly for possibly a week or two and lose maybe 5, 6 lbs. Then comes the day I say "I've been so strict with myself, this little bit won't hurt." This goes on until the 5 lbs I've lost is gained back, and I feel so depressed I say to myself, "I'll splurge today, & tomorrow I'll lose it all." Tomorrow always lasts weeks, and then I buckle down & the cycle repeats itself.

I am not going to kid myself any longer! I'm going to lose 20 lbs by this summer or I'll know I'm a flimsy-minded, weak-willed, fat failure, and I'll never be able to live with myself. I know my overweight is this basis of half my problems. I want more than anything to have a good figure and be healthy. To be a really happy person you have to have a healthy body & healthy mind. I've had more sicknesses this year; colds, headaches, flus, etc; and I know it's because my resistance is low. I'm not healthy, I'm not in shape, I'm a mess! I get tired easily, and I'm inambitious most of the time. Well, times are changing. I'll do it this time if it kills me.

This morning, as usual, I talked myself into French toast for breakfast. I've made up my mind that it's the last fattening morsel to pass my lips forever. At least till my birthday. Here's my plan:

My birthday is exactly 45 days away, about 6 ½ wks. If I stay on this diet, without a flaw, this whole time I should lose more than 20 lbs. But my goal is 10 lbs. From there on, I'll make my goal 10 lbs by Easter, & from there, 10 lbs by graduation. I'LL DO IT; I SWEAR, I WILL!

This week, I'm going to drink nothing but straight Metracal, and see how I feel. If it doesn't work out, that is, if I feel weak, I'll eat solids for dinner. Starting right now: 12:30 PM Tuesday, January 17, 1961!!!

I'm not going to be a slob on the beach this summer. If I lose what I say, I'll be able to wear a two-piece bathing suit.

Another thing I'm resolved to do is: get more exercise. I'll do acrobatics, & warm-up every night for a ½ an hour. I'm gonna get my bike fixed & take a bike ride every night after school, and longer ones on week-ends. Exercise is a vital part of my make-up, and I haven't been getting it. I love the outdoors, fresh-air, and nature. I can't wait till I go up to the mountains this week-end; I'm gonna get all the exercise I can!

I'm going to make myself a little chart to check myself with every night. We'll see this time if I don't do it …"

Between the parties and senior fever to graduate was the age-old female obsession to become thinner than a piece of paper. Laced with these dilemmas of growing up were the difficulties of navigating and assimilating into her life the development of not only her own personality, but that of her mother's as well. Bobbie felt like she was caving in at some points, and yet carried the burden of accommodating her mother's broken heart at the loss of her husband. It took its toll on her emotionally. It was not an easy load to carry. She not only worried about herself, but her mother's emotional well-being and happiness too. In an attempt to convey her own unraveling, she often wrote letters to her mother to help her understand.

Jan 20, 1961

Mom,

Please promise me you'll start thinking optimistically … don't worry about every single thing … we're all still alive and we've got a lot to be thankful for.

I'm sorry if I hurt you, I don't mean to. All I try to do is snap you out of your depression and all I seem to do is get you deeper in and me with you. You aren't a failure, as I know you feel you are. You don't know how proud I am of you; if even I don't show it outwardly I feel it inwardly.

I know it's hard for you, but don't make it harder by wallowing in your miseries. Can't you see that's what you're doing?

Please pull yourself together ... gain some self-confidence ... and just believe that I love you instead of complaining I never show it.

Love,
Bobbie
P.S. Thankyou X 1,000,000,000 again for the stereo –

Effie grew up in a loving home. Effie and Viv had an angel of a mother. However their Father was a drunk. Effie would hide under the bed when he came home from one of his drunken sprees, out of fear of she wasn't even sure what. Viv had no recollection of anything of the sort. She was younger than Effie, by a few years, but it was one of the things they fought about, how their life really was. It was interesting they each had an entirely different interpretation, and therefore, experience of the very same family. Perhaps Effie absorbed the brunt of it and Viv had no idea. Effie could be a bit of a child sometimes, even into her adulthood, perhaps searching for the lost parenting she never had. Bobbie naturally filled the gap. The drain on Bobbie may have been what contributed to her multiple bouts with sickness.

Jan. 27, 1961: "The invalid. That's me. I've been sick for 1 ½ wks now. Started out as the flu and after going to the Dr. yesterday I found out I had "secondary viral infection," a few blood counts below mononucleosis & possibly pneumonia. Leave it to me!

I went up to Big Bear last week-end, knowing I was still sick but not caring, really. I was so fed up with the situation at home that I had to talk to Aunt Viv and get it off my mind. It was getting way out of hand ... mom was constantly in a state of depression, getting upset at every little thing, crying, and living in her problems ... a martyr. I couldn't take it any more.

Monday, I didn't go to school, & had it out with mom.

Wednesday I wanted to go, but just couldn't, I felt really odd. That afternoon I went to pick up Linda & them at school James ... Neither were there, so I went to Jo's to give her some stuff for her sore throat. I was in my robe & p.j.'s, and was just leaving when who do I bump into in the hall? Clark! I was kinda stunned; I just said "hi, what're you doin' home? I'm sick so I gotta go," & left. I talked to him on the phone that night & he said I'd better get well by the week-end so he could take me out. Heh, heh ...

He came over the next day, along with Jo & his friend. I had to go to the Dr's. so they only stayed about an hour. He called again that night and said he'd come over today & see me, if he and his friend didn't go up to the Mts. Evidently they did, cause he didn't call or come over. I'm kinda glad 'cause it might not've been such a hot idea for him to come ... he tho't mom was at work ... and when he would've come & found out; there would be an air of disappointment and the whole affair would've been a flop. I imagine he found some party up there------

I'm so sick of bein' sick. I'm bored stiff; to think tomorrow I could've gone up to the mts, in the snow with Clark if I was well!

The dawn of a new month! Wonder what it'll bring, what chapter it will add to my life.

I'm still "sick" and home from school. I feel just fine, really, except for occasional headaches and being tired. I really kind of enjoy staying home and having the house to myself. It lacks excitement, but I'll make up for it.

Lin, Jo & I are planning another one of our trips to Palm Springs tomorrow night. If it's anything like last time ...!

I've been staying on my diet. I haven't lost a whole heck of a lot but I'll get there. I still have four weeks to go, plenty of time to lose ten pounds.

I thought up another past-time for the three of us: rifle shooting. We're goin' to take the lessons for a license every Wednesday night. I can just see us all going hunting!

I got my test scores back from my college entrance. I'll get in, but the scores weren't high enough for a scholarship. I never was counting on one, but mom was, and I think she was a little disappointed. I knew when I took the test I wasn't going to get any genius score: my mind wandered constantly and I never concentrated."

Feb 15, 1961: Here it is, a day after Valentines. Where does all the time go? It seems like such a short time ago that I was rambling around in play-clothes, long blonde stringy hair flying in the breeze, climbing trees, chasing cows, riding horses, playing cowboys and Indians, which gives me an idea.

As serious as I was about losing weight, I did not stay on it. (the diet). I'm the limit. Why do I do it? I went on a gala splurge and gained an extra ten pounds. I went to the Dr's. again today because of my splitting headaches and earaches. The headaches are from tension, and the earaches are from the viral I had or still have. We also talked about my weight problem. I think he wisely interpreted my emotional status which resulted in tension headaches as my weight problem. He gave me some pills.

June 15, 1961, Bobbie graduated high school. She was full of enthusiasm for the future like any young woman on the brink of adulthood. She had a high school diary of memories that she kept track of significant events and plans for the future:

Name: Bobbie, 1626 Via Vista Drive.
Today's Date (date of journal): June 17, 1961.
Height: 5' 7 ½".

Class Motto: Learn, Love & Live!
Class Colors: Blue & White
Class Flower: Daisy

"An Affair to Remember!!"
Oceanside, 1961, Easter
Chuck Farrell, Burbank, California,
Oceanside Beach: April 25
About him: Age: 17 ½, H: 6", Wt: 190, Color of Hair: BL.BR., Color of Eyes: Gray, Other "facts": A Doll; Crazy over Ray Charles & Bud & Travie, Loves to sing but can't!! "Bonsoir Madame" "Bo Diddley"

I expect to marry about 21. I hope to: have 4 or 5 children.
I'd like to marry: a doctor or a pilot.

Prom: Orchestra: Firehouse Furie + 2, Date: June 15. Decorations: balloons, beautiful! We arrived at dance 12:30. Orchestra playing "By the Eligibles". My escort was: Clark Upton. His eyes are: hazel. His hair is dk. Br. First person we saw were Linda and Tony.
The nicest piece played was: All of them. The most enjoyable dance was with Clark.
I wore: my beige chiffon w/aqua cumb.
After the dance: we went to the beach and slept.
Arrived home at: 7:00 A.M. I took off everything and went to bed.

Chapter 11

Tumalo

(2001 – 2003)

<u>*Where Did You Go, Little Girl?*</u>
Outside,
Listening to the birds and animals,
Picking flowers, digging holes,
Or just watching the green hills
That roll and unfol'
Dainty speckles of purple violets,
That's where she was.

Chasing butterflies
Catching turtles or frogs,
Getting stung by bees
Running across fields with long
Blonde hair flying in the breeze,
That's where she was.

Trudging (begrudgingly)
To school through rain and snow,
All wrapped up with ear muffs
On her head, mad because

She couldn't build a snowman
Or play in the rain instead,
That's where she was.

Skipping through his pastures
To Mr. Owen's farm
To play with the little piglets,
Chase the mad hens, help with
Milking the cows, or riding
The huge ole work-horse as they
Plugged along pulling the plow;
That's where she was.

Sliding down haystacks,
Climbing trees, running through sprinklers,
Picking blackberries for Mom's pies,
Anything that could be done
Outside
Under the warm rays of the sun,
Clear blue skies;
That's where she was,
When I was a little girl.

Bobbie, 1960

Maya sat under the tree that she and her sister had been trying to climb for hours. The rope that reached the lowest limb hung from an old abandoned tree house, and it swung in the air above their heads. Maya had collapsed onto the ground out of sheer exhaustion. Madeleine had run off to look for a ladder, or some other object as a means for getting into the tree. Maya looked out over the acres and acres of fields that surrounded her, and a large forest off in the distance, chewing a piece of grass. She was living the life of a country girl to its fullest. Maya was nine and Madeleine was seven. Jill and her family had recently moved to the farm after living overseas for three long years. Dhaka was the most densely populated city in the world at the time. There was no space or freedom from the crowds of people. Coming to the farm was like moving to a different planet. The little farm and the small country town were opposite Dhaka in every way. There was nothing but space and grassy fields that stretched on forever in Tumalo. It was endless freedom for the girls.

The tree Maya leaned against was an enormous one. The branches did not begin until a long ways up and there was nothing to grab onto to climb it. They had conquered all of the other trees on the property. They were determined to conquer this one too, especially since it held the best prize ever awaiting them at the top. There was a makeshift ladder of sorts that consisted of small planks nailed to the tree's trunk. They were spaced at intervals or at least were at one time. Most of them were missing. That must have been how the tree house was accessed at its inception, but that was no longer a possibility.

Maya stared dreamily at the fields of grass. Her eyes landed on Broken Top and the Three Sisters mountains. They were covered in snow. The mountains were very close and surrounded the property, providing the backdrop where the fields met the horizon. It was a mini paradise that surpassed words. "This sure is the life," Maya thought to herself.

Madeleine came running from a distance, hobbling awkwardly with a ladder she could barely lift and half dragged in her small hands, her eyes wild with excitement. Maya stood up and grinned. "Maya! Look what I got!" "Nice," Maya said. "Shall we give it a try? Come on, over here, like that. Now, help me stretch it out, this oughta work." Maya took over. Maya always gave the orders. "Ok," said Madeleine. She was proud of herself for thinking up the idea of the ladder. Maya had to admit it was a good one.

As soon they got the ladder stabilized Maya began to climb. "Hey, wait a minute! Don't I get to climb first? I'm the one that got it!" Madeleine complained. "No. I'm the oldest, and besides, you might fall and hurt yourself." Maya had the answer to everything. "No I won't!" Madeleine whined, and stuck out her pouty bottom lip that was mostly out all the time anyway. Maya had learned to ignore that lip a long time ago. She didn't pause for a second to argue. She climbed the ladder and got to the top of it.

She stopped once at the top and peered over the roof of the barn and the house to see where she was and how far she'd made it up the tree. She was nowhere near the bottom limb. "Hold it steady down there," Maya said. "Okay. What are you going to do?" she asked. "I'm going to stand on top so I can get as high as I can," Maya answered. "Then maybe I can reach the rope."

Despite the fact that the rope was still out of Maya's reach by several feet and the tree house was several yards up from that, Maya was fearless. She was certain she could get it. Fortunately, their father walked up at that moment, deflecting a more certain outcome, a bad accident. "Get down off that ladder Maya. It's not safe. Where did you get that rickety old thing anyway? You should not be standing on the top like that." Madeleine gave a meek smile to her Father. "I got the ladder, Dad. It was my idea." Jill came up from behind, a shovel in her hand. She'd been working in the large garden, determined to grow the largest vegetable garden they had ever had. She embraced farm life too.

"What's going on?" Jill asked. "The girls are just getting down from this ladder and are putting it away right now," Michael answered. "Oh," Jill's eyes followed an imaginary line from the ladder to the rope to the shabby little tree house. She had never noticed it until now; it was so far up the tree. "It looks pretty dilapidated," she said. "Yeah," agreed Michael. "I don't think it looks too safe," Jill added. "No," Michael agreed. "Tree house is off limits girls. Go find something else to do." "Aww darn," Maya said. Madeleine said, "Yeah, darn."

The girls took the ladder back to the barn, ending the tree house adventure. Jill walked back with them to the garden. Marley was there. She was four years old, and occupied herself for hours playing with her pot-belly pig, Wilbur. She climbed the low fence into his pen and he got down on his belly and lay against it on the other side. The pig belonged to her. They had gotten him when he was a tiny piglet. For the longest time, Wilbur ran free around the property. He was too afraid to go more than halfway down the driveway before turning back. In the mornings, the girls and Jill and Michael were often woken up to the sound of Wilbur chasing their Australian Shepherd dog around the house in circles. The girls slept in the large basement, their beds spread across three sections of it. The girls and Jill had painted murals of horses and flowers on the walls. The windows reached just above ground with a perfect view of the two animals chasing each other around and around. Cara Mia, their dog, was a natural herder and nipped at Wilbur's heels. Wilbur saw it as a game and did the same to Cara Mia. First, one would chase the other and then the other would chase them. Cara Mia was confused and a bit frustrated. She didn't care for a pig nipping at her heels and it made her mad. Wilbur always had a big grin on his face. He thought it was great fun.

Jill worked in the garden and Marley carefully climbed her way up the small fence that enclosed the pigpen that contained a doghouse that Wilbur now occupied; he no longer roamed the property after he began wandering off chasing the neighbors' horses and nipping them in the legs. The fence was just tall enough that Marley had nothing to catch her balance once she rounded the top. Wilbur waited on the other side and allowed her to use him as a step stool to get into the pen. Marley lay on him lovingly and cuddled with him for the duration of Jill's time in the garden. Jill was nearly finished and Marley decided to leave Wilbur's pen. She used the gate this time and Wilbur pushed out. That happened from time to time. However, as much as he loved Marley he hated Michael. Jill yelled across the yard to warn him. "Michael look out, Wilbur is loose!" Wilbur spotted him immediately and ran straight for him. Michael yelled, "Damn it, who let that pig out?" He chased poor Michael around the yard, with Michael hollering the entire time. "Someone get this pig! Get away from me, damn it, you stupid pig." Wilbur caught up to him, and Michael picked up a twig and tried to fend him off. "Get away from me. No, you're not going to bite me this time." With the twig in his hand he thought he had the answer. "Now we'll see who's boss. Think you can outsmart me? We'll see about that." He swatted at Wilber. They danced in circles, Michael dodging the pig, narrowly missing him several times. Michael told Jill who had caught up to them, "You can train pigs using a switch. I've read about it." "Are you sure about that Michael? Do you even know what you're doing?" "Yeah, watch this, you'll see." "Hmm," said Jill. "Well I guess I have seen the kids from the pig 4-H club using switches like that to train them. But are you sure your twig isn't too small?" "No. It'll work." Michael was annoyed that she was questioning him. He swatted at Wilbur but missed him nearly every time. Marley saw and yelled, "Stop Daddy!! Don't hurt my pig!!! Don't hurt Wilbur!!!" "Daddy won't hurt him, don't worry. This won't hurt him honey, I promise. I'm only tapping him, see?" Marley wasn't convinced, and she didn't like what was happening. She tried to call Wilbur to come to her but he wouldn't listen. "You don't think whipping him with a stick is going to make him madder, do you?" Jill asked. "No. I'm training him, you'll see. But Wilbur was determined to get his nip in, and Michael was equally determined to conquer the pig. Michael finally got a switch in, and it looked like a very light tap even though Michael swung the twig a bit hard. This triggered Wilbur and he went after Michael with an even bigger vengeance. Jill did not say I told you so. Michael got two more lashes in and the third was his last. The twig broke and Wilbur made his dive. He jumped on Michael's shins and nipped him hard right through his jeans, ripping them. "God!!!" Michael said. "I hate that pig." "No. Don't say that. I love Wilbur." Marley said. "He's a good pig. "He is not a good pig. He's a stupid pig." "No he isn't," Marley said. "Oh no, Michael, look, you're bleeding." "Yeah," he said. "I'll be fine." He had an angry look on his face. "Come on Wilbur, Let's go back to your house." The pig was calm now and he listened to Marley, following her back to his pen. Poor Michael had been the one to give Wilbur his vaccination shots months earlier. Wilbur hated him ever since.

They had four goats too. They were Nubians, tall and graceful with long floppy ears. They were entertaining to no end. Chester was Jill's favorite. He was black with bits of brown and white near his ears and feet. He followed her everywhere. They'd had him since he was a baby and Jill had mostly been the one to bottle feed him. If she sat at the picnic table in the yard, he would lay at her feet like a dog.

Ali, the baby, who they often called Alibob, and later was shortened to "Bob" or Bobbie, played in the yard during all of the commotion. Wilbur wasn't the only animal to escape regularly. Chester and Candy and her two baby goats had heard the commotion and decided to break free too. For some reason Bobbie was the one the goats headed for every time. It happened more frequently than Wilbur's escapes, at least once a day. Bobbie saw them coming and jumped up and down screaming. Jill dropped the rake she was holding and ran after them. The goats reached Bobbie first, and before the goats could knock her down, little Bobbie got down on her belly and kicked and screamed on the ground. Jill shoed them away and picked her up off of the ground. "Those dumb goats," said Jill. "Yeah, dumb goats," said Bobbie. "That was pretty smart of you to get down on the ground first this time. They can't knock you over, if you're already down, can they?" The goats continued with this game the entire time they lived on the farm, and Bobbie continued to get down on her belly and scream every time it happened. For some reason, anything shorter than they were became a head-butting game to knock over. Bobbie was an easy target.

They had chickens and rabbits to round out the amateur farm. Through their first hen, Red, and their rooster Blackie, they tried to get eggs fertilized so they would have chicks. Red, however, refused to sit on her eggs. They gave up and bought three female chicks and put them under an incubator light until they grew large enough to put out with the others. They had been assured that all three of the chicks were female. As it turned out, one of them was not. Adding the three half grown chicks, two female and one male, to the flock turned out to be a disaster. The adolescent rooster was not welcomed by Blackie.

Later in the evening Jill worked on the tomato plants in the wooden boxes. Out of survival, the adolescent rooster had learned to hop the tall fence to escape Blackie. He came running towards Jill with his wings outstretched into a massive wingspan, and his talons aimed towards her. She dropped what she was doing and ran and he chased her around the yard. He caught up to her and she turned around to face him. She knew from experience not to keep her back turned if he got too close. She had seen him run right up Michael's back one time. He was menacing and Jill was afraid of him. "Help!" she yelled. Michael ran out. "Michael, I don't know what to do. Get this dumb rooster away from me!!" "Just back up Jill." "No! He'll come after me!" "No he won't. Stay facing him and slowly back up." She didn't trust it would work, but she didn't know what else to do. "Ok, here we go." She slowly took one step back. Nothing happened, but the bird eyed her down. It reminded her of Hitchcock's story of "the Birds." If it were a movie, this one would be called, "The Terrifying Rooster," she thought. She took another small step. The mean rooster didn't go after her, but he didn't move either. She kept making her way back, thinking all the while that if this didn't work, there was no back up plan. She had no idea what she would do in that case. As it turned out, nothing happened and the rooster finally turned and walked away. Jill breathed a sigh of relief. She never thought she could be so afraid of a bird.

Tonight, company was coming over for dinner, so Jill called everyone in to take their baths. Michael started dinner while Jill corralled as many kids into the bathtub as would fit. Sometimes she could get all four of them in. They tidied up in preparation for the family that was coming over. They were friends from Bangladesh and the children knew each other. Jill was good friends with the wife and Michael got along well with the husband.

"Hey there, anybody home?" Cindy was already at the front door. Jill went to greet them. "Hey there old friend!" They hugged each other and commented how strange it was to see each other in their own country. They had only ever known each other while living in Bangladesh. "Oh wow, look at this! Farm and everything! It's beautiful!" "Yeah we wanted something as unlike Dhaka as we could get!!" They laughed and the rest of the family came into the house as Michael and the girls walked up the stairs from the basement where Michael had been helping them get dressed. The girls saw their friends and said, "Hey let's go outside! We'll show you the goats and everything!" The kids ran out of the house and Jill called after them, "Hey, don't get all dirty again!" This left the adults alone so they could reunite.

When it was time for dinner, they formed a large group sitting around the table. Fortunately, it was a large thick wooden one that they could all fit around. As they ate, a large black shadow appeared at the window and tapped at the glass. It startled Cindy. She jumped and screamed. It was Chester's head peering in at the kitchen table. He had escaped his pen in the barn again. "Don't worry. He only wants to see what's going on. He doesn't like being left out." "Well what on earth is it?" "Oh it's just our goat." Chester, who had grown quite big by this time easily climbed the stairs to the porch and jumped up to the dining room window hitting his hooves on the glass staring in at them as they ate with his big black head and floppy ears swinging back and forth. "Oh, ok, just a goat staring at us through the window while we eat … ok," she said. "Well should I go out and put him back in the barn?" asked Jill "Aww no finish your dinner Jill, he'll be alright," said Michael. "That ok with you guys if we leave him out there staring at us while we eat? He won't do anything." They were from Tennessee and had deep southern accents. "Well, I guess. I'll just try not to look at him. When in Rome do like the Romans do, I guess," said Jill's friend. Every time she took a bite of food she couldn't help seeing his face staring at her. She tried to ignore him. "Are you sure it's ok?" Jill asked. "Oh I'm fine, let me just scooch this way and look over here. Every time I look up, there he is. It's fine. I'm just not used to staring at a goat while I eat. It's fine, always something new, right?"

Jill worked at a school for at-risk teenage girls. The school was located out in the countryside across from the small town that they lived. Michael spent his days searching for jobs. The girls were homeschooled the first year by Jill until they realized they were going to be there longer than they thought. They put all the girls into the small country school the following year. During that first year, however, the girls romped around the farm and joined 4-H. They bought season passes and skied at Mt. Hoodoo while Jill read their homeschooling books to them in the car on the way. They did their lessons when they came in for hot chocolate and the lunches Jill packed. It was a small family resort and everyone knew them.

Jill took advantage of every opportunity to teach the girls about farm life, of which she knew very little. She was learning just as much as they were. The girls volunteered at a horse rescue, cleaning horse stalls in exchange for free riding lessons that year, and at home, Jill took the girls on countless nature walks for science lessons. Jill secretly relished the opportunity to learn to identify native wildflowers, trees and indigenous plants. The small pond on the property provided great samples of water to look at under a microscope. A mini world of micro-organisms unfolded before them.

Although the focus of the lessons was aimed at Maya and Madeleine, it was Marley who was most attentive. On one such day, Jill read about the different ecosystems to the girls. She tried desperately to get the older two girls' attention, asking them questions to see if they were listening. "Does anyone know what adaptations plants have made to survive the tundra?" Marley sat at Jill's feet with her cotton-white hair and blue eyes so big they had a constant look of excitement. Her hand shot into the air. "I know! I know!" Marley hung on every word Jill said and knew every answer. "Maya, can you tell us?" "Huh?" "Maya were you listening?" "I don't know, yeah, kinda." "Do you know the answer? Why don't you take a guess?" "Ahh Mom, I don't know." "I do! I do!" Jill ignored Marley. "Madeleine? How about you? Any guesses?" "No Mom, do we have to do this?" "I know the answer! I do!" Jill sighed. "Ok Marley, give us the answer. You girls listen up." "Yeah whatever," said Maya. "Marley?" Jill said. She sat up straight and tall. "Well. The plants were really tiny and low to the ground so they could survive the wind, and ..." She went on and the older girls rolled their eyes. "Nice job Marley, well done!"

Jill could tell she wasn't going to get any more cooperation from the older two girls that day. "Ok, go play," Jill said. "Yay!" They jumped off the couch and ran outside. Marley followed. The girls ran straight to their bunny cages. They each had one and were planning to use them for showmanship for the county fair. They loved their bunnies more than any of the animals on the farm. They went into the barn and opened one of the cages. Maya pulled Silver Moon out of her cage. She had a velvety soft grey coat of fur. "Here Madeleine, take her while I get yours." Midnight was next. He was just as soft and velvety, but black all over. Marley came up behind them. "Hey what are you guys doing?" "Marley, you need to stay out of the way, ok?" "But what are you doing?" They ignored her and carried the bunnies out to the yard. Marley followed. "What are you going to do? Play with Silver Moon and Midnight? Can I come?" "Yeah, come on, but you can't hold the bunnies." Marley was fine with that. At least they were letting her be with them.

The girls went into one of the fields and put the bunnies down in the grass. They whispered to each other. "Here, put him over there, like that." "What are you guys doing?" Marley could tell they were doing something sneaky. "No. Move Silver Moon like that." "Hey, didn't Mom tell you not to put them together?" "Marley be quiet. They want to play together." "Oh. But I thought Mom told you not to." "It's ok. Just be quiet. Madeleine, put him over here. I'll stand here so they can't get away. You be on this side." "Can I help?" Marley asked. "Yeah stand there and don't let them escape," Maya told her. It didn't take long before Midnight was on top of Silver Moon thumping her for all of thirty seconds. "What are they doing?" Marley asked. "Hush. They're just playing," Madeleine told her.

"Ok, let's go," Maya said. "Yeah, let's go." "Why? We just got here," Marley said. "They're done playing." "Well, that wasn't long." "Yeah, it's ok. They don't want to." "How do you know?" "I just do." "Now what are we going to do guys?" Marley asked. She was just happy to be with them. "Let's go over to the forest and play lion and hunter." "Mom says you're not allowed to go in the forest," Marley said. "Marley, will you please just be quiet?" "But there are lions over there. Mom said so." "We'll be fine. Mom freaks out about everything. They don't come this close." "But Mom said ..." "Marley, go away if you're too scared." "Yeah she shouldn't come with us anyway," said Madeleine. They looked at her and told her to go back. "You can't come with us, and you can't tell Mom." "But what if you get eaten by a lion?" "We won't get eaten by a lion," they said. "Go Marley." She put her head down and walked slowly towards the house.

"Hey what are you doing back so early?" Jill asked. "The girls won't let me come with them." "Oh yeah? Where are they going?" "To the forest." "What? I told them they're not allowed over there." "I told them Mom. They wouldn't listen." Jill pulled her boots on and went for the door. "Mom, where are you going?" "I'm going to get them." Marley was relieved. She didn't want her sisters eaten by lions. By the time Jill reached the other side of the pasture where the forest began, they were out of sight. Jill went into the forest, calling their names. Pine needles crunched under her feet and the Ponderosa Pines towered over her. It was eerily quiet but for an occasional bird calling through the trees. They didn't answer. She walked in circles, calling their names, but still no answer. She began to panic. Lions were sighted all the time in this area. One morning they even saw one run across their pasture chasing a herd of deer. Jill ran back to the house yelling for Michael. "Michael, you've got to go look for them. They've gone into the forest. I'll stay here with the baby and Marley." Michael said, "Ah, they're probably alright." "No Michael, you've got to go look for them. I couldn't find them." "Ok, I will in a minute. Let me finish what I'm doing." "No Michael! Now!!!" "Oh for gosh sakes, you're over-reacting! They're fine." "No!!! I'm not, you've got to go, right now! What if they're lost?" Michael went to look for them. No sooner had he stepped into the pasture, Maya and Madeleine appeared at the edge of the forest. "There you two are. Now what are you up to? You had your mom in a panic. You really need to tell us where you girls are. You can't just run off into the forest like that." "Yes Dad," they said.

When they got to the house Jill was on the porch. "Where were you girls? I thought I told you the forest was off limits." "We were only on the edge. We weren't in there long." "Well if you were that close how come I went around and around calling for you guys and no one answered?" "You must not have been where we were," Maya said. "Hmm. Well it was too far for my liking. When I say no forest I mean no forest." "Yes Mom." "We're sorry, Mom," said Madeleine. They put their heads down and walked in the house. Marley was on the couch and poked her head up. The girls glared at her. "And how did mom know that's where we were?" "I told her," she said proudly. "We told you not to!! Thanks a lot. Now we're in trouble." Marley didn't mind. "Well you shouldn't have gone in the forest. Mom said not to."

The girls went back outside after Jill gave them a talking to. Jill followed them out with Bobbie who had woken from her nap. Marley trailed behind the older two girls. "We don't want you with us," they told her. She stayed back with Jill and watched them walk to the barn without her. "Where are you going guys? To get the bunnies? Are you going to let them play together again?" "What?" asked Jill. "Are you girls letting the bunnies be together? After I told you not to?" "Only for a minute Mom. It's fine." "No!! It's not fine. It only takes a minute!!! I told you girls you can't do that!!" "It'll be fine Mom, don't worry." Six weeks later they had a batch of six baby bunnies.

Jill relied on Marley to keep her informed of the girls' shenanigans. However eventually it got to be a little much. "Marley," Jill told her, "No more tattle telling, ok?" "Yes, Mom." Five minutes later Marley ran into the house. "Mom! Mom!" "Now what? Remember what we talked about? No tattle telling." "No Mom. It's not tattling. Maya and Madeleine, they're …" "Marley, are you sure this isn't tattle telling?" "Yes Mom, it's not. It's really really important. Madeleine just promised me a piece of gum if I ran around the farm five times, and I did, and then she gave the piece of gum to Bobbie instead, and she didn't even run!" "Marley, that's tattle telling," Jill told her. "No Mom, I'm not tattle telling. I'm reporting."

Jill had decided to get the goats and the bunnies so the girls could participate in 4-H. It seemed like a great way to teach them to be responsible. The girls had to get up early before school to feed them and put the goats in the pasture. They raked out the barn and cleaned the bunny cages. In order to participate in 4-H, since goats fell into the dairy goat competition, they had to breed them. The show goat needed to be a milking mother. Since they only had one female to do that with, it left Madeleine with Chester, the male goat. The only competition for males was the pack goat obstacle course.

They found a stud for Candy, the female goat and bred her. Soon she was pregnant with two baby goats. The night she was to give birth, the girls packed fresh fluffy hay into the barn for bedding. They separated Chester into a smaller pen, and this he was not at all happy about. He escaped numerous times, but at least Candy was protected in her own pen. The girls ran to the barn to check on Candy all night, waking Jill up each time to report. "Mom, Mom, I think she's about to have them. Come on, you have to come see!" Jill got out of bed and grabbed a flashlight, walking out into the dark. The air was chilly. Jill wrapped her sweater around herself tightly. Candy was panting but not any differently than she had been two hours before. "I don't think she's ready yet girls. I think it's going to be a while." She went into the pen and checked her water. "I'm sorry poor old girl. It'll be over soon. I know how you feel." She gave Candy a pat on the head, and she pushed Jill's hand away. "I understand. It's no fun is it?"

Finally, they fell asleep, Jill in her bed, and the girls out in the barn. When morning came, two kid goats lay nestled on the ground, one on top of Maya, and one at her side. Candy sat behind them. Maya was sprawled on the ground with her legs apart, arms spread to either side, fast asleep, mouth wide open. This is what Jill saw when she walked into the barn that morning.

The girls were in a dither running back and forth to the barn all day to check on the babies. Marley and Bobbie were full of energy after a good night's sleep. They were more excited than ever and Jill had to tell them to leave the goats be with their mother so they could nurse. "Girls, come on, let's go inside and get some baths and we can let them rest." "Yes Mom." The older two girls came in and started their showers, but Marley and Bobbie disappeared. "Now where did those two go?" Jill asked. "Michael will you help me find them?" They searched the house but they were nowhere. Jill walked out to the barn and found the two of them in a large rubber tub. Peeking out the top edge were two baby goat heads. "Girls, what are you doing? I told you to come in and get your baths. We need to leave the babies alone." Jill had to admit, they were awfully cute. "Ok wait there guys." "Michael, you gotta come see this." Everyone laughed. The girls knew they weren't in trouble. "This doesn't mean you're not coming in to get your baths right now." "Ahhh, Mom, do we have to?" "Yes, come on. Let's get the babies out of there. How on earth did you get them in anyway?" "Like this," Marley picked one up holding one arm around both front legs and the other around the two back legs. The baby goat was half Marley's size and a bit awkward for her to lift. "Ok, well that's pretty good Marley, but here, hand her to me. We need to be very careful with them. They're babies and they're newborns. Let's let them be with their mother now."

The babies were born strategically in time for the county fair. Candy, the mother, was ready to be in the dairy goat showmanship. A few days before the fair everyone met at the 4-H group leader's home. The kids brought their goats and together gave them baths, polished their hooves and painted them with clear nail polish to keep them clean so they looked nice for competition. They took shavers to their fur and trimmed them so they looked manicured and groomed. On the day of the competition, Maya had to separate the babies from Candy so that her udder would be full and give a perfect shape of a healthy milking dairy goat. The barn was full of crying babies and moaning mothers.

"Mom, did you sew my 4-H patch onto my shirt," Maya asked. "Yes I did." Maya and Madeleine wore long sleeved buttoned down ironed white shirts with their 4-H patches and white jeans. Madeleine was in the backyard with her makeshift obstacle course and Chester, trying to get him to cooperate. He wore a backpack since he was in the pack-goat competition. He was nearly the size of Madeleine and for some reason height seemed to be significant in the hierarchy of a goat's world, Jill noticed. In addition to the goats, the girls also had their bunnies in carrying cages ready to go. Jill loaded the food for the animals in the car. A member from their club would be over soon to collect the goats and take them to the fair. "Mom, can you help me?" Jill had stepped out the front door to see how Madeleine was doing. As soon as Chester saw Jill he turned and pulled towards her. "Mom, that's not helping. Now Chester wants to go over to you and he's not listening at all. I don't know what to do with him." "Ok, well, do you have a good grip on him?" "Yes, best I can, but he keeps pulling and not doing anything. He'll walk across the ramp but he doesn't want to do anything else." Jill walked over to them and stepped in front of the two of them. "Come on Chester, this way." "Ok now he's listening because you're here, but you can't be here during the competition!" "Hmm. I know," Jill said. "In fact, Mom, I think you'd better not be there at all. If he sees you he'll bolt right for you and not do anything." "Yes," Jill said. "I'll be sure to be out of sight when your event is up." "Well do your best Madeleine. It's all you can do. We'll just hope he decides to cooperate." Trying to get goats to do what you want was a little like trying to herd cats. If Chester was difficult, Candy was downright ornery.

When the girls got to the fair, they rushed around making sure their goats' pens and bunnies' cages were set up and the animals had everything they needed. They had to run back and forth between the leaders of both clubs for meetings. The events were about to begin and the girls were excited. Maya was up first with Candy. She put a lead around her neck and led her to the show ring, taking her place in line with the rest of the competitors dressed in white. There were all kinds of goats: LaManchas, Nigerian Dwarfs, Alpines, Nubians. This event was to take place on a large patch of grass under a large white tent. Jill took a seat in one of the folding metal chairs in the sun outside the tent. Many of the parents sat outside to watch their children compete.

Jill happened to sit behind Llama Lady. She was talking to Goat Lady. Jill gave them names as a way to identify them. Llama lady was extremely serious about her llamas. Goat lady had hundreds of goats. Llama lady would tell you about her llamas and then some if you asked her. Her favorite line was, "Most people haven't a clue how to handle llamas. You just have to know how." Jill got the impression she would not easily part with this information. Jill had asked Goat Lady at a meeting at her house one day, "Do you have to stay here all the time? Can you ever leave your goats?" There were hundreds of them and Jill was impressed. The reality of the commitment hit her as she stood on the farm surrounded by all of the goats. The contrast to Jill's own family's nomadic lifestyle was a stark one. Goat Lady replied, "Of course not." Jill thought, wow, her entire life revolves around goats? "So you never leave? Ever?" "No, I do not," she replied indignantly. That is true devotion thought Jill, the life of a true farmer. "What about vacation?" Goat Lady let out a big sigh. "I don't go on vacation." She put her nose in the air and walked away. Jill stared after her and said, "Oh."

Maya's turn was next. She waited for the judges to give her permission to begin. Maya tried to act very professional, dressed in her perfectly pressed white clothes and her hair neatly pulled back. Maya had worked with her unruly goat for weeks and weeks leading to the fair. Now would be the telling moment. The judge's voice came over the microphone. "Maya, we're ready. You may begin." Jill held her breath. Maya led Candy to the stage by the lead and when she was partway there, Candy bolted across the stage dragging Maya behind her. Jill gasped. Maya came right back and tried again, dragging Candy behind her, trying to act poised and in control. Jill was impressed that she did not appear too upset. It was her first competition and Jill was proud of the way she handled the situation.

It was at this moment Jill overheard Llama Lady and Goat Lady talk about her daughter. She was sitting right behind them. "Can you believe the caliber of members these days?" Llama Lady said. "No. I certainly cannot. We just don't get the quality of kids in our club anymore that we used to." Jill tapped one of them on the shoulder and the ladies turned their heads. "Is that my daughter you're talking about?" Both ladies jumped. They realized Jill had been listening the entire time. They quickly turned back around without saying a word. Jill laughed thinking to herself, "So the caliber of my kid is determined by how well she can walk a goat across a patch of grass?" She couldn't stop laughing to herself at the thought of it. The ladies wore permanently indignant expressions, and observing the raucous, spoke in hushed voices to each other with one hand over their mouths so no one would hear, pretending to be discrete. Jill laughed even harder. They reminded her of old-fashioned characters from "Anne of Green Gables," a pair of prissy self-righteous old women.

In the midst of the county fair, Jill's mother and father-in-law paid a visit. They missed the events but got to see their son and his family's life on the farm as well as something even more significant and something very close to their own hearts. They were missionaries and therefore, Christianity belonged in the realm of their world order. Michael and Jill, on the other hand, arrived at their own conclusions. In Bangladesh, towards the end of their tour and during one of many late night balcony discussions overlooking the dark streets below from four stories up, they began discussing spirituality. Michael was a stout atheist. Jill believed that everyone was on an individual journey. She proclaimed herself agnostic. She always found religion and philosophy an interesting topic. She had, at one point or another, experienced several denominations of the Christian religion during her multiple-homed upbringing. She contemplated and proclaimed herself atheistic for a couple of years after a speaker visited her high school and gave a talk on evolution. There were many logical arguments, hard proof. But then she attended a cultural anthropology class in college a couple of years later. The professor was a stout atheist. She visited him in his office one day because she found anthropology so interesting. The professor, perhaps one time too many, embarked on yet another one-sided atheistic soapbox dialogue. At the end of one of his points he asked her, "It's absurd, how could anyone believe there is any doubt God does not exist? It's so obvious and plain to see!" This comment changed her mind forever. If the professor only knew that his extreme and very staunch views are what did it. If any good college student knows, rarely is anything ever always and every and absolute. There is always an exception, a grey area. This is what went through her mind as the professor continued to "prove his point" as if there were no question of a doubt, and as if he was in like-minded company.

If the professor had been observant, he would have noticed the slight smile on Jill's face. The thought that came to her was this, and it came in the form of a reverse sort of logic. If you can be so absolutely sure there is no way to prove it does exist, then how can you prove it doesn't? And all the empirical physical evidence in the world didn't really prove anything, because if the bottom line couldn't be answered, how could anything? The ultimate question, "How do we exist?" "Where do we come from?" "Where does the universe end, where does it begin?" "Where does matter come from?" Science had never proven any of that, the biggest all-encompassing questions that underlie everything. How could science proclaim to know anything when they only had parts of the missing puzzle? What glued it all together? There is an explanation, we just don't know it, she thought. She was agnostic from that moment onwards, but that inexplicable feeling inside of her told her there was a beauty and an order and a connection to all of life that surpassed words. Perhaps this is what people called "God," but she felt this was too simplistic. How can you give a name to something so beyond comprehension? It almost seemed an injustice to the grandness of such an unfathomable concept.

This is why she could not attach herself to religion. To claim a religion seemed to her like a claim to omnipotence, having a one-up on everybody else. But if you believe there is another power with omnipotence, how can you have it too? It seemed like a proclamation that negated by logic religion itself.

Regardless, Michael and Jill embarked on a journey of their own. Michael researched and found a place. They wanted a community and education of religion and spirituality for their girls so that they could make their own life decision. It seemed like a fairly big one. Jill bought and read books on various religions. Maya ate it up. She was so curious. "Mom, what do you believe?" They discussed every angle and Jill told her in the end, "This is a very big question and you have to make your own decision. No one can make it for you. Don't believe what everyone else does because that's their truth. You must find your own."

It was on the coattails of this endeavor that Jill's in-laws paid a visit. When they arrived the girls were excited. "Grandma, come see our baby goats!" Maya said. Michael had just driven up the long driveway after picking them up from the airport. Jill walked in the room. "Hey Maya, let them get in the door! They're tired after their long flight. Hi there! How are you guys? How was the flight? Can I get you some water?" Everyone exchanged hugs. The girls competed for attention. "Hi Grandpa! Want to see the bunnies?!" Madeleine bounced up and down. "No they're going to see the goats first," Maya told her. "Let me go to the bathroom before I do anything," Grandma said. Minutes later grandma and grandpa were led out to the barns. "I don't think we're going to get a moment's rest until we go see these bunnies and goats," Grandma said.

While they went to the barns, Jill told Michael, "Hey let's invite your parents to church!" In Jill's mind she thought they would finally be happy, the answer to their prayers. They were finally going to church! Michael said, "Um, I don't think that's such a good idea." "Why? It would be fun, and they'll be so happy! Come on!" Michael was silent. Jill was excited to share the good news and was sure they'd be just as excited as she was. Finally they were embracing spirituality, even if a bit different from their own version of Christianity, what difference did it make? It was a minor detail, and one that suited Jill. This church was a little different. They had a different view of God, allowing members to form their own definition of what God was. A different speaker spoke each Sunday even though there was an appointed minister. The topics varied between different perspectives on spirituality, and were quite thought provoking Jill thought. The music was heartfelt and beautiful. "Come on Michael, they'll love it, I'm sure of it!" Michael said, "I'm not so sure." "Why?" Michael couldn't form the words to explain why. He finally said, "Ok, I guess."

The next morning Jill had a big smile on her face. She made a big breakfast and got everyone ready for church. They piled into the van and drove down the country road into town. Pulling into the parking lot, they already saw people they knew. They said their hellos and introduced Michael's parents. "I'll take the girls to Sunday school while you guys go find a seat," said Jill. Jill got the girls settled and looked for Michael and his parents in the congregation. She found them in one of the pews and had a seat next to her mother-in-law. It was an old German church, a fairly large building with vaulted ceilings and high beams. The tall windows were stained glass. A faint hint of incense wafted down from the Buddhist monks who rented one of the rooms upstairs.

A man walked to the altar and the hall became quiet. He said a few words and then the sound of deep drums filled the sanctuary and echoed all around them. They were Native American drums and they were enormous. The drummers and their drums were positioned at the four corners of the church at east, west, south and north. Jill was captivated. She thought, what a surprise and how lovely, just when my in-laws happen to be here! She knew that the entire area was an ancient healing ground for the Native Americans many years ago. She loved how they incorporated this history into the service to recognize their part in the evolution of the area. The bellowing sound of the drums sent shivers down her spine. She could feel the reverence that the Indians must have felt during their own ceremonies long ago. Jill smiled in tranquility and glanced at her mother-in-law. Her mother-in-law stared straight ahead and was not smiling. She looked very serious. Jill thought she must be deep in thought and contemplation over the profound experience of the drums.

A woman walked to the altar and announced the speaker for the day and the topic. It was to be "Biofield Reverberation and Energy Balancing." Jill smiled again and glanced at her mother-in-law. "Oh what an interesting topic, my in-laws came on a great day!" Jill noticed her lips were pursed together tightly while she looked straight ahead. Jill thought "hmm, she must be really interested and concentrating on such a deep topic." Jill sat back ready to enjoy what new ideas would be shared today. They always stimulated thought provoking discussion afterwards and Jill was enthusiastic for today's lecture.

The talk finished and the master of ceremonies walked onto the stage to announce the choir. It was beautiful as usual. They sang, "Our Thoughts are Prayers." Jill was transfixed and glanced at her mother-in-law again, imagining she must be thoroughly transported in space and time with such a soul provoking melody and words. She seemed quite serious, however, and Jill thought it odd after such a spiritually moving song. She passed it off as probably her own expression of a spiritual experience.

"And now we have a special treat for you today. Mandy will be playing Tibetan bowls for you and will teach you a chant to sing as she takes you through a guided meditation. Thank you Mandy!" Mandy sat on a colorful piece of silk fabric on the ground with bowls of various sizes spread around her. "The Tibetans believe different sounds evoke different chakras in our energy field. I'm going to chant a sound and I want you all to match the tone as I begin the bowls." She used some sort of object and moved it around the rim of one of the bowls. It made a low humming sound. With her opposite hand she did the same with a different bowl that elicited a different tone and she began to chant in Tibetan, a sort of song. After a few moments, skipping around to different bowls to make a melody, she looked up at the audience and hummed, "ooooohhhhhmmmm." She motioned to the audience to do the same. The entire congregation hummed a deep "oooooohhhhhhmmmm," matching her tone. Again Jill was transfixed with the sound reverberating all around her as it echoed throughout the hall. She thoroughly relished the experience and smiled. She glanced once again at her mother-in-law. She looked quite stern and this time Jill thought she noticed a slight frown and her entire body was rather rigid. Jill was puzzled but looked back at the altar to follow the Tibetan bowls.

They closed the service with a few announcements and Jill turned to her in-laws and smiled enthusiastically. "So did you like it?" They didn't say anything. "Weren't the drums just incredible?" They didn't answer. "What did you think of the service? Wasn't it interesting?" Her mother-in-law pursed her lips and put her nose in the air. "Well," was all she said and she looked away with a smirk on her face. Jill was confused but passed it off as indifference. Maybe she's in a bad mood, or is jet lagged or something. She smiled contentedly. "Well, I'll go get the girls," and she bounced off saying hi to a few people along the way, and exchanging a few comments about the talk and how wonderful it was. Everyone seemed elated and full of enthusiasm. "Very interesting wasn't it?" "Sure was. What did you think about the biofield reverberation part?" one man asked. "It was fascinating," Jill answered. Before coming to the Spiritual Awareness Center, Jill never knew church could be so much fun.

The girls piled into the car. They were chatty and happy. It was never quiet with four girls. Michael's parents, however, sat in stony silence the duration of the twenty-minute ride home. Everyone got out of the car and Jill said, "I'll go put Bob down for her nap. Be back in a bit." As she read Bobbie a book she heard raised voices upstairs and Maya ran down to the basement to tell Jill that Michael and his mom were fighting. "Oh? What for?" "I don't know" replied Maya. "Hmm. I wonder what could possibly be wrong." Jill came upstairs after laying Bobbie down for her nap and the house was empty. She went to her room and Michael was there. "What happened?" "Oh it's nothing. My mom was not happy with the service." "Oh really? Why? But I thought it was great." Michael raised his eyebrows. "Yeah well, they didn't." "You're Dad didn't like it either?" "Nope." "I wonder why." "It's not their cup of tea," he said. "They only believe in Christianity." "But this is Christianity, isn't it?" Michael raised his eyebrows again. "Not their kind." "But they talk about God and Jesus at our church. Sometimes." Jill argued. "Yeah, well like I said, they believe in their specific brand of religion." "Oh, they're protestant." she half asked. "Sort of," he said. "Even more specific, Presbyterian." "Oh and ours is not one of those." "Yeah, it's not any of them." "Does it matter?" she asked. "Well to them it does." "What difference does it make, God is God, isn't he?" "Not to my parents." "Oh." "So they're mad then?" "Yeah, they're pretty upset." "So what should we do?" "Nothing. There's nothing we can do. It's ok, just forget it. It's fine." "Are you sure?" Now Jill was worried. "Yeah, it's fine. Don't worry. There's nothing we can do. They'll get over it." She couldn't believe they didn't like their church. She thought it was such a great way to study religion, and so inspiring. It felt deep and meaningful and thought-provoking. How could anyone not like it? She thought this would finally bond them together and that their relationship would blossom. She couldn't have been more wrong.

Shortly after, Maya came in the house upset and worried. "Mom, Grandma says you and Dad are evil." "What??!" Jill could scarcely believe her ears. "She says you're evil." "Why would she say that?" "Because of our church. She says you and Dad are going down the path of the devil. She says we need to stop going to our church and that they are going to pray for us girls." "You have to be kidding me." "No." Maya looked genuinely worried. "Mom? Are you and Daddy evil?" "What??! No, of course not!" "But why did Grandma say that?" "I don't know sweetheart but don't you worry. We're not evil. That's silly. I'll talk to Daddy about this. Grandma should not be telling you that." Maya was relieved to know her parents weren't evil.

"Michael??!" Jill called him. He was in one of the barns. "Michael, your Mom just told Maya you and I are evil!!" Jill tried to contain her anger but she knew she was going to have to let it out in order to make sure Michael did what he needed to do. "She can't do that. She absolutely may not do that. How could she say that against a little girl's own parents! Michael, she's only nine! That is not ok. You have to talk to your Mom, and she may not ever do that again. She can believe whatever she wants, but no one will tell our daughter her parents are evil!" "Ok," he said. "Are you going to do it now?" "Yeah, I'll do it. Don't worry."

Next thing Jill saw Michael take his mother into the kitchen and quite a lot of screaming ensued. "Wow," Jill later told Michael. "I didn't realize." "Yeah." That was all he said. "We shouldn't have taken them to our church." "Nope," he said. "Why didn't you tell me?" "I tried to." Jill was surprised. She thought he was fairly relaxed about the whole idea at the start. The magnitude didn't match the warning in her mind. Michael accused her often of not listening. Maybe this was an example. But then a small part of her felt it was unfair that they had endured her in-law's church multiple times, and their lectures and preaching and prayers and beliefs. So why can't I share mine, she wondered. It seems so one sided. And are they honestly that different? She shared these thoughts with Michael and he said, "According to my parents they are." "But I don't understand the difference in all these various religions." "It's basically how wet you get when you're baptized," he said. He always made a joke out of everything, but in a sort of profound and descriptive way. "The Baptists go in all the way. Catholics get a sprinkling ... Presbyterians go partway ..." This actually made sense to Jill. It was the only way she could keep straight in her mind the details of variation that seemed so important, and yet so trivial. How could that possibly matter, she thought to herself. What about the things we share in common? Is all this fighting worth it? Over who's right and who's wrong? The whole thing seemed downright silly.

This altercation did not bode well for their future relationship with Michael's parents. Jill could feel anger and disdain towards her and she asked Michael from time to time if it was because of the religion thing and did they blame her. He said no, they blamed him. But Jill felt a seething resentfulness from her mother-in-law, a quiet rage every time she saw her. Many years later, after Maya was grown she said yes they did. They blamed Jill for everything that ever went wrong in their family.

Chapter 12

Morocco

(1957-1958)

Writing is a comfort to me, for I can firmly plant all my thoughts and organize them and analyze them. But my handicap is Time. As ideas, philosophies, solutions or just mere twinkling thoughts fly through my mind, I promise on paper to immortalize them. These habitants of my brain are like an infinite cascade and the only way to record their instancy would be to keep a pen at hand constantly. I just can't do that so – I try to capture my thought processes as they're developed over a period of time. Therefore, a diary, as such, serves me no immediate purpose.

I can't be too general at this point, or generous, rather. Time is running out. But as I laid here in my bed at home, I think I saw a glimpse of the future.

I looked up from my bed and glanced around the room at all my endearing and familiar objects – souvenirs, knick-knacks, dolls, etc.

I looked at them this time as an outsider trying to categorize the owner of the collection. On one section, the bookcase was a prized collection of foreign artesies. My Spanish doll waved her castanets above her head and seemed to come alive beckoning me. Next to her, my handmade Arab horseman gallantly thrust his rifle above his horses spiriting head. My tiny little Japanese doll, stood demurely among her delicate setting of a casual arrangement of ebonized chopsticks, and a cocky "sachi" mushroom jar, and a significant teacup and saucer. Below this shelf, a group of continental air displayed my Holland dolls, so neat and secure; my Scottish couple, so prim and sassy; my German girl grasping a candle and my whimsy German couple, plump and memories vague and happy. Effervescent of a German child, a silly African thing, a monkeyish oddity that just took my fancy for its eccentricity; my mammy doll, black and gay, plump and full of wit and good stuff, and my ship – my Dutch ship – the transportation to the lands that my darling knick-knacks are beckoning me to. Are these symbols of my personality a signal determinent of my future? My love for travel is represented by my dolls – to me they are living and someday I will see their native lands.

Up above them, on a separate shelf – for they are a separate alien facet to my person, are my cherished steeds. They stand so proud and spirited – so beautiful and real. My wild mustang, a buckskin paint; my noble Arabian, a proud prancer – a grayish smoky white; my domestic, gentle and good-natured English saddlebred, a dark bay with a bald face; and on down to tinier and more plentiful members of the herd, decorate this portion of my being. It's no secret, this love of mine for horses. I see beauty in them that no other animal can match. They bring me a freedom to mind – wide-open spaces, fresh air, smells of heady clover or hay or earthy smells. I love that life.

Skipping across to the other side, a single picture is above my desk: Shep. I drew that watercolor of my dog. Oh how I loved my little faithful Shep. He was so cute, and entirely mine. This love is even a greater one than for horses, though the association is the same. This love isn't beauty itself; it's a gentle beauty; a loyal, spiritual beauty and love. It's a beautiful understanding between a girl and her dog. My peppy, red-pepper dog – red was his fur – a gorgeous tone of auburn interrupted by downy snow-white markings on his chest and paws. The memories he brings back – beautiful, but painful since my adorable pup is gone. Yes, tears are welling in my eyes. If I <u>ever</u> catch the BASTARD who poisoned him …!

Below is my desk. On this piece of furniture, which is just a plain old desk, but which suffices as a dressing table as well, are a many things. These belie my girlish nature. All the delicate cut glass perfume containers withholding fragrant, spiciness; petite little figures such as angels waltz among the orchestral ceramic elves; a spiral glass vase here, a hand-painted sachet bottle there from which protrudes a single daisy …

Bobbie, 1962

Bobbie walked up the winding spiral staircase from their apartment to the roof of the building. Her nine-year-old brother, James, was with her. The staircase opened onto the rooftop. They lived in Morocco across from the Medina, the center of the city of Rabat. Bobbie and James attended the military school nearly forty miles away at Port Lyautey Naval Base. After school they loved to go to their favorite hangout. There was hardly a day that Bobbie and her brother didn't climb to the roof to look over the city and watch the millions of people walking in and out of narrow streets, shopping for produce on the sides of the road, or hurrying home from work. They could see the temples and the people going in for one of their multiple daily prayers. Bobbie liked to watch all of the activity going on below. The people worked hard and for many, food was scarce. Street children rummaged through trashcans looking for leftovers. Their clothing was ragged. It was hard to endure the hardships of life in the city of Rabat.

They liked it up here because they could be alone away from their guards who followed them everywhere, and also because they could look down on the bustling crowds without being seen. It gave them something to do. Bobbie thought the women looked like colorful shadows in their djellabas. That is, if a shadow could have color this was how she imagined it would look. The women and the men tried to push past each other and Bobbie wondered how they managed not to stumble or knock over each other.

Smaller children of the lower class were strapped to the backs of mothers who begged for food and money. Bobbie wrote in her journal once, "These children live in such deplorable conditions as we big Americans walk along taking in this strange, but very interesting land." Words Bobbie heard regularly from other Americans rang in her ears, "Oh, but giving them money is prohibited – there is a proclamation of some sort we can't feed them all, so don't give to any." Bobbie thought there may have been some logic to this (somewhere) but in her thirteen-year-old mind she hated them and herself too for that and she couldn't begin to understand.

The five o'clock siren call to prayer went off. They could hear them all over the city. They watched mostly men walking towards the couple of temples they could see from where they were. Bobbie and her brother sat near the edge of the roof watching the women walk together. Many were accompanied by a male relative, most likely their husband but could be a brother, an uncle, even a cousin. Bobbie liked to think of them as personal bodyguards, there to protect the cherished women of the family who possessed the ability to create life.

The pair of them watched the women approach vegetable stalls, inspecting the quality of the day's produce and carefully selecting the best. James made his own observations. "They look like ants, so many of them. It's dirty. I like our clean empty wide-open streets. I like our country much better. At least we can play outside. I wish we could be outside down there, run around and play like at home." "Yeah," Bobbie agreed, "It's like we're trapped with no place to go." "At least we have our secret hideout to escape to." They exchanged grins because no one knew about their secret.

"I hate the poverty," Bobbie said, thinking very hard about the reasons why. "Bobbie, why is it like this?" There was a touch of disdain in his voice. She knew that question was coming. "Why doesn't somebody take care of them? Our country is so much better." James had a look of disgust on his face. "Because the government doesn't do anything," Bobbie said impatiently. "And they don't take care of the poor."

They looked past the streets directly below to the buildings in the distance. It was as if moving their attention away from what was right in front of them would take the immediate situation below away. "It's so cool we can see the whole city from here," James said. "Yeah," Bobbie answered. Words seemed unnecessary to describe their birds-eye view. She looked further still towards the borders of the city and past that towards the empty land beyond and finally to the horizon and the sun slowly falling towards the ocean in the opposite direction. It felt comforting looking at something universal like the sunset and the ocean, something they could be looking at from any country anywhere ... or even from their own. It tied them somewhat to home.

After a while, they laid back onto the hot concrete, spread out, looking up at the sky. It's a thing only kids seem to do. Bobbie didn't know if kids on the streets below did this, although they did seem carefree. In a sense it was a freedom all children share, the kind that isn't bound to time. The street kids had different outlets for fun for sure, like climbing on trash piles, jumping through dirty water – nothing really mattered for them. What would? They had nothing to lose, nothing to gain, only the pursuit of their next meal. Only. But Bobbie had seen them share their littlest morsel with each other; humanity takes form in the gravest of circumstances.

The two of them stared up at the clouds, the sun beating down hot on their faces and bodies. It didn't bother them. They played the game all American children play at some point growing up; it's almost like a right of passage. "I see a cow," Bobbie said, beginning the game. "I see a unicorn," James said. "Where?" She asked. "There," he pointed, "See the horn? And that's the tail. See it?" "No, I don't see it," she replied. The game didn't count unless all members could verify it. "Right there dummy! That puff of clouds between that big one and that medium one, see the skinny long parts coming down? Those are the legs." "Oh, I see it. But I only see two legs." "Well that's because you can only see this side of it." "Ok," she replied. They couldn't afford to be too detailed with this game or they'd never find anything. "There's a frog!" he shouted. "Yeah, I see it! That's a good one, really looks like one." It was exciting to find such a close match. "There's a ladybug," Bobbie said. "I don't see it," James said. "There, next to your unicorn, see how the head came off your unicorn's horn?" she explained. The clouds had shifted slightly. "That's the body," she said convincingly. "Hmm, ok I'll give it to you," he said skeptically.

"Well, we've been gone a while," Bobbie stood up. "We'd better go check in or everyone'll come looking for us, and either scold us, or worse, discover our hide-out." "Just one more Bobbie, please?" James begged. "No. Come on," Bobbie's voice had an edge to it. James always hated ending their games and having to go back to the world of boring bossy adults. "Come on, it might be time for dinner already." "Alright," he shuffled his feet and looked down at the ground, following Bobbie to the staircase.

Reluctantly, they walked down the spiraling stairs, more slowly than they had raced up earlier. They entered their apartment where their mother, Effie, was running around, getting her hat and gloves. She was such a lady, even in this sweltering heat. But she refused to look like anything but a princess. She was the wife of a colonel in the Air Force, and commander of the radar base at Rabat. She readily played the part. The worst was when she forced the kids to do the same. Bobbie was barely a teenager and James was nine, but they were expected to act like a perfect lady and gentleman. Their mom snapped, "Barbara Maude!" She always called them by their first and middle names when she was scolding them. "Go get some decent clothes on for dinner. We're going to the club. You look a mess. Why is your skirt all wrinkled? And look! You have gravel all over your backside. What on earth have you two been up to?" She eyed them suspiciously. "Oh nothing," James tried to cover up. He wasn't about to let their secret hideout be discovered. Effie turned to James next, "James Alfred, you go get cleaned up this instant! You look a mess. Come on guys, snap to it, we have to be there in fifteen minutes."

Pretty soon they were dressed in their miserable stiff clothes and in the car with the driver racing down the streets through the traffic and people, their guards sitting on either side of them. Military children were not allowed to go anywhere without guarded protection. They arrived at the club, got out of the car and entered the big gates opening onto the compound and life contrary to the one they currently lived. The club was like a little America inside another country. And it really looked like a little sliver of America. The sidewalk was lined with perfectly manicured flowers, the grounds were mowed and opened out onto an American style playground and tennis courts. They entered the building that contained the restaurant that was the officer's club and sat down.

Bobbie thought to herself as she reluctantly made her way to the table, and later put down on paper: *"It makes me sick to sit in our lovely Officer's Club and eat our rich and tasty meals prepared by continental chefs of high reputation and look out through big, picture windows at skinny haggard looking beggars hanging around the kitchen door, rummaging through the garbage and greedily confiscating their finds. Our garbage cans are always well filled."*

Bobbie's and James' grandmother, an immigrant from Poland, never could accustom her self to this. Her whole life growing up Bobbie and James were constantly reminded of the millions of starving while they wasted. She would tell them that the spirits of hundreds of children who had died of starvation hung over them as they ate begging them to not waste a morsel. This picture was a real manifestation in Bobbie's mind before coming to Rabat – Bobbie said to her self, *"I was never one to waste, you can bet. But, when before my eyes, in stark reality I see living, human bodies ramsacking through garbage pails while the "highly cultured and educated" Americans sit at lined covered tables with candles on red carpeted floors, it makes me sick. As we sat at the dinner table, the waiters drawing the curtains, because a number of complaints were made by members that their dinners were being ruined by having to watch such utter crudity and ugly animal behavior.*

I swear that some day, when I am equipped and ready, I will fight for all that I am worth in the eyes of God to help these people, or any people in like situations," Bobbie dramatically whispered to her self. "I've got to help, and I just have to do my part in this battle for Humanity. I want nothing in return. I will give all my worldly possessions."

Several nights later, Bobbie's Father came home. Occasionally he performed a traditional inspection of Bobbie and her brother in the military spirit. Even though it was a bit of a joke, Bobbie and James were expected to uphold military standards like he was accustomed to in his work, and he ran his home the same way. That included the requirement of perfectly folded clothes in every dresser drawer. On this particular occasion, however, Bobbie played a trick; she folded everything perfectly on the top layer, but underneath, rumpled all the rest. When he discovered the rumpled clothes he roared with laughter. He was a gregarious outgoing man everybody loved with a huge personality and a huge build to match. Bobbie adored her Father.

Bobbie wrote regularly in her journal that year. There were four last entries while living in Rabat that sharply curtailed their life in Morocco and changed their family forever after.

June 6, 1958-"Dad was sent to Germany today on an emergency. He's very sick and they are trying to see what they can do. He has had bouts with cancer off and on his entire life. Hopefully, he will pull through this one.

July 23, 1958-Dad has been in Germany now for a long time and today they informed us they will be sending him home to be treated more seriously for cancer. I am so worried about him.

July 30, 1958-Dad has been sent to San Diego for aggressive cancer treatment. He has lung cancer and they are saying it's quite serious. They say he has six months to live. The Air Force is trying to get him to retire from active duty but he will not.

Dec. 13, 1958-My father passed away today and I think my world has crumbled. He was everything to me, my confident, my advisor, my tower of invincible strength, my dear dear Father. I loved him more than anyone will ever know. I think I am going to die of heartache. How can I ever go on? Mom is a disaster. I am only thirteen and James is nine. This isn't fair. Children aren't supposed to lose their father when they aren't yet full grown. Mom will have to go back to work. There is a bit of money to sustain us; mom is considered a war widow on account of the military situation in Morocco. He also fought in World War II. Dad planned well in case of a situation like this. He bought all kinds of insurance. I think he knew the end was coming. On his deathbed he even promised the house to James. I refused to believe it was happening. He pulled through all those other times, why not once more? Today is a very sad day and I think our family will never be the same.

One day, many years after his death, Bobbie wrote a poem about her Father to commemorate his memory:

Bobbie, Spring 1960

Tall and erect as an oak tree
Was he,
Like a powerful dam,
Strong, sure and mighty
Was he.
Holding up supernal standards and
Sterling morals
Unremittingly.

In searching for universal truths
Persistently
Virtuous as Socrates
Was he.
Wise he's been and sensitive
Compassion for Humanity
Ran abreast to humble Also

Sympathy.
He served as ethical officer
In the Military
With an unflinching
Patriotism
For his beloved country
A leader of men, and however
Stern he might be,
Loved and idolized by his
Company
Was he?
A Man of the World
Was he?
He had a bond with nature
It seems,
A secret omniscient tie
Which unveiled its self through his
Love for the clear, blue skies
That he dedicated limitless hours
Flying so high.
A Pilot, You see,
Was he?
Bound to Nature in other ways
Was he?
By his fascination and admiration
Of natural scenery and
simple beauty.

One never forgot him,
His impression imbued so
Enduringly;
A stature so sound and robust
A face in which eyes shone with trust,
A nature exposing qualities
Inexhaustibly,
Such as;
Intelligence, courage, goodness,

Humility
Justice, honor, faith, modesty, and
Honesty.
And jokes he recited quite
Frequently, inciting
Laughter readily,
Himself habitually guffawing
Heartily,
Above which roaring laugh
Grew bushy red mustache!

So great and noble, this man,
Standing and fighting for
Rights
Valiantly and resolutely.
Just knowing him
Instilled in one
Insight to Life and Vitality.

To help those in need
Were part of his deeds.
He played his role sublimely
Ceaselessly contributing to
Humanity.

An immortal personality
Is he?
My father.

Chapter 13

A File of a Life
(2011)

I feel like a million little people
All running inside me asking me
Who am I?
The stars shine like diamonds,
Glittering and twinkling
With a silvery happiness
That rings and sings within me.
The world is mine!
I turn myself on from one
Magic mood to another;
Living
All gamuts of life in each
Opulent, yielding mood.
Then,
Crash!
I fall into thousands of
Tiny, little pieces.
Stormy tempo surges within me:
Turbulent, tremulous, tenacious.
Every angry movement is

Depression in its ugly
Gray coat.
Despair pushes me into a
Gloomy oblivion.
I am nothing.
Who am I?

Bobbie, 1960

The phone rang. "Jill? Is that you?" Jill was still in her pajamas. "Yes, Granny?" "It's me." "How are you?" Jill yawned and stumbled down the stairs, barely awake. "Oh I'm good but I'm really worried about James. That's what I was calling about. I just don't know what to do. He hasn't come out of his room for three weeks." Jill was in the kitchen now, turning on the coffee pot. "Three weeks? That's a long time Granny. Why? Is something wrong? Is he sick? That's strange. What do you think it is?" "I just don't know. Well he's been sick but he doesn't come out for anything for a long time now. I'm so worried." "Why don't you ask him to go to the doctor?" The coffee machine started to percolate. The smell of fresh ground coffee filled the kitchen, and the sun was just peaking over the horizon. The neighbor's dog was already barking and chasing his tail in circles like he did everyday, all day long. Jill closed the window. "I have. He won't go. He says to leave him alone." "Oh. Well, what about you? How are you getting along Granny? Who's doing the grocery shopping if you can't drive and James is locked up in his room?" "Oh, I don't know, we're managing. We don't eat much. I open a can of soup for myself. James doesn't eat at all, which is another thing that really worries me …"

Jill hung up the phone, thinking to herself 'a can of soup? Granny is not eating well.' Every day Jill checked in with Effie after that to see what was happening with James and the situation unfolding. James refused to talk on the phone. Finally she decided to call an ambulance. They pulled James out of the house against his will and they took him to the hospital. James' liver was failing and they kept him. Jill called neighbors to check on Effie and kept wondering when James might be released to come home, but as days wore into weeks she realized that wasn't happening and decided she'd better go see Effie to make sure she was ok and see what was happening with her uncle.

Jill told the girls and Michael she was going to have to leave for a while. They were living overseas again. This time they were in Bulgaria. She had no idea what she was getting into or what lay ahead for her with James' sickness and Effie all alone. "When will you be back Mom?" Bobbie asked. By this time, she was ten years old, and her name had long since transformed from Alibob to Bobbie. Jill still called her variations of all of her nicknames. "I just don't know honestly. I've never dealt with anything like this before. I'm not sure what's happening." Jill packed her bags. She didn't even know how much to pack. She brought her things downstairs the next morning. She had booked a flight for the very next day. She still had a couple of hours before she needed to get to the airport and the house was quiet. She wondered where everybody was. She walked outside to see if anyone was there. She did not see anyone immediately, but decided to take a walk around the yard. There, on the furthest hidden corner, to the far end of the house was Bobbie, sitting in the grass. She was busy with something. "What'ch ya doin there?" She already knew the answer. Bobbie answered anyway. "Making fairy houses." Jill bent down to get a closer look. They were so tiny, built only out of leaves. Somehow Bobbie had perfected the art of stacking the leaves like stacking cards against each other in a house of cards. She had spent hours in the garden perfecting the art. It was actually quite impressive. Jill thought it was enchanting. She loved Bobbie's creativity and her sensitive imagination.

Bobbie loved to write too. She had a collection of empty journals. The funny thing was, most of them remained empty. Jill stumbled on a single entry at the beginning of one of her journals one day and it summed everything up perfectly. It was titled simply "*Blank*."

Bobbie, 2014

Ever since I was young, I had a fascination with notebooks. I collected them, and liked to flip through all of the unwritten pages. I always would have some sort of plan to write and write and fill up all of the pages with art, songs, writings, anything pleasing to me. But for some reason I was never actually able to start writing in one. I collected more and more of these empty notebooks and my collection just kept on growing and growing. Although I had all these plans for my books I don't think I actually had any INTENT for writing in them, filling them up with my own ideas. I liked the emptiness. There was something about having all these blank pages with so many possibilities to fill them with that was so comforting. I found this same comfort in moving. A new place, school, new people that I hadn't met yet. That was my Blank page. Being in the same place for years it's the same as having a notebook full of "things" would have been. Everything would be set in stone, and I as a person would be defined. Ah but a new place, there are so many possibilities I could be a new person, a nobody, or a loud somebody. Either way, I could always switch next time I moved. Each of my moves is a new blank notebook to me. But I always make sure I can move to a new place, start at a new school, before I can actually begin to fill up the past notebooks.

"I might be gone for a while you know." Jill tried to prepare her for the unknown. "I know," she said. "Are you going to be alright?" "I'll be alright Mom." Jill worried about her. She was so withdrawn in her own little world a lot of the time. Both of the girls were. Marley was in her room a great deal of the time too. They weren't forced to be, but they just did. Jill passed it off as middle school blues. Her older sisters told their younger sisters, "Nobody likes middle school. It's awful for everybody. Suck it up." What Jill did not know until many years later was that in addition to the regular nonsense of middle school for Marley were the cultural difficulties of living in a foreign country, and being a new student. The tight small group that formed the entire seventh grade at the international school had known each other for a long time. Marley spent months alone before they accepted her into the group. They were extremely critical so Marley learned to keep her mouth shut, and eventually they grew to think she was cool. Marley figured if she didn't say much, there wouldn't be anything to criticize. It was a lot to bear even for Jill's boisterous intelligent and beautiful thirteen year-old. She still had her white blonde hair like she had when she was three and four years old. And her eyes were huge and such a watery blue that with her rosy red cheeks and red lips, she always looked like a doll Jill thought every time she looked at her. She had surely adopted Effie's genes when it came to her white blond hair, and Jill's mother's big blue eyes. Marley had always been so loving and ready to hug at any opportunity. If Jill wasn't receptive, she would latch onto her legs and give her a huge hug anyway.

Jill laughed at the memory of her endearing little girl. Now that she was older, she pushed Jill away like any pre-adolescent. It was difficult for Jill. And what she didn't realize was that what she really wanted was for Jill to be there, even if Marley acted out. No one acts too much like a Pollyana when they're going through a hard time. Jill realized too late. All the hugs of her childhood, Jill felt like she hadn't enjoyed enough of while she could, and now it was too late.

Madeleine had come back home to finish her last year of high school. She had left the year before because she'd had her own set of difficulties with the international school. She had spent weeks crying in her room every night when they first enrolled at the school. The curriculum was so rigorous and did not afford time for anything fun. Madeleine relished outdoor sports she loved competitive soccer in particular. It was a hard adjustment. When Jill and Michael realized how much she was struggling, they let her go home to finish at her old high school, living with Michael's parents. Maya followed shortly after.

Madeleine had been lonely however and came back to Bulgaria. Jill found another high school. Maya laughed and laughed when Jill first took Madeleine to see her new school. It was surrounded by communist buildings and when they rounded the final turn, they saw old ugly brown fields surrounding one tall building with the windows knocked out. Maya said, "Please don't tell me that's it or I am going to really laugh." Jill hesitantly admitted, "Well … actually it is." It hadn't exactly been the words she wanted to introduce Madeleine to her new school with. Jill had researched it quite thoroughly however. Cheerily she said, "Well, it's not quite what it looks on the outside. Come on. You'll see. The school is on the very top floor. It has in-tact windows and it is decorated very cute. Just close your eyes on the way up."

Going back and forth between schools hadn't been so easy for Madeleine. If Jill would have realized it was going to be this difficult for the girls, she wouldn't have agreed so readily to embark on yet another overseas adventure. Madeleine spent many hours running the trails in the forest behind their home. It was one way she coped, and it was how she indoctrinated Marley into the sport as well. Many years later, Marley confided that if it weren't for Madeleine, she wasn't sure she'd have made it through.

Madeleine was creative and reflective as well. Before she'd left the first international school, she painted a picture that hung in the school for many years later. It was an old tree with crooked dead branches. The colors were dark and sad. Caught in the sharp branches of the tree was one bright red balloon. A teacher told Jill long after Madeleine had left Bulgaria for good that all of the teachers often came to look at it. It symbolized even for them the sadness of the restrictive school, and their longing to break free. Jill's mother had painted a very similar painting of Jill before she died. In it, Jill was a little girl and she looked sad, holding one red balloon. Her mother loomed high above in the clouds looking over her like a premonition of what eventually came to pass.

Jill told the girls goodbye and got into the car with Michael. He dropped her off at the airport and they didn't see each other for two months. This was how long it took to take care of Effie and her unraveling family.

Jill arrived late one night where friends of the family met her at the airport. They told her "Jill I think you'd better go straight to the hospital. We're going to stop there on the way home so you can see James." They arrived at the hospital and walked down the long corridors and Jill suddenly realized he was in intensive care. She walked into the room and gasped. He was strung up to every machine imaginable. A nurse came in and told them, "His liver is failing, and his kidneys are beginning to fail too. All of his organs are slowly shutting down." "Why are his arms bandaged like that?" Jill asked. "It's to hold the fluids in. It's what happens when kidneys fail. There's nothing to hold the bodily fluids in." "Oh my God," said Jill. Poor James had tubes running in and out of him every which direction.

Jill drove to Effie's house with her friends. She knocked on the door. It was late at night and so dark Jill could barely see the front step. Effie hadn't put the porch light on. The air was chilly and crisp and the stars were as bright as ever she could remember at the old house under the desert skies. It took Effie forever to come to the door. "Granny! How are you?!" They hugged and their friends left them so they could reunite. Jill came inside and it looked the same as always. The shaggy yellowish-beige carpet, the aqua couches, the piano, all the paintings her mother had painted that decorated most of the walls. The large Moroccan brass plate still hung in the living room where it had always been. Dishes and wine glasses from different parts of the world were locked inside the glass and wooden display case that Effie had custom made with her name engraved inside. Little dolls from Poland and Japan were interspersed inside as well. German dishware filled the china cabinet in the living room. It was detailed with brass colored metal trim that criss-crossed over the glass. For some reason that unusual feature always attracted Jill's attention. It was part of what made Effie's house, Effie's house. It felt cozy and comfortable as usual, and yet somehow cold and lonely at the same time. It always did feel that way to her at Granny's. It was like the house was filled with old memories of parties and people from decades back, and yet with sadness and emptiness too.

"Have you been to see James?" Jill asked as she followed Effie down the hall. "No, why, have you?" Jill didn't answer right away. She waited for Effie to fill the silence. "How would I get there? I have no one to take me. Joan and Ed took me a couple of times, but that was two weeks ago." "Two weeks ago," repeated Jill. "Why? Do you know anything? How is he?" "I think we should go see him tomorrow Granny." "Oh yes, can we?!" Effie's face lit up. Jill looked at Effie sadly. Yet another impending death she shouldn't have to endure. "Of course we'll go Granny. We must." Effie smiled, delighted and happy at the thought of going to see her son. Jill fought back a tear.

The following morning the two of them cooked bacon and eggs, drank coffee and there was a happy energy as Effie got herself dressed and ready to go see her son. A heaviness hung on Jill's shoulders as she watched Granny's excitement. Effie sat at her makeup vanity, the same one she had all those years before when Jill was a little girl and she helped Granny pick out her shoes and purses to match her outfits. Effie picked out something special to wear. She was going out for once, and to see her son no less! Jill wasn't sure what to say. In the end, she said nothing. She talked to Effie tenderly. If Effie sensed anything, she ignored it. She turned to Jill a couple of times to ask if she knew anything again. Jill remained quiet. Effie refused to imagine anything was wrong.

When they arrived at the hospital, Effie was in a hurry to get in the door. "I hope he's okay," she said. "I just want to know when he's coming home." Jill decided to dampen the blow that was about to come. "Granny, you may have to brace yourself for the possibility he's not coming home." Effie's brow wrinkled. She didn't ask again if Jill knew anything. She only put her head down in consternation, like she was fighting the possibility. Jill had to practically jog to keep up with Effie racing down the hall she was in such a hurry to see James. They came to the doors of the ICU and waited outside to be let in. Effie noticed the sign and the reality of what she was about to find started to sink in. "He's in ICU?" Jill had tears in her eyes and hugged Effie. Effie looked concerned. "What's going on?" "Granny, please remember I'm here for you and I'm not going anywhere ok?" "Why are you saying that?" "Granny, James is not doing so well. I just want to prepare you …" Effie looked at the door like a wild horse penned in a corral, anxious to know what she was about to find. When the nurse finally let them in, Effie went straight for the bed where James was. A look of horror crossed her face when she saw him and she let out a moan belying the heartache of every mourning mother that ever existed. Monitors beeped, and fluid coursed through some of the tubes connected to James' body. She went to her son, and held his hand and talked to him telling him, "Oh my dear son, James, I'm here. Everything's going to be ok. I love you, I love you, oh God are you suffering? Are you ok? Oh dear God, please let the angels be with my son. Oh James, the angels are with you …" Effie repeated variations of the same thing over and over, choking over sobs and holding his arm close to her heart and leaning as close to his head as she could. James did not respond. He was unable to talk. Jill stood at the foot of the bed and watched her Granny mourn the impending death of her second and last child that would go before her. It wasn't fair.

A doctor came to the room and asked if they were the relatives. It was probably the first time a doctor ever raced to see the relatives of his patient since none had come the entirety of his stay in the ICU. Jill said yes, and he asked if he could have a word with them. "Yes of course," Jill answered. Effie hardly noticed he was there, but Jill gently put her arms around Granny's shoulders and told her "Granny, we have to talk to the doctor now." Effie looked at the doctor and nodded her head. She set her chin in a show of confidence, mostly trying to muster up the courage for what she knew was coming. "Please have a seat." The doctor pointed to a couple of chairs. "I know this is a difficult time, but we need to discuss some important details." The doctor did not mince words or sugar coat what was coming next. "Who has legal medical authority over James?" "I do," Effie said. The doctor looked at her now. The doctor needed to get some critical answers and quickly. "As you can see, the situation is not good, and I'm not going to lie to you and pretend it is. Short of a miracle, James does not have much time and I need to know what your wishes are. The only thing keeping him alive are these machines. Soon he will go into a coma. His organs are failing one by one. There is no reversing this. We can prolong the process and keep him alive as long as possible, or we can allow the natural course of the inevitable. I just need to know what you want to do." "What about surgery or some other invasive action?" Jill asked just to exhaust every possible option. "We could do that, but as soon as we'd finish one organ we'd have to move on to the next, and the likelihood of success is very low. He would need a major surgery on every organ. There is no way he would survive it. It would be a great deal of effort and expense for very little chance it would even do anything. His body would not be able to withstand the trauma." The only words Effie could muster were "Is he suffering?" Effie looked to Jill for support and asked her "What should I do?" "Granny, I don't know what the right decision is, but it has to be yours and whatever you decide I'm behind you. I don't think there is a right way or a wrong way. Whatever you feel, it will be right." A calm stillness came over Effie as she looked to Jill for strength and told the doctor "I don't want him to suffer. Let's end this." She sobbed and said over and over again "I don't want him to suffer. I don't want him to suffer." "I know Granny, I know." She looked at Jill for reassurance. "Did I make the right decision?" "Yes Granny. Absolutely. You did. I think it's the best one you could've made to be kind to James." Effie nodded and seemed reassured.

Effie got up and walked to the side of James' bed without saying goodbye to the doctor. Jill talked to the doctor a couple of more minutes and waited with Effie for some time after. Finally she said "Come on Granny, let's go get something to eat." Effie closed her eyes and said, "Yes. Ok." She looked at her son and held his hand in both of hers. "Goodbye James, I love you. The angels are with you my son." "We can come back, can't we? Tonight? Tomorrow?" "Of course Granny, as many times as you'd like."

Effie and Jill walked through the dark garage complex to the car. They didn't talk. There wasn't much to say. Effie kept her head down. When they got to the car Jill opened the door for her. "You going to be ok, Granny?" She said quietly "Yep." Jill's heart fell with the heaviness of a thousand sad words. Jill began driving and Effie put her face in her hands and cried. Jill put her hand on her leg and said, "I know. I know. It isn't easy. We'll get through this." Effie raised her head and met Jill's eyes and squeezed her hand. "Where do you want to eat Granny?" "Let's go to that good soup place." She could never remember the name. Jill knew exactly where she was talking about. She pulled into the parking lot and parked the car. She helped Effie out and they went inside.

On the way to the counter they passed two large standard poodle guide dogs. One of them strayed from his owner and walked right to Effie. Effie loved dogs, and especially big ones. She was especially fond of German Shepards. The owner followed her dog. "My dog has never done that before. He's a trained guide dog and he never leaves my side. The only reason I let him do it is because I was curious what could have been such a diversion to draw him over here. Obviously he really likes you. That really says something." The other standard poodle and her owner came over to them and Effie and Jill and the two women began talking. Jill told them why she was there and the tragedy of her poor uncle. The woman speaking to Jill said, "I knew James. We went to high school together." Jill was surprised. The women said goodbye and Jill and Effie bought their food and sat down at one of the little tables to eat their soup.

James was gone the very next morning. The doctor called to let them know when his blood pressure was dropping and that it would be a matter of minutes to an hour. Effie and Jill sat at the kitchen table with the stepladder stool that served as the head of the table for as long as Jill could remember. The sun poured into the kitchen as it always did. They sat together holding hands and the phone rang shortly after. "He's gone," the doctor said through the receiver. Jill nodded and looked at Effie. The corners of her eyes had filled with tears. Jill didn't need to say anything. Effie said, "He's gone isn't he?" Jill nodded her head. Effie was suddenly very calm and very still. "It's over."

Along with grief came the necessary preparations. The two women mechanically moved through the motions of arranging the service, going to the crematorium, calling everyone. Jill became so focused getting everything done that the logistics at times overshadowed the emotional impact of what they were doing. When Jill handed Effie the Crematorium form, she broke down crying. Jill stopped what she was doing. "Oh Granny, I'm so sorry, this is really hard." She bent over and hugged her.

There was so much that needed taking care of that it was challenging juggling the human element with all of the work. Effie couldn't live by herself anymore. They needed to figure something out. The house had to be cleaned out and taken care of. The finances were in disarray. Jill found a foot high stack of mail with bills that hadn't been paid in months. Jill sat down and called all of them, sorting out how far behind she was. And during all of this, poor Effie was in a whirlwind uprooting of her life. The house she had lived in for sixty-five years had seen generations of her family come and go amid the events that filled their family's existence. And now it was all about to be taken away.

The day of the funeral arrived. Jill loaded her car with photos carefully selected, representing her uncle's life, flowers she had arranged her self and placed in large old vases that belonged to Effie and everything else they needed that day. She walked up the old steps to the front of the church that her family had gone to her entire life, and that housed every major life event in her family, including her mother's and her grandfather's funerals, her mother's wedding, her own baptism. She had never entered from the front before. She had never noticed how tall and large the doors were. They were swung open welcoming her over the threshold to yet another life-marking event. It felt strange to Jill, all of this time. She never quite felt like she belonged there. It was like she was always on the outside looking in, and yet suddenly here she was, in the middle of everything. She walked inside the church carrying some of the flowers. She shivered from the cold breeze that blew in through the door and rustled the leaves of the tall trees just outside. It was hard not to be inspired by the magnificent high vaulted ceilings and massive stained glass windows that covered every long wall of the sanctuary. From the large altar hung an enormous cross from the rafters with a statue of Jesus hanging from it.

"Jill, over here, you can place your things on the pews to the side right there." This was the section Effie sat every Sunday, and the place Jill sat when Effie brought her every time Jill came to visit all of her years growing up. She'd never sat anyplace else as far as Jill knew. It was odd entering this section from the other direction. "I'm glad you're here. Now what do you need help with?" Several older women who were friends of Effie's and had worked with her in the past, volunteering at the church, were there to help. "Thank you," Jill said, "but I think I've got it." She put the flowers on the front pew in front of the altar as well as one of the boxes that contained some of the framed photos. She was so caught up in the moment she hadn't realized how heavy the box was. There were creases in her arm where the box had been resting. It was a relief to get it out of her hands. "The ladies are in the kitchen preparing the food," one of the women said. Jill never even went to look. She left that part to them.

Jill carried everything into the church and began arranging things where they belonged. She placed more flowers neatly at the altar, including one white lily on the small table where she put James' pictures. "Can we help you?" the ladies asked. "No thank you. I've got this." Jill wasn't about to let anyone put things where they didn't belong. The photos she had selected were ones she thought highlighted what she knew was special to him and what represented who he was. One showed him in his bright yellow waterproof fishing overalls in Alaska holding a salmon bigger than any Jill had ever seen, half the size of his lengthy and towering six-foot-two body. An enormous proud smile spread across his face atypical of any of his other pictures. Jill liked it because it was a rare moment capturing him in his happiness and she felt it showed the true inner him. There he was with his long sunny handlebar mustache that spanned the width of his face and hung down past the corners of his lips and his messy blonde hair.

It was in this capacity Jill found herself tenderly and thoughtfully presenting James to the public in a dignified way that demonstrated to all who cared to see who he really was. She thought she did a pretty good job. At the funeral she was called repeatedly to the altar to speak. She read a poem she thought befitting to him. The priest asked questions during the mass and all of them were directed towards Jill. Everyone's heads turned not towards his mother, Effie, who was much too distraught … but to her. Suddenly Jill knew more than even his friends and more distant relatives.

After the funeral, Jill approached the priest. "Father, I want to thank you for the heartfelt contribution to the memory of James. But I have to ask you, how did you know about the hats?" Her uncle had collected hats for as long as she could remember. They were his prized possessions and they hung from every corner of his claimed territories of the house, and mostly from hooks in the rafters of the garage. The priest read an unlikely series of excerpts from "Bartholomew and the Hundred Hats." It was a perfect lead-in to Jill's report on the final count. There were precisely 208. Everyone had always wondered. Jill searched every nook and cranny of the house to count them before the funeral. For some reason it seemed imperative to know in order to put her uncle to rest. Jill expressed her gratitude for the appropriateness of the priest's selection of the passages and informed him that it fit James's sense of humor perfectly. She waited for him to answer her question. He replied, "I didn't know. I just had a compulsion last night that I needed to read that book."

Jill got something to eat and talked to people, meeting old friends of James and even friends of her mother, people she'd heard about her entire life and knew when she was young, but didn't remember. When Bobbie had died, she never saw them again. Jill was surprised to see one of the owner's of the poodles Effie and she had met at the soup restaurant several days earlier. It was the one that had known James in high school. Jill couldn't believe she was there or that she even knew about the funeral. "I read about the death of James in the town paper and decided to come. I am so sorry for your loss." "Wow, well I'm so glad you came." "You know, James was very handsome in high school." "Really?" Jill was intrigued. "Oh yes, in fact he was one of the most handsome and popular boys there." "No! You're kidding?!" Jill was quite surprised. This couldn't be true, she thought. "My uncle?" "Yes, and … "She hesitated, looking suddenly very bashful. "I always had a crush on James." "Really?" Timidly she nodded yes. Jill raised her eyebrows. "Really?" she said again. The woman nodded again. She looked embarrassed and like it was a very deep secret she was divulging. Jill found it inconceivable. "My stringy long blonde-haired uncle with the handlebar mustache? Really?" Jill thought the woman standing in front of her was far too normal, well kempt, and too pretty for her uncle. He had never gotten married and everyone had always been very sad about that, but here was a woman who'd had a crush on him all this time and in his very own hometown all these years. Jill couldn't help but wonder, what if … Eventually she stumbled on some old photographs during a time he was forced to look like a gentleman, and admittedly Jill had to concur; all cleaned up he was strikingly handsome.

James was outwardly gruff and unseemly, yet his outward exterior veiled a generous and good soul. He was full of potential. Jill's Father had taught him to fly and he was a most talented pilot her Father had told her one time. It was unfortunate he quit short of his final solo. He had applied to the Air Force Military Academy. He had a likely chance of acceptance; decades old familial ties to other officers from his Father's war days and his position as a Colonel would have made for certain admittance Jill imagined.

His outward decisions in life that led him down the path he took masked a rebellious soul that was authentic and genuine. Jill felt there was no room for his out-of-the box ideas and commitment to serve it with unruliness and an unacceptable unseemly appearance and with a dedication that never earned the respect it deserved. Jill grew to love him and be his friend late in life. Jill's girls became his prodigal grandchildren and he loved them dearly. He bragged about them and showed them off proudly like any doting grandparent. It was like a last minute gift in the last days of his life.

In Jill's younger days she thought James represented the crude underside of human nature, challenging the fake personae of society and the prettily dressed women in his life. Jill wished he were still here so she could tell him that. He would have laughed for sure. It was a stark contrast, the conclusion Jill had arrived at about him in the end compared to the one she had of him growing up. When she was young she disapproved of James and his disheveled unkempt friends. She thought they were very ungentlemanly, not at all like the ladies her granny or her mother were. Jill was used to her own elegant dresses, boots and pea coats, growing up. Jill remembered when she was little, at bars, sitting on high stools, surrounded by young men with shaggy blonde hair and long handlebar mustaches just like her uncle's. They all looked the same. She remembered one time everyone thought it was funny, her mother included, to make Jill wear a t-shirt that said "Budweiser" on the front of it. It hung past her knees. Jill did not find it funny. She thought it was an absolute embarrassment and she refused to wear it. Jill tore her room apart when no one was looking, and pulled the shirt off, searching for something decent to wear. When her mother found her slinging clothes all over the place, she got a spanking for it.

The contrast between this unlikely pair, Effie and James, was extreme. There was dainty small-framed Effie with her prim and proper conservative forty's style. Jill imagined she would have made an excellent first lady in the White House. Exquisitely eloquent and just as generous with a grace that surpassed Mother Theresa, she was the epitome of a lady. And there was James, living with her in the same house, with manners and dress equally opposite, contradicting Effie's image and antagonizing her ego endlessly. The organization of the house had its representative territories. James laid claim to his bedroom, the den and the garage. No one could surpass its lack of orderliness and filth. Effie's, on the other hand, was the picture of delicate elegance becoming of a lady. Ornate white old-fashioned wood dressers, lace curtains, glass perfume trays and elegant glass lamps from Neiman Marcus adorned her bedroom. James' room contained old falling apart dressers that looked like they'd been collected from a thrift store, a TV tray as a nightstand, stacked with dirty drinking glasses and piles of coins, clothes rumpled into piles in every corner of the room, including Jill's mother's old desk that had remained right where it had always been all those years ago. They were in constant opposition to each other in every way, a perfect balance between extremes. It was an odd spectacle, and one few ever witnessed. Hardly anyone was granted access to this inner realm, Effie out of sheer embarrassment, and James out of complete obstinacy.

Following the funeral the necessary arrangements for moving Effie to a suitable living situation remained and this led to the monumental task of cleaning the house. It was hard separating Effie from this house that had seen so much. Jill painstakingly researched and took Effie to see many places to live until Effie decided on one she liked. Many of her friends lived there and it had a festive atmosphere. Figuring out what to do with all of her stuff and how to do it was another ordeal entirely. They decided to have a moving sale and the morning of it, throngs of people were at Effie's door. Effie's things were arranged and priced around the house. They had spent hours the days leading up to it, patiently deciding what to do with each item. Effie and Jill weren't prepared for what happened next.

The morning began with the doorbell ringing at six a.m., three hours before the sale was to begin. Jill answered the door confused. "I'm here for the moving sale," the man standing in front of her said. Over his shoulder Jill saw two other cars with people sitting in them, staring at the house. "The sale doesn't begin until nine. That's three hours from now." "Well, can I take a look anyway?" "But we aren't ready yet. I don't even have everything laid out." "I don't mind," he said. "Well I do," Jill replied. "You'll have to wait. I'm not ready." She closed the door and a dread sunk into her stomach realizing what was in store for them that day. "Who was it?" Effie asked. "Someone for the moving sale," Jill answered. "Already?" asked Effie. "Yep already. Can you believe it? There are more of them outside waiting in their cars too. That man wanted to come in and look right now! Somehow I think we're in for more than we bargained for." Effie scowled and Jill wrinkled her forehead. "Yep," said Jill. "This is not going to be a fun day I'm afraid."

A couple of the neighbors helped, and when the doors opened, people poured into the house like hungry shopaholics hunting for a bargain. Jill couldn't keep track. People asked questions left and right. They were everywhere. The neighbors had done this before and had assigned everyone to posts. Effie was so overwhelmed that she ran down the hall into her room, closing the door behind her. Jill followed her. "Are you ok Granny?" Effie was in bed with the covers over her head. "Oh Granny." Effie shook her head from under the covers. "I can't watch. I just can't watch. This is awful. My house, my things. I can't do it. I don't want to see it." Someone opened the bedroom door and Jill jumped up to intercept whoever it was. "Oh no, this room is off limits. Nothing for sale here." Effie pulled the covers over her head more. "Oh God, no, no, no," came her muffled voice. Two more people followed behind the first and tried to come in. Jill pushed them back and raised her voice to let everyone behind them know that everything down the hall was off limits. "Granny are you going to be ok?" A small voice came from under the covers, "I'll be ok, you go, just do what you have to do." Jill grabbed some tape and closed Effie's door behind her. The tape made a loud ripping sound as she pulled a big piece of it across the doorframe to Effie's bedroom. She went up and down the hallway to the rest of the doors and did the same, all the while pushing people back and talking loudly over her shoulder. "This is off limits people. No one is to go in any of the bedrooms except this one. Any room with tape you cannot go in."

Jill made many trips to Effie's room to inquire about items she knew meant a lot to her. "Granny, what about this? Someone would like to buy it, but are you sure?" Effie took the vase in her hands, "Oh it's so lovely. I got this in Austria." The look of nostalgia on her face at the turning over of each item twisted into pain and eventually to one of peace. "Ahh give it to 'em. I don't need that old thing." Each time Jill came down the hall to ask, the process became easier and easier until Effie didn't even care anymore. "Just get rid of it," she said before she even saw what it was. Jill wanted to make sure Effie was ready to let go, and by showing her each item she was hoping that eventually it would lead to helping her let go of the house itself.

Jill was in disbelief at the aggressiveness she witnessed that day. Towards the end, she glanced out of the back window in time to see both of the very long ladders that had been James' being carried away by several men. She went outside and asked the neighbor manning the backyard station "How did you do out here?" "Oh well here," she handed Jill a twenty dollar bill and couple of fives and ones. Jill looked around and noticed that several large items were gone. She took the few measly bills in her hand and looked up at her neighbor. "Is this it? What about those large heavy ladders?" "Oh well, they weren't worth much. Better to just get rid of stuff." "But look how much is gone," Jill said. She heard a clattering over the fence coming from her neighbor's yard. It sounded like ladders. Jill said "Oh." What could she say? Her neighbor was being kind enough to help with the sale. The neighbor smiled back sweetly as if to say, "I'm right aren't I?" She did not acknowledge the clanking of the ladders that had been taken to her house, and neither did Jill, but they both knew each other knew perfectly well what was happening. Jill didn't know what to do about it, so she didn't do anything at all.

When the crowds cleared out, the two neighbors milled around long enough to see what was left. "I'll get that piano off your hands." It was the ladder-lady. The piano was shiny and new and had barely been touched. Effie had bought it fairly recently thinking she would take up playing again, but never did. She had also told Jill earlier in the morning that she paid over $2,000 for it. "Well no, I think I'll hold off on that one. I've got several names and numbers of people interested and willing to give several hundred for it." The neighbor sweetly and very convincingly said, "Oh well, are you sure? I could take it right now, get it off your hands, and you won't have to worry about it. Better to get rid of it." Jill thought she seemed to say that same thing all day. "That's ok. Like I said. I'll wait. I've got a couple of people very interested." The neighbor looked disappointed.

Outside the other helping neighbor took Jill aside and said, "You know my son and his wife are looking for a place to rent if you need someone to rent the house. What do you say to $900 a month?" "Oh well, that's something to think about. I hadn't really thought that far ahead. I'll think about it." Jill later discovered the rent was going for substantially more in their area. Jill was grateful for all of the help but she was beginning to see it came at a price.

The day ended and everybody went home. The house looked like a wreck, even if so much had walked out of the house that day. Effie came out of hiding to inspect the damage. It was difficult for her to look.

Jill had no idea what to do with everything in the garage. There was so much. There were so many tools and equipment. Her uncle had been a carpenter by trade. She called her dad and her brother to ask them what to do and eventually they arrived at the conclusion they needed to come out to help her. The things they found surprised and baffled them and caused no end of discussion. "Hey what's that up there?" Jill's brother asked. They gathered around to look. "Well I'll be damned. Is that a lawn mower?" The three of them looked at it not knowing quite what to make of it. "How did he ever get that up there?" her dad finally asked. "How are we going to get it down is the question?" "Why on earth did he even put it there is what I'm wondering!" The three of them nodded their heads. "It's actually pretty impressive," her brother finally said. "Yeah, come to think, it is," her dad agreed. "Here, I'll climb up there and you toss me the rope Dad." "Oh are you sure? Be careful, looks pretty sketchy. That's a long ways up, not much to grab onto." "Don't worry dad. I got it."

After a great deal of finagling, they finally lowered it down. The three of them stared at it. "Why?" Paul shook his head. "If you weren't going to use it, why not just get rid of it?" "Yeah, why would you go to all that trouble?" "Seems like it would've been easier to just go ahead and mow the lawn." The three of them laughed. "Well back to work," Jill said. "Let's see what other wonders we can find tonight."

Paul had to leave late that night. He had his own post-retirement project that needed his constant attention, a cat rescue. Jill and her brother remained in the garage late into the night. At three in the morning, they were still at it. It was so interesting, all of the things they were finding that they hardly noticed the time. Jill climbed up a ladder to inspect what else might be up there. Some boxes cluttered a large plank of wood straddled across some of the beams that formed the rafters. Jill climbed higher, struggling to see how much it was going to entail pulling all of it down. She tugged at some of the boxes, pulling them closer to her to get a better look. A plume of dust covered her face and she coughed and sneezed, covering her eyes. She had trouble moving the boxes and stubbornly pushed them from side to side, inching them towards her when she noticed something green over the top of them that was obviously the culprit holding them down. She continued to wiggle the boxes until she could reach her hands up enough to get it and pull it towards her. It was a suitcase. It wouldn't have seemed significant if it hadn't been all by itself, unlike a stack of travel gear, fairly accessible for the next vacation. And on top of that, there were about six inches of dust on top. In fact, it was so thick Jill had to lift it off like a blanket.

She finally saw the handle and grabbed it. Then she saw why it had been so difficult to move the boxes that were under it. It was quite heavy. Now Jill was curious. As she got it closer to where she was standing on the ladder, she realized there was no way she was going to be able to lift it down herself. "Hey will you help me with this?" she said to Robbie "Sure." Her brother dropped the empty dog food bags he was holding into the heap of trash in the driveway. "What is it?" "I'm not sure, but it's really heavy." "I'm going to start sliding it closer to the edge, but will you help me grab it when it starts to fall?" "Yep, right here." Jill inched it to the edge of the beam, and the weight of it started to teeter-totter over the side. "Keep comin.' I got it." Her brother had his arms stretched up in the air ready to catch it. Jill tried to lessen the force of it coming down, but from her angle on the ladder she barely had leverage and it fell with force into her brother's arms. "Whoa!" He said. "What the heck's in here?" "I don't know," said Jill. "Let's open it and see."

Her brother carried it to an open space on the driveway under the floodlight coming from the garage and laid it on its side. He unzipped it and Jill stood over him to watch. "What's this?" He picked up a wallet and opened it. Jill bent down to look. Her brother closed it back up and handed it to Jill. "Wow. Jill are you seeing what this is?" He stood up and backed away as if in reverence. Puzzled, Jill opened the wallet and looked inside. There was a driver's license and credit cards like it had only been tossed up there yesterday and yet was completely in tact. Jill was confused until she pulled out the license. She turned it over in her hand. She read the name on the license. "It's my Mom's." "Yeah," her brother said, "I think we should close this back up and take it inside. Come on, I'll help you." Jill zipped it back up, still holding the wallet in her hand. Her brother picked it up and carried it into the living room. Jill followed him into the house and sat down next to the suitcase. Her brother sat across from her, looking at her, wondering if she was ok, if it had sunk in. "Do you realize what this is?" "It's my Mom's things." "Right. Why don't you get something out? Let's read it!" Jill found a daily planner, a calendar, stacks of papers, and then she noticed a large brown file strapped closed with a piece of string. It caught her attention so she gently lifted it out of the suitcase. It was stuffed full of papers and was quite thick and heavy.

She looked at her brother. His eyes were big, waiting with anticipation. He was just as curious as she was. "Well come on. Open it." She carefully took the file into her lap and unstrapped the tie that was around it. The paper was so old that it tore easily. She lifted the flap and looked inside. It was full of papers. She looked up at her brother again. He raised his eyebrows, encouraging her to keep going. Jill was slow. The moment hadn't sunk in. "Pull something out," he said. She thumbed through some of the papers. "I don't even know where to start," Jill said. "Just grab one, anything. Let's see what it is." She pulled out a sheet of paper and held it in her hands. It was a poem. "Well are you gonna read it?" "Ok," Jill said. She started to read, "I feel like a million little people …" she began, and she read the entire thing and at the end said, "It's signed 'Bobbie.'" Her brother's eyes were bright and warm with gentleness and excitement at the same time. Jill was in shock. It was such a revealing poem, so expressive of her feelings. Robbie sat back and said, "Wow. She was bipolar." Jill said nothing. They stared at each other. The significance of his words filled the room. After a couple of minutes, her brother broke the silence. "Jill, do you realize what this is? This is all of your mom's stuff!" He sounded more excited than Jill, but for Jill it hadn't registered, the significance of finding a suitcase full of her mother's things, and the writing. "Read another one," he said. "Ok." She pulled a paper out and read it. "The voice inside pushes a way to reality, whatever that is …"

Jill had wanted so badly to know her mother for so long that to find this hidden treasure after all those years seemed unfathomable. She fingered the brown file after placing the two pieces back in and closed the flap. Then she noticed the writing to one side, penned in her mother's own neat handwriting, "A File of a Life." It wasn't until weeks later she noticed on the right hand side, and in very faded cursive, was written "Bobbie."

For her brother it was a sort of discovery too. He realized there was no good reason why he was there with Jill that night. Why had he ever been involved in Effie's life? Time and again, their Father found himself at Effie's house many years after Bobbie's death, Jill's brother with him. Her brother concluded acknowledging if it had not been for her death, he would not be here. Jill's dear dear brother, maybe things do happen for a reason.

Jill held the contents of the suitcase close; she only shared the photographs. She wasn't ready yet to share the rest. She wasn't willing to risk losing her mother's writing. She felt as if she might lose a piece of herself if she let any of it go and she couldn't afford to do that. She needed time to take it in, to integrate it into herself. They were hers now, and there was no treasure she would inherit from anyone that could be more valuable than that.

For many nights following, Jill found herself alone in that house perched on top of the hill, the backyard sweeping down to the valley that began the downward descent of the canyon Effie's home looked over. Even though the canyon was filled with houses now, Jill only saw the fields and fields of sage and tumbleweed and long grasses with trails that horses and their riders wound their way around so long ago. She could still smell the strong smell of sage all around her as she ran up and down those hills as a little girl even though the sage was no longer there. Old friends and her father too, when they happened to come back to the house, stood at that very same place at the top of the hill and looked over the canyon with the same look Jill thought looked like the one she felt. It was like that spot on the hill was a portal into the past.

When Jill came to the house to clean for many days following, she found herself up late into the night, sometimes even all night. Each layer of photos, old letters, clothes and old cigar boxes seemed to represent a decade of time, and each layer was as undisturbed as the suitcase had been. The further down into the layers she dug, the further into the past she went. She came to a final layer of old cigar boxes stuffed with letters Effie and Jill's Grandfather had written to each other during WWII and some even before that while they were courting and he was attending the military academy at West Point. They were very much in love and they were waiting for him to be finished so they could get married. West Point didn't allow marriage before graduation. As it turned out, his class was the only to graduate one semester early, so the newly graduated cadets could enter the war. They were needed, and her grandfather was a pilot. Jill had heard stories about him. He was in a downed plane during the war. A movie had been made about it. Effie never could remember the name. He had been in the first bomb group to drop bombs over Germany; Jill even found aerial shots of B-17 formations taken from his cockpit window and shots of liberated concentration camps below. There was even a picture of a missile close-up and mid-flight, smoke trailing behind it. The detailed flight plans remained in his flight bag undisturbed. No one seemed to have thrown out a thing.

The rest of the cigar boxes were labeled with the price tag of fifteen cents! There were old newspapers from major world events dating back to the sixty's and the Cuban Missile crisis and some much further back than that. There was a "Playboy" magazine dated 1960. The cover girl wore a rather prudish and unrevealing one-piece bathing suit. Jill imagined it must have been quite scandalous back then.

She continued cleaning late into each night. The familiar feeling of the dark was comforting. She didn't feel alone, even though she was. Her brother had long gone. She felt as though the spirits of her family were there with her. She could almost feel their presence, as much as she could feel the presence of a real person. She wasn't afraid. She felt surrounded by love and assurance, and like she was being encouraged to discover who her family was, and how she fit into it. It was like a tunnel leading between here and now and a time that didn't quite fit into a definition of time.

An old friend and former boss of Effie's who came to be a good friend of Jill's too had persuaded Jill not to stay alone in that big empty house with a mattress on the floor to sleep. She had gotten rid of most of the furniture. They invited her to stay with them while she tied up loose ends. After one of her sessions at the old house, Jill came back to her friend's home and stood in the living room, telling her what she had found that day; it was a letter. She told her about it because it described an incident Jill knew about and was part of, but it was in her mother's words. As she stood looking at her friend she told Jill to stand still. She said she saw a glow of yellowish-white light all around Jill, as if it were coming from her. She said she had seen this one time before long ago. It was her Catholic Priest, only the light came out much further around him. She said as she sat looking at Jill, she had no idea what it meant, although to Jill it felt perfectly logical having been so close to what seemed ethereal each time she was at her family's house.

It was these things Jill came to know about her family, tying her to a past she had not known. She was grateful for that. It was an unexpected gift. Much later, while eating ice cream with her fifteen-year old daughter, Marley, Jill told her that her mother had a list of everything she loved and it was pages long. "It was so sweet," Jill said. "One of the items on the list was the word 'ice cream'" she told her. Jill asked, "Do you know what her favorite was?" Her daughter made a few guesses. Finally Jill told her, "Peppermint." Her daughter answered, "Wow, it's like she made that file on purpose, just so you would know everything about her."

Chapter 14

My Garden

What's to come of daisies and daffodils and sweet dreams? The plow is tearing them up to plant another kind. They are being turned under and buried so that the new species can increase. I can't let them die – I fight and I fight and my garden still grows, untouched by this new thing. But I am losing strength – I am so outnumbered and I wage this war with no aid. If I relinquish my plot, the new variant will not grow in my soil anyway, the seed is ugly and cannot be nourished in this pure, fine soil used only for things of beauty and trueness. So, if they take it, they can only plow and plow and be rulers of a garden of nothing.

But I cannot bear even to see my garden go thus; I have cared so long and tenderly for the perfection of its beauty. I will not see that destroyed! I will fight until I drop, I feel half dead already, but I'll go on until they kill me. And if I die, they can never touch my garden of daisies and daffodils and dreams … it lives on forever, but invisible to those greedy cruel and destructive hands. Yes, it lives on and its beauty is eternal because its care is Infinite in the Hands of the most loving Gardener of All.

Bobbie, May 19, 1964

Jill wasn't sure if the discovery of the file of her mother changed anything, aside from giving her a feeling of belonging somewhere. At least she knew where, or who rather, she came from. Realizing how many similarities, coincidences and common experiences they shared made her feel connected, almost like she knew her.

It's funny she liked to write and so did Jill, yet she never knew! She had wanted so badly to know who she was. Whoever would have imagined that suitcase was sitting there all these years right in front of her? It's like it was waiting for the right moment for her to find it. The more she learned about her through each piece she wrote, each letter, each essay, each poem, the more real she became. It was like a treasure was given to her finding all of her things, a lovely gift that was kept safe until she was ready.

Her writing had shown her something. Jill could see who she was in the context of a bigger picture. Her mother had raised the bar for Jill by the values she lived her life by; Jill wondered if she would be a disappointment to her if she could see her now, that she'd waited so long to express herself, that she'd kept it inside until now. She felt it was like she'd been sleeping all this time. On her own, she wasn't sure she'd have known how. Through Bobbie's writing it's like she showed Jill, taught her, like a mother would, even though she was never there. It's like she wrote those journals and poems because she knew Jill would need them one day, and she knew she wouldn't be there to do it.

Discovering what kind of person she was gave Jill a different expectation of her self. She could see the places where she'd fallen short. She could see what was possible, and she wondered, was it possible in her too? Seeing her differently made all the difference in the world. Jill was proud of who she was. She was pleasantly surprised to find her mother was so much more than she'd ever imagined. Even if troubled, she was a beautiful soul.

Jill thought to her self, everything happens for a reason. She did not understand why her mother left her life. Jill knew it was not because of her. Bobbie was living her own life, experiencing her own experiences and they had nothing to do with Jill. As a child it's hard to know that. What happened to her mother happened, and there's nothing anyone could do about it. Despite it all Jill thought, "I have much to grateful for. I can choose how I want to interpret the things that have happened in my life. I can choose sadness and regret – disappointment even. Or I can choose to remember how many beautiful things have happened to me and how many incredible experiences I've had. I want to choose happiness and gratefulness. Every moment counts. Like my mother said, 'Time is running out.'"

Author Description

Although her background is math education, Christina loves to write. Writing *A File of a Life* was a journey that helped her to unravel a past she did not understand. It came at a time when she was going through a divorce after twenty-five years of marriage, and with four daughters nearly grown. Simultaneously while rediscovering herself, her likes, dislikes, what she wanted and didn't want out of life was this process of unraveling the history of her family and working through it. Traumatic and a little complicated, in the end it is beautifully simple, and she has realized that life is suddenly unfolding all around her, allowing unimaginable passions and dreams to materialize.

Printed in the United States
By Bookmasters